Advance Praise
for the new novel *Rappawan*

TRACY KIDDER, National Book Award and Pulitzer Prize winner and author of T*he Soul of a New Machine, Mountains Beyond Mountains,* and other best-selling books:

I read this novel quite compulsively, in a way I haven't for quite a long time. I think it's very good. This story provides what Emily Dickinson calls transport, and it leaves me with a mood, feeling, atmosphere — something hard to name. If I had to say what it's about, I'd say aging and change. I had all but given up on reading contemporary novels but found myself eager to get back to this one.

PETER COYOTE, actor and author:

I finished this in one ravenous gulp. Part Evan Connell, part Wendell Berry, and part Elmore Leonard, the characters are so striking, evolve so wonderfully and the book is full of woods wisdom and lore. The plot swells symphonically, all its recognizable parts annealing in a completely satisfying form.

HENRY ALLEN, a Pulitzer Prize winner for criticism and author of *Where We Lived — Essays on Place* and other books:

The wisdom of nature, the nature of wisdom, the beauty of snow falling on flowing water — and a narrator who knows that doing the right thing may not save us, but it'll have to do till something better comes along...

SARA DAY is the author of *Coded Letters, Concealed Love* and *Not Irish Enough* and, as a curator at the Library of Congress, *Women for Change:*

The unnamed narrator in Conaway's latest novel has spent his life in an impoverished rural community at the base of Virginia's Blue Ridge Mountains on his beloved river, the Rappawan. Now widowed and having recently lost his lover, Esther, he is dismayed by the painful, fatal bow-and-arrow wounding of a mother bear that Esther had enjoyed watching with her cub. Acutely sensitive to nature and wildlife, producing some of the most evocative and beautiful descriptions in the novel, he rages against the threats posed to his formerly unspoiled rural environment, and the effects of alcohol and drugs on locals. Life brightens with the return of Esther's free-spirited daughter, Lurie, and her small daughter, Maeve. Renewed in purpose, he assumes responsibility for the family he never had.

THREE NEW NOVELS BY

JAMES CONAWAY

Rappawan

Tregaron Springs

Since My Baby Left Me

DARLING THUNDER PRESS
BERKELEY • CALIFORNIA

This book is published by Darling Thunder Press with the assistance of Fearless Literary Services: *www.fearlessbooks.com/AssistedPublishing.htm.*

COVER ART:
"Lost River" by James Conaway

COVER DESIGN:
Susanna Conaway
D. Patrick Miller, Fearless Literary

ISBN:
979-8-218-44813-4

LIBRARY OF CONGRESS CONTROL NUMBER:
2024911779

Contents

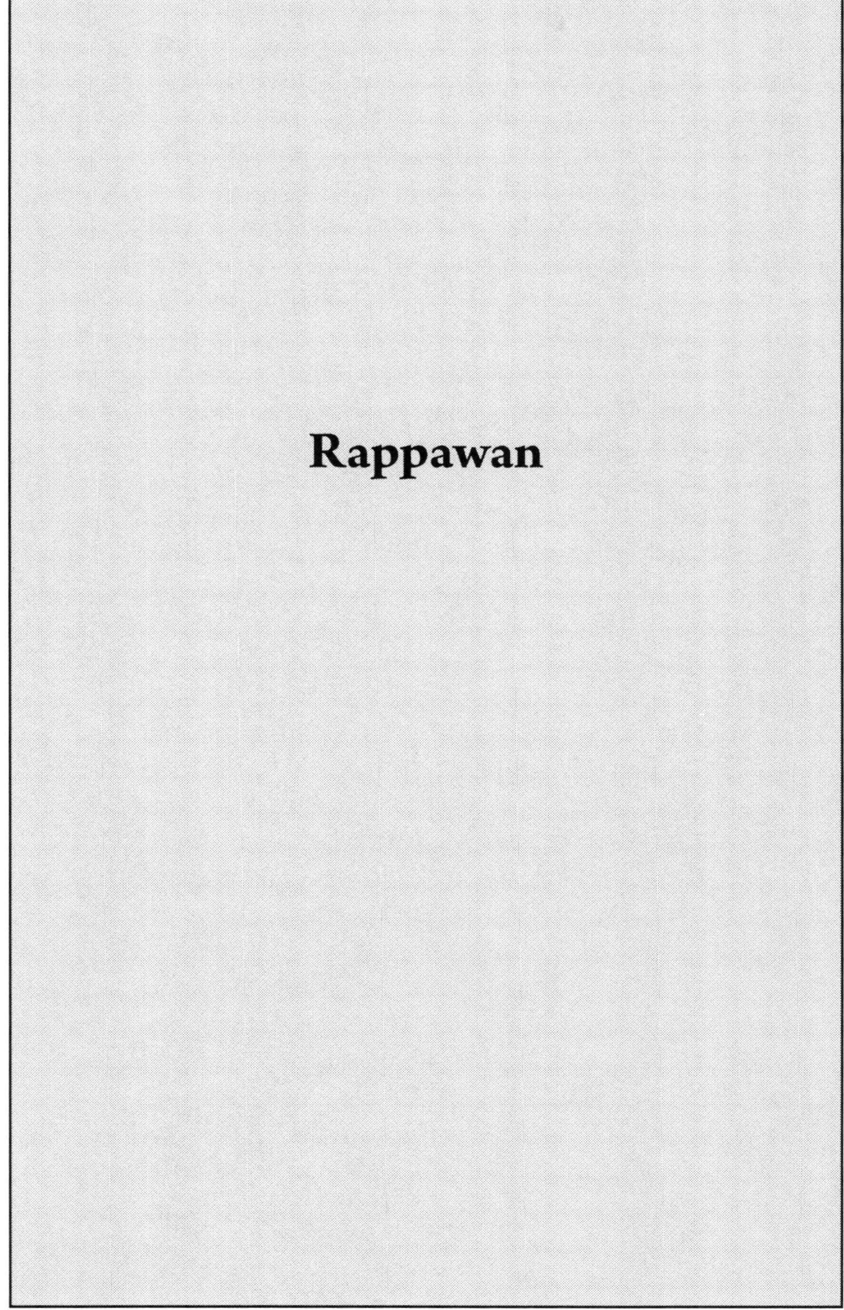

Rappawan

For Susanna, again

The people in this novel are imaginary and do not represent anyone dead or alive. The river is real but renamed, based upon others like it that rise high on the east slope of the Blue Ridge and work their difficult way across the Piedmont and down to the bay.

Start by doing what is necessary.
— Saint Francis of Assisi

ESTHER

Chapter 1

They have to take her out through the hole where the picture window had been because her coffin was assembled indoors. A front-end loader's required to get the coffin in the ground, plus two men with ropes to balance it going down. I will pay for the loader, and her daughter, Lurie, for the coffin and the preacher. There's no headstone because Esther didn't want one.

She weighed almost three hundred pounds at the end, but I loved her at any weight. She had never seen an ocean and hadn't seen her children in many years. Son Dwayne's still making license plates in Mosby Correctional, outside of Charlottesville, and they aren't about to let him out if they don't have to. Lurie grows dope out in California using know-how, I suppose, picked up working Esther's considerable vegetable garden, back in the days before Esther got so big.

Lurie arrives for the funeral in the first cab ever seen on our road, all streaky blond hair and Levis with holes in them on purpose. It's cold and she will leave before the falling weather starts and red dirt clatters on the unfinished pine of her final resting place. But first Lurie gives me a big hug. She and I always got along, even when things were really bad.

Back at my place, I sit in the truck parked on the low-water bridge and look out over my little river. Is there anything prettier than snow falling on dark moving water?

Walking to my house, I leave footprints in snow shod with new grass, next to the turkey's horny tridents. The stove has gone out and dusk's coming on. I rebuild the fire thinking about the long trail of misfortune that was Esther's life and look up to see a fox crossing the yard, a squirrel in his jaws, and slip into the brambles.

A cardinal, a scarlet dart pinning a branch of the thornbush to a gunmetal sky, hesitates to seek cover there. But even the proximity of the fox is preferable to this March wind.

I wake up after dark to the ticking of the old Wincroft stove, its spent coals bright in the cracks as in an iron firmament. The moon hangs in the sycamore as pale and wan as my abandoned dreams. What would my life have been like if I had tried harder, had been braver? Esther was always beautiful in my eyes, a strong, confident woman making the most of a hard life shaped entirely in this little county. I could have been a bigger part of it if I had followed my instincts, and now the weight of this knowledge has come down on me.

The last time we got into her bed — two camp mattresses stitched together and covered with the tattered mountain quilt I gave her long after my wife died — I took the blue pill Dr. Simms had provided as a sample, and it worked. When we were done I was still at attention, you might say, and I asked Esther what I was supposed to do with it. She just smiled in that sweet way of hers and said, Same old, dear.

Chapter 2

The woods have changed from something I took ready comfort in as a young man to a declining mix of the known and the unknown. Plants from elsewhere crowd out what's left of the big hardwoods, like the so-called tree of heaven that's anything but heavenly, flame red in spring but impossible to kill, casting seeds on the wind that thrive anywhere there's sun. Sprouts leap up in the middle of fields and gardens. Even in the shed, feeding on a narrow wedge of sunlight, they creep across the packed dirt floor and climb into the rafters.

Esther called it the chicken-foot tree and it reminds me that a walk in the woods has become a fight with strange plants that defy forward motion unless you brought along a chainsaw. New insects are as bad. Ladybugs bite and fill up your breadbox. Horny new stinkbugs fly into your food. At least the lightning bugs survive and by early summer will float over the fallow field at dusk like winking angels.

Borers have killed every white ash tree on my place. Red-tailed hawks love the snags that let them drop onto moles and mice, and I love the wood for its straight grain. Oaks are going more slowly, though it's called sudden death syndrome.

A new kind of wind howls over the Blue Ridge, pushing clouds wispy at the edges and dark as death in the center. Microbursts clear my chimney but shear off trees, and healthy oaks and poplars roll like schooners in the grip of powerful invisible waves.

At the same time, people from elsewhere — from-aways — add up to a force beyond their numbers and affect the land in new and troubling ways.

Having said that, my own forebears were from-aways, Virginia coasters known as Tidewaters. My mother, half Catholic, was educated and didn't like hearing other people disparaged, including colored folks. She used Old English words sometimes, like "squander" for "scatter," and others that still slip into my head from time to time.

We lived at the base of the Blue Ridge and my father ran a big cordwood business out of the house, our yard spread with piles of split heater wood and fireplace logs. He had a bunch of older boys with pickups hired to deliver it to suburbs within a two-hour drive and come back with stories of big houses, lawns like putting greens, top dollars paid by folks who didn't know a cord of wood from a tailgate load.

Me and my brothers split heater wood in the yard from age eleven on to earn spending money. This leaves a yoke of muscle you won't get playing football. I spent a lot of my time in the woods when I wasn't reading the old books that had come down from Mother's side, novels and even poetry. Some of it I didn't understand but much I did. I even wrote some of my own.

None of that survived, but I wish some had, like pieces of me waylaid on some forest floor. My best friend, Kyle, read some and said he liked it, and a little approval meant a lot. But Kyle was drafted right after high school, and he fell in Vietnam's Tet offensive.

I find myself to this day looking for pages torn from my old spiral notebook and toed under leaves and dirt so long ago. I walked ungodly distances then, thinking about being a teacher of English, but I got into the lumbering program offered by the ag extension service, the route to better, faster money.

The fact that I married Emily, who did teach school, helped us all think of ourselves as respectable, but she couldn't have children, as it turned out. I thought it must be me, but no, the doctor said it was something to do with her plumbing. Being childless made us sorrowful long-term, but we learned to live with it. I wish I had a family still, but they, too, likely wouldn't have a cent to spare.

I think firewood, the only commodity a poor man could get his hands on, contributed in a strange way to my father's death. He kept the house so hot in winter that my mother would move in temporarily with her sister and my brothers, and I kept our window open most of the time. My father had said he might not get rich in heater wood but by God he was going to get warm.

I'd watch customers fall back from the door when he opened it on cold days. Mother said he slowly cooked himself to death, which may have been true. He caught cold easily when he went outside in winter and died of influenza.

Chapter 3

The bear hasn't been seen since August, when I drove Esther down to see the mother and her half-grown cub. Esther wore a kerchief and smoked her mentholated cigarettes as daintily as ever. She also drank tea all the time, kept in a cooler at hand even for that short trip. There she sat, patient as a saint for something to see when the sun touched the mountain.

Looking at bears was one thing that still brought her pleasure, since she was largely housebound and disliked television. This cub was a late developer and the mother not too worried because she was familiar with my place. They would cross together at the bottom of the property and wade the river. Bears are predictable up to a point but ultimately unknowable, like people. Last July this one came to the house in broad daylight, the cub gone and the mother sitting in the shade of the big hickory like she was contemplating something. I never again saw her alive.

I went out of county to price some timber and didn't get back for two days. Coming down my road in late afternoon I smell it even though I'm upwind and the windows are closed, an almost touchable thing large enough to generate so much bad air. The smell wraps round you like a blanket and has to be outrun, while buzzards perch above like black garbage bags in the trees, their knobby, naked heads a-bob.

Dipping my bandanna into the river and pressing it to my face, I wade downstream, knowing what I will find and not wanting to. Back across the river, I push through mile-a-minute vines until I see the bear, back legs tucked under her, the ground all round clawed down to bare dirt. As anyone who has spent time in the woods knows, this once healthy, glossy creature had something terrible and painful within her and against which she was powerless.

I think I know what that something is. Also, who put it there. But I will have to wait for all the life feeding on her to finish. That will take all winter, giving me time to decide what to do about it.

Not much can be understood of this place unless you know what came before. Crop and cow country has turned into fox-hunting country, too, with farms growing cocktails instead of corn and grass for from-aways to ride across on sleek thoroughbreds fitted with saddles like afterthoughts, the riders' backsides draped in coats called pinks even though they're red. They also wear velvety polished leather you'll not find at Kmart, a striking sight, granted, while you watch them hold up traffic not to catch a fox but to chase it.

The hounds are the best to watch, as a rule better bred than the horses or the riders. Nothing wrong with hunting foxes, people used to do it afoot using dogs that could tree a coon at night while we listened to them around a campfire. The object was to kill a raider of henhouses and decimator of rabbits, and our own homegrown gray fox not as strong as the red. Someone would bring a spade and someone else a pistol, all wearing Army surplus and lace-up boots left over from work.

The problem with from-aways is twofold. First, they build a house on the property even when the house already there is serviceable. With new houses comes runoff from bulldozed slopes that clouds the streams, and more strange trees and bushes. The second thing wrong is that the new owners often get tired of each other stuck in the middle of what they consider nowhere. So one goes back to where they came from, and for a time the other lives alone, and builds a hothouse or a sauna or another residence. Then that one, too, pulls out.

What's left is two empty houses with all the plumbing, wiring, polished oak floors and well drawdowns. More from-aways parade through thinking maybe to buy them. If the houses can be assigned to different lots, then the land's broken up some more and eventually these new owners sell, too, and the whole thing begins again.

If they don't sell right away the houses fill up with two types of people — overseers who don't know what they're seeing over, or contractors in real estate deals who tend to be hard partyers and aspiring great white hunters. They erect outdoor speakers that fill up the woods with noise, or deer stands with lawn chairs and coffee-makers and fancy new rifles that can kill most anything at a hundred yards.

A bear has the best nose in the woods. Watch one cross downwind and you'll see him stop at the exact point where the wind is at your back. You could tie a string from the end of your nose to the wet, black end of hers. The head comes around and she looks directly at you, her sight poor maybe, but who needs eyes with that nose? She'll turn and walk away, raising first one paw and then another and settling each in a silent dance carrying her away from what she knows to be the most dangerous creature on Earth.

The first warm day after snowmelt I wade back across and find the bear rendered to bone and polished skull by coons, foxes, and bugs that rise with the spring in infinite numbers. I get down on my knees and rake through their leavings, using the bear's lower jawbone to turn up a dozen claws that I drop into my shirt pocket. Then I hear the metallic clink of a metal arrowhead and know the whole story.

I've never killed a bear, nor wanted to. I tried bear meat once but didn't like the taste. They say for catfish or sliced potatoes deep-fried you can't beat bear fat. But underdone bear carries the same bug that infests feral hogs and I don't eat those either.

I've seen a bear stand in this river making sounds you'd not expect to hear in Virginia and slinging a full-grown dead doe from side to side. This instructed me in the extremes to which a bear will go if inspired and also a determination never to so inspire it.

For the bow hunter the only useful way into a bear is between two ribs. A respectable shot then passes through the lungs and the bear's dead within minutes. But only if the hunter's competent. A poor or impatient shot's more likely to be a missile of long-suffered torment.

Sure enough, the broken arrow shaft I find, of carbon steel, was shattered on impact but the broadhead's as bright as when it entered her, nearly weightless in the hand. Razor-sharp edges notched by glancing bone would hurt as they worked their way deeper into her tissue with every movement.

The last time I saw her sitting under the pignut hickory she must have already been shot. I have to ask myself what went through her mind. Just an animal, you'll say, but people living here long ago made their arrowheads not from steel but from fetched white quartz that turns up winking in the riverbanks. So it's a very old transgression from the bear's point of view.

A wounded one will stop eating, but water's different. A mortally wounded animal goes straight to it, the fear of death by thirst greater than the fear of burgeoning rot.

Hanging around with hunters can make you witness to things you don't want to see. Like dead bears laid out in a row like drowning victims. I happened to stumble onto all this, and I knew the men who had killed them. If I hadn't, I don't know what might have happened.

A freshly skinned bear looks like a man, one you'd rather not mess with. Those long muscles are capable of tearing branches from grown trees. The corpses were bathed in light from a shiny Cadillac with an air freshener dangling from the rearview mirror, driven by a man in a suit and tie. He videoed the skinning and the extraction of the small bluish gallbladders some people believe, if eaten, will have the same effect on a man as the little blue pill had on me.

One bladder lay on the chest of each bear. The man with the Cadillac took the bladders and put them in an insulated metal case. He dispensed what looked like cigarettes but were in fact rolled-up hundred-dollar bills, a thousand dollars in each, and went back to wherever he came from. I said goodnight and got away as fast as dignity allowed.

Chapter 4

There's only one window in the building, and the siding's all rough sawmill slabs. The only sign's a hanging plastic sheet with a single word in black letters in the center, glock. Push open the double-hung, heavy-gauge bars and you'll find most any pistol you might want, foreign or homegrown — .357s and bigger calibers, little pink .25 calibers for women's purses. Also a classic shotgun with a hand-carved beavertail, a vintage Buck knife or a Damascus blade that's gone back down into the crucible half a dozen times.

Assault rifles, Uzis if you know how to ask, a .50 caliber monster with folding stabilizers on the long barrel and bullets costing five dollars apiece. Muzzle-loaders, bump stocks, a deer stand with a motorized lift, a rack of doe, fox, and coyote piss in little bottles, and a hanging forest of compound bows of every description.

The man folded over the workbench in the back wears a headlamp like a dentist's and a dirty T-shirt. His name's Lester and he's probing a pile of trigger springs with a metal tine. He looks up and stares.

Haven't seen you in a while, he says.

I had a death.

And I take out the plastic sandwich bag holding the bear claws, the shattered arrow shaft, and the broadheads. He takes the bag like he's expecting it. You would never know looking at him that this man owns a big pre-Revolution house and has a wife who sits on chairs belonging in a museum. He's here twelve hours a day, longer in hunting season, fixing actions and popping lead balls from jammed muzzle-loaders and advising kids on what they need to kill whatever it is they're after.

He says the name of a manufacturer I never heard of, adding, Expensive — but this broadhead's too heavy for the shaft. That means you'll be shooting low.

It's not mine. Was it bought here?

You know I don't talk about that. Your neighbor must have felt he needed such big points.

So you know the story.

Don't know a thing. How come you stopped coming to our meetings?

Because I got tired of hearing about black helicopters spying for the government.

Well, there's as much government now as there was then, and more traitors. Let me know if you want to sell those claws.

By June the field in front of the house has filled up with fireflies at night. Deer staying back in the woods come forward, their summer coats pale red, pestered by bugs. The sudden beam of my flashlight swarms with gnats and mayflies rising and falling in ecstasy into gathering ground mist.

I find the deer stand not a mile from my house, across three property lines and a fearsome stretch of bramble. The metal ladder's against a dead ash, the high seat folded back to keep the coons from shitting on it. A digital camera's been lashed to another tree, so this hunter, whoever he is, can watch the action from his bed if he wants to. When he kills something, he'll have what for him is a precious visual moment preserved for posterity.

The stock tank under his stand is half full of corn, cinnamon buns, and hot dogs getting ripe. Deer will eat most anything, including cigarette butts, but those hot dogs are for bear.

Next morning I leave the house well before light and again climb the wooded ridge toward the stand. Water in the run feeding the Rappawan downstream is surprisingly cold, the woods ahead a blackness you need a can opener to get into. I stay downwind of the man's house, no light, no sound, feeling the rough bark of a locust tree and then the smoothness of the beech wrapped with the webbed strap holding the camera.

If he's already on the deer stand I'm in trouble, but I know he's not. Late riser, house so close he can take his time, sit on the stoop in the dark putting fox piss on his boots to cover his own smell. A buck snorts far to the east, having picked up a sound on a squandering breeze, and soon enough I hear the soft implant of a boot on leaves. The faint click of metal on metal would be the tip of his bow touching the hollow steel frame of the deer stand. His movement trips the shutter on the camera, and suddenly the woods are awash in light.

I see the illegal bait and a big man blinded despite the brim of his military-style hat. His face is chevroned with lampblack and he's sheathed in new camo that has spent no time with dirt and leaves in a plastic bag to get rid of its unnatural smell. He shows teeth to the lens, saluting to the future audience of this video that will have an ending he doesn't expect.

He climbs the ladder and fits an arrow to the drawstring, then attaches the trigger just below the nock point. The camera light goes off but I've seen the slender shafts and the costly, outsized broadheads reflecting like polished mirrors. They're the same sort and size I found among the bear's bone pile.

Waiting for first light's the best part of hunting. You hear birds and squirrels in the leaves and sometimes, far off, an eighteen-wheeler coming noisily off the mountain. Or somebody dumping a load of lumber two miles upwind. The sky bleeds color and the air picks up promise that won't last, but right now the world's a new place and you're a part of it, thinking it will go on forever.

I can see him now, facing west, the direction the quarry will come from, trending southeast along the river as they do. The hunter has a solid jaw I could swear has just been shaved, on its way to a job somewhere after he kills a bear out of season. There's a bowie knife on his hip as long as his forearm and a monocular spotting scope on a spring-driven cord pinned to his vest.

I take a breath, and say, friendly enough, It's illegal to hunt this time of year. Particularly bear, particularly over bait.

To say he's surprised isn't even close. His hand goes instinctively to the knife.

Get the hell off my land, he says.

It's not your land, it's Bubba Pitchur's land. The line separating Bubba's from yours is right between your stand and this feed bin. Pretty slick. If the law happens by, you can always claim Bubba put out the bait.

I know who you are.

But he's not climbing down. Superior height means a lot to some men and they don't give it up easily. I've seen it as well among those on horseback, and in pulpits.

I don't know who you are, I tell him, but what I do know is that you gut-shot that momma bear a year ago almost to the day, out of season and over bait.

I come out from behind the tree and walk around the bait bin. I look up into a face I have seen a hundred times on a deer stand, one eager for a kill, any kill.

Didn't have the guts to follow up to put her out of her misery, did you?

He says, I should put an arrow through your sorry ass.

Well, even this sheriff won't take well to you shooting a from-here like me. You'll end up in Mosby Correctional or somewhere worse, getting your rose stemmed every night by some right rough ole boys.

They told me in the gun shop you're batshit.

I ignore this, turn around and belly up to the bait bin. I unzip my pants, haul out my equipment, and let fly into his bait right there in front of God and his camera.

A man's unburdened bladder is about the last thing a bear wants to encounter, I say over my shoulder. It'll spoil a whole tub full of stale buns.

Back home, I walk straight into the river, boots and all, and lie back against a rock. I let the water flow over me. There will be more to hear from my neighbor, I suspect, but right now all I want is relief from the heat and the bugs, settled against two slabs of rock rising from the bottom like fins of bluestone. It came down long ago from one of the oldest mountain chains on Earth that in another billion years will be gone altogether.

Something ended this morning that began in Esther's final days. Seeing the bear and her cub had been one of the last delights in her life, and not long after that last jaunt she died, the last person who meant something to me and me to her. From now on there's not a soul who cares what I do or why, something else I could have prepared for if I had known what I know today.

If I get the chance yet I'll see that someone does care, that I have ordered what's left of my life and do something — I have no notion of what — to make up for neglect and laziness and all the little omissions that make up a man's life after he's lived most of it. I will not let an opportunity pass, in the unlikelihood that it appears, or by what some people think of as God I will hold myself accountable in the most terrible way imaginable.

Chapter 5

By August the lightning bugs are going and the woods are edgy. Deer's summer coats have changed from red to a shadowy gray, one of nature's sleights of hand announcing the start of hunting season. Prey feels it as surely as does predator.

I don't kill things anymore, leaving that to others. But I have killed as many deer within a mile of where I sit on this rough brick porch as most people have ever seen. Emily and I didn't buy a piece of steer and precious little pig in those days because I tagged a legal deer each year and two when the law changed, and then three when it changed again. The bow gave way to an old rifle with iron sights, and the venison rose in a slow tide in our trunk freezer.

It was our sustenance, our industry, and, looking back, our entertainment. Emily taught school up at Porters' Gap, the kind of job I envisioned for myself before I started cruising timber along the borders of the George Washington National Forest and found the money too good to give up. Often it was paid by jackleg sawmill operators that were there one year, gone the next.

Come deer season, I used to put all else aside, shooting and gutting a deer many dawns. I'd have it hung in the shed before Emily left to deal with those rowdy up-holler kids. There's a right way and a wrong way to butcher a deer, as with most things. I used a hog spreader that belonged to my father — a polished stob wedged behind the deer's back tendons to lift it with, using an old wooden pulley and leaving the carcass to hang while I went in for coffee.

I'd come back and strip the hide down like a pair of old long johns, and work up from there. Neck meat for the stew pot, same for that between the ribs and the foreleg bits. Cut out the backstraps, then the shoulder roasts, rump roasts, tenders from the underside of the spine that are cooked as soon as they hit the skillet.

The heart goes into boiling salted water and stays there while you wash up. Then cut it into thin slices, lay those on white bread with mayonnaise, raw onion, and enough black pepper to near cover it. Your day has begun.

That night, dream on the long trail of cooking deer bones, blackened in a hot oven and simmered in kettles atop the woodstove. Wake to an inch of dark essence poured into cookie pans and, once congealed, cut into squares like brownies and frozen. Throw one of those into the skillet with a tender, and if you don't you'll never know what venison really tastes like.

We butchered and drank Bee-K's peach whiskey, as clear as air, proud of the artful disassembling of muscles instead of just cutting them with a band saw like in the packing houses. Wrap it all in white waxed paper and stack it in the arctic darkness of the freezer. Jerk any excess on a rack above the woodstove, grind any residue with a little pig fat for sausage.

Make love then, happy to have a year's protein that gives you leave to forage greens and berries and in spring grow vegetables under a heavy black plastic net. Bears tear it open to get their great heads inside, but most makes its way to your table.

For me deer hunting went the way of the bobwhites whose eggshells were weakened by chemical fertilizers and the legions of mayflies that once coated the windscreen but now leave the nights sparsely populated, and streams, too. Coarse fish have taken over where smallmouth bass once knocked plugs out of the river. Beautiful little brook trout barely hold on far upstream.

The first sick doe I saw from the kitchen window was pale as straw, unable to keep up with the others. She stumbled and fell, which deer rarely do. Not long after I heard of something called wasting disease, the animal equal of flame trees, Formosan stinkbugs, and sudden death oak syndrome. Wasting disease is no threat to people my age because we'll die of something else before it eats our brains, but you have to admit it takes something away from deer hunting.

I went out for awhile after that but never again with a weapon. I would sit in the stand in the morning and just watch the deer move, the thrill of an emerging buck at first light still powerful. Bow hunting collapses your field of vision, the hard steel cold to the hand, the drawing of it a hard task under those dark, liquid eyes.

But something odd happened after I started leaving the bow at home. A monster buck I had tried to kill for years showed me his spreading rack, the tines as thick as the handle of a baseball bat, his tabletop back as broad as a mule's. He had coughed many a doe out of the range of my arrow while remaining unseen, saving their lives and enhancing his amorous life. But now he stood in the clearing at the bottom of my property with four or five does. They had listened to me coming, as if they wanted me to see them partying before crossing the river, hooves ringing on dark rocks.

Once two bobcats walked right under my stand, offspring of a couple Emily and I had watched screw in a distant field one March, making a godawful racket. These young ones looked up at me but kept going, shaking their paws before placing them soundlessly in the dry leaves, one a tabby and the other with dark vertical stripes, their little tails like muffins.

Before long I had birds and animals all around me, including sharp-shinned hawks, turkeys, the great blue heron clattering up from the river like an unfolding card table, even a horned owl with those merciless yellow eyes, moving so fast I felt his wind.

Six months after Esther's passing I drive past her house and see a strange truck parked outside. It has mismatched front fenders, lifts on both axles, and big knobby tires. What looks like a possum skull is wired to the grille. The truck sits at an angle to the ground, the way they will when they've been in a collision. The bed's full of stuff under a tarp, and the sign in the rear window reads **I SPEED UP FOR ANIMALS.**

This road's more than two hundred years old and still hasn't been paved. Likely stagecoaches and fine carriages once came this way, seeking the ford in the river down by my place. All around was owned by an English governor who said it reminded him of home and to it he invited the likes of young Thomas Jefferson and James Monroe. I wonder what this road would remind the governor of today.

I slow down but keep my foot off the brake so the taillights won't come on. Ordinarily I'd walk up to the house since there's no one else to keep an eye on it. I pass on by and turn into my own half-mile track overgrown with warring invasives. The county fire marshal recently drove down from Porters' Gap and asked me to cut it back. I told him I preferred wearing it out with my pickup, and he said, Well, don't plan on any chimney fires because we ain't bringing our new truck down that rabbit hole.

I sit on the front porch awhile, thinking about that truck with the knobby tires. What bothers me most is the possum skull. They are pathetic creatures, run over on purpose at night, easy to kill anytime and abused in general because they're slow and ugly and defenseless. But a possum will groom itself like a house cat, and the number of deer ticks they eat in a day is a gift.

The coffee's cold but I drink it anyway, pretty sure I know who owns that truck outside Esther's old place. One of the problems with advancing age is that you know too much, knowledge binding you to a past and a world you allowed to turn into this one. Sometimes I meet a child and know from the eyes or the set of the mouth what has gone before and what likely lies ahead which leaves me in a lonely, judging place I'd rather not occupy.

Chapter 6

I don't travel with a weapon but I have them around. A man living in the country without at least a varmint gun is a fool, what with rabid coons, skunks, foxes, coyotes, and dogs. I keep a short Smith and Wesson .38 wedged under my bedside table and take it out and shove it in the back of my trousers. Then I get back into my pickup.

There's a story to the pistol, naturally. It belonged to Bee-K, the distiller, who carried it in his front pocket so long it left a visible imprint, like Jesus's face in his shroud. You can see the clear outline when he plays — Bee-K's a fine fiddler — over the mountain at Tully's and when he sells his fruit-based whiskey out of his truck at intermission while the sheriff directs traffic.

Nobody ever went blind from Bee-K's fruit-based. He doesn't use a car radiator to condense it and doesn't spike it with grain alcohol or something worse. Nothing wrong with a man with a talent making a fine local product and selling it close in. So when I saw the gray sedan with a whiplike antenna and two suits inside turn off the highway toward Bee-K's, I left my pickup on the shoulder and bushwhacked straight uphill.

Bee-K was splitting hickory, the sun glinting off an ax blade filed sharp that morning. I called out to him, and he dropped that ax like it was hot. Before long he passed me on the way back down, holding a flour sack that looked to be full of laundry. He crossed the highway and jumped off the bridge, straight into the spring flood. I watched him bob out of sight, squeezing that flour sack like it was a baby.

When I got home he was drying hundred-dollar bills on my grass. There were a lot of them. I later found the Smith and Wesson in my mailbox, and when I asked him about it, Bee-K said, Don't worry, it ain't killed nobody. I just wanted to buy something with more heft.

I park behind the truck with the possum skull and get out. Under the edge of the tarp I can see a gas can, part of an iron bed frame, God knows what else. I climb the steps, making some noise. Leaves have drifted into the porch corners, and dirt-dauber nests hang in the angles of the picture window frame, the wasps' muted buzzing marking the end of summer.

Where you goin'?

Dwayne has come up behind with me unaware. Naturally, if Dwayne's going to show up it will be at the outset of deer season, even if it means breaking out of prison. He moves through woods better than anybody I know, a natural stealth that makes him the best deer hunter in this part of the Piedmont despite his scrawniness. His habit is to tote around spikes in an incidentals bag and hammer them into trees to make a ladder. How many times have I come across sixteen-penny nails driven into tulip poplars that get enormous next to creeks and followed with my eyes a tortuous iron path leading up? What sane man would attempt that?

He wedges himself into crooks and doesn't move for an hour, not an easy thing to do. He shoots straight down and butchers on the spot, cutting along the spine with a skinny knife sharp as sheared glass and peeling back enough hide to get at the backstraps. He carries them off over his shoulders like two big snakes.

How'd you get out of prison, I ask.

Good behavior, good buddy.

That's what you might call a statistical impossibility, but I let it pass. He's grinning, the silver cap on that front tooth catching the light as does his spiky, carrot-colored hair. His father, Gatewood Doyle, had red hair, too, when he still had any at all. Dwayne would have been a decent-looking man except for the acne scars trailing down both cheeks, and the holes poked in his skinny forearms. His eyes, pale blue, are flecked with black as if something nasty got in there long ago and couldn't get out.

Lurie know you're here? I ask.

Lurie's got nothin' to do with it. None of your beeswax anyway.

I know Esther left the place to Lurie and told Dwayne not to come back. But I let that pass, too.

He adds, Lurie don't mind.

Well, if you two made up, I guess that's good.

It's good if I say it's good. What is it you come by for, anyway?

Just checking, Dwayne.

Well, then, there's not a thing keeping you, is there?

When I get back to the house I go through the numbers I wrote in the back of my old directory. You don't often see a wall phone like mine, on a party line whose other user is dead. The trouble with a phone down here by the river is that every time there's lightning it rings. Once an orb like a blue golf ball popped out and rolled across the floor. More than once the phone's just blown up. The company keeps fixing it though many people have gone to cell phones. The repairman must hate the very sight of my place.

I know Lurie's number will get only her answering machine. The voice isn't hers. Selling marijuana even where it's half legal must entail unsavory characters. I've often wondered what her life's like out there in California, her having left straight out of high school ten years before.

I leave a message that Dwayne's moved back in, but I can't get him out of my mind. He's one of those people whose existence reminds you that the model's busted and needs to be recycled. His people were split between mountain and Piedmont, a combination that rarely works, us flatlanders being regularly exposed to others and so learning to get along, whereas mountain folk remain aloners and are more easily riled.

The Doyles had to give up property on the Blue Ridge when the parkway went in. They were given money to live elsewhere and could have gone down the west slope but came down the east one instead. I never knew what old man Doyle did, if he did anything at all, but his son, Gatewood, got a job with county maintenance and immediately set about getting himself declared disabled.

You can understand how an innocent like Esther might fall for Gatewood Doyle, a big and by some standards decent-looking young guy who would come into the co-op where she worked as the cashier. He would tell Esther that everything cost too much and then mansplain the headlines in the Piedmont Trader, the differences between races, the worthlessness of all government.

Gatewood was the only man who talked to Esther persistently, though she didn't share his views of colored people. And Gatewood didn't hunt, not out of scruple but because hunting requires getting out of bed in a timely fashion, and he lacked those constraints. Gatewood wore Esther down, and they married and moved into the house on our road two years before my wife and I arrived.

Right away Gatewood drove down here to tell me to turn my electric meter upside down to halve my bill, but I declined his advice. He soon faked a tumble in the county gravel pit that ended his short working life. His pension couldn't have been much, but it was enough for him to sit on the bench outside Bartrum's Gas & Quick-Mart all day, eating corn dogs and advising his benchmate, Groundhog, a taciturn man who owned a small-bore rifle with a scope that could shoot out an eye at great distance.

Groundhog took payment for his services, plus he ate the objects of his toil. He knew as much about groundhogs as any human alive, but that didn't prevent Gatewood from telling him all about groundhogs. He also told everybody coming out of Bartrum's where they could buy cheaper milk and chew, until Bartrum finally ran him off.

So Gatewood set up shop on his own front porch, his expanding, shirtless stomach glistening like a pink medicine ball in summer, his booming voice frightening sparrows out of the house eaves. He wondered why shouldn't the few people driving past his house in a day have to slow down to get his advice, so he had his son pilfer sandbags from the county to build a speed bump opposite Gatewood's rocker. As drivers slowed to get over it they learned everything there was to know about fescue or their cars' shortcomings or the black helicopters sent by the government.

I was working regular out of county then and had to be up early and on the road, without time for Gatewood's bump. So I put two empty fifty-gallon metal drums in the pickup and went over it at forty miles an hour every morning, watching in my rearview mirror as Gatewood jolted up in bed like Dracula in that old horror movie.

Chapter 7

Sometimes I imagined Gatewood telling Esther how to mount him so he could engender a son without having to move too much. I don't think my wife ever spoke to him. When she died, Esther drove down and set a cheese casserole in a tinfoil pan on the door sill of their truck. I accepted it but was so distressed at that time I don't remember if I even thanked her.

After that, I would drive past the Doyle house and see wash on the line and a garden that over the years became an oasis, tomatoes in frames and beans on poles, broken tree branches holding up the fence in places and old boards to keep out low-traveling pests. Inside that leafy accumulation I saw a handsome woman working. She'd push dark hair out of her eyes with the back of a wrist, waving if she happened to notice me. One early morning she was gardening in her nightgown and I couldn't help but notice her silhouette against the morning light, and I still have that sight fondly in mind.

I never once saw Gatewood in Esther's garden. Dwayne was there only when very young. The garbage can on the back stoop overflowed as often as not. Gatewood was no longer visiting the dump as a matter of course because the dump master stopped standing still while Gatewood listed the shortcomings of his dump management and of letting black people into the recycling shed to finger the thread-worn suits and ass-busted coveralls all thrown together on a long table.

The dump master also let in Mexicans after they showed up in the county to perform the labor white men had once done.

Gatewood complained of lazy Mexicans even more than he had complained of lazy blacks. A house up the road from the Doyles' was owned by a good black family named Dostry, and those boys stayed on the other side of the road from the white blowhard in his rocker.

Not so their father. At first Gatewood wouldn't speak to Dostry when he walked past on his side, but he couldn't resist such an easy target and before long was telling Dostry how the different races came to be and why their separation was necessary. Dostry would stand at the edge of the property while Gatewood talked, having convinced himself he had an ally in Dostry against the Mexicans. He finally allowed Dostry to sit on the lower step and even to move slowly upward, but Dostry never gained the level of the porch.

Gatewood ended up with not one other person in the county who would listen to him. I would see Dostry's dark, lean frame on his step, bare arms like crossed butcher knives, and wonder why he put up with Gatewood's endless talking. I finally realized that the pathetic white man had become Dostry's unspoken good work. Comfort the afflicted, so teaches the Bible, and Dostry did that most every day without Gatewood ever suspecting he was a poor black man's charity.

I started pulling into the Doyle turnaround on my way to the dump. I would hoist Esther's overflowing trash can into the back of my truck and she would smile and nod her thanks from the garden or the kitchen window. She started coming out to say hello.

Sometimes Esther would catch me looking at the heft of her dark bound hair and at the way her full mouth turned up at the corners, and I think it pleased her. I didn't realize it but I was already a little bit in love with Esther. Sometimes I'd see her looking after me, like there was something she had meant to say.

One morning down at my place — it was June — I looked up from the last of wood splitting and saw Esther coming on foot. This was more than unusual. Womenfolk don't walk for the most part in these woods, having been warned by their men of the perils of mountain lions, although none had been officially reported.

Esther came across the low-water bridge, her hair up in a blue bandanna this time and her head held high though she looked sheepish. She asked for a drink of water and I got us both one, and we sat on the screen porch, away from the gnats, to drink them.

We finished our water and neither of us knew what to do next. She stood up, looking sad and a little desperate, the same expression I saw in the mirror every time I shaved. Then she seemed to make a decision and raised her arms and put them around my neck, the way a close relative might. The naturalness of it felt right, her considerable chest against mine.

The dampness of her shirt, the smell of her, all made me stupid. Then she was kissing me, and no relative's kiss. The next minute we were on the iron-frame bed that served as a couch. She peeled off her work shirt and then went for mine, a wonderment, this woman baring her breasts. Then one of them was in my mouth and I was unprepared. This must have been plain, because she said Don't worry, I'm already pregnant.

So I didn't. Worry, that is.

Chapter 8

After that I couldn't get Esther out of my mind. It wasn't just the sight of her in that sunlit nightgown, not anymore. Now it was all of her, the one big, powerful thing in my life, and I thought she had to know it. But she didn't come down to my place again, and I was afraid to go up there and make her life more difficult.

It's hard to believe, I know, and I blamed myself, having little experience with such things and hoping for a sign from her. Then her condition began to show, and I was ashamed of desiring a woman pregnant by someone else. Making love again felt necessary, though, inevitable and impossible all at the same time.

After Lurie was born it was clear that she was as different from her brother as could be. She came down here first time when she was two, naked and trailing a dirty blanket, sucking her thumb. She had the habit of running away when her mother wasn't looking, but this was the farthest she ever got. I called the Doyle house and by the time Esther came, Lurie was sitting on the back steps with me, eating sugar out of a cup, her little toes feeling the raised grain of the old chestnut.

She looks just like you, I told Esther, trying to ease her tearful relief at having found her daughter. And not a bit like Gatewood, I added, joking. But she picked Lurie up and got back in their pickup and trailed her fingers in the wind as she drove off.

Lurie grew up with a mouth on her. I would see her at Bartrum's with Esther and ask how she got all those fingers, and Lurie would ask how I got all those hairs in my nose. Before long she was overhearing and repeating all kinds of things, like No lie, frog-eye, and Get out the road, toad. Making an assertion of any kind in little Lurie's presence was akin to spitting in a tin plate because you were sure to get a retort.

She was free as only a child can be who doesn't realize it's not the common lot, a joy for herself and for anybody happening to lay eyes on her.

Dwayne at thirteen or fourteen was already a pimply borrower of others' cars without asking permission, a veteran shoplifter and scourge. He would kill any animal within range of the seat of Gatewood's all-terrain vehicle, which Gatewood had gotten a deal on and drove only once before leaving it to Dwayne to terrorize the woods with.

Gatewood would backhand him on occasion when he didn't have to cross the room to do it. He kept the keys to his pickup on a chain around his neck and generally ignored his son. Dwayne and some friends broke into from-aways' houses for salable stuff so they could buy marijuana and whatever else they craved. He spent a month in juvenile detention when Lurie was entering high school.

She made good grades, and that made Esther proud. There was a seriousness about Lurie, but in senior year she dropped out of school without warning and went to California. I asked Esther about it at the gas pump, trying not to make too much of it, but the desolation in her eyes took my breath away, and I knew I had been right to worry. I wanted to put my arms around her even though Bartrum's was the last place to try that.

Esther, I said, but she was gone again, a woman alone and I the closest, sorriest excuse she had for a friend and one-time lover.

Gatewood's stomach had become an impediment to his seeing

anything beneath chin level. His face glowed like a tomato. He had the heart attack not on his porch but on the toilet, and getting him to the hospital was quite a trial for the rescue squad, or so I heard.

The only people who came to his funeral were Esther, Dostry, and me. She cried but wanted no comfort. She did give Dostry a ride home in her truck afterward, and I thought I could hear old Gatewood banging his head against the lid of that coffin.

The next time I dropped by to get her trash Esther came out with two mugs of coffee and we sat on the back stoop. The front porch was like an open-air mausoleum, off limits, each of us keeping half an ear out for Gatewood's heavy shoes in the ruts he had worn in the unpainted boards and for his voice castigating a passing driver for dust.

You'd think with Gatewood dead and the kids gone Esther and I would grab each other, but we acted instead like the other was red hot. The memory of that time down at my place, still fresh in my mind, was no match for the thundering silence of the present. She had left half-moons in my back I could still see in the mirror a week later. I had gone to sleep that night hearing the cry from Esther's lips. But to get back to where we were on that distant day, if possible, required a courtship.

She asked to ride with me to the dump because she wanted to look in the recycling shed. It was April and the rolling hills as pretty as I had seen, studded with spring beauties opening in the sun.

The dump's fenced now, with an overhang high enough for big trucks to slip the dumpsters in and out. Flies are persistent, as are people tired of their dross. A separate structure houses clothes, books, magazines, household ware heavy on mismatches, all manner of stuff in need of repair. It's well picked over but on occasion something rises from the discards to greet you like an old friend —

a pitcher with an uneven lip, a sewing dummy.

You will eventually see everybody at the dump, gentry and those down from the back roads with long poles with hooks at the ends for reaching in and snagging the dumpster's desirables.

Esther held a white blouse up to her chin, then discovered the cuffs were too far gone. She held an apron without strings, shifting her hips in a playful way. I tried on an old sports jacket but she was doubtful. Neither of us had said much and neither wanted to get back into the truck, but we did.

The way home lies close to the mountains, skirting Boar Wallow but offering close views of the slopes I've been looking at all my life. Esther needed to stop at Bartrum's, so I stayed in the pickup, well away from the pumps. We carried her groceries into her house and she said, Macaroni and cheese?

The kitchen was a box, and in there with me was a big handsome woman melting cheese from a government-issue block. I sat at the Formica-top table shoved up against the wall, the crack between the leaves a haven for old toast crumbs and what is either unbleached flour or the long-ago remains of something illegal. What exactly went on in this house while Esther was working again at the co-op, having thought she'd finally escaped it, couldn't have been good.

Soon Esther and I were eating in silence, then bumping into each other at the sink, washing the dishes. Before we were done she led me into the bedroom, but one look at the broad depression in the mattress where Gatewood had slept drove me back.

Esther's jeans came down in handfuls and I urged her onto the Formica, my pants falling around my ankles. In my hands the softness of a waist I remembered, moving with the rhythm of a table gently bumping the wall. It took longer this time but the result was identical, her cry driving away the years.

Chapter 9

When you're young, death's often just an inconvenience, a thing that happens to other people, confounding at best. As you get older, dying begins to have more persistence and you realize it'll always be there. By the time you're my age, many people you know are gone and youth appears an oddity. You're on Earth to die, not live, so get on with it.

Animals know this instinctively. They don't sit around dreaming up religions and fancy arguments to excuse the mess they're in. They will do anything to avoid death, but alertness and persistence instead of dread is their way. Only people pretend something partial to them is in charge, that it will make the hereafter pleasant despite the fact that we all turned the garden into which we were born into a wasteland. Vanity, pure and simple.

Esther confided things to me after that, but not all, as you will see. The most important was that Dwayne provided both the inspiration and the means for Lurie's going to California, in that one of his friends had a fast car and decided to drive cross-country. At the very last minute, consulting with no one, Lurie climbed in with him. It was not romance, it was flight.

The main problem was that Dwayne had tried to mess with Lurie. Esther provided no details except to say that Lurie knocked out his front tooth with a thrown Pyrex pie plate. Though he was the main thing she was escaping, the whole nine yards of the Doyle family was intolerable to her, unfixable. No matter how well she did in school, no matter how high her hopes, the weight of the house hung round her neck like a logging chain.

No one we know has ever been to California. We all thought we knew what it was, though, a place where people walk around high on something and it's often too hot. Well, when you think about it, that's a pretty good description of Virginia.

Esther didn't know the details, except that Lurie ended up in the foothills of mountains just as she had started out in the foothills of mountains. I tried to imagine a pretty girl arriving in one piece in San Francisco, and getting from there to a community of farmers of a sort you might find here except that they were growing marijuana.

I pass Esther's house one day after Dwayne's return and see another vehicle out front, a car with flames painted on the hood before it got scorched by the real thing. The license plate reads biskit and the back window's covered with decals, mostly skulls. The back seat's door- sill-level full of discarded cans and plastic bottles.

The next time I pass a six-point buck with a gaping rib cage is hanging by the antlers from a tree, there for all to see, cloudy blue eyeballs heavenward.

Then there's a boat with a trolling motor and beat-up gunnels planted with rod holders. It sits on a trailer with two flat tires, half full of rainwater. Then the boat's up in the yard, and then it's gone altogether. Dwayne's pickup has acquired a big expensive spotlight rigged so you can climb onto the roof and shoot right over the beam. There's no sign of Dwayne, but Biskit — a man, not a dog — are in there because there's a little satellite dish on the roof now and a purplish flickering on the blinds.

Some nights later I hear a deep-throated mechanical growl far off and know it's Dwayne's truck. I glimpse a light and hear the shot. Spotlighting's illegal, but calling the law can have consequences beyond somebody's arrest. Dwayne's a former felon, so he'd go straight back to prison if caught with a gun, and I'm not looking for that kind of trouble. Not yet.

Lurie never calls me back. Deer season passes and decent weather creeps over the Blue Ridge. One night I hear a car door slam. Since nobody comes down my road by mistake, a strange vehicle at night's an event, and I open the front door.

I can hear the river in the darkness, then a child's voice cuts straight through it. I turn on the porch light and see a cab with the motor running, a batch of luggage set in the grass, and Lurie pushing bills through a slit in the window while next to her stands a little redheaded girl in a skirt, wide-eying me.

The driver can't get away fast enough. Lurie steps onto the front porch and gives me the same hug I remember from the funeral. The little girl's got a fistful of Lurie's jeans, maneuvering to keep on the far side of her.

Well, I say, not knowing how else to put it. Lurie must have come home to get her house back, or maybe someone's chasing her.

She tells me, This is Maeve.

Then she says, Maeve, say hello — and winks at me — say hello to Grandpa.

LURIE

Chapter 10

Contrary to what you might think, a person can grow up in a minute. By grow up I mean overthrow a lifetime habit of seeing the world this way or that, of thinking you arrived long ago at the doorstep of knowing and have spent the rest of your life fine-tuning your wisdom.

You will sometimes see a few seconds of that minute enacted at a revival meeting or in the exaltation of love climaxing in a wedding. All these promise more than they can deliver, in my experience. You will see it after a near death, yours or someone's close to you, but even this in time warps like a plank left out in the sun. Before long you're lost in the twistings of a grain leading back to where you began.

But sometimes that minute goes straight to the bone and lodges there. The only place to later find it is in the heart. Revealed bits of a story you thought long unraveled and gone were all the time with you. Were you.

I put them in the front bedroom because it can accommodate two and then lie down in what we used to call the hired man's room. Their murmurings reach me and then all's quiet, my mind alive in a way it hadn't been. I don't know if Lurie stopped by her house first and had a fight with Dwayne, or if she blew straight down my road.

Lurie's calling me Grandpa was a convenient way to make the

child feel at ease, I understand that. But the word struck deep. Since I never had children I could have no grandchild, and all night long I feel doubly bereaved.

There's nothing in the house to feed a little girl, not even bread, and nothing to amuse her if she wakes up before her mother does.

I get the woodstove going and feel around underneath for an implement I haven't touched in years — the cold wrought-iron handle of the waffle iron. It's like shaking hands with an old family member, covered in cobwebs. It cleans up pretty well, and I set it over an open burner and lay in two strips of bacon to grease it. I mix milk, eggs, flour, and baking powder from a can with a rusty rim in the big banded bowl with the crack. I also set dandelion honey on the stove to soften up.

When the bacon's done I move it to an old copy of the Piedmont Trader, pour batter in the iron, and clamp it shut. The first waffle's never the best, so I pour honey on it and stuff it in my mouth, looking up just then to see a carrot-topped girl standing in the doorway.

You can't tell a true story straight, and if you try, it will still contain a lie. Time curls around and comes back at you from another direction, like people. Just when you think you know someone, or something, she or it will reappear, wholly different, all you thought you knew overcome and in its place revelation.

This little girl is Lurie's. Doyle hair and Doyle eyes, but not Lurie's solid frame. At six Maeve can already make an old man hop without having to say a word. I sit her at the table and put a new waffle in front of her, and she turns in the chair to stare at the bacon. A strip of that lands on her plate, and only then does she pick up her knife and fork.

You can eat the bacon with your fingers, I tell her.

She just turns those blue eyes on me. The bacon disappears in neat little knife-cut bites. I expect her to go after the waffle then but instead she turns and looks at the other strip of bacon. I reach that over, too. When it's gone she skims honey off the waffle with the table knife and sits sucking on it like a lollipop.

We're vegetarian.

It's Lurie, standing behind me. Once again Gatewood's head bangs against his coffin lid. For him the only thing worse than Mexicans and blacks was a feedbag full of gun regulators, animal rights folks, government employees, same-sex anythings, and people who don't eat meat.

Lurie's in the same clothes she arrived in, arms folded across her stomach, dark hair uncombed. Paler than at her mother's funeral and in some distress, it seems.

You look like you could use breakfast, I say.

She asks Maeve, You like that?

The girl nods. I give Lurie a plate with only a waffle and not until she's done does she ask for tea.

I don't have any.

So I pour coffee into a mug and set that before her. Maeve's staring at the river.

You want to go down and throw rocks in the water? I ask her, but she doesn't answer.

You don't have much to say, do you?

I do, too, she says. I just haven't said it yet.

Lurie at her age would have used the word "ain't," so she's been improving the family while out there in California. I have plenty of questions for her but can see this will take time, and she's just waking up.

I go out to the shed for a length of rope and tie it to the sycamore nearest the house, in plain view of the kitchen. I have no proper swing so I make a loop at one end with a bowline that won't slip and throw it over a high branch. I tie the other end of it to the trunk.

Before long Maeve comes out to assess the handiwork. She walks over and tests the rope, then puts a foot in the loop. Before long she's swinging, the first time a child has played in a yard used by all manner of other creatures. She's enjoying it, and that's unreasonably pleasurable for me.

I take out a chair, to give her some altitude, and she swings higher. Lurie comes out and sits on the steps without her coffee, holding instead a widemouthed canning jar wrapped with duct tape that conceals whatever's inside.

She says, I'd appreciate it if you'd bury this and promise not to tell me where. And not dig it up until it's time.

How will I know when that is?

Oh, you'll know.

Chapter 11

My wife and I once had quite a garden. The remains of it lie at the edge of the property, fallow for years, overgrown with things I had hoped would return nutrition to the soil. Two of the sideboards remain and four weathered posts. The fencing I took down, rolled up, and shoved under rafters in the shed. The stacked tomato frames are rusty but still capable of supporting the riot of vine and juice-heavy incarnations of the photographs in the seed catalogs.

Hanging from the walls of the shed are more gardening tools than a man really needs, some with dirt still on them from mixing in horse manure. The watering can has sat pointing in the same direction for years.

What we need now is grown vegetables, lots of them from the look of things. That means driving up to the supermarket in Purdy.

The three of us cruise past what is now Lurie's house, not Esther's, Lurie in the window seat and Maeve between. Biskit's flame-covered car's back and Dwayne's pickup has lost its spotlight. There's another flat- bottomed skiff in the yard, more woebegone than the first, with a paddle sticking up and a hand-lettered sign saying Fishing Guide. Lurie must be thinking the same thing I am because we both laugh.

Maeve sits forward, watching the land go past, stretching toward the mountains like one big sheet of unbleached muslin. I drop them at the drugstore so Lurie can get a prescription filled and go to the bank for cash. I'm now seeing Purdy the way a little girl might, people mostly too big for their own good, the trials of a lifetime in their eyes.

The plumber and hardware dealer are struggling, and the whole place feels like it's been left beside an interstate it didn't want in the first place. Old folks gathered at the edge of the world, not wanting to peer too far over because they might fall.

We meet again at the Food Lion, where we buy what feels like half the produce department, plus milk, cheese, eggs, tofu — there goes Gatewood again — and on the way home visit the drive-thru. Soft-serve's running down Maeve's arm by the time we get home.

Lurie goes to lie down and I take a closer look at the garden. Before long I have the wheelbarrow down there and the hoe, whacking at weeds. Some people pull them by hand, as my late wife did, but I don't unless I'm looking for dandelion or purslane. Then here's Maeve again, in stretch pants now and high-top sneakers.

You going to help? I ask.

Without a word she starts slinging dead johnson grass and goldenrod like she knows what she's doing.

At suppertime Lurie comes into the kitchen, eyes bright and on her face the remembered smile. I feel so much better, she says.

She sets about making supper out of a mess of vegetables I never saw keep company in the same skillet, and serves it over rice that looks dirty but tastes all right. There's thin bread wrapped around more vegetables, fried and dipped in soy sauce.

You on vacation? I ask Maeve.

We're home-schooling, Lurie says. A little behind, aren't we, darling?

After supper they're back in the bedroom, where Lurie reads her a story I can hear from the hallway. Pretty soon Maeve comes out in pajamas with animals printed on them and outsized slippers made to look like bears. She says, Good night, Grandpa.

I say, Good night, Granddaughter. And want to cry.

When Lurie returns to the kitchen I tell her flatly, I don't like this. I'll go along for now, but only because I figure there's a good reason. I have to know what the reason is for lying to a little girl.

And she says, You're not lying.

Lurie might have been sassy as a child but she didn't talk easily about herself, and the one thing she never did was lie. Esther said Lurie was so tired of all the lying from both males in the family that she decided to always tell the truth, no matter how bad.

What in God's name are you saying? I ask.

That Esther wasn't pregnant when she came down to see you that time. Desperation gave her strength to follow through on what she craved, not just affection but to leave something behind not tainted by Gatewood. He wasn't even interested in sex by then. Ma told me all about it. She convinced him I was just born late. Made up something like spontaneous conception or prolonged conception, I don't remember which.

You mean he didn't want to know?

Because if he had he would have had to deal with it. So what I'm saying is, you're my father, not Gatewood.

I feel behind me for the chair.

Why didn't Esther tell me?

Because it was too late. Me and Dwayne were gone, you the only one to keep an eye on her. She wasn't sure you'd believe her. She had wanted a child all her own and was good at keeping secrets. I didn't find out until the end, way out in California, and she made me swear not to tell until I had to. And then to tell it without regret.

Why didn't she just leave him?

Because he was her husband. She had promised to abide with and care for him, so she stayed even though it broke her heart. You were a godsend but not the perfect one. I think she loved you — not at the beginning maybe, but eventually.

I don't know what to say.

Ma's still right next to Gatewood, she says. Listening to him for all eternity. That's hell twice over.

Lurie scoots the kitchen chair across boards sanded by me before she was born and puts a hand on my shoulder.

Why didn't you come up and take Esther away?

I didn't want to cause her trouble.

She already had trouble. You saw that. I think you were afraid, and now you've got to finally deal with it. If you had asked, she would have walked out and slammed that screen door in Gatewood's face. I could have grown up down here.

She flings a hand in the direction of the sycamore.

That could be my swing out there.

She begins to cry while I stare at the floor, noticing the places I missed with the sander. Reach out, I should have told myself back then. Take a chance. What else of such importance had I missed in life? Had I ever gotten anything really right?

I try to pull Lurie to me, but she won't be pulled.

Why? she repeats, unmindful of the tears, pounding on my chest with her mother's forearms.

Chapter 12

Spring arrives from the earth, not the air. Grass greens up, rising like something's down there, pushing. Long after you think the trees should have leafed, they're still gray and barren-looking, at least from a distance. To see the first buds you have to really look.

Embedded lichens appear on rotted wood like thrown saucers with sculpted edges. Bluebirds sit on the power line, looking for a prospective nursery. Nowadays they don't migrate because the winters are so mild, but I still find one now and then frozen in February.

Other birds are scarcer, like indigo buntings that used to chance my feeder. I glimpse them in the tangle swallowing my driveway. In spring the thrasher pursues its work in thickets made perilous by feral house cats. Early spring's also a dangerous time for fire, the rains coming but not quite yet and the woods dry as tinder. A turkey hunter scouting the woods for a spot when the season opens all too often has a cigarette in his mouth.

Ground fire can come in from the mass of fallen timber to the north, raining ashes. My roof's tin but the house itself is clapboard, which can ignite from the proximity of an inferno. Fire could also come along the power line to the well pump, everything connected, everything touchable by one little spark.

The garden's hung now with the old fencing, but the gate's new and the soil inside is mixed with new mulch shaped into rows. In years past those tomato cages were fitted with the starter plants from the kitchen window. The carrot seeds went in early and will soon have to be thinned, which will feel like murder.

We put in onions, too, me, Lurie, and Maeve. We're about to put in kale, potatoes, squash, and a number of other things Lurie wants. The only way to deal with uncertainty is work, I believe. Industriousness isn't just praiseworthy: it helps you survive doubts about yourself and your world. Work scrubs the soul when it doesn't destroy it and puts distance between you and unlikely dreams.

My professional work changed slowly with the onset of tree blights and sudden death disease. Who needs a trained timber cruiser when half your trees are bleached or fatally cankered and all you need is a saw to finish the job? And now instead of one person to feed I have three.

Other procedures are new, like farmers' markets where we see strange vegetables and from-aways and hippie types buying them, as well as herbs and natural cures. Visits to the supermarket have to be timed with Kmart trips for little rubber boots and to the drugstore for Lurie. She has her own money but not in the amounts I would have thought.

Some kind of difficulty developed out there in California, and right now she doesn't want to talk about it. I half expect Maeve's father to show up out of the sunset in one of those tie-dyed shirts and long hair, but my expectations are long out of date. All I know is that Lurie's condition — migraines, she says — have not improved, and her manner can go from anxious to content in a minute.

She sleeps late most days but by midday is up and homeschooling has kicked in. Woe be to anybody who gets in the way of that. I hear her and Maeve discuss the history of oppression, something I never heard about in school, and mathematics that makes little sense to me, and I can work a slide rule and even calculate on it. The difficulty of the things this little girl is supposed to learn amazes me, and I begin to understand why parents send their children to school — to avoid being embarrassed by all they themselves don't know.

Maeve and I are thrown together most mornings, waiting for Lurie to get up. At first I think I'm looking after her but soon realize it's the other way around. You don't have any socks on, she'll say. Deer ticks will get on your ankles and crawl up.

Or, The inside of your collar's dirty.

She thinks tree names are boring, but not bird names. She doesn't like shoes with laces, but she does like questions. How can a whole tiger swallowtail come out of this?, holding up a cocoon picked from the juniper tree? Why doesn't the river flow down the well? How can a dog and a coyote be in one animal? How does baking powder get poison out of a sting? What's an aquifer? What's dowsing?

A girl who wouldn't talk in the beginning now won't stop.

I'll show you something, I tell her, if you'll promise not to tell your mother.

I lead her out to the well.

An aquifer's an underground river, I begin. Ours runs — I point out the directions — southwest by northeast.

How do you know?

Because I dowsed this very spot, a long time ago.

I pull a flimsy branch off the white oak.

Trees and everything else are connected to aquifers, I go on, even if they're way down there. Like veins in your body. All of them don't reach your heart directly but are part of something bigger. Animals and plants need wetness, and some plants will reach for it to depths hard to believe.

I hold the branch out in front of me.

Most people don't believe in dowsing, I add, just so you know.

We start to walk slowly around the well house.

You have to hold the branch lightly. Keep your mind clear.

The tip twitches, and Maeve's big blue eyes widen. She reaches for the branch and I give it to her.

Keep walking, I say.

She holds the branch out in front of her.

Loosen up, I tell her. Unlock your elbows. Think of nothing.

Before long the branch twitches again. Her mouth falls open and she let outs a shriek. If that doesn't wake Lurie up, nothing will.

But Lurie doesn't appear, so Maeve gets another vacation from homeschooling, sitting at the kitchen table over the illustrated encyclopedia I looked at when about the same age, open to the familiar picture of a Tyrannosaurus rex worn faint by the fingers of her distant kin.

I go back and knock on Lurie's door. She doesn't answer, so I open it. She's under the sheet, hair wet with sweat. The smell of old air in the room for some reason chills me.

I have a really bad headache, she says. Got any painkillers?

I don't take pills except for aspirin, which isn't up to Lurie's demands. Years before, I gashed my thigh with the skill saw, and only the dense weave of my Carhartts prevented the blade from reaching bone. They sewed me up at the hospital in Purdy and gave me some pills. I took one, and it made me so unreliable I shoved the rest to the back of the cabinet with the iodine and stool softeners.

Now I dig them out again. The name on the label is Percocet, which means nothing to me. It's out of date, but I give her the bottle anyway and a glass of water.

Half an hour later she's up and breezing into the bathroom, running the tub until there's no hot water left.

Chapter 13

Homeschooling commences with a vengeance, and one day begins to resemble the one before. Chard thinning, changing the blades on the mower after first cranking it onto one side with the come-along and putting the chopping block underneath so I can get at the bolts without being maimed. Sweeping mouse droppings from the top of the washing machine in the shed so the laundry basket can be set down cleanly. Hanging wet sheets on the line.

Maeve watches all this in her usual reverie, but I know she's learning. Repairing a window sash, cleaning out a drain, tightening the leg of a chair, if you don't know how to deal with these things you'll succumb to a relentless piling up of jobs, like drowning in a slowly rising cattle pond. Work is treading the water of life: it keeps you out of the poorhouse and sometimes out of the nuthouse.

I show Maeve how to drill holes with the power drill. These are wood screws with Phillips heads, I explain. You have more grip with them.

I show her how to put the bit in the power drill.

Will it hurt the washer if I drill holes in the side? she asks.

Probably not, but that would be a silly thing to do.

But I'm bored.

Then go do something else.

I've told her not to put her hand into a hole in the stone wall, not to suck on a hollow piece of wild grapevine that might be full of ants, never mess with a snake that smells like sliced cucumbers, because it's a copperhead.

Now I say, Pay attention to what's a ways off, not just right in front of you. Stay in sight of the house. Never run from a bear, but instead walk slowly backward and scream, realizing as I say it that Maeve's lungs lack the necessary power.

After lunch I leave her with her mother and drive to Lester's gun shop. It's warm for early spring, the sky blue and without obstruction, the mountains just beginning to green up in the creases where the big trees are. I find the shop empty except for two turkey hunters in camo who've been listening for gobblers all morning and have the tired eyes of men up since four with nothing to show for it.

Lester leans over his workbench, still in winter clothes, his felt vest creased at the waist. He looks up at me and says, I hear Lurie Doyle's back.

You got any bear-scaring devices?

He points to a display rack behind me jammed with canisters of pepper spray and air horns on compressed- gas cans. I choose the smallest and pay cash. It's a problem that needs solving. A girl's mother is supposed to decide what a child does, and Maeve needs socializing as well as homeschooling, but poor Lurie has her hands full taking care of herself. So I take Maeve to lunch at Bartrum's, where we split one of those mahogany hot dogs that go round and round all day and homemade tomato soup in Styrofoam containers.

The county examiner sitting at the common table asks, Who's your friend?

Maeve. She's visiting family.

He asks her what kind of name is that, and Maeve says, Celtic. It means intoxicator.

The inspector laughs. What's intoxicator mean?

Maeve shrugs, bored now. She attacks her package of saltines, then attacks mine. Others join us, and she listens to every word said while pretending not to. I see no harm in it. These are hardworking men — a mechanic, a part-time farmer with moldy hay in the back of his truck, a lineman. Usually the likes of us just eat and watch people buy cigarettes, soda, candy. From-aways mostly buy their high-octane outside and rarely come in except for the New York Times. They look back at our table, but that's about it.

Lurie needs to see a doctor to get her prescription refilled. I send her to mine, Dr. Simms, a country practitioner on the outskirts of Purdy, as old as I am and of similar mind. I go to see him every half-dozen years, and he always asks what I'm doing there. He thinks people spend too much time worrying about their innards, but he did ask me once if I wanted a prostate examination. Naturally I said no.

Lurie borrows the truck to go see Dr. Simms, and Maeve and I set about making her a scabbard cut from a piece of tanned deer hide for her new air horn. It has fringe and a drawstring. Maeve likes the pouch but not the idea of carrying a can in it, so I sweeten the deal with a little sheath knife with a bone handle, an item long in the family, found among old hunting paraphernalia in a cabinet smelling of gun oil.

We go outside and string the pouch and horn on a leather belt shortened and skewed twice with an awl.

Remember, I tell her, knives cut. Never point the blade toward yourself, never cut toward your hand or you might lose a finger. Hold the scabbard while you're shoving the blade back inside.

The air horn's a bigger problem.

I can't get it out, she says.

You don't have to. Just push down on it as it sits.

She tries, and the blast shunts her sideways. This is the first time she's laughed like that since she arrived.

Now, I say, don't go more than two see-fars away from the river.

What's a see-far?

I'll show you.

We go into the woods. I ask if she can still see the river, and she says, Kind of.

That's one see-far. Now go another see-far and then turn around and see if you can still make out the river. If you can, that's two see-fars. Go on.

There's cobwebs in the bushes.

I tear off a little branch. Wiggle this in front of you as you walk.

I stay put. In two minutes she turns around, a little girl in new rubber boots with the jeans bottoms tucked in, a knife and air horn on her hip and an old Harris Feed cap giveaway on her head. Her eyes are wide.

I wave. She waves. I turn and start back to the house, wondering if she'll come galloping after, but she doesn't.

I sit on the back steps and wait for the horn blast. Lurie drives up and I can hear from the way she slams the door that the visit with Dr. Simms didn't go well.

Where's Maeve?

In the woods.

In the woods?

Her eyes are red-rimmed and she looks like hell.

You can't just leave her in the goddamn woods.

She knows where she is. In five minutes she'll come walking out.

But Lurie doesn't wait, putting her hands to her mouth, and is about to shout when I take her arm.

Don't. You'll make it seem like something's wrong. She'll see you're scared then she'll be scared, too. What happened with the doctor?

He wouldn't give me a prescription. Said I don't need it, if you can believe that.

What did he say about the headaches?

That they're imaginary. I wanted to give that old man a headache but didn't.

She sits on a step.

He said I take too many painkillers, that if I don't stop I'll end up in the substance abuse clinic.

I've worried about Lurie's past from the beginning, and what tendencies she might have brought back with her. I expected her to walk around smoking marijuana but she didn't. Not in secret, either, because I know that skunky smell picked up sometimes around the gas pumps at Bartrum's.

Maeve comes out of the woods dragging a length of rotten log embedded with big yellow lichens. Lurie studies her getup.

So now you're arming your granddaughter?

A person sometimes need a knife in the woods.

What's next, a Glock?

Maeve has the knife in hand and is prying at a lichen. There are dark streaks of earth on her cheek where she pushed the hair from her eyes. She looks like a capable redheaded kid in a feed cap.

Well, I tell Lurie, I guess you better stop.

Chapter 14

Drop even a small rock into a river and you give rise to an expanding circle of disturbance. The ripples get smaller and broader but still ride on the current until they wear themselves out and again are part of the river. This has always seemed a small miracle to me.

Your troubles are like that, ripples atop a deep, unstoppable thing that will eventually take them in again, solved or not, and move on to a place where they no longer matter. Seem to no longer matter's more like it.

For a long time Lurie's tale has been mashed into a ball of yarn so tight that finally, in the telling, it unravels so fast I can barely keep up. I don't ask a question because I'm afraid she'll stop.

One would be how did she get west of the plains where she left Dwayne's friend in a roadhouse. A nice southern girl, she says, carrying an old canvas bag containing the things she valued most, walks up to a group of women about to board a bus chartered to take them to Denver and asks, Do you have an empty seat? Because I'm broke.

Then I see Lurie sitting next to the nice gray-haired former teacher who gives her forty dollars to take the Greyhound from Denver to San Francisco, where she steps out onto Market Street and asks where are restaurants needing waitresses.

Then she's setting plates of home fries and ham and eggs in front of men with beards and the tourists come to look at them. The neighborhood's called The Haight, and Lurie spells it for me. One young man tells her of a place in the foothills of the Sierra Nevada where people are getting rich growing pot.

She makes her first mistake by sleeping with him in his communal house. Then she takes off with him the next day still riding shotgun, finds a dope farm, and her young man keeps going after Lurie is hired.

She trims buds, piles up weed, bags it. She's promoted to field supervisor, they call it, which means shading the plants from the sun and the law passing overhead in a helicopter. The law knows what's going on down there but they don't land, and pretty soon no one pays them any mind.

Growers on nearby farms try to poach their crop, and the head farmer goes out and fires a semiautomatic rifle into the darkness. He rigs up trip wires attached to devices with shotgun shells inside that will take out a trespasser's knee.

The money comes in fast, too fast, everybody stuffing it where they hope it won't be found. Lurie's problem now is that she's pregnant, and when this can no longer be hidden she attaches herself to a fellow worker named Ocean, his hair up in braids. She takes his last name for convenience and shares a bed with him, but little else.

Pretty soon she's doing the farm's books and helping sort out who gets how much money and making communal tubs of soup on the side. Maeve's born in the kitchen. The other women help out, the men stand by, and when they see Maeve's red hair they all cheer. There's comfort in that.

They named the baby by popular vote.

This setup holds long enough for Maeve to grow out of babyhood and everybody to accumulate so much cash that hiding it's a real problem. The head man keeps his in a locked trunk freezer under the basement stairs, wired with an alarm and one of those shotgun shell devices that will kill anyone trying to find out how much is in there. How he himself gets to it without being buckshot nobody can figure out.

The others are now hiding their money under floors, in the guts of disused farm equipment, in holes in the ground, in trees. Lurie's stays in plain sight in leftover but like-new diaper boxes shoved under the bed. Not even Ocean suspects this. She buys herself a car just before the helicopter finally lands and armed men in camo and face paint pile out.

The head man takes off in his van with what Lurie estimates to be a million dollars. She and Maeve are sitting at the picnic table at the time pretending to be visitors and they stay put, reading a story while everybody else scatters. She tells the law she knows nothing about marijuana and only stopped by to use the restroom and read her daughter a story.

She shows them her driver's license with Ocean's last name on it and the address of a boardinghouse in town. One writes all this down and tells her not to leave the area. Her diaper boxes are already in the trunk of her car because they were safer there than under the bed. So she and Maeve get in and drive away, leaving everything else they own in the bunkhouse.

Here the tale picks up speed. Lurie rents a furnished apartment in town and puts the diaper boxes under the bed. She lets the law know where she is, and buys another car and hides it in the garage. When Esther dies she and Maeve take a chance and fly back to Virginia for the burial. Little Maeve waits in the cab the whole time, unnoticed. They return to California and two days later a friend of Ocean's shows up with another guy and tells her if she doesn't hand over her savings, they'll take Maeve.

Lurie doesn't believe him but is afraid to risk being wrong and gives him a diaper box. The trial of the others is coming up, and Lurie's to be a witness. But she and Maeve slip away in the middle of the night and don't stop until they get most of the way to Denver. They live on coffee, milk, apples, mixed nuts, and sweet buns. She sells the car, throws away the phony driver's license, and buys two tickets to Dulles airport using her expired Virginia license. A big woman agent gives her a strip search right in front of Maeve. The remaining diaper box is in her checked luggage, and they board the plane.

So, I say, how much money did those guys take?

A hundred grand.

That takes some wind out of me. It's late, and darkness is thick against the kitchen panes. Who would guess the kid who once walked down here naked would end up in such a desperate place?

What's in that jar I buried?

Lurie shakes her head. Not money, if that's what you're thinking. Not dope, either.

All of a sudden she looks weary beyond her thirty-odd years.

Maybe I should dig it up, I say.

I know you won't because you promised not to.

Chapter 15

For an appreciable stretch of time Lurie gets herself out of bed in the morning, though she's irritable. She sweats with the slightest effort. Working in the garden drenches her. We lift out tomato stalks and stack the cages behind the shed for next spring. We pull the drear remains of the annuals and prepare the ground, build a chicken house using old lumber and wire, and buy South American hens Maeve falls in love with.

Lurie is inclined to weariness still, a sad thing to see. Sometimes tears cut trails in the dirt on her face. She talks no more of the past, and I don't ask. Maeve roams her two see-fars wearing her knife and air horn. Two or three times a day she checks the henhouse for eggs. Those chickens are as companionable as dogs, settling onto your feet if you stand for a minute chuckling without pause, and there are never enough kitchen scraps. They lay pretty pale blue and even green eggs, the yolks dark orange. We eat them every which way.

Bears seem content digging out yellowjacket nests along the old stone wall by the river to get at the larvae and grazing blackberries at the far edge of the woods. Groundhogs patrol the garden fence in late evening, coyotes yip at night, coons overrun the henhouse but can't get in. In the morning we see the fox running away with nothing in his jaws, his backward glance a curse.

Maeve has to stay in the yard after black powder season starts. The muffled bump of muzzle-loaders firing sounds like far-off thunder. I think of the amount of lead these old trees carry after all the missed deer, turkeys, varmints, and people shot at for hundreds of years, an invisible load of fury embedded in the cambium.

I used to live for gun shooting, any gun, and remember well the sense of power it carries. Also the company it brings you. Carrying a gun makes you feel you're a match for the world, for no good reason. But calibers and magazines and the speed of bullets keeps rising beyond what's needed to kill things, another sign of our ailing species. To say this is to risk being shunned, even if you vote, even if your days are spent working for a living.

Not just rich from-aways carry fancy guns. I've seen boys with no more to spare than they can scrape off the soles of their boots walk into Lester's and put down six hundred dollars for a stainless-steel high-powered pistol fitted with a scope that's about as useful as spit.

Some of every day is now spent splitting heater wood. There's a rhythm to it once you spot the weak point. The first ax stroke's reflected in every one that follows. Do it right and on the final stroke the log will open like a flower.

I'm splitting down-property when Lurie comes out and calls to me she's borrowing the pickup. She doesn't say what for and I think nothing of it. She comes back at dusk, all smiles and hugs for Maeve, eyes bright, step lively. She's not sweating or meeting my gaze, and her nose is running.

Where've you been?

I stopped by the house to talk to Dwayne.

I suppose that's addiction, her taking stuff from the one who once attacked her.

There was stuff we had to work out, she adds.

What'd he say?

Not much.

It doesn't take an hour to say not much. You talk to him about paying rent? After all, Esther left you the house, not him.

That didn't come up.

I drive the next morning up to Purdy to get advice from Dr. Simms. He listens a while and asks, She your paramour?

Hell no. What would make you ask such a question?

She's attractive and she's living in your house. Is her child yours?

Same answer.

But I'm thinking that's naturally what most people will assume. I can imagine them at Bartrum's gas pumps: You hear about Lurie Doyle coming home with a child and living with a man more than twice her age?

She's my daughter, I tell Simms.

Which one?

The mother, goddamn it. Why didn't you give her that prescription?

Because she doesn't need painkillers. Your daughter's addicted to something the doctors out there in California must have given her. If you want to help her, get the stuff away from her and her away from the place where she gets it. If you can keep her away, she has a chance.

I pay him in cash. He says, Now, if you're going to start taking care of a family you've got to take care of yourself. You've never had a prostate check and you're seventy-odd years old. God knows what's up there. Drop your pants.

For once I do as he says.

Now turn around and bend over.

What happens next is impossible to describe. Mostly it's humiliating and it hurts.

I'm sorry, he says, handing me a tissue. He hasn't even taken off his suit coat. Your prostate's got more bumps on it than a horny toad.

You need to see a specialist.

Specialists are people you pay a lot of money to tell you you're about to die.

I think the prostate needs to come out.

He writes a name and a phone number on his pad and hands me the sheet of paper.

Call him. If you want to be on this earth a while longer, that is.

Chapter 16

The likelihood of dying clears the mind. Decisions you put off a lifetime ago get made, and not wholly by you. They say dying brings up your whole life, even if's been as uneventful as mine. Doomed people start going to church and looking around for a good cause. None of that appeals to me. It sounds silly, but I don't have the time. As for the hereafter, I have no expectations after a life watching and sometimes assisting in other things dying. It left me expecting more not of the hereafter but of the right now.

A woman and a child come down your overgrown driveway in a taxicab and make themselves precious. Whether they're kin or not doesn't matter as much as the feeling. Now I can't tell the grown one what to do, even if she is my daughter, but I can attempt to change the odds in her favor.

It's clear she's getting something from her brother that goes beyond painkilling. Lurie's nose is always running when she comes back, and she's more active. But the aftermaths get worse. Home-schooling falls off, Maeve gets quiet and unsure of herself. Days get shorter, nights longer, and there's not enough for a little girl to do. She needs company her own age, proper schooling, better clothes. Lurie should be dealing with all that and she isn't.

What's Dwayne giving you?

Either cocaine or some pill he crushes with the hilt of his knife.

The confession sets me back.

I don't take much, she adds, just a pinch now and then. To keep me steady.

What do you pay him?

He calls it rent money.

It's not rent money, it's what's left of you. You've got to stop. If you don't, social services will take Maeve away.

You wouldn't let them do that.

I've got no legal say.

You do. I've written what I guess you'd call a will. It says you're Maeve's guardian.

How will I manage that? I don't have enough money as it is, and Maeve needs things requiring more than money. She needs her mother. She needs friends. You're high right now, aren't you?

I'm contemplative.

I just shake my head.

Why don't you dig up that jar? she asks.

Because whatever's in it will end up with Dwayne, the state you're in. You've got to stop, Lurie. You've got to stay away from him.

That night Maeve and I play checkers. I ask what she thinks of Uncle Dwayne, and she says she doesn't like him.

Why not?

Because he squeezes my leg when Momma's not looking. Hard.

When she's asleep, I tell Lurie. She closes her eyes and sits with her elbows on her knees, hair hanging down that can't hide the blotches on her cheeks. Nowadays about all she eats is sugar, and she drinks a lot of milky coffee that still doesn't keep her awake.

I won't take Maeve back up there, she says, as if that solves it.

You shouldn't be up there, either. Dwayne's a pestilence and you know it. He's got to go, and you have to get into that clinic up in Purdy. Don't make me be the one calling social services. You could end up in jail.

Why don't you just kick us out and be rid of us?

I don't want to be rid of you. Even if I did, Maeve would still be without schooling. You'd be without whatever they'll give you at the clinic. Dwayne's the one needs kicking out, brother or not. He tried to rape you, for God's sake. He might try something a whole lot worse.

Autumn comes a bit later each year, September hot and dry as dust well into October, brittle leaves on the ground making soundless walking impossible. Foraging squirrels drive hunters on deer stands crazy and often get blamed for a kill-less morning.

Geese, goldfinches, many kinds of bird that would ordinarily be headed south by now spend their winters here, their scant bodies pathetic in early spring as they wait for bud-break. Bare survival seems a sign of things to come, not cold but heat, drought, wind.

I go to a specialist over in the Shenandoah Valley, and Lurie and Maeve come with me. We get soft-serve on the way, not talking much because there's so much to say. We look like a family to most, I suppose, but Lurie's problems are still with us. Something has to happen to change that.

The specialist probes around, takes pictures, goes after a piece of it with a snaky thing that makes all former pain seem benign. Sometime after that he sends the results to Dr. Simms, who tells me the cancer's slow growing and there are two options. Have it out, or don't have it out.

Choose the first, he adds, and there's a chance you'll lose control of your bladder and may have to pee through a plastic tube. Choose the second option and you'll have a front row seat at the race between your natural longevity and the cancer's unholy appetite.

Laurie still goes up to the house she owns and her worthless brother lives in. But Maeve stays with me. You wouldn't think such a thing could get routine, but it can, as pitiful as that sounds. My money's nearly gone so one of us needs a job, but Lurie can't pass a drug test, Maeve's too young, and I'm too old.

One afternoon while Lurie sleeps Maeve goes far down the yard. I'm reading the Piedmont Trader on the back steps when I hear the air horn. I run toward where she stands, her back to me, looking into the woods beyond. She turns, her face pale.

He was right there, she says. He had his bow. He was smiling.

Uncle Dwayne?

I thought he was a bear.

She laughs and starts back to the house. There's no sign of him, and I follow Maeve, the weight of the thing almost insupportable. I can't tell Lurie because she'll confront Dwayne. He'll say he was just funning.

I swing a stick against a goldenrod hard enough to take it down in a cloud of pollen. There has to be a way out of this. Maybe it's the only one, though no pastor or judge would agree.

One thing a man my age knows instinctively, or thinks he does, is that certain people need killing. There's no way out of this when the life of a child's involved. Report the crime and let the system work, you'll hear. But sometimes that's not a solution, just a postponement. In the meantime terrible and unfixable damage can be done.

I park down the road from Dwayne's truck and wait. I have thrown the shovel into the back of the pickup and put on my old camo jacket that still smells of dirt and rotten leaves. My boots are the oldest and most worthless because I will be burying them. Bee-K's old revolver's tucked into my belt, the cold, hidden handle pressing against my stomach.

The possum skull on Dwayne's grille has been replaced by fresh antlers off a spike buck, the rest of him hanging upside down from the sycamore tree. Big knobby tires have grown on Dwayne's truck that jack it up so he can drive over fences and through rivers when he feels the impulse. The sedan with the flame-covered hood and the Biskit license plate's gone, as is the metal boat and woebegone trailer. So he's living alone. The satellite dish on the roof's full of bullet holes.

I get out and start for the house. I clomp up the steps to announce myself and tap on the door. It's jerked open and there he stands, in camo since it's deer season.

Hey, Dwayne.

Hey what?

I need help.

He squints at me, the silver tooth winking, his eyes slits in a knobby, now shaven head.

With what?

A bear. He's the biggest I've seen and hell on my compost pile. I'm baiting him back in the woods with hot dogs and buns, but I'm not sure I'm up to dealing with him.

So you want backup?

No, you can kill him yourself. Should be real easy.

Dwayne looks me over. Something's going on behind those black-flecked eyes.

I don't want any of him, I add, except maybe a tooth. The gallbladder in a bear like that has to be worth twelve hundred dollars.

Is there a stand?

No, a depression. Which is better. He can't scent you, and there's maneuvering room. A good upward lung shot's dead certain, and probably the heart.

I don't know about that.

I'll be nearby. I'll help open him up once you've killed him and to move him later.

The room behind him is full of glasses, Styrofoam cups, cigarette butts, plastic plates of pig rib remnants, empty canisters of store-bought coleslaw, hot sauce from little red bottles lined up on the mantelpiece.

He comes back with his bow.

Okay, old man. Let's go.

From the road I watch for the two-tread track overgrown with ailanthus and creepers leading off to the northeast. We step out of the pickup and Dwayne gently, almost tenderly, lifts out his bow.

I pick up the shovel.

You're the only person I ever heard of to bring a shovel on a bear hunt, he says.

I want to dig out a step. Makes getting in and out easier.

There's a rushing in my ears as we walk, Dwayne making not a sound. I never noticed before, but he's almost delicate looking, slipping the thong on the string trigger over his right hand, pulling back the clasp on the left side of his belt to free that wicked knife.

He says, No bear's gonna take Dwayne Doyle by surprise, by God.

The woods had been cut over and are still a dismal sight, a big tree here and there, but mostly runty trunks. Stone walls run this way and that, built long ago by men more determined than those of today. Ash borer paths in the trunks look like the markings of a lunatic.

You said it was half a mile. We done come that.

See the pile of rocks?

When we get there, he looks down.

God a-mighty, I guess that's a hole.

Somebody's fine cellar once.

A single standing wall blocks the southern view.

That's the way the bear'll come, I say.

He climbs down without waiting for me to dig, and I follow.

I don't know about this, he says.

You'll be protected by the wall. I'd set up right below it.

And I toss three still-frozen hot dogs into the weeds.

While he dines you can put two arrows in him.

If it's so easy, why ain't you doin' it?

It's been too long. This is a young man's game, somebody with experience who's as good at it as you are. But don't do it if you're scared. Nobody'll blame you when I tell the story.

He shoves me away. I ain't afraid of no god-damned bear. Just not accustomed to ground blinds, is all.

No way he can see you until it's too late.

He moves over, careful to keep the steel bow away from the rocks, finds a better perch, and settles. In one smooth motion he draws the bow, limbering up.

Go on, he says, get out of here. I'll take care of your problem for you, old man.

He nocks an arrow with a serrated broad-head.

Don't come messing around until the sun's down, he adds.

My right hand's under my jacket, on the pistol butt. I slip it up and out and jam the barrel against his forehead, as certain about this as I have ever been about anything. The astounded, almost adolescent face I look down into loses what little color it had. Instead of lunging for me, as I expected, Dwayne spreads his lips tight against his teeth in silver-studded astonishment, the back of his head against stone dug up a century before and his bow clattering to his feet.

You're going to die, Dwayne, and I want you to know why. You raped your sister and ruined her life. You left your mother when she needed you most and caused all manner of grief to all manner of people and animals.

I lean harder on the pistol.

The law'll never know what happened to you because they'll never find you. I'll push the rest of these rocks over you.

I've heard stories about Dwayne's prison exploits, where he supposedly led a gang and forced men to do what he ordered. I always suspected it was the other way around, that Dwayne was the bitch, but he hasn't pissed his pants and he's watching me for an opening.

I've heard of a frozen trigger finger, and that happens to me now. I can't do it. Nothing to do but pull the pistol away, leaving a neat white circle in the middle of Dwayne's forehead the size of a .38 slug.

I reach down and slip his knife out of the scabbard and step on the blade. I lift until it snaps, and toss the haft away.

You're a lucky man, Dwayne. Now here's what's going to happen. You're moving out of Lurie's house and out of this county. If I ever see you around here you're dead, simple as that. I don't care if you're in your pickup, in a bar, or at the gas pump.

Chapter 17

I spend the rest of the afternoon on my porch, facing up my long driveway. I will stay away from Dwayne's place until tomorrow, give him a chance to leave. If he's still there I'll have no choice but to pull that trigger, because you can't not kill a person twice after announcing it.

Night falls, the lights go off, me on the porch and the pistol in my lap. I listen first to Maeve, then to Lurie settle down inside, then to deep-throated crickets in dry grass, trying to recall summer.

I wake up cold, the thin gray light of reflected dawn outlining the woods. The crickets have gone to sleep and only the river makes a sound, barely detectable.

At breakfast I tell Lurie I want them both to stay inside today, raising a hand before the objections start.

That's all there is to it.

I wait all morning but there's no sign of Dwayne. After lunch I get into the pickup with the pistol and drive slowly up the rabbit hole to the county road. Dwayne's pickup's gone. I park nearby and wait, my armpits slick.

Physical fear is debilitating and boring at the same time. I wait an hour, then another. Finally I see a car coming, the battered sedan with the faded flames on the hood owned by Biskit. He jams on the brakes when he sees me, reverses, and is gone in a boil of dust.

I can't wait any longer. I go up to the house and pound on the door, knowing he's not there. The old key Esther kept under a rock's still there and I let myself into the usual unholy mess. Now packing boxes are stacked against one kitchen wall and a single stroke with a machete has opened two up. Bottles of red cough syrup wink inside one, in the other marshaled bottles of what I know to be Oxycontin, all picked up in Purdy, I'll bet, which is near the intersection of two interstates and at night the scene of wild exchanges of stolen merchandise.

A propane furnace and the metal tub fitted with turnscrews sit in the middle of the floor, the temperature gauge smashed. I would bet that in there the fundaments of crystal methane come together under heat and pressure, bottled and sold as easily as ice cream from a Good Humor truck for a lot more money.

The decision is instantaneous, since calling the sheriff is useless and staying is suicidal. Candles make good fire starters and I get one from the living room, light it, and leave it standing the middle of the kitchen floor. Then I wrap the handle of the tank with my handkerchief, not wanting to leave fingerprints, and turn it ever so slightly until I catch the smell of propane.

Supper's over by the time I get home, and Lurie and Maeve are in bed together. I can't eat or sleep for the life of me, so I turn off the porch light and get back into the rocker with the pistol.

The blast never comes. Instead, later than I thought likely, in the frigid night air I hear a woman's distant scream. It drops off, rises again, gets closer: the fire truck down from Porters' Gap. The sky's now black as the sole of a miner's boot, except for a bright red blush in the treetops.

The three of us sit in the front seat of my pickup, as close to what's left of the Doyle home place as the volunteer fire crew will let us get. Maeve's in her pajamas and Lurie's in a nightdress. Neither wears slippers. They lean forward, faces lit by the flames. The fire crew has used up all the water from their truck, and there's no pond or cattle tank to drop the end of the hose into, a common problem in the country.

Two men in flame-resistant suits work closest to the blackened edges while the rest stand by and watch the final consumption of Gatewood's house. The last stud on the ground floor lights up like the charred rib of some prehistoric beast. The roof sags, offering a foot up, and quick enough, it's burning, too.

The collapse releases a storm of sparks rising counterclockwise in a spiral as if pulled from above. The smell of it gets past the rolled-up windows of my pickup.

Then I see the passenger door hanging open and, in my headlights, the figure of Lurie running toward what's left of the home she grew up in. Maeve has her knuckles jammed into her mouth, and I pull her to me. The firemen are watching Lurie, too, transfixed, but she ignores them, ignores us all, in fact, dancing on cinders in her bare feet, hands raised to the sky as she did when still a child, the silhouette of her body so sharply drawn against the thin cloth of the nightdress that she might as well be naked.

MAEVE

Chapter 18

Time's the only thing. In the beginning it doesn't seem to move at all, but at my age it's a light but constant wind. Stand at a closed window and feel it. See something walk past — a deer, say — and look away and then right back, and that deer's halfway down the property. How did that happen? Then the deer's at the bottom of the property. Then it's gone.

By October the Rappawan's down to rock, more trickle than river, the sound of it lost unless you're standing on the bank. Wildflowers have taken over the lower yard — blue lobelia and cardinal flower at the edge of trees where shadow gives way to sunlight in late afternoon: wild aster, goldenrod, tiny white flowers waving on the tips of a weed I still don't know the name of.

Lots of moss underneath, its tiny arms reaching up but releasing no spores now in the three inches of air that is its whole world. Everything's waiting for first frost. There might as well be no animals in the woods, since there are none to be seen, except an occasional young buck stupid with desire and likely to meet a lead ball head on.

The woods hawks are active, low-flying and fast. Crows are hysterical and pileated woodpeckers high-flying, strident. Autumn on the banks of the Rappawan is a time of death, and escaping it depends on wile and learned ability.

I drive up to what's left of the Doyle house and spend half an hour wandering around in its ashes. The place seems smaller than it seemed before. A blackened metal sheet is the kitchen table with the Formica scorched off. The fire marshal's convinced that Dwayne torched the place himself before taking off, so he now has an arson charge in addition to receiving property stolen from eighteen-wheelers up in Purdy.

The detox clinic is on the top floor of Purdy hospital. The door has to be opened by somebody on the other side, seen through a big glass panel. Lurie and I are buzzed through to the administrative desk since Dr. Simms has called ahead and set things up.

A woman in street clothes instead of a uniform, hair up in a bun, gives us a sheet of paper already filled out.

All you have to do, she tells Lurie, is sign it.

Can't my father sign for me?

No ma'am, has to be you. Otherwise we can't let you stay.

Lurie signs and pushes the paper back across the counter.

You'll have to take off your jewelry and leave it here. Also any scissors, clippers, nail files, anything metal or sharp.

Lurie surrenders a little gold chain Esther gave her and the wooden skewer holding up her hair.

All right, now say goodbye, ma'am. He can visit most days. Jean here will show you to the room.

Lurie has brought only a clear plastic bag of clothes and a pair of slippers. She gives me a hug and a kiss on the cheek, then walks back to the glass door to wave to Maeve sitting outside, serious as a stone. But when Lurie kisses her hand and presses it to the glass, Maeve jumps up and does the same thing on her side, their hands a pane apart.

Then Lurie's following the broad-shouldered nurse through the lounge where people young and old sit looking at magazines or at nothing at all. I hate like hell to see her go, and I was the one who talked her into it.

We'll come see her tomorrow, I tell Maeve when I get on the other side of the door. And anytime you want after that. Mama's going to be fine.

When will she come home?

They're not sure but it won't be too long. Now let's get some soft-serve.

Afterward we go to the supermarket and then to Target. She ends up with new pants and a skirt, sketchpads, pencils, and a silver backpack.

Lurie cleared everything with the grammar school, which tested Maeve and said she could start a month late. I'm more nervous than she is as we drive there. Miss — Ms. — Alexander, Maeve's teacher, is younger than Lurie but clearly in charge. As students go indoors after recess she takes one aside and introduces her to Maeve. What happens next amazes me. The two girls stand looking at each other, and then they're both smiling and walking off together like old friends.

Maeve doesn't look back, and I know I'm supposed to be glad about that. Something big's coming, and then it arrives and you aren't prepared. For weeks I've been if not the center of her attention, at least close to it, and that's now over for all time.

I drive home and eat the same lunch Maeve's eating at school, made for both of us that morning by Lurie before she went away. Tonight Maeve and I will be together but I'll have to wait to hear the whole story of her first day at school, because that's Maeve's way.

Lurie also made us dinner, which Maeve and I eat together, me trying to fill the silences between her little pearls of school experience. That's the reality, and once you're part of it you have to be careful not to drop even the smallest piece because you'll never get it back. It's a breathtakingly short interlude in retrospect and a source of lasting regret for anyone who's known it.

I decide to get a television set and a satellite dish, links to the outside. Lurie likes Maeve as a wild child, but that's bound to change. Money-wise, we're down there. I use the credit card for most things, even soft-serve and the Medicare co-payment. I dread every time the bill lands in the mailbox. I have a job interview at Walmart to be a greeter, one of those who tell people where to find what. It'll help if I get it.

After lunch I take the shovel from the shed and go down-property. I used two trees, an oak and the sassafras, as coordinates for finding the jar again, and the shovel touches glass on the second stroke. I bring it up, dirty but with the duct tape still in place. Cut around the lid with my sling blade, get it unscrewed, look down at wadded-up newsprint.

Underneath is a small red envelope with a snap, and printed at the top the names of the bank in Purdy and Lurie Doyle. I unfasten the snap, open the envelope and a key falls out. Six digits, mashed into shiny metal.

Chapter 19

The morning after her first night, Lurie and I sit in the lounge of the detox center with all the others. I've dropped Maeve off at school and will pick her up again until the school bus driver gets the route figured out. In her loose-fitting green stretch pants and her own slippers Lurie looks better than some. She seems drained but is smiling.

You dug it up, she says.

I assume that key's to a safety-deposit box. Why didn't you say so?

Because I had to be certain. If you'd dug it up early I'd be snorting crushed-up pills and cocaine with Dwayne, and there wouldn't be any money left.

How much is in there?

One hundred and two thousand, seven hundred and twenty dollars. That was in the second diaper box.

Dear Maeve, I'm leaving my house, land and tools to you and Lurie. My property touches Lurie's down here so someday the combined pieces will be worth real money. I wish I had more to leave.

I want you to know some things about the past, good and bad, because it's best to have the whole story and easier to make your way in the world when you know what's gone before. Your life, too, will be hard, what with the world as it is, but no matter how bad things get, always remember that you were and are still loved. Your mother loves you and I love you and if your grandmother Esther had known you, she would have loved you, too. You are brave and industrious and you made my life meaningful toward the end. I'm more grateful than you will ever know that you came into my life and became part of it.

I spend some time thinking about Dwayne. It must have taken him a full hour to get home that day, trying to decide what to do. My attitude hasn't changed. If he shows up again, he's dead unless he sees me first.

Lurie's home in under three weeks and seems to have recovered something of her old self. She gets a half-day job at the garden center south of Purdy, owned by a widow who's a plant lover like herself. So Maeve's driven to school by one of us, and the school bus drops her off at the top of our road in the afternoons.

Lurie buys a second-hand Japanese pickup, then a double-wide. She has the trailer set on the foundations of the old house, with a little porch and a television satellite on the roof. She's having a hardwood floor put in and buying some nice furniture and decorating the place with a new hanging plant every day or so, so it'll look and feel like a real house.

After dropping Maeve off at school I drive on up to the Walmart. In a room in the back greeters have to sing a little song each morning about making people feel welcome before we go onto the floor.

The first time was one of the strangest experiences of my life, the manager pushing us forward, telling us to say hello to people as we've been taught to do. We wear identical vests with slogans printed on them. Some shoppers are as old as I am and clearly worried about finding what they need. They're so grateful for help it soon takes away the useless feeling and makes the job seem worth doing. I find I like helping them, and many will remember me in the future and the place will begin to feel like a community.

Months later I read in the Piedmont Trader about a fire down toward Charlottesville, on the edge of federal land. Three men were making methamphetamine using cough syrup or something stolen in bulk and boiling it. The whole operation blew up, as such things are apt to do, and only one of the men could be identified, so badly burned were the other two.

That made me think. I spent money talking long-distance to the sheriff's office down there, trying to find the right deputy. I tell him I might know who the other two men were, and he says, I'm listening.

Did one have a silver tooth?

As a matter of fact, one did. Incisor, on the right side. Melted down to a puddle and stuck to the lower jawbone.

I say, lying, No, the one I knew had a silver molar. And I hang up.

It has to be Dwayne, who burned himself up. I'll bet money the other one was Biskit, owner of the sedan with flames on the hood. Some people would say they brought the fiery end on themselves, driving around with the skulls of dead animals wired to their grilles.

Chapter 20

I see the man coming toward me where the oaks and hickories gather in deep, downriver shadow slashed at by the pale trunks of blighted ashes. In my experience things coming upstream are unwanted — wet weather, lost dogs, people. This man's clothes are wet, and a cloth sack hangs heavy in his hand. He's been shot, I'm thinking, or drunk. Maybe both.

Things coming downstream, on the other hand, are mostly welcome. Clean water, animals out of the Blue Ridge, the last of early spring sunshine. My stretch of river's close to the headwaters and so is mostly free of trash, though one man upstream drinks beer from silver cans with screw-off tops, then puts the tops back on, throws the cans into the river, and shoots at them with a .22 rifle.

Like many, he thinks a river once past somebody's property is up for grabs and that any object floating on it that's not human, canine, or income-producing deserves to be shot at.

Now the stranger's in my yard, when a minute ago he was a quartermile away. Then he's on hands and knees, crawling. Another city fool, I'm thinking, off pavement for the first time and lost to his world and to mine. Outsiders are usually grateful for directions and a lift up to the road, though I don't always offer it. Once you're nice to them the next thing you know is they're sitting under the sycamore with others, eating sandwiches and looking around at what they call foliage.

This one's wearing a shirt not made for canoeing, and his canvas shoes belong on a ball court, not the bottom of a river still cold with spring runoff.

I go out and sit on the back steps, some of the last planks in the county cut from native chestnut still deep-grained and silvery, that Lurie once sat on as a child. After that a nice woman from something called the Chestnut Society came, stared at these planks for the longest time. We can get seedlings to grow, she told me, but the young chestnut trees sicken and die.

Ordinarily I would have gone down to see if the man was all right. But nowadays a crawling stranger with a sack of something is a potential problem, maybe on a mission you don't want to be at the end of.

I carry the sling blade, though a working knife's worthless against a pistol. And I'm too old to run. Truth be told, I'd almost rather get shot than have to try. My doctor told me again I wouldn't survive if I didn't have my prostate out, but I never had. And now, a dozen years later, that doctor's dead and I'm still here.

The man has seen me. He leaves the sack and crawls on, then stretches out in the grass. Not the best time for a nap, I'm thinking, soaked through, in March. The river's too shallow to drown in, unless you're determined, but deadfall's thick and those ancient rocks are slippery.

He's tired, neither young nor old, sandy hair cut by somebody who charges more than a barber, eyes that at this distance look like fresh-popped corn. I get up and walk to him. Blue lips, fingers, too. I know something about hypothermia, not just chill but galloping heat loss, and his body is unable to generate more.

He struggles to get his mouth around a word. Forty- five minutes in the pickup might well be too much for this guy, then somebody will sue me for not having a fast enough truck. But if I take him into the house, I might not be able to get him out.

I help him stand and we walk to the steps. I don't always bother with a fire in the kitchen stove this time of year, but luckily I did today. He's dripping and his teeth are telegraphing each other. I get him inside and tell him to take off his clothes while I get blankets. Ordinarily I'd drink a beer before watching the news, but not today.

My guest's standing naked in his own puddle when I get back, hugging himself. Well built, pale as lard. He ought to get into a tub of hot water but the heater's busted. I wrap him up and shove the rocker next to the stove and him down into it. Put the kettle on, squeeze a lemon, lace it with enough sugar to stand the spoon up in.

Talk, I tell him.

No houses. Nobody.

It's an educated voice from someplace else.

Those vines, he says.

I pour a dollop of Bee-K's peach liquor into his empty jelly glass. His eyelids droop.

Go to sleep now and you won't wake up, I tell him. What's your name?

Simon.

You need to eat, Simon.

I feed him beans straight from the can, heated on the stove. Then I put him in the hired man's room.

He's in there for ten hours. Then he's eating four eggs and a quarter pound of bacon while I stand at the kitchen window. The nicest thing about early spring is the pink nubbins on the redbud branches and the wild white dogwood peeping out. Arriving robins stand flat- footed in new grass, jerking worms and eating them like spaghetti.

What's in that sack out there? I ask Simon.

Rocks.

He goes out, hauls it back, upends it at the foot of the back steps.

Holding up a rock he says, These are really old, tools used by the most primitive Homo sapiens. They lived here long before what we think of as Indians. They didn't make arrowheads — the Clovis point was the Paleolithic version of the steam engine — but used these rocks as tools and votives.

He holds up a dead ringer for a goose head.

They've been worked on, so crude you're not always sure. But the corners and grooves couldn't have been cut by wind or water.

He hoists what looks like a stone penis. I find a lot of these.

I've heard enough, and say, Let's go get your vehicle.

Headed up my road, Simon's rocks in the pickup bed, I ask what he does for a living.

Work in the White House basement.

I just look at him.

I'm a historian. I thought I could do some good in government. My PhD thesis was on the drastic effects of human migration in second-century Mesopotamia. Some White House advisor assumed I oppose immigration, which I don't. They just hired me to do backup research for the president's twisted speeches. I couldn't take it anymore.

We pass Lurie's land where she's put up a barn with a little riding ring with split rails and hay bales. She quit her job at the nursery after getting a veterinarian's certificate, but about the only animals she deals with now are horses.

Where do you live?

Lived, he says. In Spring Valley. Big houses and gardens where everything growing's brought on a truck. People busy making money, shaping what they call the debate. The prevailing sound's not birds but leaf blowers.

Why'd you leave?

My wife divorced me and took the house after I quit my job.

So you're out here searching the banks of the Rappawan for rocks, and for yourself.

I turn onto the county road and head east, thinking

I know where Simon left his car. I ease though wild rose and mile-a-minute. Tire ruts but no car.

Should be right here, he says.

Was the key in it?

Under the mat.

That's still in the car, Simon.

Chapter 21

The sheriff's office on the outskirts of the county seat has two deputies. They take turns manning the desk and warning tourists against drinking too much in the one good restaurant. The presiding deputy takes down Simon's information and studies his D.C. driver's license.

He says, This is expired. What's your address?

I don't have one at the moment.

Give me your phone number, then.

I lost it in the river.

You're just a mess, aren't you? Check back tomorrow and we'll let you know if the car turns up.

But we all know it won't.

Back outside, I ask if Simon wants me to take him to the Trailways terminal.

Why?

Well, to find yourself another job.

My clothes are all in the trunk of the car. Just drop me over there.

That's the county gun store, Simon, not a bus station or a Kmart.

The parking lot has more chrome in it than before. Stickers in pickup windows don't say Lock Her Up, as they did a few years ago, but Stand By. I'm reminded of the day Lurie and I drove Maeve down to Charlottesville after Maeve had been accepted by the university, her suitcase in the pickup bed and all of us so proud we could hardly stand it. We arrived to find Thomas Jefferson's capital full of out-of-state license plates and men beating up people on the street while the police stood by. Lurie and I drove straight back and that night on TV saw the woman run down and killed on the sidewalk.

Simon gets out. You saved my life, he says, and I thank you.

The greater the distance I put between us the more bothered I get. Simon's about as unhappy as a man can be, and a gun is the last thing he needs. Killing himself would be his business, not mine, but at some point another person, even one you've just met, becomes yours too. Then I remember his rocks in the bed of my pickup.

I could just leave them there, but something special about those rocks has given them added weight. So I make a U-turn across the median strip.

The gun store offerings have been mostly bought by people getting ready for God knows what. What's left are pink .25 caliber ladies' poppers and a few double-barreled shotguns. The men at the counter, with long hair and wearing leather, look more like pregnant women with gray beards and silver studs. In the midst of them stands Simon.

Then I'll get a Virginia driver's license, he's saying.

Lester's long dead and his son's behind the counter. He knows nothing about gunsmithing and a lot about automatic weapons and sniper gear.

Bring that driver's license back here, he tells Simon. I'll sell you that hoss in a heartbeat.

On the glass countertop in front of him lies an enormous brushed-steel revolver.

I'll buy it for you, says one of the black leather boys. Just give me the money, plus a little something. Then I'll hand it over.

That's illegal, I say.

They all turn.

That's right, says the kid. I could lose my license.

I grab a handful of Simon's sweater and ease him toward the door.

Back home I mow the grass even though it doesn't need it. The mower's decades old and missing a hood after I collided with the woodpile, and the seat's worn down to metal. Simon, in my old Carhartt coveralls now, the ones with a gash left by the chainsaw, is weeding the garden.

Next thing I know he's back in the river in my old hip boots and a couple of hours later up-ending the sack again at the foot of the steps. And I'm down on my knees poking around among rocks.

He points to a groove cut in one. Mortar, he says. Probably for grinding acorns. And here's a buffalo effigy.

Buffalo?

They provided food not for the organized tribes but for clots of primitives dealing with horrors we can't imagine. Single puny human beings couldn't survive by themselves.

He passes a hand across the view.

Riverine flats like these offered a level place for crude shelters near water. Dinner would have been a circle of hunched shoulders around a fire, a pile of plants, half-cooked meat bones for breaking to get at the marrow.

My telephone's ringing. Lurie's calling to tell me a foaling's going on in her barn and she needs help.

Well, Simon, I say, it looks like we have a real job to do.

Her horse trailer's parked at an angle to the paddock, and the exhaust fan's running in the barn. Simon follows me inside where there's a warm, wet smell. An impressive black mare stands with her legs splayed, eyes wild, Lurie behind her, hair tied up, gray streaks among the blond. She's wearing jeans and a T-shirt, and her left arm's up to the shoulder in that mare, next to a dangling chain attached to something deep inside.

The contractions have stopped, she says, but the mare won't help. We've about run out of time.

The thing about horses is this. They're docile one minute and diabolical the next. I don't know of an animal as smart and as dumb at the same time. I've never been a rider but have been around plenty of horses. Put your hand on a horse's flank and you'll feel the muscles twitch, and by the time you take your hand away that horse knows more about you than you do. The same horse will nuzzle you and then rear up and take a piece out.

Horses are not just a rich person's concern, and women are better with them. They may look all trim and proper in their red jackets, slapping riding crops against their legs, but young or old, pretty or plain, you can bet their hands are rough as rat wire and their grip can bring you to your knees.

A horse is finicky, though powerful, and faster than reason allows. Yet a horse can break a leg just waking up in the morning. They cost the Earth, worse even than boats, one man told me.

This horse is glossy and I don't know how many hands tall, but plenty. It doesn't take an expert to see she's ungodly valuable and on the edge of calamity. Lurie didn't grow up with such things, being poor, but night courses in veterinary school made up for that, and she got good at it quick.

People with expensive horses are willing to pay for a decent vet. Horse doctors are more welcome in their homes than those planting their bushes for them, she discovered. Vets have stories to tell, though these send guests without horses straight to the canape table.

Get that rope, Lurie says, pointing with her free hand. Make a loop. No, one big enough to go over a colt's head. Not a slipknot, a bowline.

I stay clear of those hooves as I do it. The mare's thighs are like sides of beef but farther down as delicate as a ballerina's. It's clear what's at stake: a well-bred colt dying in birth is a big hit for any owner, and not just the rich ones. Both mother and colt dying is a true catastrophe and a lasting black eye for any vet.

Lurie's arm comes out like a slick python, bloody to the fingertips. The chain's still in there.

Hand me the rope, she says.

She puts the loop over her thumb and the arm goes back in, her cheek hard against the mare's flank.

Damn, she says, almost sobbing. I'm two inches short. She draws the rope out again.

My arm's longer than Lurie's but arthritic and near useless when extended. The last time I tried using the splitting mall it flew out of my clunky hands and broke the birdbath.

Lurie calls out to Simon, You.

He comes, flat-footed as an ape on a spaceship.

Push up your sleeve.

It's too tight, he says.

So she unbuttons it for him, right down the front, and strips it away to expose that pale chest.

Flatten your palm, she tells him. Stick up your thumb.

She drops the loop over it.

Now, without letting go of that rope, slip your hand in there. Go on, it won't bite. What you're about to feel is the colt's hooves with the chain looped round them. Just keep going.

Simon's shaking. After a bit he says, All right.

That's the head you're feeling now. It's caught up in the pelvis somehow and you've got to pull it down and get the loop over. If you can't, we're likely to break that colt's neck pulling on just the chain. Might kill mother, too.

Simon can concentrate, I'll give the man that. No sound other than breathing and the exhaust fan, his cheek planted on the other flank and his eyes inches from Lurie's. He's younger than she is, but not by a lot. I've heard of two people putting out some scent or other, binding them before they've met. I don't know about that, and there's nothing to smell in this barn but horse. But Simon might as well be cast in salt. Lurie, too.

Simon says, Okay.

They tug in unison.

Easy does it, says Lurie.

Rope and chain start to pile up between their feet. Here come the miniature hooves, polished black. The nose follows, glossy black, the colt's chin pressed flat to its forelegs and its dewy eyelids pressed together. Then one of them opens.

Lurie eases the colt down into the straw.

What a beautiful little mare, she says.

Simon's soiled with sweat and afterbirth, his flushed face awash in tears.

No, no, says Lurie. The colt's fine. And you were wonderful.

She hugs him and he hugs her back. Bound up in each other's arms they seem reluctant to let go, and in a way they never do.

Chapter 22

That was all both an age ago, and yesterday. Now Maeve has the imprint of that colt's hoof on her forehead — faint but detectable — left after they both grew up and Maeve learned to ride and shoe her.

Simon proved to be more than a vet's assistant. He started teaching at the middle school. He stopped collecting rocks and moved into the trailer with Lurie. They put in a wood floor and more plants until you wanted a machete when you visited. Now they're building a house.

I asked Lurie why she didn't marry him first. She said, I don't want a husband, Pa. Just a man will do.

The veil of time's so thin now I can feel an eyelash through it. Another year passes, and my pickup's gone. Now, any man could have let the front tire of his vehicle slip over the edge of a low-water bridge and any man could find himself staring down through clear water at bottom-feeding fish thinking they're about to be hit by an asteroid. Fortunately, the pickup stalled.

If you're old you're no longer judged unlucky in such circumstances, but deficient. Mentally and morally. The brain's not working right, they say. Neither is he, turning into an animal when he was one of those all along. It never occurs to them that the brain might be working just right finally, going straight to the source of things, to the fundaments.

Memory's a different problem, of course. Not just the fading of a once vivid former world but also the signs we hung on it. Is it confusion, or was it the right name for the thing or the person all along? Crazy talk, they say. But maybe it's just that the signs have all fallen off objects and people, opening them to reinterpretation by an onlooker seeming either addled or indifferent. Which happens to be me.

Lurie is talking to a tall man in a tie, standing in a hallway of a place called Bright Hills. It's lined with chairs, some of them on wheels. Sitting in them are people of what Lurie calls a certain age. The woman next to me — not really blond — has been smiling. Finally she asks me if I'm interested in sex, and I tell her that's not the same thing as doing it.

Can be, she says.

Lurie's talked to that man long enough. I don't like the looks of this guy anyway, and besides, Lurie's already attached, in her way. I get up and walk over and inquire if I'm going to have to knock the man in the tie down.

Well, sir, he says, I certainly hope not.

Out in the parking lot, Lurie tells me, Pa you've done it again. Now there's no good place left to get you into.

Maeve has her academic degree in art history but is trying to support herself by making paintings instead of teaching about them. She works in my shed and sleeps in Lurie's barn, after being bumped out of the trailer like a pinball by Simon. But she seems to like the arrangement well enough. And she has found others in the county who share her interests and her views.

She shows up one day at my little house in the pickup, followed by a young colored woman in a Japanese car. Maeve introduces her as Grace, who lights up as if she knows me, her teeth bright and her eyes a deep liquid brown. Maeve asks if they can stay overnight so she can show Grace around one of the county's last wild places, adding, I brought dinner.

I'm already living in the spare bedroom where a hired man would stay if I had one. There are two iron-framed beds in the front bedroom, and there they dump their bags and go off walking, their happy voices carrying across the field.

I don't see them again until dinnertime. It's Lurie's cooking, a casserole of tasty imponderables but also pork chops. Maeve never gave up meat and has learned to cook it pretty well. We all fall on it like starvelings.

After dinner we drink a little of Bee-K's fruit-based, one of the last jars I bought before he died. Maeve tells the story of her and Grace meeting at the tavern on the highway where Maeve works part-time in the kitchen. Grace's fish was undercooked, so she took it back herself and saw Maeve standing at the fry basket, her mass of ginger hair up in a net.

They met on the steps when Maeve's shift was done and an hour later they were still there. Young men from the co-op came by for a drink and one asked, Aren't you two supposed to be around back?

This kind of joke is never a good idea. The women weren't sure if he was referring to Maeve as a part- time employee or to Grace as a colored person. Maeve got up and said. Aren't you supposed to have brains in your head?, and bumped him in the chest with the heel of her hand.

The argument was over before it got started, but she and Grace were now friends. After supper they drag my television set into the living room to watch flickering ghosts of shows and laughing.

Next morning Grace comes out in a dark skirt and stacked heels, ready for work. She analyzes things in the new laboratory up toward Purdy and will put on a white doctor's coat when she gets there, she says. There's a purposefulness to everything she does, from drinking coffee to hefting her briefcase.

Maeve comes out in a blousy-sleeved shirt, scuffed canvas vest, jeans with the natural-worn holes in them. On her hip she carries the little sheath knife I gave her long ago and doesn't mention Grace at all. Soon she's out there knocking around in what we now call the studio, not the shed.

I go into the front bedroom to gather up and move the last of my stuff and see that those two iron-framed beds have been shoved together. Those young women really do like each other.

Chapter 23

Maeve has her grandmother Esther's habit of coming over and giving me a kiss for no particular reason. She regularly goes into the woods and comes back with bags full of plants — moldering black walnut shells, wild rose, sumac, acorns, moss, lichen, even poison ivy vine, hairy and wrist-thick, which she chops up with the hand ax and boils on the woodstove in water and vinegar.

Now don't breathe that steam, Grandpa, she tells me.

What she eventually does with all that stuff is make ink, using gum arabic as a binder and cinnamon cloves to preserve it, lifting scabs of mold off with a fork. She writes the name of each ink on labels and lines the jars up on a shelf where they catch the morning light. With the ink she pulls images from sheets of homemade paper that will wake you up late in the night.

She makes the paper in the bathtub with nothing but rags, glue, and boiling water. I have sat and watched her lash the paper with weeds dipped in ink. She took some of the bottles and paintings up to the little art supply store in Purdy, though I told her nobody was likely to buy. Well, they did, and for money you wouldn't believe.

In the beginning she and Grace came to spend the night, and before I knew it they had moved in. A satellite dish soon followed, then a big TV screen hanging in a corner of the living room ceiling. A new sofa appeared after the old one was hauled to the dump, a food blender found a spot on the counter and then a microwave. I feared the things but now can't imagine living without them.

In the bathroom are new towels with heft, replacing the limp remains of the old. Competing scents move into the medicine cabinet, and the sound of Grace cutting loose in the shower. I will never again listen to a man sing when I can listen to a woman instead.

On hot days Maeve opens the windows in the shed and more music emerges. The plywood workbench has been turned into an easel. On Grace's days off they talk out there for the longest time, their voices carrying to me on the front porch. Whatever the talk, it's precious.

One afternoon I go into the studio and find Grace stretched out buck naked. The smoothness of her skin, the soft lines, will not let me look away. She raises herself on one elbow, sees me and says, Oops.

She's been painted, throat to toes, with pale green ink, beautiful against her rich caramel skin one nipple leaving a green bullseye on the table.

You'll never get that stuff off, I tell them.

Oh, Grandpa, says Maeve. It's just pokeberry and spring water.

I turn around and there in front of me is the field I've looked at forever and now has Grace's lines in the dips and rises. Shoulders, waist, hips, thighs, all live in that very old human topography. Grace under grass.

After a bit Maeve comes out and sits beside me on the porch. She has that burnished look pale-skinned people get from coming and going out of doors. Grandpa, she says, I have to tell you something.

I know, you're leaving. It was bound to happen.

No, we're not leaving. We're getting married.

Chapter 24

The first thing I notice that has moved on its own is the spade. I used it in the garden an hour ago, scraped off the dirt with a piece of old shingle, and hung it in the shed. But when I look from the kitchen window I see that spade's back down-property, leaning against the fence.

Grace is at work and Maeve has gone up to see her mother, so it wasn't one of them who moved the spade. I wait until she gets back and casually ask if she knows how the spade got moved.

She says, I don't.

I often forget where I've left something. Then I find it, like a trail marker along my route. But this is different. Same with the long-handled wrench I used to install the makeshift shower on the side of the house so the girls — the women — could wash more easily. Next time I look, the wrench's not on the nail in the shed where it's supposed to be, not on the flagstones we dragged up from the river for the shower, not anywhere.

Then I find it under the couch on the back porch where Lurie was conceived and no human being would ever leave a wrench. I may be absentminded but I can't accept that objects walk around on their own, though real things do occasionally creep about the edges of my vision. When I look, they're not there. Sometimes they are, but if I walk closer they change shape.

Downriver there's someone I know but can't name. Then he's gone. I look away and look back, and he's still not there. Then he is.

You can't talk about this to people close to you because it's worrisome and puts them in the same predicament you're in, one with only two choices: learn to live with phantoms or check into the nearest insane asylum.

The downriver figure disappears for a day, then reappears upriver. Clearly something's been set in motion, and I'm determined to find out what. I remember the sack of Simon's rocks at the back of the shed, which is ignored by day and locked up every night. Simon may have forgotten the rocks but I start to think they haven't forgotten him.

Maybe the rocks have been here long enough, I'm thinking. Maybe they're missed by somebody. Maybe if you're twelve thousand years old you resent being deprived of your goose head and your stone penis.

Next day I load some of the rocks into my sturdy old seed bag and drape the strap over my head. It's ungodly heavy at first, but with a staff cut from a dead ash I can walk easily enough, lightening my load all the while.

I don't dump the rocks in the river because that's not where they were found, but where the land flattens out. There I fling them. Sometimes I walk in the river itself, happy to discover that with the staff I'm as steady as I was on all fours as a child and almost as steady as in the past when, a walking fool, I covered thirty miles in a day.

I sow the stretch of bank directly across the river from us with rocks and that night sleep straight through.

Downstream where Simon first put in is the hardest stretch. Then I'll be done. The last artifact I fling is what Simon called a votive, mysterious markings on smooth, seemingly impenetrable stone. At that moment, I smell Dwayne.

Familiar, disgusting, a long-unwashed body with some semblance of humanity, a fearsome barrier to trespass, I would assume.

CHAPTER 27

The things I wrote down from time to time about Esther, Lurie, and Maeve seemed a good idea when I started. But the closer I get to the end of the story the less I think this. Two have lives now of their own, and a life being lived is far better than one written about. Those pages accumulated in the old cardboard box I kept under the Sears catalogue long after Sears itself was gone. So after the weather turns cool I carry the box down to the river, along with the wire frame I put over zinnia sprouts to protect them from the rabbits in spring.

My chair's set up there and shows the high-water marks on the legs tied to stakes in the ground so the current won't take the chair away. I spend a fair amount of pleasurable time in it, often asleep.

The river has become the one predictable thing in my life, awake or dozing. Its direction doesn't change, like everything else does. Whether calm or chaotic, it still goes west to east, mountains to sea, the surface sometimes bearing the faces of those from the past, glorying in their final ride.

I stack the pages on the bank, and drop the wire cage over them because it's fire season. Writing this has left me uneasy that, after all this time, Lurie would read them and suffer all over again. Maybe Maeve would too. Happening upon them in the beat-up box wouldn't tell her anything she doesn't already know on some level. Writing them has been my solace, but finishing is something else again.

So I lean over and strike a match to the upwind corner. Old paper burns more slowly than new but is used up quicker, another riddle. I want to say goodbye to everything I scribbled there, say goodbye good-bye, but I can't think of anything appropriate. Then I'm asleep.

I wake to a lowering sky lap-seamed at the edges in orange, at first not sure where I am. The kingfisher's scold reminds me. The sun's going down, too cool for what I'm wearing, but someone has draped the old plaid comforter over my legs.

The sheets of paper are perfect ghosts of their former selves, the edges still sharp. I set the wire cage aside and kick at what's left, and the breeze picks up the white ashes and pushes them out over the river.

Yes, nothing prettier than snow falling on dark, moving water.

Tregaron Springs

For Mark Borthwick, in memoriam

In and between the wood and wine
there will be no separation…
Go back, go back to mystery.

Roland Flynt
SKIN

Prologue:

The Bottle

It rides like a weapon under his Macintosh, protected from another atrocious London spring. Chilly rain trails from the brim of a hat between him and the oncoming headlights, the stench of exhaust and rubbish bins on the curb and, from the depths of Holland Park, the faint promise of spring.

Clyde Craven turns under a sign of a king in burnished armor and pushes into the murmurous warmth of the Windsor Arms. Now his nostrils must deal with damp wool coats on pegs, old beer, sherry dregs, whiskey splashed from dusky bottles behind the bar, and gin and smash in the hands of two pretty women. Also, fatty sausages girded by crisp baked bread, cheddar released from its glass prison, pickled eggs, and logs ablaze on ancient andirons.

Next comes a warring floral miasma: perfume, hair spray, hothouse peonies, and tobacco. Clyde's nose is overly sensitive, the doctor said many years before. He may grow out of it. But he hadn't. At thirty-five years he has never smoked a cigarette but can identify the hint of roasted hazelnuts in Player's cigarettes just by being around those who smoke them. And the dinge of Turkish in Camels, the ghost of burnt tires in Gauloises. Cigars are more interesting, abounding in smells of dense growth under a tropical sun.

"Clyde!"

An up-raised hand in the corner booth, the perennially stricken smile, belongs to his oldest friend, Gerald, a bachelor like himself but lacking Clyde's cleft chin and abundant hair he knows not what to do with. Gerald is also an oenophile but lacks Clyde's phenomenal sense of smell. He watches as Clyde sets the bottle on the table, peels off his Macintosh and slides across the board.

Gerald says, "Label's a bit over the top."

But Clyde likes its low, lavender mountains, exotic trees and long shadows cast across a valley floor too brilliant to believe. Does the place really have that shimmering lucidity?

The bottle levitates, held now by the waiter. "Please open it carefully," says Clyde.

The man draws the long cork and Clyde sniffs it, then takes the bottle back and waits for the glasses to be set out. Dark solids have fallen out of solution, but the wine remains a deep garnet. He already smells the hint of cassis and briary black fruit. This vintage was in the famous Paris tasting that pitted American bottles against French and although it didn't win, it did place, an amazing accomplishment.

The two old friends sip. The long shaft of flavor doesn't falter. "Nice," says Gerald, "but what's that odd component?"

"Mint. It's considered an attribute by some over there."

"Will you be writing about this?"

"I'm intrigued. There may be a market in Britain for such a wine, though Lily & Sons pays me to scribble about Bordeaux and Burgundy."

There are vines on the label, too, in an alien land touched by a ferocious setting sun.

"What would it be like," he asks speculatively, touching the label, "living in such light?"

"Provence with buffalo. So, what news?"

"Uncle died. And it appears he wasn't rich at all."

"How unfortunate."

"What's more, the cellar's bereft."

A sharp intake of smoke, dismay in Gerald's pale gray eyes. "Not the case of '29 Cheval Blanc, surely."

"Afraid so. Consumed, purloined, or both. Likewise, the Latour, and the vintage port. I'm grateful he let me taste such things when I was young."

"What about the money?"

"To get what's left I must take his name. He put that in the will."

"Oh, dear. Jones, isn't it?"

"Afraid so."

One of the two young women at the bar is smiling at him. He looks again at the label, makes a quick decision, and shakes Gerald's thin hand, noticing how his friend has aged. "I'll leave you the bottle. Anon, Gerald, and try not to smoke so much."

Passing the bar, Clyde says to the welcoming eyes, "That lad over there has something special to share with you."

"And where are you going?"

"California."

Part I:

Foundlings

Chapter 1

Trew climbed the long, dimly lit flight of wooden stairs, reciting to herself as she had as a child mounting to her father's office high above: Tregaron Springs... valley of the Catarina... the Bear Republic... California... United States of America... Northern Hemisphere... Planet Earth...

Steep, conifer-furred slopes visible through the window on the landing: rock, big trees, loamy earth, St. Bart's peak. This section of the old winery was segregated from the crushing, fermenting, blending, bottling, storing, and what passed for science at Tregaron Springs. The twenty-foot raftered ceilings were untouched since Gold Rush days, and the tight-fitting doors on heavy iron straps. Yet even this sacrosanct space could not elude the essence of billions of microbes cavorting in moistness of the cellar. At once sweet and vinegary, an indelible smell of fermentation that crept unseen up the stairs during more than a century of the winery's existence had taken up residence in floorboards and massive mortise-and-tendon Douglas fir beams and planking. These were cut by the old-timers with water-driven drop-saws and nailed up forevermore with long, square-headed nails.

She pushed open the door of her sister's domain and stepped into a lair of light, the wall of westward-facing glass framing a bit of the big house and a slice of dark, lily-choked moat. Reeve stood with her back to it all so that Trew could see only her sister's angular frame, the corona of her hair afire, a deeper red than Trew's because Reeve avoided the sun and the streaky blonde incongruities it left.

Closing the door behind her, Trew waited for her eyes to adjust to the light but already she sensed the presence of her brother-in-law, silhouetted on a chair propped against the wall, his familiar blue blazer emerging from shadow. Trew's irises opened a bit more, and there was Julian's tie — cream and lime stripes — which meant he would be driving into San Francisco for lunch with someone at the Pacific Union Club, on a membership he had inherited. Because Trew and her sisters each owned a third of the winery, as well as of the view and all that it suggested, Trew would pay a third of the cost of Julian's lamb chops or trout almandine because Julian was employed by Tregaron. Worse, she would lose a third of the value of the rare wine he would sneak out of Tregaron's historic cellar. She said, "This looks like it's going to be a whole lot of fun."

"Hi, Trewdy," said Reeve, smiling brightly.

Julian said nothing and neither did he rise. It struck Trew as odd that a man so meticulously well brought-up would sit balanced on two chair legs and pop his knuckles. His hair was a tad too dark these days, she thought, or was it mean to notice?

Julian elevated his chin in greeting, but Trew pushed it. "How're they hanging, Julian?"

"Free and clear. How about yours?"

Said Reeve, "Let's start over, shall we?" abandoning the window for the only fashionable desk in the biggest office in the winery, an oval of transparent aquamarine glass upon which were arranged a telephone console, a Mont Blanc fountain pen, a leather organizer by Coach, and an arrangement of calla lilies from the garden in a long-stemmed vase.

Reeve had fit her narrow hips into tight denim and now she propped elbows on her open calendar and knitted long, shapely fingers unsullied by barrel bungs and sloshed wine down in Trew's domain. Reeve said, "Well, there's something we have discuss."

They were such opposites, Reeve's ecto to Trew's endo, Reeve's above-it airs to Trew's in-the-middle-of-it, her sister's thrice-milled French soap and loofah to Trew's homegrown pig-bristle scrubs. Reeve had beautiful hands and Trew's avocation, not wine making but painting in oils, left stubborn traces of burnt umber, forest green, Phthalo blue. She smelled of turpentine and linseed oil as well as cabernet lees and pomace, whereas Reeve left in her wake the barest essence of flowers from a finely stoppered little bottle.

Trew loved her big sister and had to admire the gutsy cocked hip checks Reeve gave to any pushy supplier or distributors who dropped by, and to anybody else who supposed her an air-headed inheritor. Trew couldn't have managed all that as well as her sister did, although she probably would have to take her turn at it someday. She said, "I'm all ears, Sis," and sat.

"I've received a serious offer for Tregaron. Wait…" Reeve of the downcast eyes and lofted palm, Reeve the referee. "This isn't more Abruzzini bullshit or a pod of San Diego real estate developers. It's somebody from outside the valley with a long reach in the business and a desire to get into the valley while the getting's good."

Julian said, "Just tell her, Reeve."

"You take the pleasure out of the simplest things," she told her husband. "Do you know that?" Then, to her sister, "It's Consolidated Brands."

"They make whiskey," said Trew.

"Do they ever. But they want to get into wine and naturally they want the oldest and one of the most prestigious names in the valley, which is us."

"Can you believe it?" said Julian to Trew, as if they were suddenly buddies. "It's so great. No more patchwork proposals, tentative offers. Just cash. From parvenus in New York who will need all the help they can get in the valley."

"In fact," said Reeve, "they want us to stay on if we agree to sell. You and me, Trew. It's our address as much as it is the wine, and Consolidated being able to brag about it and use this place for hosting. They can put Tregaron on their brochures once they've spruced it up, working with us as minority partners. It will be a new start."

"How minority?" asked Trew.

"Three per cent — one for you, one for me, one for Cain. Plus, one hell of a buy-out. And they'll pay for all the stuff we've talked about for years — replanting, barrel storage, a new roof." Reeve's clear blue eyes tended toward angelic even when triumphant. "They want a visitors' center and a hotshot winemaker we could never afford. You and I will have money for things like travel. You could live for a while in France, Trewdy."

"Or open a gallery," said Julian.

"I don't want to live in France or open a gallery."

That would be the answer to Julian's dream, she thought, get her off somewhere pushing seascapes on tourists, out of his so-black hair. It had to have been Julian who approached Consolidated and promised them a classy enclave in California, an inside deal. She knew him. This would explain his plane ticket to La Guardia — first class — she had seen on his expense account, and she would have to pay a third of.

She said, "No."

Reeve's gaze lifted and stayed up among rafters cut generously even for the old days from the hearts of bigger trees than were seen now, that could hold up the universe. Her pose, as close as Reeve would get to drama, told her sister that, yes, she and Julian had rehearsed this. Now

Reeve would lose all affect, those lovely orbs of blue dropping back to earth, she sitting in judicial silence to let two advocates of utterly different points of view scrabble for supremacy. It occurred to Trew that Reeve should be running Consolidated Brands, not enabling a husband's pander to them. Trew repeated, "No."

Julian's chair was shoved so forcefully back that his head bounced off the wall. "Why not?" he moaned.

"Because selling would mean the end of everything we've known and our family has accomplished," said Trew. "Our family, Julian, not yours. We'd be vassals of an East Coast conglomerate of weasels as indifferent to us as they are ignorant of who and what we stand for. Do you honestly think they'd give us a real role? They'd just crank out crappy cabernet and other drek and send us around to peddle the stuff before selling out to someone even bigger."

"We don't have a choice," said Julian.

"We do have a choice. And what's this 'we' shit? It's our decision — mine and Reeve's alone, since Cain's taken herself out of it. Not yours."

"Oh yeah, your hippy sister. Another problem Consolidated can get us out of."

"You're more of a hippy than Cain is," said Trew. "Cain doesn't drink, remember? And she believes in something, remember? And she actually works."

"Growing tofu." The word came out like spit. "You and Reeve should have her declared incompetent a long time ago and taken control."

"Cain incompetent? She's anything but."

"Trewdy, what do you propose?" asked Reeve.

"I honestly don't know. More belt tightening, I guess, getting rid of non-essentials." Like Julian, she thought, vice president of "legal affairs" who kept a small office across the landing. "Get another loan, re-plant Green Buttons and a couple of other vineyards, get another intern from

Davis, pay somebody qualified to come in here with a fresh palate and appraise everything and tell us what's needed. Take on more duties ourselves. Patch the roof."

"The winery doesn't make money," said Reeve.

"In case you haven't noticed," added Julian.

"It doesn't lose that much. Let's keep re-jiggering. The price of fine wine is on the rise, everybody's talking about California cabernet, including ours, thanks to that tasting in Paris. The future could be great. If not, why would lumbering Consolidated even listen to you, Julian?"

Her hunch only, but his silence confirmed that Julian was acting as the go-between. "There's something else," said Trew. "We owe a lot to this valley, and to the people in it. The last thing most of them want is a big corporation coming in. The valley's not set up to resist that. If we did sell out this would be a signal to other big, soulless bureaucracies. The barbarians would pour over the Burros range and things here would never be the same again."

"Maybe they shouldn't be. This valley's too stuck in the past, stuck on itself. What would you do, Trewdy."

"My sisters call me that, you don't, Julian." He swam in refracted light that almost blinded her, this remnant of the man her sister had married eight years before who then said he believed in good land use, which was a front.

"Come on, Trew, solve the problem for us. Are you going to man the bottling line? Prune? Maybe just stand out on the highway wearing a sandwich board, the youngest of those scrappy Vassy sisters?"

"I could do more, yes. You could do a lot less. That might save us… what? A hundred grand a year if you found a real job. Stop buying airplane tickets to the wrong coast for unauthorized chatter with industrial big shots."

He was just another useless product of San Francisco's Pacific

Heights. Yes, there should have been a great-grandfather in the Stanford-Hopkins clutch of robber barons who sacked the United States treasury to build a transcontinental railroad. But Julian's family had somehow missed out on that, and this scion had to look elsewhere for money, starting at the University of Southern California where he found more leisure but no heiress to claim. He had come back to join a middling San Francisco firm and marry Reeve in what Trew now saw was desperation.

Now Julian stood and touched the candy-striped silk under the perfect knot in his tie, tacit announcement he was departing. He had decided three years before to leave his law firm and set up shop at Tregaron Springs, but he was soon bored with torts and piddling land squabbles, drawn to the supposed glamour of the wine business and knowing zilch about it. A depressingly familiar story: spouses, lovers, children in jobs created for them when there was no need, making of them red-nosed leches and entitled non-entities.

"Oh, Trewdy," said Reeve, after he had stalked out.

"I'm sorry. I wish Cain could be enticed to come back in, if only for a bit. It would make life so much easier for us. Maybe we could resolve this stuff once and for all, with the three of us."

Reeve got up and came around the desk. Almost a decade older than Trew and on the dreaded actuarial edge of 40, she was as beautiful as ever. Trew would have done anything for her, except this. Reeve perused Trew's shirt and khakis for old oil paint that yearned to attach itself to Reeve's sheer blouse and designer jeans. She put her arms around her little sister and said, "Oh, Trewdy, it wasn't supposed to be like this."

"Was there ever a 'supposed,' Reeve? We supposed, not them. Our parents never actually said anything like that, did they? Don't you wonder sometimes if they really believed it, that we would carry on?"

Reeve said sadly, "To tell you the truth, Sis, I try never to wonder about anything."

CHAPTER 2

Trew went out through the massive front portal. The specter of light still haunted the dreamscape beyond the rough stone columns, the glare wiping out depth perception and making of the shadows between the rows of vines, in the lee of oak, madrone, and Douglas fir spilling down from the peak of St. Bartholomew's, a menace. Below the lip of the waterway, in the shadow that followed the long drive out toward the highway, were harbingers of things as intriguing now as they had been to her as a child.

The regimented cubes of volcanic rock holding up the banks of St. Bart's Creek had been cut and set by legions of Chinese in another century, the same cohort that had built the house, winery and out-buildings, the paths and pond and island with its peaked bridge and elaborate Chinese fretwork. Their lunch tins and tight-fitting tunics lived in stories she had heard as a child, and in the pages of children's books that had come down from her grandmother. They lived in the gloom under the bridge, part of her great-grandfather's fantasy stalking the creek-side when shadows grew long in the evening and the mountain moved closer.

Those strangers built the railroads, too, making white men richer, channeling California's incredible resources. They were decimated by the rage of a later generation of settlers' and heirs, an inexplicable act before the marauders themselves became outcasts to history, more ghosts than real little men in braided pigtails.

Don't step into that sun casually, her grandmother often told her. It will leave in its wake another complexion, another person. But step into it Trew had and stayed there, light-enhanced to burnished brass in summer, her auburn hair streaked with blonde despite the cowboy hats and bandanas she wore when painting, never ball caps that let the rays in sideways where they went for the irises. She needed these eyes more than she needed smooth skin. There was no real hiding from this light, just moderation of the eventual destruction it eventually wrought everywhere.

The sun had scored her hands, cheeks, neck. But how could a painter in California remain in-doors, obsessed as they all were with capturing what lay at the edges of light and substance, to render in pigment on a flat plane something not there? Exacting, endless, never perfect, that was painting even her beloved Tregaron Springs, she resigned to perpetually, ecstatically falling short.

The touch of the column framing one side of her view was cold. How could a thing in a solar oven already heated by ten in the morning be so cool when only the shadow's knife edge lay between it and punishing sunlight? An overhang cut to block the morning sun was just one of hundreds of cunning features of a winery bigger than any other in the valley when built, designed not by an architect but by a Victorian engineer from far-away Vermont who knew much less about winemaking than he did building barns and wineries.

She doffed the beat-up straw, pulled the brim low to her brow and plunged across the frontier, glorying in the sudden warmth and prickly feeling laving shoulders and thighs. She would paint today, but not now when the light was so hard, vaporizing the range bracketing the far side of the valley, adrift in thermals. Puddles of frigid shadow lay under live oaks, and she waded through them as she crossed the lawn, caressed by extremes of temperature to finally step onto dusty, sun-punished tarmac.

She followed it toward the highway, past ancient olive trees, the trunks painted white. These marched beside her as they had since childhood, stalwarts in a Dali landscape, she a fairy queen at her own coronation with wild mustard rioting in the fallow vineyard, electric yellow, impossibly bright. She heard Julian's BMW bearing down on her from behind, waited a moment longer and then turned, stepping deliberately into its path, eliciting a shriek from the punished tires.

"Jesus Christ!" he shouted. "I almost ran you down, Trew!"

Smiling, she walked past the open convertible and stood over his rolled shirtsleeves iridescent in the sun, barely wrinkled even under the bind of yellow suspenders he might have worn to match the blooming mustard. Julian's eyes were obscured by smoked lenses, making of him more a priest than an attorney. From this angle she could see that his hair had indeed begun to thin at the crown. Things like that weren't supposed to happen in a top-down world kept safe from falling eucalyptus buttons that could dimple even this, the very best black enameled German steel.

Julian's jacket was neatly folded in the back seat, but he hadn't taken pains to properly conceal the bottle lying under it. All Trew required was a glimpse of the neck label — 1947 — and envision the gap in the long, dusty row of similar ones locked away deep in the earth below the winery. "That's a library wine, Julian. It's not supposed to be touched by anyone but Reeve and me. And Cain if she was here."

"It's for a special occasion. The exception's justified."

"If it leaves the property, you're going to owe the estate three hundred bucks. I'll make sure you pay it."

He turned and with an athletic reach grasped the bottle by the neck, she thinking he would hand it to her, punt-first, but at the last moment, without looking, he hurled it up and back. With a gasp Trew watched it turn in the air — once, twice — dropping into the sickening finality of disintegrating glass, a shard-studded star black as ink.

Julian's tires were trying to dig trenches in the tarmac. They finally bit, the car leapt forward, fishtailed, in seconds reached the highway. Then it was gone.

Kneeling, Trew took the bandana from her back pocket and spread it. She began to pick glass from the redolent puddle. The aroma was as old as anything she knew, and she touched a finger to her lips, the olfactory lights coming on one by one: cabernet sauvignon, merlot, cabernet franc, the tastes reaching back past the palate into her origins. Better for the wine to lie in the sun that created it than in the gut of some old prep school lacrosse chum of her brother-in-law. His behavior told her Julian was unreasonably emboldened and this meant the prospect of selling the place was more advanced than he had let on. She needed help and there was only one person she trusted who could help her, Saul Stubin.

She tied up the bandana, Little Red Riding Hood style, but kept the label separate. This she held up to the sky, shattered glass still clinging to the paper, spider-webbing the unknown artist's rendition of Tregaron's western horizon. She matched it to the real one now: green valley, bluish range sloping down from St. Bart's, luminous sky. Then out of it, in her mind's eye and for the thousandth time, came a small plane more gnat than Cessna, banking into a north wind, the cockpit tilting almost perpendicular to the ground. Trew, astride her Appaloosa at the age of eight, was looking up, thinking she could reach out and touch her father's unshaven jaw fresh from barnstorming the Mendocino coast. She sees once again his aviator glasses and next to him her mother's beautiful face behind dark lenses in tortoiseshell. So steep is the angle of the plane's banking that Bev Vassy hangs above him, her white teeth stellar, directing down at Trew a beneficence that carries to her youngest daughter below unspeakable love and joy. Her mother thrilling to the steep descent, her light-shot hair wind-blown, sleeves rolled to reveal the wink of beveled glass in what Trew knows to be an antique watch strung on woven gold.

What happened next remains unbelievable, always will, the Cessna's trajectory unchanging — down, down past telephone lines toward the pathetic landing strip where an old windsock flaps in the wind. Trew hasn't yet heard of time standing still but, in her world, anything can be altered, even the past. Her father never makes mistakes, before every take-off calling aloud even when there's no one to hear but his wife or a daughter or two strapped into the seat beside him: Stand clear!

The prop would kick into motion, the delicate craft shake and sputter. Their father would have checked every dial up in Mendocino and written mysterious things on paper held by a clipboard's rusty clamp. Yet the plane that day so long ago had flown into its own bright smoke. It would rise again into view, she knew, engine howling, swinging round to settle in on the next pass, but it never did. Suddenly there was no plane in the sky, and the next thing Trew remembered was her little horse jumping the fence at the edge of the vineyard, squeezing its withers until her thighs hurt. Racing past vines, the pony rearing then, Trew on her knees before a charred, smoldering mass like a burned fruitcake studded with metal: a glasses frame like her mother's, a checkered blouse and a make-believe face not her mother but a party balloon, splattered with dirt, Trew hearing herself screaming: "Where are you?" and feeling someone behind her, pinning her with strong arms — the winemaker, Teodoro. Still, she screamed — That's not my parents, where are they? ... That's not my parents, where are they? ... That's not my parents, where... — and didn't stop for two days.

Everyone had said it of her parents: They're wonderful. This became an abbreviation for things more complicated and, over time, a social imperative: ... such a well-suited couple, the Vassys.... Nothing they wouldn't do for each other.... Nothing they wouldn't do for you.

Her mother, from southern California, had been born early enough to take water for granted, and to be stamped with the optimism inherent in that blessed land in the early twentieth century. Endless orchards, lots of money. Beverly Corrine Phane, later the inimitable Bev Vassy, really wanted to know how you were when she asked and if not well, then a note would follow.

Now, dropping broken glass into the barrel outside the winery, Trew was struck by the perfect couple's very imperfect ending. The reason for the crash eluded the authorities but the awful truth Trew had learned that day, so long ago, was that awful events possess their own finality and in the end it doesn't really matter what happened. You are forever pursued by a countervailing force of equal ferocity and must forget, make the memory, too, go up in smoke.

Chapter 3

Trew's Toyota was too neat to be a farmer's — or a winemaking painter's, for that matter — and she had accepted the gentle joking of Raoul and other workers in their soft sibilant Spanish when they spoke of the pickup's pristine demeanor. Now she put the hat on the seat next to her and drove out to the highway, then south. Later, crossing the trench of the Carquinez Strait, she looked east toward the Central Valley and the far Sierra, trying to imagine the immensity of the flood that in the Pleistocene had scoured that stone to such a depth, sweeping everything before it to the coast range and breaking through at the Golden Gate, leaving behind flotsam, volcanic ash, the bodies of creatures still being dug up by scientists.

The highway passed through rolling hills dry as fluff, scored by distant houses, and beyond the distant bridge the horizontal blue slash of the incoming Pacific Ocean. She was in the urban tangle of the East Bay, San Francisco hanging out there under an inverted cloud while everywhere else the sun shone brightly.

Turning west, she took the rickety old iron bridge west, past windowless buildings squatting at waterline like tumuli, backed by industrial spaghetti. It must have been hard in the old days, deciding where to put the ugly stuff in a seascape vast and uniformly gorgeous. Never did oil storage tanks have a better view.

Abalone's was a seedy little bar with a great view over the bay and kelp at low tide. She parked in the lot and walked toward an assortment of mismatched windows strung together with plywood sheeting overlooking an expanse of black kelp. Inside, eleven-fifteen in the morning, four bearded men were playing shuffleboard, their beer glasses trembling on the rails and their tie-dyed shirttails covering impressive beer guts.

A single figure at the bar, his back to her. Cuffed trousers, a knit shirt that has, she knows, an alligator stitched on it. Bald head, thick forearms resting on the bar's bevel, a square hand economically lifting and then setting down a squat, faceted whiskey glass containing pale amber liquid. Some men are built to sit on a barstool, she thinks, and Saul Shubin's one of these.

"Hi," taking the stool beside him.

"Look who's here." He doesn't turn, having seen her in mirror behind the bar. "What brings you to paradise?"

"Bee's wax." She meant business, an old joke.

"Which sister this time?"

"Reeve. Her husband."

The bar's owner appeared: gray ponytail held in place by a rubber band. Trew ordered an Anchor Steam which she would sip and then set aside. "Julian wants to sell," she said.

"Who to?"

"Consolidated."

His anvil jaw and brutal under-bite were belied by his eyes: soft burnt sienna, some pain way back in there. Saul said nothing at first and that bothered her. Trew had entrusted much of her life to him when she came of age and needed advice, legal and otherwise. And this tough little guy from the South Bronx, retired in the East Bay, had driven up to the valley and let Julian know that he, Saul Shubin, and his new client were taking not one ounce of shit from anybody, including her new brother-in-law. Finally, he said, "Bunch of monkeys," meaning Consolidated.

He had been in the liquor business in the five boroughs and New Jersey for years before taking a speedy departure. There was mention of the Mob, Trew remembered, but what did that mean? All so East Coast.

She had her own reasons for trusting him, one being that her former guardian, Vladimir, had recommended Saul. How a Russian émigré like Vlad, who had never lived in New York and in middle age had found himself saddled with three difficult daughters of friends, knew Saul she never learned. But Saul had given backbone to a younger, insecure Trew Vasey when she needed it most and charged a pittance for his services.

"I don't know how much they offered," she said. "And I didn't want to encourage Julian by asking. Must be a lot. We're not a money-maker, though we could be, and maybe I'm reading this wrong but why would they be content to buy and spruce up Tregaron just for its traditional value?"

"Consolidated would shit-can tradition on principle," said Saul. "If Reeve and Julian think that outfit's going to let them have cotillions and live there in baronial dishabille, they're crazy. Consolidated's into a lot of stuff other than booze and they're not nice. I'm amazed that they're even looking in the valley, but if they are it isn't for whatever your brother-in-law thinks it is."

"Julian brought up the idea of going after Cain, somehow eliminating her influence if she won't take part in financial decisions. Can they do that?"

"No. But they can try."

A whoop came from the shuffleboard and one tie-dye shirt brought a cluster of empty glasses to the bar. Trew pushed her full glass toward him, and he smiled and then drank it while Abalone filled the others.

"This is where the 'Sixties came to die," said Saul, after the man had returned to the board. "Those poor bastards waited too long to get out of North Beach, and now they all have incurable Hepatitis C from sharing needles. Some won't be here when Abalone gets around to buying a new shuffleboard if he ever does. Is that what Catholics call purgatory?"

"Wouldn't know," said Trew. "I'm descended from Huguenots,

remember? French Calvinists."

"Wet Presbyterians," says Saul. "You still seeing that guy who welds chunks of steel together?"

"He's a sculptor, Saul. And no, it's over."

Saul poured ginger ale into his vodka and held the glass up like it was a urine sample. "Know what an alcoholic is?" he asked.

"I have a pretty good idea."

"Alcoholics love booze and lack proper nourishment. Alcoholics aren't Jewish and don't get enough sleep. Well, I drink much of the day, am Jewish, and hate the taste of booze. I eat three balanced meals a day and snore from sunset to dawn. Ergo…"

Without asking, Abalone poured him another shot. Far to the south the clouds were lifting, exposing the hem of the city's resplendent white petticoats. She smells popcorn — at Abalone's it's free — and says, "I don't like this business with Consolidated. I can't believe Reeve does either. The offer must be huge."

"Want me to get into this?"

"I think so."

"Okay. Clock's running."

She hooked back north at San Leandro and was soon lilting out across the flats of grass moving in the breeze. The bay had gone silty and sullen. Cars on the sparsely driven road rose and fell in unison, as always in California bound for a place different from wherever you happen to be. When she got home it was late afternoon and the light no longer hurt. Her little house, a cameo of the big one, built of the same quarried stone, had the big house's features but was in scale, sitting in its own lake of shadow at the edge of the tree line with its own path among blooming lavender. The garage had been converted to a studio with bubble skylights and a little deck. Chairs and couch both had heavy oak armrests and Navajo throw rugs. Kachina dolls on the shelves, and Pima knock-off baskets under dusty rafters that had so delighted her mother.

Famished, Trew cut open an avocado and brought the blade down hard into the seed, twisted and tossed it and butcher knife into the sink. She poured olive oil into the cavity and ate with a spoon standing up. There were tasks yet to do in the winery, but she was exhausted. A winery once set up tends to run itself, after a fashion, if it has good grapes. But maintaining quality without money was akin to shooting the moon on a broomstick, and she would be back on the job tomorrow.

Her easel was all aluminum tubes she had drilled and strung together with wire and brackets, a sturdy, three-legged alien. She carried it and the paint box in a converted frame backpack, the canvas under one arm or, if wet, above her head with both hands to avoid the sticky accretion of bugs and seeds that wet paint and linseed oil seem to generate.

She liked the expeditionary feel of plein-air painting and had learned to live with the curious stares of animals, including humans, struck by this encumbered, red-headed apparition in the middle of nowhere. Shadows were reaching for the Green Buttons vineyard, hundred-foot conical fingers in the lee of Douglas fir and redwoods, and she waded through the thickly growing wild mustard, outpacing the shadows, if just, the light almost loving at this time of day. Ordinarily it drove California painters to think they could handle it if Redmond and St. Clair and others like them had. But most painters contracted what she thought of as chromatic madness — too much illumination, too much color — that made of the world something unreal. You had to paint your way out of it, she had learned, and it takes years and acres of canvas.

The mustard was underlain with the palest cadmium green and an infinite weave of umber and viridian that never failed to thrill her. Green-buttons vineyard was named for the little reproductive button-like discs that rained by the hundreds from the ancient eucalyptus anchoring one corner. Here was one of the three wells for which Tregaron was named, like a town in Wales where her grandmother had been born. The well was just an old elbow joint in an iron pipe, but it and the vineyard meant the world to her, Tregaron Springs best, site of the crash, the one place she wanted to be when her time came.

Chapter 4

Clyde Craven-Jones had discovered rolled tortillas and wrapped inside them darkly redolent shreds of unidentifiable meat. They proved nourishing, economical and quite delicious. His room at the El Pescador motel smelled of cigarettes but also of an exotic spill-over from what he imagined to be a desert, sweet and feral. Blooming oleander reared beyond the patio where water sprayed from the earth at night and beyond that was cool, fragrant air alive with conifers.

Much of the floorspace was taken up by his enormous steamer trunk, cosseted with wooden bands. At the Oakland airport he couldn't get the trunk into the back of the taxi, so the driver had taken him to a used car lot in a wasteland of wire mesh where he bought for cash a station wagon with a gate-like rear door. He drove north through a daunting confusion of highways. Flying to the United States had taken long enough, but then he had flown across it, studying his alphabetized list of Americanisms: Can you dig it, dream on, phony, the Man, to the max, book it. Also cheese eater, fool that you are, get down, right on, airhead, bread, bummer, bunk, busted, chick, chill, chump, cool beans, you copy? Doobie, dork, funk, gag me with a spoon, gnarly, copasetic, deadhead, groovy, hey sunshine. Confusing him was Jack squat, primo, righteous, solid, stoked, stop dipping in my Kool-aid, sweet, TCB, tight with that, totally, and wicked.

His eight-track player had been replaced by one for cassettes. He had earlier tried watching The Dukes of Hazzard on television and was dismayed. Saturday Night Fever he liked but not Earth Shoes, pet rocks, mood rings, leisure suits, water beds, swag lamps, beanbag chairs, shoes with giant heels or women's hair "stacked and packed." He was baffled by Governor Ronald Reagan, too, and the oil crisis, but not James Taylor playing on his old car radio. He preferred the occasional blues rendition coming out of his single speaker, particularly B.B. King. The Rolling Stones were as disturbing as ever until he realized that he, too, was now a rolling stone.

In El Pescador the trunk reminded him of home and served as a kind of valet on which he lay out clothes for the following morning, including his signature silk handkerchiefs washed and hung to dry in the shower stall. Mornings he brewed tea on an electric coil and made calls to prospective sources for what was to be a book about California wine. The publisher in London had agreed to publish it but the advance was piddling. Articles he would write for Lily & Sons, the two-hundred-year-old wine merchants, would go into the collective pot, and so would what was left of his inheritance from Uncle Jones. But talking to New World vintners was proving more difficult than he had anticipated. Calls made on the rotary phone often went unanswered and the vintners he dropped in on were suspicious and some rude. Others overly enthused, insisting on showing him technological embellishments like stainless steel tanks replacing the old fermentation vats of redwood and Douglas fir, and feeding him not tortillas but liverwurst or a local cheese known as Jack. Twice when he finally returned to his station wagon, he found cases of wine put there by his hosts.

So, Clyde gave bottles to the desk clerk, the maid, fellow dippers into the diminutive motel swimming pool, and the tattooed handyman with a hand-rolled cigarette appended permanently to his lower lip who called Clyde "professor". The most popular resident of El Pescador, Clyde began to receive extra day-old buns and creamer for his tea. One day blended with the next and he found himself pleasantly adrift in bright, beautiful days, writing up his notes, taking more by phone and wondering if his money would last.

However, the primary inspiration for his coming to California, Tregaron Springs, remained elusive. He heard that the winery was stressed financially, and his telephone calls to the estate weren't returned. One afternoon he drove out to see the place for himself and sat on the shoulder of the highway, gazing across parched blonde grass and vineyards at shadowy assemblages of stone. He was reminded not of Bordeaux or Provence. The giant trees making of this as much a wilderness as a wine estate, the setting of house and winery identical to the label he had seen in London, now breathing massively of the past.

Then, when he had returned to his room, a bit of sorcery. The phone was ringing when he came in and when he answered an efficient female voice invited him to visit Tregaron the very next day. She added, "You sound British."

"English, actually."

"Cute. See you tomorrow."

The gardener outside Tregaron sent him to the top of a very long flight of stairs. What Clyde discovered looked more like a grand tack room than an executive suite: raw boards hung with saddles, whips, sombreros, horned heads, brass plaques from Rotary and something called Sons of the Golden West. A whole section of wall was dedicated to awards from the Caterina Valley Vintners, another to fierce-looking bearded patriarchs in black suits out of another century in gilt-framed daguerreotypes and their bustled women posed in haughty profile. A more recent photograph showed a hatchet-faced man in wing collars smoking a pipe.

"That would be Daddy," Reeve Vassy was saying, a pretty woman in flared, tightly belted trousers sitting on the opposite side of a glass desk.

"Now I assume you want to taste our current releases, so I've arranged a tasting in the Trader's Room down in the winery. Then we'll have lunch on the patio with my sister, Trew, who supervises the wine side. She can show you around the property, too. Our history's interesting — Native American, Chinese, Spanish — we're in the journals of Junipero Serra. And Italians, Germans, a Hungarian but no Englishmen, I'm afraid. Lots of French including four generations of us Vassys."

"That would all be lovely."

"All right. Now do you mind if I call you CJ?"

"Why?"

"Because 'Clyde' just doesn't really work in California. Clive might, but not Clyde. Please don't be offended, it's just a suggestion. Clyde's very nice, really it is, but if it happened to be somebody's name here, they'd change it. CJ's short, catchy. And it stands for that wonderful double-barreled last name of yours."

Astounded, he followed this remarkable woman back down the stairs and into a cavernous room full of disused redwood casks, light showing between the boards. The place smelled of fortified wine and generations of resident microbes. The free-standing cubicle in the middle of the winery's broad stone floor served as Tregaron's front office but they passed it and entered what she called the Trader's Room. Damask-covered walls, north European floral designs pressed into the backs of oak chairs, carved claw feet on a table supporting long-stemmed glasses and four cork-less bottles. On one wall hung a tapestry antique with harts and hinds.

"My great-grandfather lived in San Francisco and imported all this to make a proper tasting room. He didn't drink but had the foresight to hire people who knew how to make good wine and then learned how to sell it."

"The Romans used their country villas the same way," Clyde —

now CJ — said. "It's a noble tradition. The farthest flung in Europe were fortresses against the barbarians."

"These chairs are from Alsace."

Reeve settled her lovely, long-legged self onto one, adding, "I thought we could start with the claret."

"I'm accustomed to evaluating wine alone," he said, "if you don't mind awfully. First impressions are very valuable."

Her eyebrows went up but without a word she left him and took the perfume with her, which was the whole point. Now he sat in sepulchral quiet, picked up a glass, and was soon scribbling.

So-called claret well-made but unmemorable... Something called petite Syrah an inky but imminently drinkable except for the very alcoholic floral essence... Merlot promising, some red fruit, toasty, no Pomerol but with a decent finish. Cries out for spine-enhancing cabernet sauvignon...

Eventually he sat back and ate a wafer. The last glass brimmed with the scents of cassis, cigar box and voluptuous fruit, underneath everything a suggestion of mint. Even the distinct nose on this wine took him back once more to the Windsor Arms in London where he first tasted it and glimpsed the label's blue hills and abundant light. The finish was long and elegant then, and still was.

He stepped out of the Trader's Room strolled about the stone amphitheater. He could see that wine had in the old days flowed down from above to come to rest in these ancient redwood tanks, now empty. Stainless-steel ones stood back among the shadows, but the tell-tale aromatics of yore, as precise and evocative as cave paintings, hung in this olfactory Lascaux. The far-flung associations called up were powerful.

Before him yawned a dank stairwell. He went down it to see marshaled French oak barrels on their sides, dark red stripes about the midriffs where wine spilled from the bung holes, and sunlight glimmering in narrow cracks between hand-set stones. Surely this was a unique American chateau, as beautiful and romantic as anything he had encountered in Europe. A wine thief lay on an over-turned crate, its antique glass tube wearing a bluish brass collar and a ring for the forefinger, a device designed for slipping into casks and bringing up thin columns of pubescent wine for tasting, the only overtly sexual aspect of winemaking that bordered upon the illicit.

"I hope you're not planning to use that."

The voice came from behind him, and he almost dropped the wine thief onto shattering stone. Turning, he made out a young woman with wild, light-streaked hair. She wore smudged dungarees, a tight black jerkin and blue work shirt with sleeves rolled up from sturdy forearms: the proverbial cellar rat, denizen of wine-making's depths the world over, though rarely so striking.

"Of course not," he said, carefully replacing the thief.

"I assume you're the British writer Reeve was expecting."

"English actually."

"How did you like the wines?"

"They're lovely."

"Can't do better than that?"

"Well, there's room for improvement. But the cabernet from the Green Buttons vineyard is extraordinary, if flawed."

She laughed aloud. "It placed in that Paris tasting and is selling out. Too bad we don't have more."

She offered her hand to shake, a habitual Americanism he was still trying to get used to. "I'm Trew Vassy."

"Clyde Craven-Jones, though your sister has re-christened me CJ."

Trew laughed again, revealed perfectly aligned teeth, an apparent requirement to live in California. "Well, CJ, welcome to the valley."

Reeve waited for them at the head of the cellar stairs. She led them directly to lunch on the back patio: loaves of sourdough split and filled with sliced roast fowl and more Jack. Trew Vassy took from her jeans a bone-handled folding knife and cut strips from the green chilis standing in a glass. One she ate outright, a daring move, and left untouched the bottle of Tregaron Springs claret standing open on the table.

Reeve said, "I understand the wines are acceptable, CJ."

"More than acceptable."

"This book you're working on," said Trew, "when's it going to be finished?"

"I've just begun. I must assemble my research. There are already quite a few notebooks, though I've had difficulty contacting some winemakers."

"Let me guess who." Trew gazed up into the towering branches of a Douglas fir. "Well, there's old Joe. He's a trained chemist who worked in the Central Valley where he blew oak chips into oceans of industrial wine to give it some character. He can be a prick . . . ."

"Trewdy," cautioned her sister.

"… but his wine is good."

She mentioned the name of a woman who had also ignored CJ's overtures. "She's an airhead who takes off her clothes and jumps into pools at parties. But she has good vineyard land and a good if uneducated, ruthless vintner who bangs her gratuitously…"

"Stop, Trewdy."

"… and destroys every tree in sight. She lets the grapes hang on the vines until they're so ripe only skunks will eat them. Her cabernet's got a wallop and what wouldn't with all that alcohol, so heavily extracted you could almost spread the stuff on toast."

He was writing in his notebook by now. "Do go on."

"I know you've already talked with the Abruzzinis," Trew said. "The old man's Mister High Culture now, when he's not Mister Take-off-your-panties."

"Trewdy!"

"His father shipped Central Valley fruit to Mafiosi in Chicago during Prohibition, but he talks about 'sculpting' wines, wine and art, all that. Our sister, Cain, married one of his sons and that lasted less than a week. Terry Abruzzini took her to Rome for their honeymoon and when she came out of her hotel bathroom on the Veneto, she found him sitting on the bed with two prostitutes."

Reeve said, "No more," and with a forcefulness that surprised him, holding aloft an antique silver coffee spoon like a weapon. Just then dishes of fresh berries in crème fraiche arrived, dispensed by an aging Mexican woman in white. Trew shrugged and attacked her dessert.

Reeve asked, "CJ, have you ever done consulting?"

"I have made suggestions to winemakers when asked, though I seldom am."

"Any suggestions for us?"

"Well, you have so many wines. You might consider eliminating one or two, and there's the question of the minty component in your best cabernet."

"What question?" asked Trew.

"Well, the wine's fascinating but also highly uncharacteristic. It's the first from California wine I ever seriously considered, but the mintiness will always be a problem with wine critics."

"Fuck them."

Reeve sighed and dabbed at her lips with a napkin. "Maybe, CJ," she said, "you could advise us more generally. Perhaps taste the young wines and tell us what you think might be changed. We wouldn't insult you by offering money, but we could provide a place for you to stay while you're here if that has any appeal. Our guest cottage has a kitchenette and a view up St. Bart's."

"Well," he said, "that is a possibility."

"Tonight, you could stay in the big house while the cottage is cleaned. What do you say, CJ?"

Chapter 5

He checked out of El Pescador, gave the handyman his last bottle of wine, and returned to Tregaron Springs. The maid who had served the luncheon now showed him to a room on the second floor of the mansion, where he ate cold tortillas from a paper bag and was asleep before the sunlight had seeped well away. Much later he awoke to something in that big, echoing house and waited to hear it again before switching on the bedside lamp and padding out into the dark hallway.

Narrow stairs led down to the kitchen where a punched button flooded light onto dangling cooking implements and framed posters for French aperitifs. Family photographs massed on walls of knotty pine captured Thanksgiving and Christmas celebrations, sweet sixteen parties, vinous events. There were signed shots of movie stars: Humphrey Bogart holding a cut crystal whiskey glass, Rock Hudson smiling imperiously, Ronald Reagan as a B-movie cowboy in a bandana.

Vassy family members tended toward stripes and broad collars, hairdos, tight neckties, bright lipstick. What he assumed was the Vassy sisters' mother had a lovely elastic smile and the frankest gaze of all. All these Vassys were presided over by what must have been the girls' father, bemused in his tennis whites, austere when he wore a tuxedo and daring in a leather pilot's jacket as he leaned against a small aircraft with a pipe clenched in his teeth.

The most intriguing photo was of the three girls in a ballroom, all wearing tight black sheaths, their arms entwined, their collective mass of hair a ruddy conflagration above. The one who must be Cain looked askance at the camera, as striking as her siblings but slightly to one side, her stance proclaiming: I'm joining in, but I know something my sisters don't know. She and Reeve looked much alike, whereas younger, Trew, was more darkly complected and clearly the outsider.

CJ opened the refrigerator, hoping for some delightful surprise, but all he found was congealed salad dressing, saltines in waxed paper, and an open box of baking soda.

When he awoke again the sky was cloudy as Shropshire's in November. Decidedly cool air tumbled through his open window and from abroad came the murmur of machinery — a fork-lift, a raspy device for blowing leaves. He saw an aging Mexican in hip-waders in a pond plucking lily pads from dark water. For an estate supposedly on the edge financially Tregaron seemed to employ a remarkable number of workers.

He put on his new Bermudas, sandals and a flannel shirt, to be in the California spirit. Back down in the kitchen, he was met by Trew, who said, "I've come to show you around."

She led him onto a path among lavender, then tangles of undergrowth and huge trees he couldn't identify. "We're at the southern-most point of a temperate rain forest. This is one of the largest biomes on earth, and it has the most diverse biological profile. Trees like these have survived drought and fire that left those black scars, the worst threat being us."

"Us?"

"People. At the time of settlement vast stands of untouched forest covered these coastal ranges. Then creeks ran high even in summer and a raindrop falling here took days to reach the earth, so thick was the canopy extending down the Pacific coast from Alaska."

Accumulated pine needles silenced their way through the forest, his guide rolling off the balls of her feet while looking up, always up, passing exotic slugs the size of bananas to point out an acorn woodpecker. He sensed in her muscular figure and thick multi-hued hair gathered in a bandana, a knife on her waist, a passion he hadn't expected. He said carefully, "The forest must have offered refuge to the natives."

"Yes, and they depended upon acorns and other plants for subsistence. Life in the valleys was easier and the steepness of the terrain isolated them. They spoke a hundred distinctly different languages often incomprehensible to those living just one valley over. Having so much primeval forest eventually cut by us crippled them permanently."

"As the Romans felled the great oaks in Ireland, laying bare the druidic mysteries."

"Yes, cut the trees and kill the gods. I wanted you to see what this place is really all about, which is land and water, not grapes. Not that we don't try to minimize impact. Green Buttons vineyard is dry farmed, but not the others. We have more water than most places in the valley, and it doesn't come from the creek but from ancient springs. Every night this concrete holding tank fills and at dawn the water flows down through plastic piping to the vines."

He expected a dank irrigation project but what they came upon was the estate's swimming pool. No statuary, just lounge chairs and a table with an open umbrella and brimming, beckoning water. Side by side. He and Trew stared into its mesmerizing depths. "You can drink it," she said. "I do every morning, before anybody's had a chance to jump in."

And with that she knelt and put her face in this beautiful water, her hair floating like a weedy mass. Her shirt rode up from the small of her back: unblemished skin kept from the sun, flexed back-straps, softly flared hips. He had a powerful urge to touch her but didn't. Kneeling, he too lowered his face to the cold water, drank, and rose to see Trew rocking back on her heels and running wet hands through her hair. She lifted her face to the sky. "They'll never get me out of here," she said.

"This is where I belong, and this is where I'm staying."

"I pray the end find me here," said Clyde, showing off his scholarship, "and here shall ask a reckoning of the vanished hours."

"Who wrote that?"

"Petronius. I'm a medievalist by training, not a wine critic."

On impulse he reached out and covered her palm with his, struck by the roughness of it, the calluses. "That was quick," she said, withdrawing it. "Must be lonesome, driving around by yourself, so far from home. California can seem so friendly and yet utterly remote. We're very self-protective here in a way difficult for newcomers to understand. I sympathize with your needs but I'm not the girl for you, CJ. And I've just ended a relationship with someone, and I don't believe in jumping straight from one to another." She laughed. "You'd have better luck with my sister."

"Your sister's married."

"Oh, yes, I tend to forget that part."

Reeve was waiting for them at path's end. She wore tennis whites and little cotton balls attached to the back of her shoes. Her fitted tank top that did not conceal an athletic brassiere because she wore none. "Tennis?" she asked. "I assume you play."

Trew kept walking. He said, "Yes, but I have no shoes."

"Oh, Julian has loads of that stuff." She pointed to a metal racquet and a pair of old sneakers, laces knotted, on a bench. "Those should fit, close enough anyway. I feel the need sometimes in the morning before it gets too hot. Do you mind rallying a bit?"

"I suppose not. You said something early about a mission for me."

"We can talk about that on the way to the court."

She picked up a large manila envelope and led him to the court. "I have an important document here I need to get to our sister, and you could help us with that, CJ. The problem is that Cain doesn't communicate like normal people. She won't ordinarily answer letters and refuses to talk to anybody — lawyers, accountants, anybody including us. I sent her a telegram asking if this nice Englishman might drop off a document crucial to all our futures, that all she must do is sign and hand it back to him. To my surprise she telegraphed back to say yes."

He could see the court now, below the level of the swimming pool. Reeve approached it with the utter familiarity of someone who has grown up in an unwavering arc of privilege so constant she never questioned it. The prospect of his having to face this lissome and no doubt formidable opponent while wearing Bermudas, a collared shirt, and her husband's shoes was unsettling.

"Cain lives on a kind of commune. It's called Sanandra. They'll let you in apparently, so just make the delivery and then wait until she's had a chance to read and sign it. Then you're to bring it straight back. Don't worry, we'll pay all your expenses if you agree. If you do this for us, CJ, it will cover a lot of rent and eventually help us a great deal. Well, here we are."

The court was enclosed by rusty vine-draped fencing but had a well-kept surface. He had seen worse on baronial estates. At one end of the court was an old, mounted telescope of bluish brass set low enough for children to view the forest that Trew had discoursed on so eloquently. Reeve waited while he sat on a slatted bench to replace his sandals with the tennis shoes. He swung the racket as he marched onto the court, where Reeve fired a ball at him. Clyde hadn't played tennis in a while and though he admired her clean, powerful strokes, obviously the result of many hours of lessons, he resented her maneuvering him effortlessly around the court with savage returns directed at his feet. Soon he was panting.

"That was a nasty drop shot, wasn't it?" she said apologetically.

These Vassy women were dangerous, he was beginning to realize. Meanwhile Reeve's attention had moved to activity up at the swimming pool/irrigation tank. She dropped her racket and walked to the big telescope, bending to the lens, and presenting Clyde with a pristine view of tanned, tapering thighs and spotless white panties draped with a pleated skirt. "This telescope came off a Japanese destroyer," she said. "Somebody gave it to Daddy after the war. Now something's going on over at the pool that shouldn't be, CJ, I suspect. Could you look and tell me what you see?"

She stepped aside and he leaned to the big lenses and saw a man and a woman lying side-by-side on a lounge. He was dark-haired and handsome, she younger than he and she had very large breasts, one dark nipple pointing at Clyde.

"I see two nudes," he said.

"One of them is my husband. Now what are they doing?"

"She's sitting up."

"Where is her hand?"

"On his stomach."

"This I have to see."

He stepped away and Reeve took his place. Clyde — what the hell, CJ — saw that in those two minutes she had removed her panties. How? And where were they? His purview now included what looked distinctly like Reeve's slightly moist pudenda and an under-bush of dense red hair. Mesmerized, he couldn't look away. How long had it been? Not since he left London and another furious woman wanting to marry him, and he refusing. Now he heard Reeve say, her eyes remaining fixed on the distant couple, "Oh, go on CJ."

His hands rose as if on wires, his fingers digging into those lovely, muscular orbs. He expected a violent reaction, but none came. Reeve, still peering through the binoculars, said, "Flounce up my skirt please, it's just been ironed."

He did as instructed and then unfastened and dropped his Bermudas. His undershorts followed. Erect, ruddy in the California sun, grasping what felt like twin grips on a lovely valise of the softest leather, he lifted her until her feet dangled, the white cotton balls signaling her surrender and the tips of her sneakers tracing half-moons in the court's composition.

He planted himself without further ado, and Reeve gasped, "My God!"

She began to move rhythmically but never took her eyes from the telescope. "She's kneeling now. . . ."

Out of Clyde flowed months of longing, desire, and self-doubt, a spasmodic propulsion seemed to come up from deep in the Earth, and inexplicably he began to weep.

But Reeve remained riveted on the lenses. "Why," she said, "the little bitch!"

CHAPTER 6

Trew found Marta cleaning the guest cottage. She had gained weight in her bright floral day dresses but was still dainty as heavy people can sometimes be. She and a handful of others were from the state of Michoacán and were in a way wards of Tregaron, long in service without formal arrangements, some hired by Trew's father. Now they served as a collective bulwark against change, anchors of grace in a sea increasingly menaced by the likes of Consolidated Brands. She and all the others would be swept away if Julian's plan prevailed, so Trew was also working for Marta and her people — a two-fer.

The mop and broom stood in one corner of the old cottage, Marta holding aloft the feather duster like a weapon. "I knocked it off," she said, indicating a little tin box on the coffee table. Trew had never seen it and her gaze followed the line of the duster up to the heavy redwood beam bisecting the room eight feet from the floor.

"Looks like somebody forgot something up there," said Trew, "a long time ago."

Marta stopped gathering her things for the next job and laid a hand on Trew's arm. "It's not going to be easy, Trewdy," she said enigmatically, this woman who had practically raised her and always tarried, if encouraged, to talk about her joints, the early harvest, the truncated schedule at Tregaron that would require her to work the bottling line. But not today. She patted Trew's cheek and went out, leaving Trew alone with the mysterious box.

It was too small to accommodate a scroll, or a telescope. A geometric design had been pressed into the metal. Trew raised the lid and removed a rolled sheet of paper. Spread on the bench, it revealed a penciled list of expenditures and the date: August 1947. Trew added up the numbers. Almost seven thousand dollars, but for what? There was more in the box: a folded scrap of cream-colored watermarked stationary Trew recognized as her mother's. It had been torn as if in haste, unlike Bev Vassy's other notes on the same sort of paper and sometimes whole letters that went out constantly when the phone would have been easier and faster. Because her mother had liked writing them — introducing friends to others or, at a time when cocktails meant mixed drinks and boiled shrimp clung to the rims of footed dishes full of ketchup and Worcestershire, serving country pate instead. When beef was usually well-done, she served rare steak cut cross-grain and laved it in a dark sauce Trew could still smell when descending the back stairs to the kitchen of the main house. There Trew had a special place on the landing where she could linger and listen unseen to her mother in apron and heels, laughing with other voices Trew knew, not just her father's and Vladimir's but those of friends and visitors, too, some of them famous.

The falsetto she remembered best belonged to the big woman performing cooking miracles on television, Julia Childe. And, when Trew was six, she walked into the second story bathroom to find a man leaning against the sink, staring at a handful of pills. This is my bathroom, she had wanted to tell him. A decade later she had watched him rub salt onto black leeches in African Queen and realized how sick this Humphrey Bogart had been when she met him.

She unfolded the piece of stationery. Emblazoned on it was the familiar imprint of her mother's lips, crimson and puckered, the creases as fresh as yesterday. Often Trew had watched her mother blot that beautiful mouth, she had felt those same lips pressed to her cheek. Her words had been invisible balloons lofting up through the talk and exotic stove smells to hang against the kitchen ceiling, where they remained.

A single line had been written with her mother's gold fountain pen: *I am unleashed.*

Trew drove into town and sat outside Caterina's finest facility for assisted living, Bright Hours. Here their — her and her sisters' — guardian Vlad had gone to live after his difficult rule at Tregaron, a one-handed tyrant without an army to enforce his orders. Vlad's thunderous disapproval had served as a kind of governor on them. Trew as the youngest had been his favorite but the old man brought now into the common room by an orderly was barely recognizable — hank of white hair askew, deep wrinkles about the eyes of what had once been Lieutenant Vladimir Umansky, hero of the Great Patriotic War, survivor of Hitler and Stalin.

She said, "Hi Vlad," and bent to touch his cheek. He managed a smile, the rheumy eyes willing but uncertain. "Trewdy," he murmured.

"I'm so glad to see you, Vlad. How have you been?" She pulled up a chair. "Is there anything I can get you?"

His gaze started with her hair and moved down to face, throat, the buttons on her shirt, finally her hands, where it remained. She had scrubbed them before coming but they still bore the residue of paint, and cellar grime. Vlad was registering, she realized, the transformation of an adolescent child into a full-fledged adult now on the wrong side of thirty. Vlad's own gnarly knuckles gripped the armrest, blue-tinged with veins under thin skin. His nails were in better shape than hers, so someone at Bright Hours was paying attention to him. The cuffs of his shirt had been buttoned, the blunt left wrist protruding. As a kid she had stared at the folded flesh where his hand should have been, fascinated by its absence. He had employed the stump with great skill and utter disregard for on-lookers, turning the pages of a book with a deft nub, holding down a slab of meat while assaulting it with a steak knife.

She said, "Vlad, I'd like you to help me with something. I've been thinking a lot about. I've been wondering if Mommy had a, you know, special friend. Way back. A lot of time has passed, I know, and it doesn't really matter now but it nags at me. Was there ever anyone, you know, anyone other than Daddy?" It was the question she tried to put to Martha after reading the note, but Martha was nowhere to find. The censure of asking such a question would come down on Trew, no mattered who answered it, but Vlad's demeanor was changing so slowly she couldn't tell if it was his memory, or something deeper. "Just me asking, Vlad. You remember Mister Bogart. Were he and Mommy, you know, special friends?"

Vlad's gaze wandered. Boredom, or flight?

"Was there someone else then, Vlad?"

He moved his lips, as if rehearsing what he might say. "Not that one."

She leaned closer. "You mean not Bogey but someone else? Who?"

Hindered by the babble of patients, the amplified televised talk show, the clatter of metal walkers and orderlies in pale green tunics passing, Vlad said nothing. For years he had withstood her sisters' hysterical reactions when prevented by him from taking young men to their bedrooms and other infractions — driving without a license, demanding money, neglecting studies and, once, swimming naked in a grape gondola filled with water and hauled down the highway by an accommodating worker. Trew fished the scrap of stationary from her shirt pocket and turned it so Vlad could see, but his arm came up to ward her off. He was afraid.

"Oh, Vlad, I'm sorry. It's nothing, really. Just lipstick on a piece of paper."

She touched the bony shoulder of what had once been a powerful man, probably attractive to women. Did that stump once trace her dear mother's topography? No, she decided, it had not.

"I'm so sorry, Vlad. But if not Bogey, then who?"

But Vlad wanted deliverance. He signaled an orderly crossing the room, who came and seized the handles of his wheelchair, Vlad's gaunt old frame retreating but his eyes still on Trew. Out in the parking lot she drove her palms against the steering wheel. She had abused a defenseless old man who had done her family great service. He knew something.

The smell of cleaning lingered in the guest cottage. Trew stared at the tin box on the table, opened it again and turned it upside down. An old key rattled to the floor.

It was late when she scooped flour from the tin into the bowl and added yeast salt, pepper, and a splash of olive oil. She mixed the dough and set it aside to take a bath, avoiding the answering machine full of messages from their cut-rate vineyard management company and bottle salesmen. Then she put on a sweatshirt and flannels and went back to the kitchen.

The dough was rising so she turned on the oven and stood with her back to it, looking at the lumps on the table: whole-wheats, baguettes, fusilli's. It was a joke among the help who viewed her as part mistress, part beneficent witch who stalked old growth with her easel and filled the freezer with bread stacked like cordwood. Once harvest got underway, she would distribute warmed-up, tin-foiled lengths of bread to the itinerant pickers. Fresh would have been better but these were never turned down. Lady of the Bountiful Loaf, one of the pleasures of life competing with walking her family's land, painting, and that other thing.

On impulse she picked up a pencil and wrote on her notepad:

Kneading focaccia
thinking of your hands on me
the dough squeaks.

But there were no hands these days. She slipped the baking pan into the darkly gaping oven and sat down at her desk. In the warm circle of light thrown by the lamp she tried to envision Mrs. Joseph Vassy dealing with mid-life, as Trew was anticipating. Raising her eyes to the window she saw the outline of the guest house next door. Had it been the scene of some unseemliness, a haven of adultery, or something less damning? She must talk to Marta about this, as awkward as that would be.

Just then Trew saw in the window her own reflection and then, taking its place, that of her mother, lovely brows arched, lips parted as if about to speak, gazing not at Trew but through her. Then a blaze of light obliterated Bev Vassy, causing Trew to cry out and grip the table. She rose, driving a knee painfully against unyielding wood, realizing it was just CJ in the guest cottage, stuffing a sandwich and a sweater into a valise. But Bev Vassy had been driven back into the shadows and Trew felt abandoned, again, her knee throbbing. Doubly bereft.

Chapter 7

When Trew got up the next day CJ's car was gone. She drove into the town of Caterina past autumn-trending vines, the grass searing in the heat. It hadn't rained in months, good conditions for harvest, maybe, but for little else. Wine pourers were straggling into their tasting room jobs, traffic lined up on the main street behind north-bound tanker trucks.

At the stoplight she dug the mysterious key out of her jeans. It might provide entry to a safety deposit box or a bus station locker but there were none of those in this little town. The only logical slot she could think of was a mailbox. She parked and walked into a lobby that never failed to thrill, its murals painted during the Depression with money given to the artists by the government. The work now served as a testament to a valley that no longer existed, when white Americans did the work in the vineyards, men and women, hefting wooden boxes of grapes, leaning into the handles on mechanical wine presses, wiping sweat from their faces with bright bandanas.

The postboxes had ornate metal scrollwork and little windows offering shuttered views of the mail. Heart beating, Trew read the numbers, one after another, searching for 133. Then in the corner where the box should have been stood a display table for brochures and the numbers jumped from 120 to 140. Twenty post office boxes had simply disappeared.

"Those were taken out a long time ago," the clerk told her, squinting at the key when she showed him.

"What about the contents? If anything was in there it still belongs to my family."

He led her into the storage room and searched among the cartons on metal shelving scrawled over in black ink. He took one down and together they peered in. Random papers and, underneath them, a small book bound in pale blue leather. The rubber band binding it had long since broken but she took it, thanked him, and carried her treasure out into the morning.

People passed and nodded, and she nodded back, tempted to open the notebook right there. But she waited until she had taken it into the gift shop across the street, once a lunch spot with round, marble-topped tables, chairs of twisted wire with round wooden seats. She remembered her father and Vladimir sitting in the window with Caterina's banker and sometimes the mayor — the power circle. The subjects of their conversation would have been the House Un-American Activities Committee in Washington, high taxes on agricultural products, the sanctity of small business. Joseph Vassy had inherited a fortune and the valley's prime estate but was the loudest defender of free enterprise which in fact he never practiced, heavily dependent upon servants without ever recognizing that fact. How many times had she seen him standing at the open trunk of the Lincoln and a pile of luggage or a recently acquired antique, turning automatically to see who had arrived to handle the burden, his hand going automatically into pleated gabardine trousers for coins to dispense.

Bev Vassy had been more aware even though dependent on a cast of young women working about house and gardens, constantly in flux, the senior Vassys usually off somewhere, wine their magic carpet. It also attracted to them other inheritors, politicians, movie stars. Trew suspected that Tregaron Springs's finances had been a bit perilous even then and tried not to resent the fact that they hadn't been better managed. Only Cain had the nerve to voice this when barely a teenager, suggesting at the annual Christmas party that Marta receive the mother of the year award and with it a magnum of wine for taking better care of the three Vassy girls than their real mother. This had brought out her father's disapproval, never far below the surface: a chiseled part in very fair hair, bright blue eyes, standards for living. Cain had been banished to her room yet again.

Trew walked to the pickup and, one shoulder resting on the warm steel, finally opened the book. Unmarked cream-colored end papers, the first lined page covered with her mother's familiar azure cursive. A recipe for lemon tart. Looking up into the sky, Trew laughed aloud, there was nothing clandestine here, nothing shameful. It was just a record of Bev Vassy's culinary progress through the dailiness of Tregaron: dishes, meals, guests at family events, an innocent record out of a time lost.

She opened the truck door and climbed in, thumbing up another page, and read: *... seeing you in the last light before the sun goes behind St. Bart's, angling through the space above the curtains. The sun's allowed in for a minute, a divine snoop, but nobody else can see what the mountain sees. Which is you, shadow outlining your ribs and chest and collarbone, lean, stark, beautiful. Don't be offended. I even love your droopy drawers. Then the sun's gone and the long shadows hungrily wanting more. ... the way you hold me, who would think it could be so different? Not fair knowing so little about you. No one could possibly imagine this, not me anyway, and you lost to me until next time...*

I know you won't blame me or misinterpret. Men just don't understand. To hold is to risk a kind compact that might bind them, as if touching those parts of a woman not involved in the act has no purpose. But women look at men less as lovers than as holders, as odd as those sounds, a way of measuring beyond the other. Holding is in its way more sensual because sex distracts (don't we know!) from seeing a person whole. When you hold me and knead with those rough hands I adore, I feel closer to you than when I'm coming...

Trew carefully turned the volume over in her lap, suddenly breathless. This was no diary. It was an extended love letter, fondly conceived, carefully wrought. The experience itself had been brief, that was clear, and the fact that the object of this passion had never read her mother's words seemed tragic, whatever else it signified. Who had so lovingly kneaded her mother years ago? It could not have been Vladimir because Vlad had only one hand, and not Bogart because he was the first to die. Then who?

...I don't mean to diminish what happened but just to say it's quite different. I know you know, though sometimes I want to hear if you've done the same with other women. (DO NOT TELL ME). However you came by it, I envy you. My father never held me, in fact he barely touched me. Don't know why because I was a good girl, dutiful as we all were then. What I got was pats and precise kisses on birthdays and graduation, when what I wanted was the soft force of flesh, the weight of the real.

The sad irony is — I know this is hard for you — that my husband's the same, almost as if the two of them got together and decided to continue the tradition. The gap between the precipices is just too much for some men to attempt. Mother was better, but even she was afraid either of losing authority or of my father's disapproval...

My life was so different from yours. I'll bet you never had to worry about finding someone to hold you. I feel those people through you, although I'll never know, couldn't, the warmth of those generations. They of course probably couldn't possibly imagine me...

This strand as thick as a tree, rooted so deeply that everything else seems new and unrealized and insubstantial. That's what I feel when you hold me, a progression infinitely slow, so gradual yet never still. I sometimes come before you're there, even when I try not to, but it's the holding that unburdens me...

I feel the power of your unknown life, its branches pushing into and out of me. Much I admit is lust. Your face, the bones so severe, the eyes so soft. The flat of your stomach, hips like a toreador's although I know that's a stupid comparison, your lovely you-know-what. So expandable. I have to admit it fascinates me, the mechanics of it. How can human tissue behave like that? As you know, my experience is limited and in fact until now I wasn't sure exactly sure what the word meant. I never met one like yours and find it a wonderful contraption — a hood revealing the fierce face, a sheath miraculously absorbed into the whole…

Enough, Trew thought. Close the book and stick it under the seat. Much known, more not, including his name. Whoever he was he wasn't and never would ever be the governor of California who was almost certainly circumcised. The grandiosity of Trew's earlier speculations now shamed and amused her even as the audacity of what her mother had done was thrilling.

CJ didn't get back to Tregaron Springs until late afternoon. He had done as Reeve asked, handing over the manilla envelope to the receptionist at Sanandra in the high Sierra, waiting an hour before the document had been signed, and then driving back to the valley. He never met the third Vassy sister. Now, exhausted, he slipped the envelope under Reeve's office door and went back to his cottage where he fell into a profound sleep.

The sun wakened him to the sight of his manuscript on the table in Tregaron's guest cottage, the pages of the typescript foxed at the edges. He got up and fondly squared them, marked as they were with dark circles wherever his tea mug had stood. He was at last writing his book, commissioned as a treatise on recent vintages of California Bordeaux sauvignon but becoming something more, an exposition of the culture behind these wines that was a complete mystery to wine drinkers in Britain, the revelations passed on to CJ by Trew.

Some of the wines were not just good but also unique. Some of the vintners were simply outrageous. Soil and sun had produced an abundance of personality as well as luscious fruit rainy Bordeaux would never enjoy, a wild taste he attributed to volcanic effluvia spewed forth during the Sierra Nevada's creation had also produced extravagant personalities, too.

Here in the Caterina Valley the West ran out, Trew had said. These stone walls framed blueish hills with halos of dry, dusty chaparral, backed by dark, huge, twisted branches. The smells of sun and wood created a cedary continuum not unlike the inside of a wine barrel. Now CJ felt himself taking on characteristics of sawn fir and gnarly valley oak and the fragrance of lavender pushing constantly in under his front door.

He opened it and saw on the worn welcome mat a baguette wrapped in bright aluminum foil.

Chapter 8

Trew's phone was ringing. She plucked it from the wall and heard her sister Reeve say, "Cain's signed Consolidated's offer."

"How on Earth did she get it?"

"CJ hand-delivered it."

"The bastard."

"He thinks it's not a bad idea, considering our financial difficulties."

"So, I guess you signed it, too?"

"No but I intend to."

"Please don't before we talk."

"We've talked this to death, Trewdy."

"It isn't much to ask, just let me come over first. I can't stand the idea of you writing your name on that document alone, under the eyes of all our forebears. And wouldn't it be better, legal-wise, for me to witness it?"

"Julian says it doesn't matter."

"I think it does. Somebody has to witness, and it might as well be me."

"Well, I must get my teeth cleaned at nine-thirty and can't postpone it again. Then pick up the dry cleaning. Let's say noon?"

Trew hung up and slapped her Rolodex, thrusting a forefinger into the Ss and surfacing Saul's card. The attorney's home phone rang for a long time. Finally, she heard the familiar Bronx growl: "Good morning."

"Cain signed," she said.

Two hours later he called back. "I talked to a guy on the inside at Consolidated. You were right to have doubts about this, they want the Tregaron name and the facility but what they really want is the land. I'm not talking vineyards, but water. Somebody — most likely your brother-in-law — got hold of an old map and had a facsimile made and shipped it east and Consolidated's development team flipped."

So Julian was stealing not just library wines but also documents to buttress his pander. The land in question would show up on county charts, of course, which could be unearthed easily enough, but a historical document carried extra weight. She could see it: hoary verisimilitude, discovery. The lost treasure of Tregaron. Her grandfather and great-grandfather had put together their domain piecemeal. Some leases went back as much as seventy years. They ignored parcels that ran up into steep, forested slopes of the Pima range. Strung together, it all snaked a mile toward the Bay, some of it fallow, crossed by hikers and horseback riders and a wealth of wildlife. Even as Trew recalled this neglected extension of the estate she saw its awesome potential.

"What development team?" she asked.

"The one that looks for real estate. Land to be 'improved,' big time."

"You mean houses?"

"And more. Golf course, clubhouse, tennis courts, condos, pools, and get this, a casino. All they need is a handful of descendants of Pima or Wappo or whatever Indians to sign on."

"That's ridiculous."

"Maybe, maybe not. But first they need the land, and all that good water under it."

"Cain would never have gone along with that, had she known."

"Maybe, maybe not. You never know. But she's already signed. Somebody will make a lot of money out of this, and one of them can be you."

"I don't want a lot of money."

"Not to sound crass but there are worse fates. What if you didn't have a choice?"

For the second time that day Trew wanted to cry. It was not yet noon and she was facing the prospect of roulette wheels in the big house she could see out the window, backed by the red and green trunks of madrones. The density of black manzanita and poison oak was formidable, but not to dozer blades. So were the Douglas firs, even the redwoods. The sagacity of faceless people on the wrong coast impressed her mightily, and their audacious vision for a place they hadn't even seen. Yes, my home would make a wonderful resort. It had been one for generations.

"Trewdy?"

"What?"

"I think you should talk to your sister, get this out in the open, particularly since we know Julian's officially in Consolidated's camp. I'm on my way up. Try to put off the signing until I get there."

The winery's façade in the noonday sun was a towering mass of broken stone and deep shadow, a crazy harlequin pierced at the base by a door hanging open to the staircase, the edges of the horizontal treads picking up the light. Before going in Trew gripped the rough, warm jamb and leaned out over the plantings and threw up into little peeping blue annuals.

She had eaten nothing and swallowed only coffee, so the event lacked spectacle but left her momentarily weak and confused. She could see Saul's car parked in the lot, where it had been for half an hour. Maybe Reeve had already signed, the transformation of Tregaron Springs a fait accompli.

The stairwell yawned, ominously silent: they were waiting. Trew wished for a mint to suck on, water, something, feeling her way up the walls under the visages of farm workers long since dead, and those of state and county grandees who had once blessed Tregaron with visits and honors and extortions. Then the winery had epitomized the valley — as it might again — as insular and farm-bound as any in Iowa, grapes just one of a myriad of crops, their luster barely exceeding that of grain or prunes, its owners part of the exotica traipsing around California in the previous century.

Positions had already been taken in the office: Reeve at her desk, elbows adhered to the glass, stunning in fresh white poplin. If she had been surprised by Saul's arrival, she had adjusted. What Trew assumed was the contract lay on the table before him, the clasp removed. If there was any hope, he gave no sign of it. Today Trew's attorney was dressed for a world far from Abalone's: pinstripes, slightly faded, probably bought about the time Trew's parents were killed. His tie was all funereal blossoms, the diminished knot never untied but passed over Saul's head whenever he wore it, and later hung on a peg — first in the Bronx, now in Walnut Creek.

Julian by contrast looked crisp enough to cut your fingers on. His double-breasted blazer was as dark as his eyes, the white shirt collar open, signaling readiness for combat, his chair was tilted back. Pleated slacks, tassel loafers but not for lunch in the city, not today. Trew felt like his miserable female antithesis, rumpled beyond the habitual, her hair a manic sheave bound in the soiled blue bandana, and murder in her heart. If only, she thought, seeing all the blank spaces that could have been filled in over the years to complete that sentence, and had not been.

Reeve said, "Well, Trewdy, this was supposed to be just the two of us."

"I thought Saul should see the contract. He had to eventually."

"Not that it makes any difference," said Julian. "Not that it can."

Saul raised his chin. His hair was plastered down and his face pale, but he looked ready. Trew asked him what Consolidated was offering, and he said, "Three, as is. Plus, an incentive for prompt signing and some money for any new equipment in the interim. Basically, each of you girls would get a million bucks and the right to a couple of stipulated family heirlooms. Otherwise, everything — and I mean everything — would convey. They want to own your family and its past, as well as the land."

"Will convey," said Julian.

"Also, you can live here gratis for six months if you choose. One of you would agree to help with transition, for a fee, as a kind of..." He paused, flipping a page. "... temporary major domo, whatever that is."

"Hostess," said Trew.

"I guess. Not bad, considering what they'd be getting."

"Will be getting. It's a good price and you know it," Julian added, but not combative. He was trying, Trew gave him that. "This place is a wreck, a money sump. Capital improvements on the house and winery alone will top a million, easy. The brand's good but no great shakes. The vineyards need replanting. The money's a gift."

"To somebody," said Saul, "but not to my client. If you sign this, Reeve, we'll sue. It will take a long time to get un-kinked, I promise."

"And more money than Trew has," Julian went easily on, "and more time than you have, Saul. And you'll lose. So, what's the point?"

Trew's attorney seemed older in this light, diminished, a little white around the gills, as her father would have put it. Saul needed another drink to buttress the couple he must have had somewhere. She said, "Reeve, don't do it this way. We can work something out."

"No," said Julian. "This is the deal. They won't accept anything else. No changes. I've been through this with them, and it's 'go for it now, or go down.' Their line."

Saul had found something about Julian that interested him. Trew took a chance and asked, "Would they pay less?"

"What do you mean?"

"Maybe we could carve off a parcel for me. Reeve and Cain would get their money and I'd get less and some land. It would cost Consolidated less, maybe get them — and us — some goodwill in the valley where the reaction to this will be awful."

"No," Julian repeated. "They want all nine hundred and seventy-three acres, period."

Reeve turned to Trew. "What parcel?"

"Green Buttons." The idea had come to her while climbing the stairs, a bitter, desperate move. "It's less than twenty acres, all on the northern boundary and easily separated from the rest. Consolidated wouldn't even miss it."

Julian snorted, tipping his chair further back until it rested against the post: the victor's rest. "It's the one good vineyard. They wouldn't even consider it."

"They don't give a damn about vineyards," said Trew. "They're going to turn this place into a resort anyway. They can have their demo vineyards anywhere. Green Buttons has its own water and a dirt road over the railroad tracks connecting to the highway. It even has its own line of olives separating it from the driveway. A natural boundary." She looked Reeve full in the face. "Please. It won't cost you a cent, and something will be left in the family. The Vassy remnant." A horrible phrase.

Julian was shaking his head. "Non-negotiable, like I said. They want it all, and your sisters agree. It's over, Trew. Even this English gent in the guest house thinks we should sell."

"How do you know? "

"I asked him. He's supposed to be advising us, isn't he?"

Reeve asked Julian, "Couldn't we at least ask Consolidated?"

Trew held her breath. She was so angry with CJ she couldn't speak.

"Don't start," Julian told Reeve. "I've explained this to you. The deal's barely hanging, and some weird land swap proposal would cut it down. They'll take their toys and go back to Connecticut, and we'll still have an acre of leaking roof, an antiquated plant, a miserable market share, and an undependable product that breaks backs and bank accounts."

Julian rolled the barrel chair to and fro, the rounded backrest and corresponding foot rail lolling against hewed Douglas fir. His smugness was infuriating. But Trew was fascinated by his effrontery, too, this California boy-man who saw existence as primarily sportive: smart, talented, privileged, useless, he was forever on the look-out for a pick-up game, an easeful deal. Poor Reeve, her husband choosing a perilous position to test his athletic ability, enjoying the risk of rolling the chair too far one way, too far the other. Closely approach the limit and then, with a deft touch of a loafer, reverse direction, that was Julian, in command of a lovely old assemblage of thin oak struts and worn leather designed by Frank Lloyd Wright. The uncomfortable chair attracted and then punished the sitter, chosen an age ago because of its affinity with real barrels in the cellar, burnished by decades of passing posteriors.

Saul, seamlessly picking up Trew's argument, said, "Now why would they back out just because we asked for a little change? People fine-tune real estate deals all the time. That's what a deal is, Julian."

"Maybe in your day, Shubin. Things have changed in the last twenty years, so you wouldn't know."

A mistake, Trew thought.

"Corporations aren't run like family businesses anymore," Julian added. "Let's get on with it."

Trew opened her mouth again, but Saul raised a hand. Blunt fingers, one lavender nail he must have hit with a hammer between trips to Abalone's. "I guess I am out of it, Julian," he said evenly. "But I know a juvenile delinquent when I see one, even in a case of arrested development like yours. Know what I think, sonny boy? I'll tell you what I think. They're paying you a big fee for this, and it's all contingent upon this" — tapping the assembled papers — "signed, as is. I think it's a take it or leave it deal for you only. That's because, if your wife or sisters-in-law demand alterations, your little arrangement with Consolidated's off. Ka-putt. That the problem, Julian?"

The rolling of the barrel chair had ceased.

"You're an employee of Tregaron," Saul continued evenly. "As I understand it, anyway. If that's right, and you entered into an agreement like the one I'm describing, without the knowledge of your superior — that would be Reeve — you could be charged with fraud. All sorts of possibilities come to mind."

It was past noon and the sun cut through a corner of the plate glass, situated to fully catch the light in winter and so let in its intimation at harvest time. Trew felt a quite dangerous impulse. "Reeve," she said, speaking quickly, "whatever's going on between you and Julian is your business. But let's at least put this idea to Consolidated and see what they say. If they agree, I'll sign, too. Then we can be one big happy family again."

They smiled at each other in recognition of that bad old joke. Time rushed in on Trew, on all of them, having been somehow postponed and with it awful demands: all three sisters stood on the threshold of middle age, encased in a rosy, spent placenta of wealth and tradition, knowing it would eventually be stripped away, yet unprepared.

Reeve asked weakly if what Saul had said was true.

"Don't," warned Julian. "Just sign the goddamn contract, and let's move on. Like I warned, they're playing you."

"Answer me," she told him.

"I swear to God, Reeve, you refuse, after all the time and effort I put into this, and I'm gone."

"Did you make your own deal with those guys?"

His barrel chair came down hard, its staunch, upright back jolting and transforming him from potentate to defendant. Trew found herself loving that silly piece of furniture, the chair's artfully wrought wood suddenly Julian's straight-jacket and a testament to Wright's perverse genius.

"Just sign," Julian demanded.

"You would actually walk out if I didn't?"

"This time, yes. And you'll regret it, believe me. I'll divorce you and take half your share of this wreck, whatever it sells for."

"That sounds like a threat," said Saul. "And you won't take anything, Julian, if I have anything to do with it. Sounds to me like you've violated your fiduciary duties, which could be grounds for disbarment. Also, both a civil suit, and divorce." He turned to Reeve, utterly reasonable. "You should put a hold on any joint accounts you have with Julian, right now. You'll also want to give him written notice of whatever actions you decide to take. I could help you with all that, even file whatever's necessary at the courthouse on my way out of the county."

Trew asked, "Who're you representing, anyway?"

"You, Trewdy, of course. But also your sister if she wants it. This is a very different matter."

"You son of a bitch," said Julian, staying put, hands in lap, everyone trying to catch up with this and get ahead. "It's unethical," he added lamely, and Trew thought he might have a point.

"That's good, coming from you," said Saul. "And your insult's unprofessional, counselor. All you've got to do to prove me wrong is agree to take Trew's proposal back to Consolidated. Ask if Green Buttons can be split off from the rest, and what value they'd put on it. You'd be saving them money, Julian. Trew's the one who would take the financial hit. Like she said, what's between you and Reeve is your business, but

Reeve can make it mine, too."

The moment had arrived, all of them looking at Reeve, isolated by an expanse of hand-cut planking and the slab of glass upon which the panoply of the chief executive's life was spread. If Julian got up and crossed to her, and took Reeve's hand, the game was lost. But he didn't. Trew suspected that he couldn't bear the humiliation, not in front of another man, and tried to recall when last she had seen Reeve and Julian touch. Maybe not since their wedding when Reeve had thrown her arms around the neck of her handsome Pacific Heights Percival and, to the dismay of the minister, wrapped a leg around Julian's waist, white chenille hiking up to reveal a tanned thigh and impertinent carmine panties.

Chapter 9

Reeve no longer seemed to recognize her husband, her surprise and disappointment lodged in her spine, as straight and unyielding as Julian's. She turned to Saul. "What if he's right? What if they withdrew the offer?"

"If they don't want to lop off a vineyard, they can say so," he said. "Things are starting to happen in the valley, Consolidated's setting up to take advantage of a tourist bonanza and Tregaron's got everything they want — brand, reputation, location."

"And water," said Trew. "Look, Sis, do you really want a knock-down drag-out with me, after all the juggling we've done together? Is our very own protracted shoe-string operation, the fact that we kept it going, mean nothing to you? If you do go through with this, your only ally will be Cain, and how's that going to feel?"

Oh, wicked, she thought. Reeve and Cain had never been each other's allies, but to reach down now and pull up their collisions from the past — who put mashed potatoes into whose hair, who scored Terry Abruzzini who turned out to be the worst husband imaginable — was mean. Tregaron was possibly sailing toward casino-land or some other real estate play and Trew's heavy guns felt justified.

Reeve told Julian, "Get out."

He stood. "Saul doesn't have grounds for any of this, Reeve."

"Sounds like I have grounds for divorce. Maybe it's time. You're fired, Julian, now get out of this building and out of the house." She turned back to Saul. "Please take over negotiations with Consolidated, put this counteroffer to them."

"Reeve," said Julian, "let's talk after they've gone."

"I said get out." She wouldn't look at him. "If you don't I'm calling the sheriff. Same thing if you take anything at all from the house, and that includes my father's Limoges shaving mug. You can keep your stupid little car."

What happened next, as Trew would recall, was a marvel of contained rage. Julian turned and in one easy motion picked up the chair and swung it hard against the thick wooden post. Only in the second collision did the wood complain and begin surrendering in the joints. He set it back on the floor and stepped onto the foot rail, grasped the back and squatting to bring well-developed thighs into play, stood to the accompaniment of splintering oak. It released a drift of ancient powdery glue and a half-human screech. Pleased, Julian did it all again and tossed the broken bits into a pile.

Turning to face them, he dusted off his hands, a scene out of a silent movie. No one else had moved during the minutes of demolition and Trew had the strange sensation of living in the future: they were seeing Julian for the last time and wouldn't much remember him beyond the mock triumph of his stride to the door and his failure to close it behind him, as always.

Trew got up and stepped behind the fancy contortion of tubular metal that was Reeve's chair. She leaned over and kissed the top of her sister's head, which smelled of the exotic herbal reductions, noticing the trace of gray roots. Of course, such radiance required the regular attention of a hairdresser, with Reeve about to turn forty, but Trew felt ashamed and naïve not to have noticed the graying before, aware that her ignorance of such things had become a liability. She whispered, "Thank you. I'm around if you need me."

Reeve's eyes were dry but in them a measure of defeat. "Don't worry about the Frank Lloyd Wright chair, Trewdy," she said. "It was a reproduction."

Trew went straight to her studio and took a frozen baguette out of the freezer. She took it next door to the guest cottage and hammered on the door. It opened, and CJ said jovially, "Ah ha, the culprit," meaning the one who had dropped off the earlier loaf.

"No, CJ, that would be you."

She swung the loaf savagely, catching him on the side of the head with a resounding thwack! He fell against the doorjamb.

"My God. What…"

"You're ruining my life, you limey son of a bitch. You told Julian to sell, after I explained to you how much this place means to me."

He stared at the loaf, which had acquired an elbow. "No," he said. "I didn't. I just agreed that Tregaron Springs is special and surely worth a great deal of money."

She turned away, wanting to believe him but afraid she would start crying. And saw Saul standing at the end of the lane, watching.

As she approached, Saul said, "That was childish. Julian probably exaggerated whatever it was the Brit said. Things are about to change here in ways you think you can imagine, Trewdy, but you can't. You must get a grip. There will be more meetings, most with people you don't know. You can't come to those swinging baguettes. Meanwhile wash your hair, buy some new clothes, leave your knife at home. Play the role for the time being so Consolidated can think it's getting what it's putting up big money for, which is the real thing. Find a guy to squire you around in the meantime and not another artist monkey. The Brit's handy, decent looking, well-spoken. Has a rep of sorts. Why not use him? Because you're going to need all the help you can get."

CJ watched Trew bound onto her porch with the Vassy's natural athleticism and disappear inside. He picked up the bread, cold as ice, and went back in and turned on the oven. He had eaten the earlier loaf and now he would eat this one. He tended to girth if he wasn't careful, but he was hungry — again.

He shoved the loaf into the oven and started to pack. It would be back to the El Pescador, his Tregaron adventure ill-conceived and disastrously embarked upon. He should have recognized this the moment he was wantonly assigned a new name by Reeve. These sisters were quite unhinged and clearly dangerous.

An unexpected wave of regret washed over him. He was losing an asset without knowing its precise nature, having glimpsed a unique world whose face was only partially revealed before being turned away. He felt the weight of the unspoken here so profoundly that it left him nostalgic for a place he had known only briefly, imperfectly, but valued. Now he must leave it behind.

He slumped in the desk chair, overcome by the power of the unnamable. It had drawn out of him emotions he long suspected were there but could never quite touch. But here feelings and ideas came to him as he sat at the typewriter. He anticipated what he would eventually imagine — an illogical, inexplicable progression that nevertheless felt quite real. Several times in the last few days he had stopped writing and turned expectantly, as if something or someone stood behind him.

He smelled the warming bread, part of the reality at Tregaron, part of the seamless blend of past and present that quite possibly could have made of Clyde Craven-Jones the whole and happy thing he yearned to be. But that would not happen here, nor anywhere.

He gazed across the tangled growth between the cottages and Trew's studio and saw her opening a window. In it she set a sign, the letters slathered onto cardboard in bright viridian that only one of the mad California plein-air painters would dare.

The sign read: *I'm sorry!*

Part II:

Beasts and Maidens

Chapter 10

As Saul had predicted, Consolidated Brands accepted Trew's conditions and made a prodigious down payment on Tregaron Springs. Now, inside the winery's massive stone entranceway, the two sisters stood shoulder-to-shoulder, Reeve in another silk blouse and tight slacks, blonde hair radiant. Trew wore a new plaid shirt and clean jeans, her streaked auburn hair artfully piled. She wasn't wearing a knife and even her hands had been thoroughly scrubbed. She was ready.

"This woman called and told me to have someone pick him up at the San Francisco airport," Reeve was saying. "I told her that's an hour and a half away and we don't have a spare car anyway. There was a long pause. Then she asked if there was a closer airport. I said sure, Oakland, and she said, 'We don't do Oakland.'"

A black limo turned into Tregaron's long drive and both sisters watched it approach, broad smiles in place. "What's his name again?" Trew asks.

"Ronnie."

"Surely not."

"I was hoping for a Nelson or a Gilbert."

"It's waspy enough."

The limo stopped and the driver got out and hurried around and opened the back door. A foot in expensive black leather protruded and a hand gripped the limo roof. Dark suit and white shirt, tie, in the other hand a tooled leather briefcase. His hair was cut short and his face determined. A hard-head on a mission, she decided.

Reeve whispered, "Daddy must be rolling."

"Daddy never made it to the grave, remember? Not all of him, anyway."

"Ouch."

They descend the steps together and Reeve began. "Ronnie, how nice to meet you. I'm Reeve Vassy and this is my sister, Trew. She manages the cellar while I take care of business upstairs. Try to, anyway. How was your flight?"

Ronnie began to cough. Reeve said, "You need water. That's always the first thing with visitors, Ronnie. They forget until it's too late that it takes a full day out here to drink your way back to feeling normal." She laughed. "Wine isn't the real treasure in wine country, water is."

Good point thought Trew. "Raul will get your bags," Reeve was saying. "We've given you the master bedroom overlooking the valley. You probably want to rest a bit."

"Actually, I'd like to get down to business."

"Well, I want to properly introduce you to Tregaron Springs. That means tasting library wines in the Captain's Room."

"Maybe, but not with me. I don't drink."

"Consolidated Brands is an international dealer in alcohol," said Trew. "How in the world do you avoid it?"

"Good asset management and brand advancement don't depend on the sensory satisfaction of those making the decisions. It's not a problem."

"Well, I've got to take care of some things in the cellar, Ronnie.

Nice meeting you."

Later, stretched out on the Prairie-style sofa in Reeve's office, the oak armrests banked with cushions, Trew watched her sister decisively push her chair away from the desk and rest her feet on the glass slab. She thumbed through her datebook as if it had offended her. Consolidated Brands may have bought the place but turn-over was a week away. She and Trew had much to talk about but, as they had done in the past, they chose instead something utterly irrelevant.

"Do you think Mommy could have had an affair with Humphrey Bogart?" asked Trew.

Reeve stared at her. After a bit she said, "I wonder what that would have been like."

"Reeve, for God's sake, it's a serious question. We're talking about Mommy."

"What in the world gave you such an idea. She wasn't exactly the affair sort, you know. In fact, she was the last person anybody would have suspected."

"Which doesn't necessarily mean she didn't. I've been thinking about that time, all the socializing and stuff. But I remember so little. What did our parents really think about all those people passing through the halls of Tregaron? What did they think of each other, for that matter? I mean, not what did they pretended to think. What did they find comfort in? You're the oldest, Reeve, but you never talked about all that."

"Well, we called him Mister Bogart. He was here a lot but only for short periods of time. He and Daddy once flew off to Tahoe and Mister Bogart got drunk in the Cal-Neva casino with Frank Sinatra. The two of them crawled around in the bar looking for some woman's earring in the carpet. But not Daddy. He would have been outraged by such behavior and flown off somewhere, our north coast Charles Lindbergh. Taking off was always what he did best."

"Landing not so much."

It had been the worst day of Trew's life and yet here they were, joking about it. The winemaker, Teodoro, had been the first to reach her. She recalled endlessly the strong arms encircling her, the musty smell of his shirt, being jerked off her feet and carried screaming into the house. By the afternoon of the following day the wreckage had been cleared away with a front-end loader and no real investigation ever done, no explanation ever offered. Freak accident, people said. No one to blame. Her father's pipe with the broken stem was all they found and a lens from Mommy's sunglasses in the middle of Green Buttons vineyard. Old dirt removed and new dirt going in, and new vines. After the second season she couldn't find the spot of impact, no matter how often she looked.

"Mister Bogart was just a guy who smoked and drank too much," said Reeve. "And said things that made Mommy laugh. Most men tried but he succeeded."

"How did Daddy take that?"

"He shared the spotlight, that was about it. Reflect the glory of Bev Vassy. I think he liked Mister Bogart well enough, a real man and easy in his skin as Daddy never was."

"Did Bogart stay in the guest cottage?"

"Don't know. Lauren Bacall was with him once. I don't think they knew quite what to make of all of us. Somebody else from southern California who knew Mommy from the old days, when she wanted to be an actress, must have introduced them. It wasn't Rock Hudson. All he did was make that stupid movie about a winery, using footage taken earlier around Tregaron. And there was that actress married to Reagan, the one whose career was taking off while his was tanking."

"Too bad our parents didn't keep up with Reagan. He could have done wonders for the Tregaron brand after he became governor."

"Vlad tried to get in touch with him, but nothing came of it."

"I wish Mommy had kept a list of parties," said Trew. "And guests. I never thought I'd care about that stuff, and now I do."

"The one person who would know if there was anything like that would never talk." Reeve meant Marta. "Vladimir was Daddy's friend, his creation, kept around as an exhibit of triumphant anti-Communism."

"I never knew quite how to think about Vlad." Trew hadn't mentioned her trip to Bright Hours.

"He wasn't much use in a tasting, was he?" Reeve mimicked him. "Dees vine invites me to drrreeenk eet… How many times did he say that?"

"With that guttural thing at the end."

"Mainly he went fishing with Daddy."

"Steelhead on the Mendocino coast."

"I never saw him tight," said Reeve. "Vlad tended to disappear in the evenings. He must have been lonely, but no woman ever came here to see him. He did technical stuff in the winery in the beginning, but he had been an aeronautical engineer before he lost his hand. I thought of him as a sort of uncle. We owe him a lot, Trewdy, but I can't bear going over there and trying to reconcile what he is now with the man he used to be, standing at the end of the driveway every time I came home late and refusing to let boys get out of their cars."

"Nothing matched the gondola melt-down. The three of us naked in the water, being towed up the highway."

Reeve nodded. "I was the oldest, I caught the flak."

"Even though it was Cain who propped her boob on the gondola rim."

"Because I had already flashed a nipple and she had to one-up me. She had Fred Abruzzini running down the main street of Catalina with his tongue hanging out. I'm convinced that eventually led to his asking her to marry him, then to treating her like a whore."

"You two were so competitive. Pushed it to another dimension."

Trew could still see the astonished faces on that hot September day, long ago, beholding the Vassy sisters naked in a hauler meant for grapes but filled instead with spring water and two of them — not Trew — splashing around buck naked, back-stroking, while one of the muchachos drove the truck. That would have been Jesus. He had been cajoled into the cab of the old International Harvester by Reeve and Cain and, returning to Tregaron, fled into the vineyard before Vladimir could get his one good hand around Jesus's neck.

It had started out as a lark but once underway, the older girls took it all off while their pubescent kid sister hid her budding womanhood against cold steel. The stunt became an overnight legend, Cain's bikini bottoms lost, only to eventually wash out of the drain in the bottom of the gondola.

"God did Vlad have a temper," said Reeve. "Daddy couldn't have matched it. Maybe that's why he picked Vlad to be our guardian. I think the idea of anointing a Russian émigré as master of Tregaron amused Daddy, never suspecting he might have to suddenly take over."

"Poor Vlad."

"Poor Mommy and Daddy."

"Poor everybody."

They both laughed.

"You know, Vlad was a decent-looking guy, but it never occurred to me he and Mommy might have had something going. He was a war hero, all that stuff about Russia's Great Patriotic War and bombing the Germans? What was it he used to say?"

"Vee bombed dem back..."

"... to dere cuckoo clocks."

"Daddy refused to believe that Vlad hadn't taken part in the siege of Stalingrad, remember?" Reeve seemed happy for the first time in a long time. "It was all part of Daddy's narrative: Vlad helped defeat Hitler, then renounced the Soviet Union and helped others escape it."

"Remember the story about Vlad sitting back-to-back with the pilot in the bomber, navigating, while the Germans strafed them?"

"Dey flew hup hour hasses."

"Only to lose his hand in a turbine factory."

"Tregaron must have been the answer to Vlad's dreams," said Reeve, "until he got saddled with us."

"And a winery barely afloat on worn-out family capital."

"Our parents lived way beyond their — our — means. Not something easy to square with Daddy's rep for fiscal prudence."

The light had altered, the sun almost at its zenith. Instinctively they averted their gazes from the big window and the gathering radiance of Reeve's golden hair. Trew said, "I do wonder what Vladimir thought of Mommy, don't you? What she thought of him."

"She liked most people with gumption. But I don't think Vlad was her type, or Mister Bogart. Daddy either, for that matter."

"Who was?"

The past was lying there now like the tattered rug, useless but too valuable sentimentally to throw out. Reeve's eyes glistened. She had never recovered from the failure of the future to coincide with the promises made to her by their parents, who believed — or claimed to — in their own God-given good fortune. "In my book," she said, "Daddy was just a happy-go-lucky, end-of-the-liner with some business slogans and no ability to change. Mommy's job was to make life appear as if it would stay the way it was until we were all out of it."

"In the end not even they got through," said Trew.

"Daddy was a big kid, Mommy his enabler. Everything flowed from that. He had no talent for dealing with the real world and without her would have had no access to outsiders. As for her having an affair, I can imagine her needing something in life, even another man. But the consequences of being found out would have been awful to contemplate."

"Maybe not."

"Give it up, Trewdy. Whatever I might know is buried and I'm not about to go back and dig it up. Life's too short for the past."

Chapter 11

The big house even at this late date still backed into wilderness. CJ passed the Roman urn on the porch that brimmed with lilies and one empty bottle of Veuve Cliquot. He went straight into the bright array of upholstered heirlooms and collectibles spread about the large sitting room that could have been a museum. The promotional dinner had already started, and Reeve hurried toward him in pale green silk plunging to the navel. "Oh CJ, you lovely man," with a tad too much enthusiasm. Since their spontaneous tryst on the tennis court and CJ's mission to Sanandra she had showed little interest in him. "We were afraid you'd forsaken us. Ronnie's pissed, as in angry."

He had met Consolidated's designated representative for the official handover of Tregaron Springs and now Reeve led him to the long table of burnished tiger maple he sat at the head of. CJ was seated between New York publicists — dark suits: vacuous, opalescent smiles and self-consciously firm handshakes. Svelte Ronnie Staunton, however, wore European-tailored dark blue worsted with wide lapels and he stared balefully across the table at CJ before plunging into his sole mousse.

Next to CJ sat Trew with what passed for a make-over — a touch of lipstick, hint of mascara — her natural complexion heightened by alcohol and the fire in the hearth, laughing dutifully at some pleasantry from Ronnie. CJ had developed an instant, palpable dislike of the guy who now boomed, as if they were old friends, "I know you don't like this sort of thing, CJ, but please indulge us. We all have before us a red wine brought up from the cellar put together by the girls' grandfather long ago, just one of the European exemplars in the creation of Tregaron Springs cabernet sauvignon collection. Would you make a stab at identifying this one, Clyde?"

CJ looked at the inky red in the decanters being poured for each guest, mostly wine critics CJ knew slightly. He took a deep breath and examined the wine. "Bricky meniscus," he said, and tasted. "Prunes, suggestions of tar and more black fruit. I would venture to say a Latour."

"Very good," said Ronnie. "What vintage?"

"Oh, I don't know, possibly a '53."

Ronnie took an empty bottle from beneath the cloth, revealing the distinctive label stained with wine. He set it on the table. "A bit younger, but very close. Congratulations. Now ladies and gentlemen, some of you may think I tipped Clyde off in advance, but not so."

This much was true. Then came the smooth corporate elide into the big lie. "This is the sort of critical judgement long brought to bear here at Tregaron Springs that will long continue."

CJ would never work for these people. He felt like a performing monkey in need only of a tambourine. Trew was smiling at him encouragingly but he was oppressed by the assembly and all the over-sized glasses, the scalloped trays of fresh-cut celery, crushed walnuts, veined Stilton, the inevitable biscuits and cut-glass decanter of port that would eventually skate round the table like a squat friar, just as it might have in England. All staged, costing the Vassy girls a fortune and seriously depleting their cellar. But it was necessary, they felt, to get the deal finalized the next day, when Consolidated would then own not just the cellar but also the houses and the property except for Green Buttons vineyard with its monstrous eucalyptus tree.

Clyde excused himself and went back out into the hall and kept going. Trew caught up with him on the porch. "Thanks," she said. "That just what they had hoped you could bring off."

"Who knows what those dreadful people are going to do to this place."

"At least I'll have a piece of it."

The black sheath molded to her full figure, her abundant auburn hair piled on top, the dark cast of her skin accented. She wore a lovely string of some forbearer's pearls.

"My book's finished," he said, "more or less — endless evaluations and profiles of a decidedly mixed cast of characters. Your help has been invaluable. Thank you. I hope I don't end up wondering why I took the trouble."

"You have wonderful sensibilities, CJ. Trust them. Your nose is unnaturally sensitive, and valuable. Sometimes it blinds you to ordinary things, even as it exposes their essence. You're over-endowed smell-wise, my dear. It's your own cross to bear."

"And I can't turn it off, damn it." He was still registering smells: hair conditioner (aloe), the residue of somebody's cigarette (Marlboro), the decanted port (probably Taylor's Reserve '48). Over her shoulder he saw Ronnie Staunton step onto the patio. "Trew!" Staunton demanded.

"Just a minute," she said.

"People in there have questions. You need to answer them."

"We're almost done," said CJ.

"You're right about that, Craven-Jones." Ronnie took her by the arm and pulled. "You are done, we won't be needing anymore help from you, if that's what it has been."

Trew was off balance and almost fell. Ronnie pulled harder, infuriating CJ whose reaction was instinctive: drop a shoulder — the Greco-Turkish wrestling technique learned at Cambridge — reach quickly across the opponent's midriff and grasp his lapel, then in one quick move lift. The look on Ronnie's face as he went butt-first into the Roman urn was not resignation, but terror, the empty champagne bottle protruding from between his legs.

Trew pounded on CJ's back. "Stop!" She drove him toward the steps, still pounding. He walked down the stone steps and heedless of direction crossed the driveway and entered the woods. For some reason he thought of the early death of parents he barely knew, of the wealthy uncle and enophile who had raised him kindly but distantly, exposing him to first-growth cabernet sauvignon and merlot before he was a teenager, CJ's later wandering among the world's vineyards in search of a profession which by default became that of critic.

Thinking of England, not California — its antithesis — he collided not with an oak but with a giant redwood. He dug his fingers into the deep grooves in the bark and pressed his face into the bark's unyielding roughness, breathing in the smell — wet tannins, so close to the smell of aging wine while out on the highway an ambulance passed, gradually subsumed in the persistent murmur of water trickling down from St. Bart's peak, fresh from the rock, through vale and vineyard in what he realized with dismay had become his adoptive land just as he would have to leave it.

A light shone in the window of the guest house from a lamp CJ had not left on. Someone was in there, and he paused on the threshold. Pushing open the door he saw, sitting on the sofa in the center of the Pima throw rug, was a woman in a white linen sheath. As he approached, he saw one brown eye and one aquamarine, both depthless in the lamplight. "You must be Cain," he said.

She crossed her legs. Thin ankles, expensive leather sandals, high arches. "And you must be Craven-Jones." She smiled. "Sorry but there's a guy in a suit up in my old room with what I think is a pistol under one arm. The guest cottage seemed a better bet."

"That would be Ronnie Staunton's bodyguard," said CJ. "How did you get here from the Sierra?" There was no car parked outside.

"Some Sannyasins dropped me off on their way to Big Sur."

"Sannyasins?"

"Members of Sanandra, like the one who met you when you came up."

"Comrades."

"A bit more than that. They're all quite dedicated, I'm proud to say. You have to be dedicated to make sixty thousand acres support everybody and keep up with your spiritual duties. Five types of meditation, too. It's a beautiful, purposeful existence. We have many visitors and are responsible for much salvation."

"A destination resort without ski lifts?"

She showed her very white teeth. "Something like that, though that's a snide remark. We even have a small vineyard. It produces a ton of wine grapes, surely that meets with your approval. You being one of those."

"One of what?"

"Snoots who think the world rotates in a sea of wine, a substance without nutrition or any saving grace, really, other than taste and the ability to numb. And so pretentious! Of course what was there before was even worse — thousands of sheep trashing the place. We put in a million dollars' worth of water systems, topsoil, equipment, and a dozen types of vegetables on thirty acres — a hundred pounds of sunflower sprouts a day, five hundred pounds of tomatoes. Our quick mobilization would be the envy of the Imperial Valley if the Imperial Valley knew about us."

"And you're going to spend the money from Tregaron up there?"

"Most of it, yes."

The tanned head and bicolor eyes made of her a pretty amphibian, he thought. And those ankles. She reminded him of her sister, Reeve, both quite unlike Trew. "As a wine critic," Cain was saying, "you could help us."

"Do you make wine up there?"

"Not yet but we will."

"It's unlikely I could ever recommend it."

"Why not?"

"Because there are so many things against it, including the weather."

"So smug," she said. "Just give us a break."

"I try not to do that. A matter of principle."

"If you're so ethical, why are you here?"

"Good question. Well, my opinion of Tregaron Springs's wines hasn't been affected by my living arrangement. I've merely offered advice and am leaving tomorrow."

"And what have you advised my sisters to do?"

"Stop making so many different wines. Lose the eucalyptus in the best one, if possible."

"That's to be Trew's vineyard, her pride. You told her that?"

"Yes. She rejected the advice."

Cain seemed thoroughly at home, stretching out on the couch and smiling up at him. He felt light-headed, not from alcohol or the scrape with Ronnie Staunton on the patio. Something else. He couldn't stop looking at Cain's eyes. You're done here. Yes, maybe, yet here he stood over a mesmerizing stranger and an impressive stack of typing paper stained with tea and inky scribbles.

"I have a request," Cain said. "My assigned room up there" — she gestured toward a window in the main house — "and I simply can't abide it. Memories up there won't let me sleep, I know. Neither will the ghosts. Can I crash here on your couch? It's still partly mine, you know, for another day. But you won't know I'm here, Clyde Craven-Jones." His confusion seemed to please her.

"Your sisters call me CJ," he said.

"It sounds like a breakfast drink. Clyde's a perfectly nice name, I think. The double-barreled Craven-Jones suggests wanton desire for wealth and stature and a ruthless willingness to go after it."

Annoyed, he said, "Speaking of names, why do you have a man's and a biblical name as well?"

"Because of my great-grandmother. She was Welsh and in Wales a woman may be a Cain as readily as a man. It's a Celtic thing, nothing to do with the Bible. Now, Craven-Jones, if you're going to get other people to buy your book in this valley, you're going to have to say flattering things about them and their wines. This isn't Bordeaux, you know, it's still the wild West as Trew is fond of saying. But most of those wearing cowboy hats these days are wannabes and corporate scoundrels like Consolidated Brands." Her smile broadened. "And our saviors, of course."

"From what I know you and Reeve are the ones getting saved, not Trew. She's taking on the Sisyphean task of preservation all by herself."

"Yes. Why don't you help her with that?"

"Because it's not my role. I'm a critic, not a vintner. And besides she hasn't asked me."

"Is my former husband in your book? And his family?"

"The Abruzzinis? Yes."

"The Abruzzinis' are Mafia, you know. You may not live long enough to finish your tour."

Her deep-seated laugh seemed inappropriate in such a delicate looking woman. "Just kidding, Craven-Jones. The Abruzzinis don't kill people anymore, that's why they became vintners in the first place. To wipe away the blood. Reeve is flirting with Terry Abruzzini, these days, as you must know."

"I don't."

"Oh my. Reeve has screwed everybody in the valley over the years and now has her eyes on him. Has she screwed you?"

"None of your business."

"That means yes. I'll bet you haven't slept with Trew and never will. You're just a sheep in a wolf's clothes, Clyde Craven-Jones." And with that she pulled the crocheted quilt over her, propped her head on the pillow, and was soon asleep.

He followed her example, disconcerted but exhausted, too. He awoke sometime later to the sound of her measured breathing and could make out her raised chin and that supple back, slightly bowed, rhythmically rising, and falling, her palms and shoulders pressed into the couch. What on Earth was she doing? An invisible string attached to her navel seemed to pull her flat stomach heavenward, and after a bit this seemed to affect him, his body emulating hers as if she, not he, was in possession of it.

CJ's bridge of tremulous flesh rose, and fell, until finally he collapsed, his pajama top soaked with sweat. He stripped it away and lay panting in the darkness. Then a hand alighted on his thigh, and he heard a no-nonsense whisper: "Don't move." He saw her silhouette pull the gown over her head, revealing lapidary, darkly opalescent skin. Cain took hold of his waistband and stripped away the shorts and straddled him.

CHAPTER 12

Trew had imagined this scene many times. Now that it was upon her and she knew exactly what to do, she was also afraid. Here in the wine cellar, it felt like theft, however justifiable. Theoretically it could kill or at least greatly complicate the handover of Tregaron the day after the harvest party, but she had to do it. Saul had smoothed over the clash between Ronnie and CJ the night before but if they were looking for an excuse to pull out, this had potential.

The dim light from the scumbled cellar bulb barely illuminated the old bottles, their ranks greatly reduced after the wine writers' dinner the night before, precious Tregaron Springs cabernet sauvignon and cabernet franc going into the stomachs of strangers, most ignorant of its real value but more than willing to drink it. And Ronnie Staunton had also taken bottles for his own use from the cellar when she wasn't around, no doubt to give to other corporate executives.

There were gaps in the collection of Bordeaux, lesser ones in the collection of Tregaron cabernet. Some bottles had grown beards like old men, an occasional drop of precious wine having seeped past a faulty cork to glisten even in this imperfect light. She had touched them as a child and touched one now, touched her finger to her tongue and instantly rode the experience directly back into childhood. There remained notable vintages that Ronnie hadn't taken but no doubt would: a Cheval Blanc '49, a Lynch Bages '53, a Margaux '58. Consolidated would never miss them, but theft was theft and Trew and her sisters no longer owned them.

The Green Buttons's vintages were different, something she couldn't articulate but knew to be true. She had the legal right to be down here since possession was passing to Consolidated late tomorrow, but there were larger rights — obligations really. She would keep one of every vintage of Tregaron Springs wine still here with Green Buttons in it, and that was that. It had been influenced from the beginning by the huge eucalyptus tree in the corner of the vineyard, raining little pods that looked like buttons that she had collected as a child. CJ said the network of eucalyptus roots marred the taste of the wine, that the tree should be cut. But some things are more valuable than proper taste: allegiance to place, even blemishes if they define the thing.

There were gaps in the collection already. The 1845 had survived because that was the time of the Bear Republic. She had seen it as a child, but it had disappeared, damn Ronnie's eyes. Most of the rest of the nineteenth century was also gone but it was undrinkable anyway. The early twentieth century was still down here, at least after 1920 when wines from Europe were hard to get. Her great-grandfather and great-uncles had gotten serious about vertical tastings after they realized they helped sell wine to hotels in Chicago, New York, even London.

There was no '37 or '38, and the '40s during the war were a big hole. After that the line grew more consistent. She began to lay bottles side-by-side in the wheelbarrow with the iron wheel that was as old as the oldest wine. Once you got it going it was manageable. She imagined the bottles cooperating, sensing their own liberation, joining up with kin in some far-off refuge that was in fact just the far edge of Green Buttons vineyard where stood an ugly cinderblock shack. It was originally built to house wood brought down from the heights after storms, and now the only structure she owned. The lumber had been milled on site, some before she was born, and stacked, some of it as makeshift shelves. Douglas fir and redwood but also tanbark, even some big manzanitas that later went berserk as it dried, twisting into amazing shapes as if for an audience.

She could transport forty bottles at a time, she figured. Three cases. They would be heavy and difficult to manage in the vineyard, but she could do it. And if she got caught, she would claim to be cleaning out the cellar, something no one would believe. But Consolidated was so far into its own plans they were giddy, planning both a pr bonanza and another pipeline coming down from the springs to god knew what kind of new development, the wine itself more symbol for them than substance.

Late afternoon sunlight blinded her as she came up from the cellar. Roll, she thought. This isn't the time for tears. But they came anyway as she crossed the palatial drive, deserted in early afternoon, its new owners in yet another meeting, and she wiping her face with the back of her hand. Marta and the muchachos were laboring inside, but they wouldn't say anything even if they saw her. They all hoped to get hired though Trew knew they wouldn't be. She had wanted to stipulate it but Saul said no, not possible. The new owners have plans for imported maintenance crews, vineyard management companies, tourist outreach, convention consultants. All holdovers were expendable.

Soft earth around the olive trees, with their whitewashed bases, sucked at the big, spoked wheel. The dirt tract leading past what was now the north vineyard was firmer but tough going anyway. Green Buttons beyond the neater row of Tregaron vines looked overgrown. Yes, there were some weeds, she would admit, but so what? There was also vetch and wild mustard. Consolidated planned to build a wall separating Trew's property from its own, which was fine with Trew. But not so the new, showy trellising they would install, instead of the traditional single strands holding the vines. Soon a glaring web of steel would hold Consolidated's fruit up to the sun, but the juice of that fruit would never equal Green Buttons' in quality, and they knew it. This was a likely source of conflict in the years ahead as the regally ambitious corporate giant fully realized what it had given up by getting the house and land but not the best vineyard. They would alternately resent her presence and covet it.

She shoved harder on the ancient handles and the wheelbarrow lumbered into Green Buttons. She bore down on the cinderblock shed.

Far behind her the suits were coming out of the main house, blinded by the dying sun. Lean in, she thought. They won't notice, on their way to a restaurant, which appeared to be their greatest interest. And she wouldn't go to jail even if they caught her taking wine, but there was enough animosity already and this would add to the problem.

The vines closed behind her, and she headed for the shack. Some strips of Douglas fir had long ago been hurriedly fashioned into a door, a dangling hank of rope the only handle. She hauled on the knot and stepped into shadow. A skylight would be nice someday, she thought, but so would a floor, a bed, a sink. She began to carefully lift the bottles one at a time and lay them in the dirt, starting with the oldest, resisting the urge to inspect each because a hundred more bottles awaited her in the cellar.

A massive shadow now lay across Tregaron's lawn, the night close behind it, when she returned to her studio. This was the time of day she should be painting, and she wondered when and if she would ever get back to that. So much to do, so much uncertainty. Her supplies, including two easels, a host of pots and jars, canvases bound with clothesline were piled in the bed of her pickup parked in front of the cottage no longer hers, waiting for a new home. She pushed the wheelbarrow into the cellar to wait until darkness had begun to enwrap house, buildings, vineyards. Cars came and went, the outdoor lights blazed on as one, deepening the night beyond their reach.

Finally, she set out again with the last load, feeling the strain in her shoulders. Her hands ached. She wanted this to be over with and accomplished for posterity, done. Just across the path between the vineyards the wheelbarrow's iron wheel slipped into a furrow between path and vines and there it stuck. She pushed harder but it wouldn't move. "Goddamn!" she shouted, kicking at the old trooper, and tried again. "Move, you bastard!"

The whole pathetic enterprise came down to this, stealing wine at night with nowhere else to take it, sweat soaking her shirt, grime on her face and bare arms. Exhausted, she heaved at the cold wooden handles, the shed close but black as night. She had forgotten to bring a flashlight.

A dark figure rose up, framed by headlights out on the highway, and bore down on her. Broad-brimmed hat, the bright tip of a cigarette. "Who's that?" she asked.

Without answering the figure grasped a handle and pushed. "I could hear you cussing all the way to my back porch."

"Teodoro?"

How long had it been since they had spoken? A year? Two? He stepped ahead and pulled open her shed door, then struck a flame from his cigarette lighter. She remembered it — a Zippo with an old peso piece fixed to the steel. He used it to fire up those evil Mexican cigarettes the pickers, too, still smoked. He snapped the lighter shut and together they began to transfer the last bottles to the long line resting in the dirt. He asked, "Now what?"

She couldn't say. He had carried her screaming to the house the day her parents died, his arms around her like cables. It was Teodoro who that night stood in her bedroom doorway in the big house, keeping an eye on her throughout the night. It was Teodoro who cleaned up after the crash, Teodoro who planted the replacement vines, and Teodoro who hung around the cellar doorway when she was a teenager, watching the Vassy girls' antics and only occasionally waving. He was the watcher. Then one day he wasn't, replaced by an Anglo winemaker from the University of California at Davis hired by Vladimir, who didn't like Mexicans. After that Teodoro slipped out of their tumultuous lives, though sometimes Trew would see him outside his little house, gardening, or smoking on the back steps, and he waved every time, a couple of strands of wire separating his life from hers and from Green Buttons, strung with white mallows.

"What are you going to do now?" he asked.

Trew heard him blowing smoke. "Could a couple of the men build an outhouse?" she asked, since there was no one else. "Think they could build a solar shower later, first redirecting water from my allotment? Think they could?"

"Yeah, but harvest's only a week away. I went ahead and reserved you a spot at the custom crusher's across the road. You'll be needing tank space, too."

"I've got another plan," she said, but he was already gone.

She left the wheelbarrow and walked back to her studio and showered, then put on clean clothes. When she stepped out CJ was standing in her doorway.

"Where's Cain?" he demanded.

"I have no idea. What's wrong?"

"She came into my cottage uninvited and took my book."

"She took it? Why?"

"How do I know? Where is she?"

"What did you say to her, CJ?"

"That her commune would probably never produce a decent wine."

"You shouldn't have said that. But don't worry, Cain's no thief. You just may have to wait to get your book back."

"What's the matter with you people?"

And he stomped off into the darkness.

Trew crossed to the big house and climbed the stairs. She saw that Cain had not slept in her room and that there was no sign of her in the kitchen, either, or anywhere on the sprawling first floor. Trew knew of only one other place Cain might be found but not until tomorrow, before the Beasts and Maidens party.

Chapter 13

Below the moribund tennis court where showers had once stood was a room that now stored outdoor equipment and elaborate old masks propped on the shelves. And standing in front of them when Trew arrived the next morning, in her fist a mug of coffee, was a woman in a soiled white gown with the hem looped around her waist and pale yellow hair tied up in a knot, standing on a table.

"Cain. Where in the world did you sleep?"

"In one of those chaises. It was a little chilly, but I found some old beach towels."

Cain jumped to the floor and wrapped her arms around Trew's neck, smelling of sex. Had she already gotten involved with Ronnie or one of his crowd. "Cain ..." she began, then reconsidered. It was none of her business. "Cain, did you steal CJ's book?"

"I'm just taking it for a walk. Some of it's quite good."

"He says you stole it. Well, better not let it off the leash. If I know CJ, there's no copy. Did he make a pass at you?"

"No. Now will you give me a hand with these masks, Sis?"

Cain picked up the cuckold, a rooster's head big enough to envelope her own, with angry red eyes and a comb fashioned from wood in another century. She put it on, and Trew took down the bear mask. She had always loved it, the fur patiently cut with a chisel and its stone eyes opaque. The view out was overhung with teeth of obsidian. The sisters began to dance, cavorting around the room menacing each other. They began to pile the others on the table. Trew had forgotten how many there were.

Cain attached a hose to the spigot and blasted the table and shelves with water, the dirt running off and dripping onto the concrete floor from the mouth of a dragon with a foot-long tongue, the lips of a lion with moth-eaten skin. Other faces leered — a witch with a nose of twisted manzanita root, a blonde coquette whose lips had acquired a patina like old blood, a demonically wholesome milkmaid, and a Pilgrim mother with no eyes. She took off her mask and rinsed it, too, then gave herself an impromptu shower, hair falling to her shoulders and her nipples showing darkly though the linen. "I've been meaning to wash this gown for ages," she said. "Looks better, doesn't it?"

"How many of those do you have?"

"Two. But I left the other up at Sanandra."

The material clung to a body so beautiful that anyone, man or woman, would have been drawn to it. "Cain, you're about to become a millionaire, you could afford to buy another gown, you know?"

"There are better things to spend money on. Now help me lay all these out, so people can choose as they pass by, just like in the old days. And some will bring their own." Trew, quiet, finally said, "Cain, what was going on back then? Why did our parents stage stuff like this? Who were they and did they have other lives we knew nothing about? Was Tregaron Springs ever more than a distraction from something more important?"

"So many questions, Trewdy. You're thinking about all this now when I thought about it all the time I was growing up. So much made no sense to me in the beginning but as I got older it began to. I thought Reeve and you would catch up with me with the questions, but neither of you ever did. You had the plane crash to get over, and Reeve had, I don't know, whatever she had besides competing with me most of the time. She never really wanted anything but to be the boss. She made a good one, I'll admit. But I had to get out of here because of all the unanswered questions. I finally married Freddie Abruzzini because he was available."

"And rich."

"Yeah, that. Plus not too bright."

"I was too young to know what was going on anyway," said Trew. "Some things I decided I would never understand, then I discovered something you might be able to help me with, since Reeve won't."

Cain smiled. Trew knew before she asked what the answer would be but asked anyway. "Did Mommy have, you know, someone else?"

Cain touched her cheek. "There are limits of conscience to what I can say, mainly because I don't really know. I don't want to betray Mommy or Daddy, but I can say I wondered about some of those guys around her. Still do. She was just too beautiful and obliging for her own good, putting off whatever it was that ate at her until it was too late. But maybe it wasn't too late. If she had a secret love Marta would have known but she will never, ever talk about it. Even being asked would ruin what's left of Marta's life. This sale's going to be hard on all those working here. I suspect, Trewdy, that at Tregaron Springs as with everything else it has to do with the wine and you're going to have to follow that."

That evening, CJ lingered at the edge of the drive, watching as the cars disgorged guests, some of whom he knew. Clearly happy to be here, they approached the big house holding out bouquets and gifts wrapped in colorful tissue paper, paper bags dangling from arms. Out of them peered more weird fairytale incarnations, masks to be put on later. Others wore Lone Ranger half masks as they crossed the porch, or held up faces mounted on sticks, portable new identities making them more interesting because they were unknown.

CJ joined them, nodding to a down-valley vintner he had interviewed and intended to expose, not for making faulty wines but for stealing a neighbor's land through an abomination known as a "lot-line adjustment," one of many schemes for acquiring land that wasn't yours. A woman who sold bulk wine that wasn't hers reared back in alarm at the sight of him. But he went into the house and deeper into what had become a crowd, people asking why the Vassy girls had finally sold out and who were these new vulgarians?

CJ thought he would know Cain no matter what mask she wore, so obsessed was he. Almost as unsettling as losing his book was the fact that she mesmerized him. He wanted to strangle her, but also to kiss her, a humiliating turn of events. Where was this mysterious, smart, impossible woman?

Tregaron's notorious neighbor to the north, Fred Abruzzini, stood in the stairwell. He hadn't worn a mask, not needing one after disguising himself for years as a studious vintner instead of the descendent of Mafiosi. Abruzzini, CJ recalled, had married, then humiliated Cain by bringing two whores to their honeymoon suite on the Veneto. Now he pressed his shoulders flat against the wall, and there she was. Same white gown, lovely ankles, physical elasticity: Cain in a cuckold's mask. She put her arms around Abruzzini's neck as if she was still married to him and pulled him to her, dipping her head as if to kiss him with that grotesque beak.

Enraged, CJ stepped forward and grasped her wrist. With his other hand he lifted her mask and demanded, "Cain!" Only to see a pretty face, but not hers. It was Reeve instead.

Abruzzini shouldered him aside. "Watch it, asshole." But he was smiling broadly.

"Why, CJ," said Reeve, "how nice to see you on this last night. I assume you've met Freddie."

"No," he stammered. "I thought you were your sister."

"'Fraid not. Cain's gone back to her hippies, or whatever she calls them."

"She just got here."

"I'm afraid it's true."

Abruzzini now laughed. "You poor bastard," he said to CJ.

"Now, Freddie, be nice." Reeve touched CJ's cheek. "We've decided to get married. Won't that be nice?"

"Who's getting married?"

"Me and Freddie. That way I can just move in next door with him. Couldn't be more convenient, and Freddie's going to put me to use, which is smart of him, dear boy." She kissed Freddie. "I hope, CJ, that you'll…"

But he was already pushing toward the broad staircase behind the band. He maneuvered past the bass and took the steps two at a time. Lining the broad upstairs hallway were bedroom doors, all closed. CJ headed for the other end of the hallway, banging on each door as he passed. Cain must have retreated to one of them, he thought. There might be ghosts in this house, but those now actually living in it were worse.

He kicked open the last door. "Cain! Give me my book. Now!"

But the room was empty.

"I told you to be off this property before the end of day, Craven-Jones."

Ronnie Staunton stood behind him in a ludicrous silk smoking jacket and mauve slippers, dressed as he obviously thought the heir to Tregaron Springs should, though this was Consolidated Brands's house, not Ronnie's. And behind him stood the stumpy, amorphous bodyguard with big hands dangling at his side, a half-smile on his face as he happily anticipated throwing CJ back down the stairs.

"I'm pressing charges, Craven-Jones," Ronnie said, "and you're now going to jail."

"Stop!"

They all turned to see Trew at the banister's turning. She came forward without hurry, almost leisurely, as if her being here was an afterthought. She wore the same black gown as the night before, but no mask. "You don't take possession until midnight, Ronnie. And it's only 10:30 p.m. Come on, CJ. We're going to get you packed and out of this silliness."

"I'm not going anywhere."

"Yes, you are," said Trew. "Cain's gone. Come on, I'll help you pack and explain in the process."

The night was already growing cold. They walked together across the gravel, and CJ, suddenly dejected, said, "Please tell me she has my book."

"You never know with Cain but I'm pretty sure she does. Probably just wants to make sure you didn't make up anything lurid about us. And if you said anything to her that could have been interpreted as negative about Sanandra, then you were asking for it. You critics get too full of yourselves sometimes, too judgmental. It may just be the way you live — nothing of your own, really, and nothing to back you up but what you know. Maybe you disdained something she cares about without realizing it. And caring with Cain can sometimes amount to a blunt instrument."

She led him into his guest cottage. CJ's trunk sat open on the floor.

"I thought maybe she hid it," he said lamely.

"Well, let's get you packed and out of here before midnight. Otherwise Ronnie really will call the sheriff."

Together they tossed clothes into his hulking beast of wooden struts and leather straps. "You won't understand what I'm about to say," Trew added, "but I owe you a debt you're not even aware of. If it hadn't been for your coming, I would never have understood this place or my place in it. I would never have had the courage to take the vineyard instead of the money. Marta discovered a box on that beam when she was cleaning, and inside it I discovered a key. Trust me when I say this has been life changing."

"So what am I to do?"

"Go get your book. Go to Sanandra."

"My god. And how would I do that again?"

"Remember? Just drive north to Sacramento, turn right, take the interstate east, up into the Sierra. Before descending the east face toward Reno take another right on this county road," and she scrawled the number on a piece of his leftover typing paper. "There's a sign and you must watch or else you'll miss it. Quite possibly it will have been torn down again by locals."

She put her arms around his neck and hugged. For a bit they both held on. Then together they dragged the trunk out into the gravel and heaved it into the trunk.

Trew looked toward the big house and saw Ronnie, the bodyguard, and another suit watching them. CJ got into his car and pulled slowly away. In the rearview mirror he was watching Trew, and he raised his hand in farewell. She wondered if she would ever see him again.

Chapter 14

The metal sign when he finally found it again, hours later, looked like Braille because it was full of even more bullet holes. From there the dirt road mounted through hairpin turns toward the sunrise, past fence posts in piles of stones until before him lay a tree-studded aridity behind high steel mesh. A scattering of dun-colored prefabricated buildings with bright metal roofs stood in the distance, casting knife-edge shadows, and row upon row of irrigated crops.

CJ parked outside the gatehouse and got out, assaulted by the smell of sunbaked chaparral and liquid fertilizer. He entered a barren cubicle of blonde wood, the air infused with incense, where a young woman in a pink pants suit and a locket containing a cameo photograph of an old man with a gray beard, sat behind a simple desk.

"Who's that?" CJ asked.

"Indusan, who else? I know you're Craven-something but before you go in your car it will be washed to eliminate invasive species, including seeds and microorganisms traveling on tires and undercarriages. And both it and you will be searched for firearms, which are not allowed in Sanandra except in the possession of the Vigilants. Same for alcohol and drugs other than the okay ones. Now take off your clothes."

Out in the parking lot two of the so-called Vigilants in burgundy shirts and mauve ties were going through the contents of his trunk, a German shepherd looking on. A young man in a denim work shirt and baseball cap escorted him and his valise to a golf cart and drove CJ down to a prefab A-frame.

"Ravi Shankar Grove," the kid said.

"What's that?"

"A pad, man."

Ravi Shankar Grove had no trees, just willow plantings next to an artificial pool full of cattails. On the floor was a rolled tatami mat, a low table, and on the wall a photograph of the same bearded face he had seen in the receptionist's locket. CJ drank deeply of tasteless water in the jug on the table and stretched out on his mat. Soon Cain would arrive and hand over his book, and he would drive down and out of these beautiful, desolate mountains.

But he fell into an exhausted sleep and awoke to find the view in deep shadow. He walked out onto the dirt street and followed it into what the young man had called the Palace of Sustenance. Inside, it reeked of un-husked rice, squash and various other vegetables of nutritional rectitude. There was no black tea but a mug of sweet liquid resembling it. He carried his meager tray to a table where a slight, bearded man in a jaunty blue bandana said, "Hey man, I'm Vida. Harvard '75. Visual arts, environmental studies. What's your story?"

"Well, I'm Clyde, Cambridge '70. Medieval studies, with a first in…" It was hopeless.

"I met Indusan in the Himalayas."

"I don't know him at all. Where can I find Cain Vassy?"

"Sorry Clyde can't help you there. But if you're still hungry you might try Boddhisatva Pizza down past the Buddha Grove."

There he ate most of a spelt and wild dandelion pizza and went back to his A-frame. No sign of Cain. He fell asleep again and awoke in the night, nothing but a thin synthetic coverlet between him and the cold. There was someone else in the room and he stiffened, smelling sweat, a touch of lavender and something else he recognized. Had she come to him again, or was this some acolyte of the apparently mad, bearded Indusan? In this new world of wild swings in temperature, topography, and longing he now took a chance and addressed the darkness. "You're a thief."

"No," Cain said, "you are. You eavesdrop on human weakness, write it down in your notebook and turn it into something benefitting you alone, leaving those whose words and lives you've stolen to wallow in their impossible dreams."

He was stunned. No more succinct description of writing had he ever heard.

"And now you want to know what I think of it. Oh, the vanity. Well, I can see some value in it, and may give the book back to you and may not. But for the moment don't move."

CJ felt her hands on him — again — and almost wept with gratitude. Whatever this woman wanted of him he would do, a thought both humiliating, and liberating.

Finally, a rosy light struck the opposing hill, and he heard the distant generators come on. He imagined transplanted flowers out there opening to the sun and rolled toward Cain. She was gone.

He found her waiting outside in that once-white sheath, running a wooden comb through her Chablis hair. Except the muscles and the dirt on her knees she could have been her older sister. Cain said, "We need a bath," and began to lead him toward a whitewashed cinderblock building. "Work here is everything and has produced wonderful results. We equate it with worship."

"Orwellian."

"More like Huxley."

Inside the building was a swimming pool, the smell of chlorine powerful. "We don't cover here," she said, stripping. Sun-tanned to her nipples, grime shadowing her angular frame like impasto on a portrait from the Italian Renaissance, she held up two pairs of swim goggles.

"You'll want to wear these."

She put hers on and stepped into the water, CJ following, his heart quickening like a Huxley among the Sanandrans. The surprisingly hot water moved in a circular flow.

"There are metal rings set into the bottom of the pool," she said. "We like to grab one and let the current wash away all conflict."

The goggles made of her an alien as she dove. A flash of that lovely backside, those delicate ankles. When in Sanandra, he thought, and followed suit.

In the subaqueous glare he saw their two figures reflected in the mirroring wall of black glass, he with a drifting mass of dark hair and a pale English ass, and Cain upside down, her waist slim enough to encircle with two hands, her hips flared, a bright bush of pubic hair.

His own profile morphed salaciously into an erection. What this woman could do to him! He clawed upward through the warm water and glimpsed a flash of light within the blackness of the reflecting glass, not a mirror at all, he realized, but a window, he and Cain the sole performers in this aquarium and someone on the other side watching them. The bearded face inside all the lockets — Indusan — was out there and had just lit a cigarette.

She drove the golf cart between stands of wild mustard, up to a sloping tableland of rocky soil planted with straggly vines covered with reams of cheesecloth. "It provides a touch of shade," Cain explained. "These are Rhone varietals, some from north Africa that can stand the sun. Irrigation is from the black plastic drip pipes. Drop, drop, drop."

"How old are these vines?"

"Three years. Next fall these grapes will go into a crusher and the juice into stainless steel tanks down there in the sheds. Then into barrels made from local wood."

"What kind?"

"I'm not sure. And that's when you could do us a favor by writing about what we're doing here. Just taste the new wine and admit you think it has potential."

"Do you really believe this will turn into something people will buy?"

"What one believes is unimportant. It's how one behaves that matters."

He thought of Tregaron Spring's immovable old stone reliquaries, the fragrance there of sun on dust and conifer, the Mediterranean miraculously flowing with water from the mountain. Sanandra was by comparison a rocky wilderness.

"I want my book back," he said.

"I know you do. It's okay, but it won't make you famous, I'm afraid. England doesn't care about California wine, not yet. A New York publisher might, but all the gossip would stand a better chance. If that's published they will make some of our neighbors apoplectic."

"And you think I'll trek all the way back up here to see how your wine has turned out?

"You have to promise you will if you want the book back."

She drove him to the front gate, neither of them speaking, and CJ watched her raise the seat of the golf cart and take out a lumpy package bound with twine. They had been riding on top of his book all the time.

He followed her into the welcoming center where the same young woman with the locket eyed him with the same skepticism. Cain ripped open the package and took out the manuscript, a bit worse for wear, but intact. "There's a lot riding on our success here," she told him. "And you can help us. You could even be a part of it."

And with that she turned and walked back out into the brutal sunlight.

An hour later CJ got out of his car at a crossroad and peed on the front tire. To his left lay the endless variety of California, to his right the even greater immensity of America. He would drive down to Reno, sell his car and fly to the East Coast. There he would have a copy made of the manuscript and leave it with a New York publisher he had corresponded with, and then fly on to London, his money gone. But there was the last, small payment from his advance to look forward to. There was hope.

Part III:

Green Buttons

Chapter 15

Trew wasn't sure exactly when the transformation of the old shed began. First she noticed that boards from blown-down timber, cut back in her grandfather's time and stacked inside, were climbing the inside of the cinderblock walls. The boards were newly cut to length on an old table saw someone had hauled over and then covered with a tarpaulin when the work was done.

Then her stash of old Tregaron Springs vintages moved to a makeshift rack, the neck slots cut with a hatchet. The planks' dark and grainy fir, redwood and oak matched only in their antiquity but were beautiful still. The young men doing the work were wary, peering apprehensively around the sides of the shed or resting out of sight in its shadow. Trew brought them a case of soft drinks and salsa and an enormous bag of corn chips and left these just inside the doorway. The men ate it all and drank half the orange-flavored Fanta before crossing the railroad tracks and the highway in late afternoon and disappearing into Browntown.

Then, a week later, she discovered that someone had knocked out cinderblocks in the shed and framed two windows there. Eventually she planned to have all the cinderblocks at the west end of the shed replaced with glass, but she couldn't afford that yet. Her view would then be of St. Bart's and that alone, no Tregaron Springs big house, no Tregaron

Springs vines, just hers. She would pay for it all with money from a daring plan which required cunning and luck.

First, she cancelled the deal Teodoro had made with the custom crusher across the highway. When her crop was ready, she would ask him to get the men to pick it, while he kept a running tab. Once harvest was over, she would have them install the solar shower on the back wall, plus a freestanding outhouse with a crescent moon cut into the door. The sight of the outdoor privy would drive Ronnie Staunton wild, hastening whatever plan he had for blocking his view of Trew's evolving existence, but that was fine with her.

She drove to the payphone up the highway, at the Mercado on the edge of Browntown, and dialed Reeve's number. As soon as she answered, Trew said, "I have to talk to you. Right now. I'll be in the old shed where the wood was stored, which is now my house... Yes, that's right... It would be faster and easier if you just walked over."

Trew watched Reeve come out of the Abruzzini vineyard that had supplied grapes for illegal wine during Prohibition. She wondered if Abruzzini's connections to organized crime were the same as Consolidated's and decided no, Abruzzini would be Chicago, Consolidated New York. Morning sunlight lit up Reeve's hair and the ruffled white blouse she wore under her jacket, her slacks protected by knee-high boots.

Abruzzini's heavily watered ground was bare of weeds and everything else, whereas Green Button's lush understory contained a rich mix of weeds and vetch to keep the soil loose and nutritious. Turn over a spadeful and you would see worms and all manner of other creatures that Reeve wanted nowhere close to her body. "Trewdy," she called out, waving. "You've turned into a hippy!"

They hugged. Reeve had yet another new perfume — where did she find them all? — and there was an ease in her stance Trew remembered from their time as teenagers. She was over Justin, had in fact forgotten him. He was just another burden associated with Tregaron Springs that was no longer hers.

"Love the cinderblocks," Reeve said.

"No, you don't. You hate them. Well, they're going to be covered with hay bales."

"Hay bales? Whatever for?"

"Insulation."

"Whoever heard of that?"

"People have been doing it for a hundred years, Sis."

"Consolidated's really going to like the look of that. Listen, before I forget, Freddie wants me to tell you he's happy to take the Green Buttons harvest off your hands. And he'll pay you a good price."

"I'll bet he will. It's the best fruit in the valley. Tell Freddie it's negotiable but that I have a plan of my own. Want to hear it?"

"Sure."

"He pays me twice the going rate for valley cabernet. He'll make a new wine just from it, no blending, and ...." Trew held up a hand. "... and put the name Green Buttons on the label, prominently. And he'll charge more for a bottle than he does for the top Abruzzini wine ... wait, there's more. And put his name on a three-year contract with the price going up each year."

Reeve looked at her in amazement. "My, you do have a plan. He'll never agree to all that. He thinks he's doing you a favor."

"No, he doesn't. Reeve, you know, you're the expert. Don't let him get away with any crap. I'm doing him a favor and if he says no then I'm going straight back to Ronnie Taunton. Tregaron needs all the good fruit it can find."

"Logistically, it sure would be easy," said Reeve. "Freddie could just send his guys over to pick and then truck the fruit straight into the winery."

"No, Teodoro's already put together our crew. We'll deliver the picked fruit to Freddie. And he'll have to let Teodoro have some say in the winemaking. After all, Teodoro made the wine here for years before Vlad fired him. He knows the place better than Freddie does."

"If I help you with this, will you be a nice sister-in-law to him?"

"What in the world do you mean?"

"Freddie and I are getting married."

"That's crazy, Reeve. He married your sister Cain, remember? How did that turn out?"

"I'm no Cain. Freddie thought those two prostitutes would help him perform because he was so nervous. You know how Cain can intimidate people. He was already afraid of her, poor guy, after lusting after her for all those years. Besides, we're not going to Rome for our honeymoon, we're going to Paris."

"There are prostitutes in Paris, too."

"The wedding night problem's already been taken care of. Freddie's sweet, Trewdy, and still the best man in bed in the valley."

"For God's sake, Reeve."

"You're thinking I should know, right? Well, there are plenty of men I haven't slept with. Did you ever sleep with CJ? He was quite good, by the way."

"No, I didn't."

"Why in the world not?"

"Reeve, why do we still have these asinine conversations? They haven't changed since I was fifteen and you were trying to manage my non-existent sex life."

"Cain slept with CJ."

"What?!"

"Then she made him crazy because that's what Cain does. He'll never get over her now, as we both know. No man ever does."

Trew sat down in the grass and leaned against the sturdy cinderblock. Suddenly she felt very tired.

"We're going to be happy," said Reeve. "Freddie badly needs somebody to help him run the place now that the old man's dead. That person is going to be me."

"I'm glad, Sis. And a lot depends on him — and you — taking my grapes and paying me what they're worth. It'll provide me with enough to live on, at least. I'll leave the winemaking to Freddie and Teodoro. This arrangement will work because I owe no one money and so no interest, and I'll never expand which is what always ruins good wine."

"You're the only person I would believe who said that. Everybody else just wants to be rich."

"Green Buttons cabernet as a separate label will sell, once the word gets out. And it will boost Abruzzini's reputation, too. Freddie can even take credit for the single label idea if he wants. It could raise the bar for the whole valley, and it will be you and me, Sis, working together again, like old times. But now we won't have to worry about replacing a million-dollar roof."

When Reeve left, Trew went into her new house and picked a random early vintage of Tregaron Springs cabernet from the shelf. She laid it horizontally in an empty nail tray and carried it into the dusty yard behind Teodoro's house. She stepped over the barbed wire, crossed the yard and rapped on his screen door.

She could see Teodoro at the stove, making coffee. The battered aluminum drip pot was ancient. "You might want to wait," she called out to him. "I've got something better. Bring a corkscrew out here and a couple of glasses."

She sat on the steps and looked at the label. A 1912. The import of that registered in Teodoro's dark, liquid eyes as he stepped onto the porch. "You could sell that tomorrow and pay the men what you owe them so far," he said.

"But then I'd be a thief. As is, I'm using it to maintain the family's vital enological link to Tregaron Springs. As stipulated in the contract."

"No one would know," said Teodoro.

"I would."

A shiny purplish drop winked at the point where Teodoro's corkscrew met the glass rim. She drew out the long, dark cork.

"Should we decant it?"

"If there was any fruit left it's being smelled by the angels right now. There'll be nothing left to taste."

She tilted the old bottle anyway, first into his glass and then into hers. The foxed label held the view Trew had watched the Cessna fly out of when she was eight and two minutes later she was an orphan. She raised her glass to eye level. "Too bricky."

He was sniffing anyway. "Still pretty good," he said, surprised. "Cigar box."

She smelled too. "And good black fruit."

"Plums."

"Mint," she added. "Craven-Jones didn't like that, remember?"

"What does he know?"

The old wine had no tannin left, and the alcohol was low as it had been in the earlier years of winemaking at Tregaron Springs. But the taste astounded. "It's good."

They both drank deeply.

"I want some answers, Teodoro." An abrupt transition, but it was now or never. "Like, why did Mommy write you a note saying you owed her seven thousand dollars?"

"I don't know what you're talking about."

"Yes, you do. Marta found the note in a tin box when she was dusting the rafters. She showed it to me."

"She didn't find it there, she just told you that so she'd have an excuse for not showing it to you sooner. Marta had it for years, finally decided that you had a right to see it. That it was time."

"Why?"

"Because your mother gave me money to help bring people up from Michoacán. Illegally. One of them was Marta."

"Why Marta?"

"Because she's my sister."

"Marta's your sister?!"

"Other family's here, too. Two cousins, a nephew — Raoul. I never paid that money back to your mother, and so I am now, helping you with this vineyard, and the house if that's what we're calling it."

"There's more that needs explaining, Teodoro, and you know it. What about the key to the post office box? How did it get under that tin box?"

"We've let the wine's fruit escape with all this jabbering," he said. "This bottle's just a dead old thing now. Not even worth finishing."

"I'm finishing mine."

He took a National out of the blue work shirt pocket, elaborately dug into his jeans for the Zippo, and flared it up. The exhalation was abrupt.

"Did Marta leave the key there to be discovered, or did Mommy?"

"How the hell should I know? And now I'm going to bed."

He went back inside, the screen door banging. Trew tarried over her glass, taste or no taste. Teodoro could build a little fence between his place and hers, she thought, with a garden gate. That would be nice.

She slept in her truck and in the morning went back up Teodoro's steps. "Aren't you going to invite me in?" she called.

The smell of warmed-up coffee reached her. He pushed open the door with one foot and handed her a mug, but Trew followed him into the kitchen without an invitation. Nothing on the walls but a calendar, a cross, and an old photograph of a kind-eyed woman who must have been Teodoro's mother, quite possibly Trew's grandmother. Then she saw her old saddle on a chair at the foot of Teodoro's iron frame bed in the next room and went straight to it. Ribbons worked into the splices would have appealed to the eight-year-old girl she had been when last she saw it. Soft leather seat, cantle still worked with saddle soap. She remembered gripping that horn as the one dependable thing on Earth when the horse was spinning, spinning, and her parents gone.

"Why?" she asked.

"My father kept his saddle at the foot of his bed in Mexico so he would always be ready. I never rode that horse before the day of the crash, and you never rode it afterward. So, I kept the saddle in shape, thinking someday you might. Then Vladimir sold the horse to Abruzzini's foreman and fired me. I never gave back the saddle."

"What happened that day, Teodoro? Daddy was a good pilot, why did he crash?"

"Don't, Trew."

"I have to."

He crossed the room and took a suede bag from the dresser drawer. The veins in his dark forearms stood out. A working man's arms. Out fell her father's pipe with the broken, crooked stem. "See those little marks?" he asked. "The pipe was caught up in the rudder wires running to the back of the Cessna. Somebody said the take-off over in Mendocino that morning might have been too steep, and that the pipe had fallen and scooted back to the tail section. There it slipped under the floorboards and got entangled in the elevator cable. That's why your father stalled and spun on landing."

Trew passed her thumb over the scratches. "Did Vladimir accept that theory?"

"I don't know, he didn't talk to me about anything but wine-making and nothing after that. He hired out my job because he didn't think a Mexican like me could handle it. He would have taken this house if your parents hadn't already given it to me."

"Teodoro, is Marta my aunt?"

He closed his eyes. There they stood, side by side, for what felt like forever. Finally, he said, "Your mother was a good person. So was her husband. I want to leave it at that for now, Trewdy."

She took her mother's lovely little notebook bound in pale blue leather from her back pocket and placed it on the bed. They both stared at it. Trew had anticipated this moment for a long time and wondered who else in Browntown knew she was kin. What other stories lay unturned in Green Buttons' deep concealing earth?

She kissed Theodoro's unshaven face. Stiff white bristles, the smell of an old man bound to her by a passion so illicit no one would have believed it.

"I have work to do on my house," she said. It stood in plain sight, not a hundred yards off, bright in the warming day.

Chapter 16

Harvest began before dawn, Green Buttons vineyard loud with the palaver of the pickers, that long familiar sound. Trew retrieved her stack of baguettes from Tregaron's big freezer in the basement, on what would be her last visit, and carried the box out among the vines as the pickers were finishing up. The metal bins brimmed with blue-black fruit and the pickers leaned against them in the late morning sun and hungrily ate the still-warm bread.

Teodoro supervised the passage of the gondolas across the line to the Abruzzini winery and the weighing of the fruit. Thirty thousand gallons, she learned when it had gone to press, which penciled out to about ten thousand dollars an acre. She owed no bank, but she did owe the pickers, the men working on her new house, and Teodoro who stayed at Abruzzini most of that afternoon, making sure the grapes went into their own fermentation tanks with access to them when he wanted it.

Freddie Abruzzini had not only agreed to Trew's proposal but took credit for dreaming up a separate, vineyard-specific wine, as she had predicted he would. He also paid a lot more than she would have for a customized label. The wine critics were already speculating about the new mystery cabernet, but she took none of their calls, referring them instead to Reeve next door in her shiny new office. The tasting of barrel samples by outsiders other than Teodoro and Trew was months away.

The total, Trew learned, was five tons of grapes an acre. She had a livable income, if just. Additions to her house would absorb any extra cash she possessed for years to come, but she had nothing else to spend it on except paint — and canvas, of course, if she ever took up painting again.

She found herself invited to gatherings in Browntown across the highway, casual affairs where teenage boys who may well have been her kin misbehaved on their bikes or kicked soccer balls into parked cars. Everybody feasted from picnic tables, far from legendary Tregaron on the other side of the railroad tracks. This might as well have been on the other side of the world. She found herself smiled upon by strangers and their children, hugged by women who sometimes kissed her, nodded to by men who seemed to know this new, aging senorita. Teodoro was nearby, and Marta, too. She had been fired by Consolidated but was unphased, wearing new party dresses and waving to Trew as before. Had her brother told her? Trew assumed he had, but Marta gave no sign of it and never would, for she too belonged to the vanished world of Tregaron Springs.

The voice at the other end of the line when Trew got home was barely audible. "Trewdy! Thank God you answered."

"Cain? Where are you?"

"In the Miami airport. I'm about to get on a plane."

"Where to?"

"Delhi. Just ahead of the posse."

"Cain, what the hell are you talking about?"

"The feds. It's Indusan's fault."

There was an edge to her voice Trew hadn't heard before.

"He lied to me," Cain went on, "saying he had paid all the local taxes and bills sent by the Bureau of Land Management. He lied. I'll never forgive him, even though he's dead."

"The head of Sanandra? The old man's dead?"

"Yes, arsenic. The bastard. The feds moved against us, seized the property and our equipment, loaded it onto flatbeds and were about to arrest me, too. I spent all my Tregaron money in four days trying to stop them, and now they're charging me with fraud."

"How?"

"I counter-signed his agreements, believing he knew what he was doing. He knew, all right. Riding an old con apparent to others, but not to me. That's my problem, isn't it, Trewdy? I wanted to believe too badly, and he knew it."

"Reeve could help you."

"You know I wouldn't ask that, Trewdy. She's not rich enough, anyway. And if I did that it would make her the winner of our long struggle." She laughed, but there was an edge to it. "Can't have that."

"Cain, don't go. Come here instead. We'll figure something out so you can stay. Saul will help, too. Reeve's marrying Freddie Abruzzini, by the way. So if you come, you can attend the ceremony." Trew would suggest anything that might convince her.

"That's hilarious. Maybe I will. Getting busted by the FBI just as Reeve's about to say, 'I do.' That would be hard to beat, but no, the valley's the first place they'll come looking for me. Then I would go to San Quentin for twenty years and your new lives would be messed up for the duration. No, India it is."

Trew was crying. "Why?"

"Because in India being a swami is a career decision. My last. I just wanted you to know. There's a little retreat, you might call it, already established near Gangotri, at the headwaters of the Ganges. It's leaderless now, but not for long. You won't be hearing from me again, Trewdy. Please don't write or think about coming to look for me because I'm over California, period. I love you, Sis."

And she hung up.

The old woodstove went into a corner of Trew's new house and hand-split oak piled up outside her door. She got most of it inside before the storm that would become famous. It arrived from the Pacific and parked over the valley for three days, dropping an unprecedented amount of water even by the standards of winter in Catarina County. Recently planted shrubs bobbed in standing pools, and trees came down, and still the rain fell.

Then a gale began to blow, the warmer air trapped beneath the cold, gathering strength as it came through the gap in the coastal mountains. Trew heard something in the night and got up and peered at utter blackness beyond her newly glazed windows. She could hear the grand old eucalyptus whipping in the wind and was so familiar with the tree that she didn't have to see it to know the massive, bone-white trunk was stressed, dimpled with age, and holding great sheaths of shed bark in the towering branches of the seven trunks. They extended from the main stem and would be lifting and accelerating away into the night.

Finally, she stepped outside in nothing at all, her feet suddenly cold in the sodden weeds, her bare shoulders lashed with rain. A pale luminescence hung about the hundred-foot tree as it rocked and sawed, the dark orb of the bole that had grown at ground level like some pregnant giant's stomach, eight feet across, a phenomenon. She had often thought of having it cut off and scooped out and made into a boat. But tonight, she feared the destruction of the whole tree in this wind, the likes of which she had never known.

She could feel with her bare feet the snapping of roots far underground, could hear something like muffled gunshots. This tree, brought all the way from Australia more than a century before, was planted by her great-grandfather. Today it wasn't the valley's reigning giant but it was huge, and it was going over, masses of leaves falling, then the tree itself, colliding with the earth with a resounding shudder.

She stayed in bed the next morning as a personal protest, refusing to look out at the disaster until this became unavoidable. The eucalyptus lay along the vineyard's edge, no vines of hers touched but half a dozen rows of neighboring Tregaron's mashed flat. Ronnie Staunton would want compensation, which he wouldn't get from Trew, plus his vineyard manager would be glad to be rid of the reigning eucalyptus.

Two of the pickers stood next to the tree, holding the handles of a twelve-foot crosscut saw left over from logging days, the so-called misery whip. They were cutting the bole away on what must have been Teodoro's orders, and she wanted to kiss his unshaven cheek again. When the heavy bole tumbled and rolled into her weeds it was indisputably hers and, yes, might make a sweet little boat for poling in the marshes of San Francisco Bay. But now she had an even better use for it.

By afternoon Tregaron's hirelings were sectioning what was left of the tree and feeding it into the raucous gas-driven chipper. And, almost miraculously, as if summoned by the disaster, the tree's chief critic stepped out of a new red convertible, jamming his fists against what were becoming plump hips under a stylish cashmere sweater: Clyde Craven-Jones.

"Where's Cain?" he asked.

"No hello, CJ? No greeting? Just 'Where's Cain'?"

"Sorry. Are you trying to live in a Monet?"

"Excuse me."

"Those hay bales all around your little house. Monet had the good sense not to try to live in his."

"They were stacks, not bales. So, you're back after… what? A year?"

"Yes. Bought the car in Reno, stopped by Sanandra on my way here. Highway Patrolmen wouldn't let me through the gate, but I could see it's a God-awful mess in there, the disciples or whatever they were all gone. Cain too. Trew, where's your sister?"

"In Gangotri."

"Where's that?"

"India. So how are you, CJ? Did your book get published?"

"Oh, yes, in London. It's flopped — a non-event. The English made French wines famous, and they aren't really interested in the California sort. Major miscalculation on my part."

"Well, you look prosperous enough."

"Because another rich relative died, aunt on my mother's side. Had to take her name, too, to get the money. Now I'm the tripled-barreled Clyde Craven-Jones-Severs."

"My God, what a mouthful."

"Still Craven-Jones to my readers, however. What's left of them. And a publisher in New York is looking at the book and might just bring it out. All the behind-the-scenes stuff, you know. Tregaron Springs is prominent, of course." He pressed palms against the new flannel trousers, trying to hide his disappointment at not finding Cain. "Why India?"

"To avoid arrest. It's a long sad story. Would you like coffee?"

They sat on lawn chairs with a view of the half-finished solar shower and St. Bart's beyond. Trew talked but CJ seemed distracted, anxious. "I'm through with England," he blurted out, when she was done. "California's done it to me, and I'm thinking of moving here and starting a monthly review about New World viticulture, calling it Craven-Jones on Wine. I have four hundred subscribers and the first issue's not even out. I say, have you an address for Cain?"

"She doesn't want to be contacted and was quite explicit about that."

"Balderdash."

"I see you've been re-Anglicized, Clyde Craven-Jones-Severs. Too bad. I think I preferred the old CJ. Will you at least taste our barrel samples from Green Buttons's? It's our first vintage."

"Yes, of course. But not now."

"It's gotten some attention. Michael Broadbent wants samples, believe it or not."

"I'm thinking of moving back to the valley. But there's something I must do first. Do you think I might leave my car here for a week, possibly longer?"

"There's not room, CJ. But Reeve could probably find you a space next door at Abruzzini. They have lots of room."

Chapter 17

CJ slept badly on the flight to Delhi and again on one of those great, swaying monochromatic monsters that seemed to ceaselessly prowl the sub-continent. He got off in the morning in Haridwar, a name that meant "gateway to the gods" in Hindustani, a reference to the Himalayas. But this was still the baked plain of northern India, the mountains no more than distant shadows under the haze of a building monsoon.

The Ganges was the color of cafe au lait and brimmed with Hindus renewing themselves in water that had descended, they said, from a glacier almost three hundred kilometers away, near the place called Tapovan. CJ was already exhausted by the heat, the dust, and the low-grade hysteria that seemed part of daily existence. Certainly, it was the most redolent place he had been, every imaginable smell competing for ascendancy, threatening to drive him into an olfactory frenzy.

That night he asked for chicken in a restaurant in nearby Rishikesh, realizing too late that eating meat was sacrilege. Then in his airless hotel room he dreamed of violence on a mountainside and of blood welling up from the bottom of a deep blue sea. Six hours later, in the back seat of a hired jalopy plying relentlessly dangerous roads, he saw a battered blue bus side-swiped by a truck and the driver get out and wipe blood from his face.

Hindus put more faith in instinct than in reason, he was told. Dreams were prophetic, with little distinction between the conscious and the unconscious, both aspects of life as varied as the terraced rice paddies in the foothills reflecting almost infinite shades of green, a vivid mosaic. He stopped in Uttarkashi, the last town of any size before the road assaulted the mountains, to rent trekking equipment for the climb into the mountains. The outfitter had only a faded Patagonia "syn-chilla" and a backpack standing in a corner. He had read of fierce winds in the mountains in June, of snow even. He had no stove or pots, just a dozen high-protein power bars and a bottle of tablets for purifying water.

He had read Rudyard Kipling's *Kim* on the plane: "All India is full of holy men stammering gospels in strange tongues; shaken and consumed in the fires of their own zeal; dreamers, babblers, and visionaries." But not a word about holy women. The country nurtured more religions and sects than any other country, with a staggering array of gods and demigods. Plump, androgynous, bestial faces gazed from beneath the eaves of temples and shrines, out of shop windows, from rickshaw dashboards, postcards, necklace pendants.

He saw pilgrims in battered busses spewing black smoke, bound for shrines, bare toes pressed against cracked windshields, their impassive faces marked with red or yellow daubs of sandalwood paste. The busses hung out over frightening thousand-foot drops to the Ganges and dirt switchbacks opened up to reveal the mass of the Himalayas rising straight out of the earth. It began to rain and by the time he had reached Gangotri he had changed from shorts to trousers and a sweater. Mist rose in waves from cataracts eating into the marly stone above the river.

Disgorging pilgrims, bundles on their heads, the women wrapped in saris and Punjabi sikhs wearing Nehru hats. Some had come from as far away as Madras and Calcutta in white pantaloons and turbans of the Rajasthanis bobbed on the human current past stalls of incense, bead mallas, bottles for taking water from the Ganges, flowers for floating prayers on it, and staffs for climbing to the glacier above it.

Mixed with locals were carters piled with suitcases, mule drivers wearing ropes, hawkers and bearded sadhus, the poor spiritual seekers, and beggars under black plastic sheets. Intermingling in the air were the smells of incense, dung and smoldering cannabis. On impulse he stopped a pilgrim in jogging shoes and asked if he spoke English. He did, being a diamond merchant from Bombay with his wife, a plump, pleasant woman in a white sari, with a large diamond in her nose. He took CJ's hand and led him to the Tourist Rest Home — kerosene lanterns, communal baths, toilet stalls and hot water in buckets. They ate curried vegetables, roti, dal, and tea while the generator gasped in the stairwell and the darkness was pierced by candles and lanterns. "That is where you are going," said the wife, pointing to the silvery black peaks visible far up-valley under a fingernail moon. "And you don't speak a word of Hindi."

In his pack now were a sleeping bag, a mat, rain gear, Sierra cup, and the power bars. The next morning he took the trail east and up from Gangotri, past mule drivers and women bathing in the river, wrapped in saris. Ahead the mountains had massive granite corridors above the deodars and birches, and above them the high plateau of Tapovan. Half-naked sadhus with metal tridents sat beside the trail, pulling on pipes of ganja, their hair wrapped in soiled white cloths and their eyes glassy. Later he stopped for parathas and ginger tea, waiting for his lungs to adjust to the altitude. The peak of Shivling in the distance was a claw-like up-thrust with a crest of snow.

Alone now, he climbed the trail above the glacier and was soon standing on a high plateau, blowing in the rarefied air. A dwelling had been fashioned under over-hanging rock, with wood shutters and empty rice and lentil sacks spread on the stone porch. On them sat two blanketed sadhus, servants or disciples or something. A dark figure emerged from the house in a wool cap pulled down over a mass of fair hair and he watched, transfixed. This woman carried a blackened pot in one hand and a rag in the other, her blanket coat cut with holes for her elbows and red wool socks in high-topped sneakers. Cain.

At the sight of him she pressed her hands together in the traditional Hindu manner. “Clyde,” she called, “you’re getting fat.”

The sadhus brought him butter tea, rice, and dal on a metal plate, and he collapsed on the porch to eat under Cain’s bemused gaze. If she was glad to see him, she gave no sign. Neither did she seem to object, just sweeping the porch around him, fetching water, washing more wool socks and spreading them on the rocks to dry. More pilgrims with bundles and head straps arrived, mountain climbers bristling with equipment, then two western women in beads and blowzy skirts, sunburned, barefoot, bowing down to Cain Vassy and one even kissing her sneaker.

Then a party of young professionals from Delhi crowded into the little house and sat on the stone floor, clearly expecting to be fed. These, CJ learned, were advertising executives, one suffering from altitude sickness as the sun began to set, promising a bleak Himalayan night. Cain lit a candle in the adjoining cave and seemed to pray, her now gaunt frame silhouetted in the guttering light, amidst the smells incense and cooking rice.

She barked out a single order in Hindi, driving her guests back against the wall. A servile young sadhu rolled black plastic sheeting the length of the floor — this was to be the table. Soon it was crowded with tin plates full of steaming basmati, vegetables, and mugs of chai, all whipped up on a single-burner kerosene stove and a smoldering pile of charcoal. No one spoke. Afterward Cain dispersed old blankets and the young professionals disappeared beneath theirs and stretched out, shoulder-to-shoulder, cold air pouring in and the darkness soon filling with snores.

Cain stayed in her rocky nook, no room for CJ. After midnight he crawled outside and lay on the stone porch, under every bit of clothing he had brought. A southern, star-pierced sky scored by meteors seeming to fall out of neighboring Tibet. Shivling, the phallic mountain backlit by the moon, trailed clouds across broad, luminous snowfields and seemed to mock him.

At dawn Shiva's tip lit up like a light bulb and the advertising executives left, full of chai, dribbling rupees over the stone floor. The sadhus, too, departed, and only then did Cain crook a finger at CJ. He crawled in and saw, on the ledge, a framed painting of Krishna, a conch shell, a candle, and a basket of scarves.

"This is cozy," he said.

"This winter the temperature fell below zero. Ice covered the front door and after a while I started hallucinating. Spring thaw was a literal re-birth."

He touched her face and saw something new and disturbing in those remarkable eyes: blue and brown shot through with a deep reserve that hadn't been there before. "You must have gone through hell."

"It's all relative. At Sanandra I came so close to prison it terrified me. I was lucky."

She took a malla from a peg in the wall, put it around her neck, and stroked the dark wooden beads. "Prayer and chanting has helped me here. I have always craved belief of some sort, but I never knew it. Mine was a faith of will. Now I'm going to really believe up here or die trying."

She lit two incense sticks and prepared an offering: scented paraffin in a metal cup set atop a lantern, a twisted wick of cotton strands, a flame from a plastic cigarette lighter. She opened a notebook so battered it barely hung together and with a pencil stub recorded the date and something else she didn't show him. Then she took a mirror from an ancient wooden case, dipped a fingertip into a tin of sandalwood paste, and made two bright orange streaks from eyebrows to hairline.

"The color of chrysanthemums," she said. "Floating on the Ganges." He had a question, sophomoric he knew, but asked it anyway. "Life," she answered, "is for discovering who you are."

She led him out onto the porch. He left most of his gear for her and sprinkled rupees and dollars on top.

Cain said, "Tregaron Springs was lost long before you got there, I hope you know that. You couldn't have saved it even if you hadn't got caught up in the tailwind. Enough of Vassy women for you, Clyde. But you still owe Trew a lot and could help her if you would. Then, find yourself a new sort of woman and spare her the tedium of wine. Take her to the movies. Buy her a dog."

He walked toward the edge of the precipice. Far below were more pilgrims climbing to Tapovan, their colorful regalia bright in the thin light. The two sannyasins in black followed with more supplies on their frail shoulders.

CJ turned to wave, but Cain was gone.

Chapter 18

The reservoirs were full all over the valley by spring and wild mustard rioted once again, almost painfully beautiful. This was Trew's season. All winter she had stared at the pile of easels in one corner, the stretchers, brushes, cans of solvent, odds and ends, all jumbled together. The oil paints themselves were entombed in rigid tubes that required a pair of pliers to unscrew. The smells of linseed oil and turpentine rose to further chastise her for neglect as the warmth of the April sun pulled her into the vineyard every morning.

She had planned to paint a portrait of her new house, with all its uneasy accumulation of stuff, but decided the hay bales were homely. So were the shower and the privy, and even Mount St. Bartholomew towering above redwoods didn't move her. The allee of olive trees Consolidated put in to hide her rough homestead was too new. That left the mansion itself, a bit forlorn these days, the winter unkind to the new owners.

Their scheme to subdivide land on the south side into ten-acre "wine estates" for millionaires failed to pass the county board of supervisors, despite Ronnie Staunton's repeated pleas for exceptions to zoning laws. Then he threatened to pipe Tregaron's water to another county and was told this was illegal. Infuriated, Ronnie attempted the ultimate revenge, a casino. He spent an amazing amount of money courting who he was led to believe were the descendants of Wappo Native American Indians only to learn they weren't.

New York had grown tired of Ronnie's schemes and the endless problems of farming — growing grapes, labor, and unpredictable weather, wildly fluctuating costs when buying wine in bulk, a fickle market. Now the new Tregaron Springs was reputedly considering selling out to a movie director who, according to local presumption, would be an improvement over a shadowy conglomerate with headquarters on the far side of the country. Trew assumed the opposite, that the movie director would be worse than the conglomerate, with unreal dreams of playing out his family's imagined past and ostentations as yet unimagined.

Meanwhile she began to paint her childhood home, canvas after canvas capturing shadows under the deep eaves that lent it an almost living demeanor. She was thrilled by the constant intimations of forms and faces at the windows, in the doorways and surrounding shadows. The hint of life still hanging about the bit of vineyard where the Cessna had crashed. No, not faces or forms but something animate at the edge of vision that would disappear when she turned to it, only to return in an unguarded moment. She wondered if Teodoro noticed this, too.

She set up her easel most mornings now, opening the tubes of new primary colors and squeezing the paint onto her palate, then picking up a palate knife instead of the usual brush and leaning into the physical assembly of an image with both depth and shadow she couldn't achieve with a brush alone. She was building paintings now, excited by the lack of precision, the freedom. When she looked up again an hour later the light had radically changed, the old house looking sad if not deserted, the deep doorways now dark while blazing sunlight climbed the columns like fire.

Walking back to her house, equipment reloaded onto the pack frame and her new painting held aloft, she attracted as usual insects that happily got themselves stuck in the thick paint, a kind of living impasto. She looked around and saw that Teodoro was rewiring the younger vines to the cordons, an essential if tedious job that determined in advance the amount of sun the new grapes would receive, and regulating somewhat the furnace of summer that would soon arrive.

He waved. She returned it, and called out, "Teodoro, come by the house after work and bring Marta. I'm opening another old bottle."

She left her gear outside because she didn't want the smells inside today and washed her hands and face at the outdoor sink. Only then did she enter the ongoing adaptation that was home: childhood bed now a platform on which carefully folded clothes were stacked, and under which every manner of thing was stored, from metal bathtub to the heavy iron stew pot to the tatami mat on which she slept.

Her collection of Tregaron vintages had been re-racked in the far corner from the stove and three Navajo saddle throws, her grandmother's, hung in front to block heat and light, a pathetic way to store heirlooms until she could have the wine moved and properly stored. It might draw wine writers eager to taste the old stuff and then she could give them Green Buttons's new vintage.

But she had another objective. Teo would not talk about her mother unless some subterfuge led him into remembering. Talk he must, sooner or later, and she wouldn't let it rest until he did. At some point some things just had to be said.

Trew had set up this bottle, 1947, her twin since they had both born in the same year. The lees had settled, past and present to meet on the tongue. It would take guile and persistence because he was the most taciturn of men, but there must have been a link between the craft he had practiced and the love he had felt.

Marta's presence would prevent this, but Trew knew she wouldn't come. Marta disliked wine and, more importantly, she disapproved of Trew's new life, particularly the hay bales, the outdoor privy, and the hot tub fashioned from the enormous eucalyptus bole.

She heard Teodoro washing his hands at the outdoor sink. He came in tentatively, as always, and saw the bottle on the table. "What have we got there?" He looked at the label and a shadow passed behind his eyes. "You've jumped thirty-five years since our last bottle."

She carefully drew the cork and tilted the bottle, the thin blue-black stream playing first into his glass, then into her own. They sat. She held hers up to the light and said, "Great color."

"You and this bottle are the same age. You knew that didn't you? Shouldn't have opened it. Might have developed further, and it's really valuable."

"I think it's at its peak. So am I, Teodoro."

They tasted. "It's good," she said, surprised by how well the wine hung together. "But it won't be giving up its secrets easily."

"It's trying."

They sipped again. This time they swallowed together. There was a pause, both thinking. Then she took his calloused hand, still cold from the wash basin. "Father," she said, "please tell me everything you know about this wine."

ÉPILOGUE:

Craven-Jones on Wine

What is it about wine that makes of critics liars? I don't know. I came to California as a supplicant and a lover of the wine for its freshness and unpredictability. You introduced me to tortillas, blooming oleander, redwood forests and versions of cabernet sauvignon possessing uncommon freedom. I want to further explore this and other qualities in the greatest beverage on Earth, and hope you will put aside natural caution and believe me when I say I will not lie.

Wine remains the truest, and most perfidious, of beverages. Its world includes those who make, deal in it and, yes, write about it. But you, gentle drinker, who merely reads about and drinks it, need a way to grapple with its complexities and its human purveyors, and the best way to do this, I have concluded, is through ratings. Yes, numbers. They don't lie and by ranking wines, least to best, we render them serviceable. In this newsletter I will deal with Bordeaux and Burgundy, of course, and other manifestations of Vitis vinifera but my focus will be mainly on the American West Coast, a geographical entity equal in mass to much of what I call Enotopia — winemaking in the world at large. To properly judge it I will use a scale with a nadir of 0 and a pinnacle of 20.

Don't expect a wine to achieve a 20 because that is utter perfection, a near statistical impossibility but still possible, nonetheless.

Today I want to mention a new and rare wine from the Caterina Valley. It is called Green Buttons after a vineyard formerly in the possession of the Tregaron Springs estate. Green Buttons is now an independent producer vinified and bottled by another winery but under the strict guidance of its next-door neighbors. The owner of Green Buttons is Trew Vassy, of the renowned former owners of Tregaron Springs, and her winemaker is Teodoro Sepulveda, a long-time resident of that place.

Tregaron Springs itself was recently acquired by Consolidated Brands and its long list of different wines remains at best uneven. Breakaway Green Buttons, however, has achieved a stunning ascendancy with an assault that is full, rich and tannic enough to last and a complexity like an unwavering arrow carrying straight through the finish.

I have therefore assigned Green Buttons, in its first year as an independent, a score of 19. That uncommonly high ranking recognizes a signal flaw, the distinct note of mint historically detectable in fruit in this vineyard, but no longer because that massive eucalyptus tree went down in last winter's storms. Who knows what will develop now in Green Buttons's future. This new vintage heralds greatness and I predict it will outlast you and me too, Dear Reader.

Since My Baby Left Me

For brother Dan and for Chuck 'Ohio' Riggs

"I want to love you so bad."
— Leadbelly

1

On hot August nights Harmon Brown would sometimes turn off the lights in the snack bar and stand outside for awhile, listening to tree frogs shriek on the edges of Memphis's finest golf course. Then he would walk home to Orange Mound, his shiny work shoes under his arm. On this fine evening in the middle of the century, a time that had once seemed impossibly distant to him, he considered taking off his red jacket and bowtie a few minutes early. Then he saw Tuke Harrington come up from playing poker in the locker room and knew his work wasn't done.

A big man, Mister Harrington hadn't the habit of concealing his feelings, and everything about him said that his life had gone wrong: the set of his jaw, his golfing shirt half out of his trousers, damp with perspiration, the way he hauled a chair to the edge of the pool. He told Harmon, "Bring me a Jack Daniels."

"Pool's closed, Mr. Harrington."

"Don't you think I know that?"

Harmon stepped into the cabana and took a deeply faceted whiskey glass from the tray and dragged it through the bowl of melting ice. He opened the familiar heavy bottle and carefully poured for one of the city's best lawyers and a personal friend of the mayor's, placed the glass on a silver tray, and carried it outside. He carried it all the way around the pool railing and, bending slightly at the waist, presented it as he had been taught to do.

Tuke Harrington took the glass in a muscular hand and, before Harmon could get the receipt book in his back pocket open, had drained it. He then did something Harmon Brown had never seen anyone do: he tossed the glass into the swimming pool.

Both men stared as it sank and rested there, under four feet of green, luminous water.

"Harmon," said Mr. Harrington, "I'm having a drink. Why don't I feel good?"

Harmon wasn't expected to answer, although he had definite ideas about why Mr. Harrington didn't feel good, one of them being that he was carrying on with the wife of Mister Wallace. That very afternoon the two men had gotten into an argument over cards and Mr. Wallace had gone after Mr. Harrington like a sleepy bull. Mr. Wallace was lucky it was just his golfing pants that got torn, since Mr. Harrington was a former football player and both big and quick for a white man. The pants ended up in the trash bin, and Mr. Wallace had gone home in his tennis shorts.

Harmon was sent back for another whiskey. Mr. Harrington drank that one, and two more, and tossed those glasses, too, into the pool. With each splash Harmon's solemnity deepened. It was late. He had heard the high fidelity system die inside the club but he waited until Mr. Harrington finally stood and said good night and walked unsteadily but with command out to the parking lot. Harmon watched him get into that Cadillac and pilot it slowly between iron gates.

Still holding his tray, Harmon switched off the pool lights but could still make out the glasses. "Some child could hurt his self," he said aloud. After the war he had sat in the narrow alley between the golf pro shop and the tennis court hedge, pitching pennies until he was called out into the sunlight to heave a big padded bag onto his shoulder and set off across that blindingly green fairway. The money had been good, but spotty. Working on the grounds crew had been better, but being a waiter was better yet.

In summer he carried malteds and club sandwiches and tried to anticipate the demands of members; sometimes he had to pause and think about how to handle a situation. People drank too much gin and went to sleep in the afternoon sun, and Harmon had to haul over an umbrella, careful not to make too much of it. He had to correct children who ran on slick tiles, mindful of the limits of his authority. Now Harmon had four of Tuke Harrington's signatures in his receipt book, each less legible than the last, and four high-ball glasses on the bottom of the pool.

In the soft, insistent drone of the night insects he made what seemed to him an unavoidable decision.

Harmon went down to the basement and passed through the empty changing room to the cubicle in the back and hung his jacket on the steam pipe, thinking of kids who threw themselves into the pool every morning, crazed by the water; they would stay there until their teeth chattered and women in bright suits would order them out. Harmon had to laugh at the thought of children running around like pink monkeys with blue lips, in August.

When he emerged into the darkness he was wearing Mr. Wallace's discarded yellow golfing pants, rolled up, voluminous on Harmon who was aware of his bony rib cage, his knees like hickory boles. He sensed the residue of the sun in the slabs of Ozark slate beneath his bare feet. In all his years at the club he had never felt the flagstones with anything but the soles of his shoes; he had never touched the water that caressed him like cool guilt, covering his knees, then his thighs as he felt along the bottom with his feet for splinters of glass.

He found a whole glass, sitting upright, gripped the rim with his toes and carefully raised it. He poured out water purged of every conceivable germ by the heavy doses of chlorine from fifty-pound bags, the process done with great solemnity, the lifeguards like preachers, pale versions of the man who had baptized Harmon in a stock pond in Mississippi so many years before. Then Harmon had feared not being let up in time to breathe and passing directly from being blessed by God to living with Him.

He set the glass on the side of the pool and retrieved another. There were four lined up when he heard the footsteps. Hoping the person would pass by on the far side of the gate, he recognized the ring of Mr. Quinn's heel taps.

"Who's that in the pool?" Mr. Quinn loudly asked.

Harmon said reluctantly, "Me."

"What in God's name..."

"There's a bunch of glasses in here, Mr. Quinn. Mr. Harrington was having himself some drinks and..."

"Are you crazy?"

"No, sir."

Mr. Quinn's wife had long, thin legs and talked too loudly; at least once she sneaked down to the pump room with a lifeguard at night, when the pool was being refilled for the weekend and the noise of the pumps covered the sounds she made. But Harmon had heard it all, leaning on his mop handle behind the snack shop.

"I can't believe this, Harmon. They've just changed the water!"

"Yes, sir."

Mr. Quinn whined: "A swimming nigra. At the club. Now I've seen everything."

"I ain't swimming."

"What do you think you're doing, lame brain?"

"Standin.'"

"Don't get smart with me."

The water felt suddenly cold. "Some of them glasses might have broke," he said.

"I don't care, you're not supposed to be in there. Git git git. And you tell a soul about this, Harmon, and you won't even get a reference."

"What do I need a reference for?"

"You're fired, that's what. And I don't want to see you around here again, you hear me? Get somebody to pick up your check for you."

Mr. Quinn stalked off, taps striking stone.

Harmon emerged streaming from the pool, retrieved his tray, loaded up the glasses and, holding the golfing pants in one hand so they wouldn't fall down, carried the tray to the snack bar. He left it on the table, along with his receipt book.

In the basement, he took off the pants and put them back into the trash. He didn't want to be accused of theft, too. He stood for several minutes in the darkness while his body dried, then dressed and put on his street shoes and headed home.

2

Tuke Harrington awoke the next morning to merciless light reflected from the leaves of the oaks, the air-conditioner providing a feeble stream slightly cooler than the outside air, smelling faintly of mildew. In its draft his wife had once sat brushing her hair and talking on the telephone, and it had never occurred to him then that he might someday yearn for such an ordinary sight, his tongue thick from yesterday's drinking and his mind full of his dimly recalled transgressions.

In there among them was a naked woman who was not his late wife but whose body was familiar, and today the thought of her drove him, like a desert wanderer, from bed to bathroom, where he groped for the water tap, thinking that her husband would be at eleven o'clock service at St. John's Episcopal and she alone in her bedroom.

Tuke stepped almost daintily into the shower and pressed his increasingly sparse hair, still sand-colored, against the tiles while the spray engulfed it. Water ran off a body that had retained the contours of a man not too long past his prime: muscular calves, discernible hips and abdominals, veins in a forearm with a white shackle where his golf glove bit. He toweled off and put on the silk robe bought by Lois, shortly before she died, one of the first allowed in from Japan after the war.

He started down the broad steps of his large Tudor house, then sat abruptly, calling out, "Carlin!"

Her solid presence was already rooted in the hall below: white uniform, dark, capable arms folded, the upward tilt of her broad, handsome face in no way sympathetic. "Carlin," Tuke said, "bring me a little something."

He waited, one hand on the banister, gazing out at the park-like lawn, until Carlin reappeared with a glass containing the important elements, the most important being vodka. He drank slowly but steadily and set the glass on a stair.

There was a shift, a softening about the edges of the settee, the window mullions that always reminded him of a monastery, the flowing drapes. His mouth burned with the residue of Louisiana peppers in brine, and he closed his eyes, grateful for something on a hot day: he was alive, if unloved.

He went on down the stairs and into the kitchen, determined not to be unduly bothered by the hangover. The disarray of the *Commercial Appeal* on the breakfast table told him that Carlin, back at the stove, had been kept waiting too long for him to wake up.

Tuke said, "A little slow today."

"You go any slower you'll be walkin' backwards."

The newspaper told him only what he already knew: It was another Sunday in August, 1954. Our boys were coming home from Korea without victory; the United States Senate was chasing Communists among the Presbyterian clergy; President Eisenhower had played another mediocre round of golf up at Gettysburg. And, yes, everybody was making money.

Outside, the glare of a formidable sun had shifted to the burnished flanks of his car, and on impulse he walked on out the kitchen door. Mossy bricks pressed against the soles of his feet as he crossed the patio to the Cadillac.

He got in and surveyed the chrome-ringed dials, the ashtray, cantilevered graveyard for a cigarette butt ringed with red lipstick left there by Onie Gay Wallace on her brief ride to the club with Tuke. Encapsulated in three thousand dollars' worth of Detroit's finest steel and E-Z-Eye glass, the Signal-Seeking radio transmitting disembodied voices of race musicians before he switched it off. A hint of perfume lingered in the pearl-gray upholstery; the keys were still in the ignition.

Tuke fired up the engine, reversed, and rolled down the driveway. A man could drive his own Cadillac in his bathrobe on a Sunday if he felt like it. He realized too late that he should have brought a Bloody Mary with him. Other big houses drowsed in their lairs of trees and flowering shrubs, everything bright and metallic under the sun, no one to see him in this broad, church-emptied, lawn-smitten land.

The proximity of the Wallace house was both a convenience, and a problem. Some nights Tuke thought of Onie Gay making a Manhattan for her husband and serving it to him in their sunken living room, then turning the pages of a magazine, wetting the tip of her finger with her tongue each time. Tuke would be drinking his Jack Daniels in his own living room with the diamond-shaped windows, alone, and sometimes he would go and get into the car and drive with the heavy crystal whiskey glass between muscular thighs that had out-distanced Alabama and Georgia Tech linebackers not so many years before. He would get out and stand amidst the Wallaces' azaleas, looking in, and wonder what had brought him to this place at this time in his life.

Now he turned into their driveway. Her husband's car was gone, and Tuke parked behind the box hedge and got out. The gravel hurt his feet but he persevered, entering the house by way of the kitchen where another large black woman in white looked up from the sink. Tuke said, "'Morning, Willie."

"'Mornin', Mistah Harrington."

"Mr. Wallace here?"

"No, sir. Gone to church."

"Well now."

Tuke pushed his hands into the pockets of his robe. "Miz Wallace upstairs?"

"Yes, sir," she said, barely audible.

He nodded and cleared his throat and with deliberation walked into the hall. Bronze sconces above the stairs, polished brass rods on each step, holding the runner in place, and at the top a portrait of Onie Gay in a riding habit, displaying Memphis's accomplished orthodontia. He climbed noiselessly and turned toward the bedroom, where he could hear her humming, imagining her show of delight and misgiving when she discovered him. Tuke had decided not to speak, he would simply kiss her and retreat and later they would both laugh at his audacity.

She sat at the vanity, her back to him, in her nightgown. Bright auburn hair hung about her shoulders as she stared into her own unadorned eyes, the skin about them whiter than he remembered. Tuke whispered, "Hi."

The reflected eyes grew large. "Tuke!"

He stepped quickly forward and kissed her on the lips, tasting toothpaste, and ran hands lightly over her breasts. But instead of leaving as planned, he knelt next to her, lifted the nightgown past proof that her hair was indeed dyed, and took into his mouth first one thumb-sized nipple and then the other.

"Tuke, this is unwise."

Her accessibility, like her placid acceptance of her role as someone else's wife, made him that way. He had no obligations to Onie Gay, or she to him, but he yearned for a show of sentiment now and then. He sat on the edge of the un-made bed, opened his robe, and urged her on top of him. She hesitated, then spread her legs accommodatingly even as she said, in that melodic, twangy east Tennessee voice, "Oh, Tuke."

A blush appeared at the base of her strong, well-formed neck and spread upward over fine bone structure. Tuke held her waist. She descended further and canted her hips the way she did, listening for footsteps. Respectable people did not do so abruptly on Sunday, in front of God and each other, what then transpired in the moil of sheer cotton and Japanese silk.

From far away came an unintelligible voice, and Onie Gay, without missing a stroke, called, "What is it, Willie?"

"Mistah Wallace, he..."

Tuke was up and out, gathering his robe around him, incommoded by the reluctance of the most significant part of him to forego the most important activity. Willie stood at the foot of the stairs, eyes wide, and he passed her, nodding, a show of dignity, and walked to the front door, aware that one of Memphis's noted attorneys, a former football star, should not be emerging from another man's house, barefoot and in his bathrobe, on the Sabbath while that man's wife was upstairs and the man himself coming in through the kitchen.

Buff's Oldsmobile sat in the carport. Tuke re-crossed the driveway but before he could get the Cadillac's door open he heard shoes on gravel and saw Buff Wallace in a seersucker jacket with half-moons of perspiration under the arms, tie undone, holding a side-by-side shotgun. Tuke knew that gun: a Fox, inherited from Buff's grandfather, which contained nothing heavier than number eight shot for dove-shooting, if it contained any shells at all. It was used once a year at the outset of hunting season. This made Tuke think of Billy Covington, who had died of cancer after telling Tuke and others in the boundless expectation of opening day of dove hunting that he wanted to be cremated and his ashes put into a shotgun. Tuke was to fire it at a dove. "And don't you miss," Billy had said.

Tuke felt assailed by sadness, not for Billy Covington but for Tuke's own dead wife, Lois, seeing in his mind the cranks at the foot of her bed, the tubes, and hearing again the Cumberland accents of her relatives, their distress amplified by long-distance.

Tuke made a vague if uncompromising gesture in Buff's direction and was turning toward his Cadillac when a gale struck him from behind. The glossy painted surface of the door dimpled and deformed, giving back the dull gleam of exposed metal. Only then did he hear the shot. Twisting toward his scalded backside, he saw bright, precise ovals of blood freckling silk, and he called out, "Goddamn it, Buff, you just ruined this robe!"

3

Harmon Brown boarded the Southern Avenue bus early Monday morning while it labored west, sucking electricity from overhead cables, air coming in through the open windows full of the smells of crabgrass and asphalt softening in the early sunlight. He fell asleep and awoke to find the bus full of people, the white women all up front in blousy dresses, going shopping, and the men in their straw hats, jackets draped over the backs of the seats.

At the turn-around Harmon got off and walked toward the river. Beale Street Baptist Church stood in a welter of clapboard houses at the corner of Hernando. He started to buy a Dr. Pepper from the vendor, dipped from the haze of dry ice in his battered cooler, but decided to wait. The sun reflected off the Daisy Theater's pale yellow facade, and beyond it lay the juice shops and jive joints, the eateries — Johnny's, the Green Castle — not yet awake.

The tamale wagon waited outside the Club Handy. In the glass case under the marquee were photographs of a singer with teeth like a string of pearls above a white bow tie, known as B.B, whose music didn't touch Harmon. He paused under three tarnished brass balls and took notice of the snare sets, saxophones, and old low-end Stellas imprisoned in the pawn shop window. Harmon could not look at a guitar without imagining it in his hands; he could hear the keening of his fingertips on wrapped steel, could feel the calluses, translucent scales on the only pink part of him that had come off like onionskin when he quit playing.

Two women sat smoking in the cafe next door, elbows on the table. One had her hair up in a bandanna, the way his woman had once worn hers. Eyebrows arched, lips parted, she lowered her lids against the drifting smoke. He was reminded of the nights in the Elks Club when he had played for hours in high-waisted, baggy trousers with knife-edge creases and cribbed his cigarette in a clothespin taped to the neck of his guitar.

The big names all came to Beale then. The high-tone girl running the house on the corner of Second made chili for them and they played harmonica, mandolin, guitar, into the dawn. Harmon remembered amateur night at the Palace, the house-rent parties, the most famous bluesman passing through town in a pair of shoes with the sides cut out, like a field hand's — Robert Johnson, a legend. He remembered the walking bass, the gut bucket and the boogie-woogie piano and dice games at the back of Peewee's pool hall.

Through the open door of Schwab's he could see racks of plastic collars, hair clips, mojo candles and drawing oils. There he turned south by force of habit and worked his way through narrow streets set about with shotgun houses, long and narrow. On the familiar stoop stood two empty white port bottles and inside the house Leadbelly stoked a radio.

He knocked. Out of the shadows stepped a woman in a sack dress, all angles. Harmon said, "Hey Artice."

"Harmon!"

"How you been?"

"Fine, just fine. Lord."

"'Simmon around?"

She nodded, and he entered and crossed the room to the shirtless figure sitting on a mattress, sweat glistening on the rolls of his stomach. 'Simmon said, "Harmon Brown?" in that high-pitched, gleeful voice of his, and Harmon took the blind man's hand and looked down into milky, rolled-back eyes. "Hey 'Simmon."

"Sit yo ass down. How you been?"

"Fine, just fine. You doin' any good?"

"No good a'tall. Artice, bring this man some port. Bring me some port."

"It's morning, 'Simmon."

"Morning's the best time."

Artice brought the white port bottle, holding it as if it might bite her. Harmon declined, and she asked him, "You still totin' gin for white folks, Harmon?"

'Simmon said, "Now now, white folks needs they gin, Artice. What you doin' downtown?"

"Taking the day off."

"Ain't we all?"

Persimmon Smoot and the Boys had been known on Beale, 'Simmon playing the twelve-string and Harmon backing him on his Gibson. Some people had said Harmon was the better of the two, but when 'Simmon got going his hand looked like a big garden spider on a bucket of flies.

"Any work?" Harmon asked, but he didn't even have a guitar now.

"Them days are still gone, Harmon."

Claudet, Harmon's woman, had seen it coming. She and he had argued about this as the money grew scarcer, other musicians getting the work. He had given up playing one day, clean, and taken a day job "toting golf sticks for white men," as Claudet had put it. He had managed to save some money to put down on a house in Orange Mound, worth next to nothing and far from Beale, and Claudet never forgave him.

The fights had been rough after that. He still recalled the only time he hit her, and holding her down on the stove, coffee slopped all over and the gas flame scorching Harmon's fingers, the acrid smell of her burning hair a torment to him now.

"'Simmon," he said, "let's hear it."

"Ain't up to it."

"Yeah, you is," said Artice.

Harmon fetched the guitar and placed it across 'Simmon's knees. "Don' think so," 'Simmon said, strumming. "Nobody wants to hear a blind man bangin' on a box." He fiddled with the cranks and strummed again. "*Nobody wants'a hear an old man sing.*"

"Oh, yeah," said Harmon.

"*Ain' nobody carin' 'bout the way that it was.*"

He moaned a while, the saddest way, then played some Johnson. No matter that his voice was squeaky, it was real, but he always changed the lyrics, including those Harmon wrote, and made them dirty. Those girls in white net stockings used to howl, but many of 'Simmon's songs had bothered proprietors even on the street and couldn't be recorded. Harmon could have changed that, he could have closed his eyes and opened his own mouth and used his own God-given voice, but just the thought of it still made him sweat.

In the mirror he saw a ghost of a man stumbling over memories. He had been known on the street and he wanted all that again so strongly. At the country club he had no past, but somewhere on Beale they must need an experienced guitar player who knew the old style, without the hollering and the heavy beat, who could let the sound and the words lie flat on the world, making strong what had been weak and confused.

Harmon had written about back roads and clapboard shacks:

Git out of them fields.
Right here's where we belong...

'Simmon was singing, "*I've got a woman that I'm lovin'...*" and when he was done Harmon asked, "What happened?"

'Simmon stopped turned his face up to his friend, mottled eyes hinting at the rich unseen world of people and dreams bearing no resemblance to the ones on Beale today. "Ain't nothin' we did. The music changed, is all. Got all loud and electric. The blues, ain't nothing blue about them now."

"We just got old. But so did others. Ole Furry Lewis's trying for a come-back."

"You two ain't Furry," said Artice, "and he's sweepin' streets."

Claudet had seen it coming and slipped away. It was as if she and Harmon's guitar were bound up together, and his talent went out the door with her. Harmon now saw not a beautiful light-skinned woman but an aging blind man drinking knotty-head port under a window scored by crazy wash lines.

He headed north on Main, past the Green Beetle, toward the stores, keeping to the morning shadows thrown by boxy buildings. Another black man sat inside an open elevator, waiting for riders, his feet extended into the narrow foyer and a newspaper on his lap. The worn uniform jacket, open at the neck, exposed his undershirt. That was one job Harmon wouldn't have, he told himself, hauling people up and down in a box, going nowhere. Truth was he'd take anything he could find.

He wanted water but there was no colored drinking fountain on south Main. He calculated how bad it would be by the time he found one. The bigger problem was relieving himself, one he had dealt with all his life, knowing that the charge of public exposure could send a black man away.

Water ran in the fountain in Court Square, over little naked children made of concrete, all white. The magnolia leaves behind it looked black in the sunlight. Harmon crossed the street and went into Kress's variety store, the aisles of goods — candy, greeting cards, hats, underwear — stretching before him. He could have gone to Schwab's on Beale for a drink but didn't want to see the guitars again in the pawn shop windows. He had once made a kind of guitar out of an old radio case and an ax handle, using baling wire for frets. He had played it with a bottle neck.

Later, he got so good on his uncle's old Stella that people said Harmon had been to the crossroads, that old tale of a man appearing at midnight and taking your instrument and tuning it, and after that nothing you played could sound bad. But if you showed your face while playing then they could see the Devil in your eyes.

He was very thirsty now. The store was empty except for him and two white girls, one hanging day dresses across the aisles and the other behind the lunch counter, smoking on a slow morning at end of summer, few cars ploughing Main Street, too late for breakfast and too early for lunch.

Harmon walked over and stood at the end of the counter, near the nuts display. The girl's pale green uniform dispersed the light from the show window. Her butt was hard against the cold box, her hair up in a net, and she tilted her head back and blew smoke rings that disintegrated in the fan's down-draught.

Harmon said, "Missy."

She looked at him, not rude but without whatever it is that makes a person recognize another. Harmon had never understood how that worked, how he could blend with different landscapes so utterly that white people did not see him until they wanted to or were forced to.

She asked, "What you want?"

"Could you sell me a Doctor Pepper, please?"

"Colored section's closed."

"I could take it outside."

"We don't serve you this side of the railing."

She lit another cigarette and went back to washing dishes. She lined them up on a folded dish towel while Harmon listened to the hum of the overhead fan and a few cars rolling past on Main. You didn't blow your horn in Memphis, you didn't disturb folks.

Harmon without warning even to himself slipped onto a stool in the white section. The girl looked up, her hands in the soapy water. She had pale blue eyes and a high, shiny forehead and her thin lips held the cigarette with difficulty.

She came slowly erect. Harmon took out a quarter and placed it on the counter, his hand trembling. "I want a Dr. Pepper," he said. "Please."

She started to remove the cigarette, but her hands were wet and the towel too far to reach. She couldn't take her eyes from Harmon, his elbows resting on the counter, his heart beating against his ribcage. She hissed, "You git off of that stool."

He stayed put, and she looked across the room, steadying herself on the lip of the sink. Harmon thought she just might serve him, so he could go on his way, but she just closed her eyes and slid limply to the floor.

He said, "Aw, shit."

The other girl back at the register was bent over her magazine. Harmon could just walk out, but the one who had fainted might have hurt herself. The cigarette might be burning her. It was even more risky but he had to make sure and he got off the stool and stepped behind the counter.

The girl lay on the slats, skirt above her knees, her hairless legs pale, blue-veined. He knelt, careful not to touch her. "Wake up, missy."

Her lids rolled back and she took in the fan, the griddle, and only then Harmon. Her face twisted and she clawed her way backwards, along the cold box. Harmon pleaded, "Please don't, missy," but she screamed anyway.

4

Tuke crossed Court Square and walked into the Tennessee Club. Boss sat with his back to the square in an ill-fitting linen suit, in the company of two other men. The Tennessee Club was the antithesis of the Memphis Country Club, being downtown and without a golf course, strictly for business, politics, cards. It was full of people Tuke would not have dreamed of inviting to the country club. One exception was Boss, the most influential man in Memphis, not at all the same thing as being socially acceptable, but Boss would not have accepted anyway.

Boss had once been capable of delivering the biggest block of popular votes in Tennessee, but that influence was waning. Now he ran his machine with almost mechanical predictability, fueled with money raked off pleasurable, legitimate activities and with insurance premiums sold to anyone in Memphis who wanted a permit. Any permit.

Tuke reached across the table for Boss's brittle fingers, feeling the bandage on his backside pull.

"Tuke." The old man kept one liver-spotted hand on the tumbler of iced tea that had soaked the napkin to transparency.

"Morning, Tuke," said another of the men, Cooper Paine, Tuke's friend and the district attorney, as portly as Boss was lean. The fourth member of the luncheon party was Skip Blanding, editor of the *Commercial Appeal* and probably the fourth most influential man in Memphis. Skip just nodded, his gray seersucker bought off the rack at Alfred's.

They all consulted the mimeographed sheet of daily specials: tomato aspic, fried chicken, Jello. "Well, now," said Boss, after they had ordered. "Ain't this a mess?"

"An unusual accident," Cooper conceded. No one needed to be specific: they were talking about Tuke's getting shot.

"I'm wondering why this has to amount to anything a'tall," Boss said.

"Because it happened," said the editor, adjusting spectacles with thick, square lenses into which little gold screws had been set.

"Things happen all the time that're no one's fault," Boss said. "These didn't necessarily have to be reported on and spread over newsprint, where they take on an unnatural significance."

Tuke said only, "Pass the lemon, please."

"It did happen," Boss continued, in what was in fact a north Mississippi accent, not west Tennessee. He had been born in Atcho, a long time ago. "Does that mean a little squabble has to be in the newspaper?"

Skip said. "It should have already been in."

The aspic arrived, topped with a generous dollop of mayonnaise. It occurred to Tuke that maybe Memphians behaved so unpredictably because they all suffered from mayonnaise poisoning. The aspic wiggled as the men went after it with their silver-plated spoons.

"Surely not on the front page," said Boss, "since no charges were filed."

"No."

"But where?"

"Where I decide."

"We wouldn't want it any other way," Boss said.

Tuke looked down into Court Square. The leaves of the big magnolias shined, throwing deep shade. The bandstand was empty. A bus glided silently up Main, the passengers looking out the window at some altercation outside Kress's involving the police. The long summer had exhausted the city, making people edgy.

"I suppose," Skip said, "it could appear on the society page." And to Tuke, "You Harringtons have certainly been on that page enough, what with Lois's worthy activities."

The mention of Tuke's wife caught him unprepared. He felt her memory sullied by association, and he sat with his mouth full of chicken, staring at white linen.

"God bless her," said Cooper.

That was the end of it. They talked soybeans and the pursuit of Communists in Washington, and then Skip Blanding said, "I've got a newspaper to put out," and Cooper said, "I've got loan sharks to prosecute," and they both dumped their big napkins into their chairs, shook hands all round, and went out past waiters guarding the water stations.

Tuke and Boss sat while others in the room looked at them, aware of some transaction, and curious. "What's happened to you, Tuke?" Boss asked, peering at him from behind hazy glasses, too cheap to buy new ones and he owned Memphis. "You could'a been mayor, Tuke. You should be about to announce you're running for Congress, not Cooper Paine. You could'a been a goddamn senator what with your family name and football history."

Tuke had once considered it before he started to make serious money. The thrill of that, in the war's aftermath, and the ease of it transcended all else.

"Sometimes men's wives die, Tuke. You got to get a handle on it. She was a wonderful person, and she's gone. Find a woman who's not married. You can't let something like this happen again, not and stay in Memphis you can't."

Tuke didn't go directly back to the office but walked down Court Street to Front, his jacket slung over his shoulder. The river looked tired, an immense tan ribbon ironed flat by the weight of the sky, threading the brackets of the Hanrahan Bridge linking Tennessee and Arkansas. He tried to imagine Indians signaling with ritual fires here on the bluffs. The river had always felt alien to the city's strict ways, though there had been ruffians in the far past, and whiskey in casks from which his family had prospered before Memphis's remarkably brief resistance during the War of Northern Aggression.

Big iron rings were secured by bolts that had been driven into the river bank, to hold the paddle-wheelers. The rings had shed rust in scales. The *Memphis Queen* still berthed here, but the other vessels were gone. Memphis had become the quietest city in the country, prosperous, undisturbed, its face turned toward the yawning eastern suburbs and away from the warehouses and the old Cotton Exchange, away from Confederate Park with its Howitzers left over from the First World War, away from Mud Island like a sedimentary creature adrift in inexhaustible brown water.

He could see President's Island to the south, the last bit of land on the Tennessee side before the wilds of Mississippi. Presidents deserved islands in their names. Tuke's president had been a tall, pale soldier who defeated Hitler and inspired the little general's jackets in fashion. The photo of Eisenhower standing in his white Eldorado convertible reaffirmed the necessity of men of a certain age who represented the standards.

Tuke had seen no action in the war. Although too old for the draft he had insisted upon volunteering, and gone in as a lieutenant for little more than a year spent in the Pacific, doing paperwork on a carrier. He knew he was on a boat when the whiskey ever so slightly climbed the sides of the admiral's decanters as the carrier shifted. Once Tuke had ridden in a PT boat along a blasted white coast, the sun illuminating as if in a dream little naked Japanese soldiers standing on rocks in surrender.

Talk of war experiences now drove him to haul out, over cocktails, the samurai sword and the orange sun on tattered cloth, proving nothing but the fact that he had been close to the action. A man should rise to an occasion but there were so many. The trick was determining which occasion deserved rising to and then deciding.

Tuke read the story in the newspaper the next morning without much interest, under the headline: *Shotgun Mishap Disturbs Sabbath Calm*. It didn't mention his wearing a bathrobe, for which he assumed he should be grateful, and it made Buff Wallace sound like a fool, which he was. The ringing of the telephone disturbed the morning ritual and he got up to answer.

"Seen the paper?" asked Cooper Paine, who he had just had lunch with the day before and so didn't need to again anytime soon. "I don't mean the story about Buff shooting you in the ass, I mean the one about Kresse's."

"No, why?"

"Because we've got ourselves a rapist problem."

"Come again."

"Just read it."

Tuke took the wall phone back to the table, stretching the cord, aware of Carlin's broad back at the stove. He opened the paper to *Negro Charged in Variety Store Incident* marshaled over a one-column story in the lower right hand corner of the front page. The victim of the assault was identified only as a 27-year-old white female employee of Kress's. He then read the name of the perpetrator. "Can't be," he said.

"Can too," said Cooper. "It's our Harmon, all right. We got to minimize the damage to the club and do it now. Turns out Quinn fired Harmon for some reason at closing time Saturday, so at least we can say Harmon was a former employee."

Had Harmon Brown been fired for serving him drinks after hours? Had Harmon actually tried to rape somebody behind a lunch counter? He asked, "What do you want?"

"Make this disappear."

Tuke hung up and called Billy Quinn, the club manager, assuming his lawyer's voice. "Billy, Tuke Harrington. How come you let Harmon Brown go?"

"He took liberties."

Tuke thought of a potential felon serving Manhattans and crackers in cellophane with little butter pats stamped with the club's initials. "Like what?"

"He went swimming."

Tuke opened his mouth but didn't know what to say, so he hung up. Carlin asked, without turning from the newspaper, "What's a grand jury?"

"A collection of citizens that decides whether or not a crime's been committed."

"And what's a arraignment?"

"Formal charges made in front of a judge. Everybody gets his time in court, no matter who he is or what he's done."

"What if he ain't done nothing?"

"He can plead not guilty."

She moved stony-faced to the table and set the eggs and grits down harder than usual.

"If he didn't really do anything the judge might reduce his sentence to a few years at the Penal Farm. The police don't make these things up," he added, knowing full well that they did.

The county jail and courthouse shared a classical sandstone facade with a Roman soldier gazing down, lamps with spiny brass crowns, and heavy brass doors that swung inward. Prisoners were brought over from the police station across Second Street and bound over to the state for serious offenses. Tuke had often seen them in cuffs.

Inside the courthouse it was dank, the wooden floors scarred with cigarette burns. Dust had collected in the etched letters of the names of functionaries and the closed doors of the courtrooms needed shellac.

He went on through to the county jail where a short, thick-set man in shirt sleeves sat, his pistol in an old leather holster molded to the cylinder's hard edges. Tuke told him, "I'd like to see this Harmon Brown."

"You a lawyer?"

"Yes."

"Well, he told Judge Jones he didn't do it." The deputy's name plate said Tiller. "But this grand jury indicts faster than it takes a penny to drop in that weighing machine out there."

"Did he hurt the girl, officer?"

"Not so's you'd notice." And he pointed Tuke toward the stairs.

When court was in session defendants were brought down, Negroes from the second floor, whites from the third. Tuke climbed to a narrow door set with a rusty metal grate. The room beyond contained two wooden chairs and a table, and there he sat to wait.

5

Harmon smelled baked beans and gravy poured over white bread served on tin plates that passed him by. They had battered edges engraved with the words, *Shelby County*. The white inmates got fed first and then the kitchen help brought down what was left. Harmon stood against the bars as far from the bucket in the corner as he could get while the other prisoners filed past, punks and hooch-heads from back of Beale and some real rough boys going to lunch.

They looked in but didn't say anything. Harmon was a curiosity, picked up on Main. What he remembered was turning his head as the blackjack struck, in the back seat of the cruiser. The police had dug an elbow into Harmon's stomach while the other watched in the mirror.

They had taken him to the alley that ran between Fire Engine House No. 1 and the police station. The policeman's cap had been held in place by a little black strap that barely found purchase on his chin. Silver whistle, badge, black belt with silver buttons and a revolver nosed into the holster. Harmon had felt the warm line of blood down the side of his face and seen the tracks on his shirt.

Beyond, black arms trailed in the open air and black faces mashed against the bars, watching. The door of the cruiser had opened and the other police leaned in and hit Harmon in the face with a billy club. The sun went out, Harmon twisting his body away, pushing his face into the seat, but it was no use.

His cell was windowless. The door at the end of the corridor opened and three men entered — two white guards and the black trusty, Dink, who waddled as he walked. He carried Harmon's plate in one huge hand

and pushed it through the slot in the bars.

Harmon set the plate on the bunk. Dink waddled off, and the big guard said, “Guess he ain’t hungry. I guess chasing white women makes ‘em forget how to eat.”

“Makes ‘em dead,” said the other.

Mr. Harrington sat with his polished penny loafers on the table, looking at Harmon as if he didn’t recognize this man with the lacerated lip and eye swollen shut. He asked Harmon, “What the hell have you gotten yourself into?”

Harmon didn’t answer, humiliated by prison issue that hung on him like drapery and the fact that his feet were bare.

”You shouldn’t give the police a hard time, Harmon. You know they won’t stand for it.”

“I didn’t give them nothing, Mr. Harrington. But I wouldn’t say I done it. They tried to make me write it out, say I was after that gal, but I wouldn’t.”

“Tell me exactly what happened.”

“I ain’t touched her after she went and swooned behind that counter. I went back to help her and she woke up and started screaming.”

“Why did they say you tried to rape her?”

“Because they got to say something after beating on me like that. Somebody should talk to that white gal, Mr. Harrington.”

“Tell this to your attorney, Harmon.”

“Ain’t got no attorney. And I ain’t taking no Vance Avenue funeral parlor lawyer, either.” Harmon gingerly touched his temple. “My head feels like a sack of walnuts.”

“I’ll see what I can do. Meanwhile, Harmon, don’t... *do* anything.”

The police named Tiller came in, and Mr. Harrington asked, “Did this man resist arrest, deputy?”

"You could say that."

"I'd like to know why he doesn't have any shoes."

"He might use the laces to hang hisself."

"Can't somebody take the laces out so he can have something on his feet?"

"We don't spend a whole lot of time pulling laces out of colored boys' shoes."

Mr. Harrington thought about that. "Well, I'd like some more time with him."

Tiller went out again and Harmon glimpsed black faces at the cell bars. The other prisoners knew about Harmon having no shoes, just as they knew about the charge against him, but what they talked about was Harmon refusing to eat.

"Did you sit at the counter, Harmon?"

"Yes sir. In the white section because I couldn't in the colored one."

Mr. Harrington closed his eyes. "Good God," he said. "So you tried to integrate Kress's?"

"I didn't. I was just trying to git a drink. I was thirsty."

Mr. Harrington dropped his feet to the floor. "The district attorney might be willing to reduce the charge to assault if you'll go along. That means some time at the Farm but nothing like what you'll get otherwise."

"I ain't assaulted nobody."

"So you want to go with a trial? Do you know what that'll mean, in Memphis?"

"Can't see no way around it."

"I'm offering you a way."

"Mr. Harrington, after what they done to me I'd go to hell before I'd go along. Does all this mean you're my lawyer?"

That afternoon the little deputy with squinty eyes came to Harmon's cell with another police holding Harmon's shoes.

"I do believe he's barefoot," said the little one.

"Why don't I give him some shoes?"

"Did you *polish* 'em?"

"I plumb forgot," said the big one. "And he's got important people coming round."

"A *attorney*."

They both laughed and the big one pushed Harmon's shoes through and dropped them to the floor. When Harmon went to pick them up the little one raked a nightstick across the bars. "Better not think," he said, lips pulled back from tobacco-stained teeth, "that some rich man's gonna save your black ass."

Tuke caught up with Cooper Paine outside his office. "Harmon said he didn't do it. He said the girl fell down behind the counter. Fainted, I guess. And he went to help her. Maybe she got confused. Maybe the police were a shade too quick on the draw, as they have been known to be. Maybe they figured Harmon was out of line, and maybe he was, and beat the be-jesus out of him. Then they had to charge him to justify it."

"Got it all worked out?"

"This kind of screw-up could happen any time," said Tuke. "It's just too bad it's Harmon and that it got into the paper. Maybe the city ought to drop the charge. Call it a mistake, something, but not attempted rape."

"Do you think the state would impugn two police officers and a young white woman on the word of a black man?"

"I don't think Harmon tried to do a thing to that girl."

"Well, I've read her statement."

"Would it stand up?"

"You sound like a lawyer, Tuke. The girl's down there behind the counter, and so's Harmon, on the floor. She's screaming her head off. What else do you need? What Harmon — our Harmon — had in mind was a hot pork injection."

"Did he hurt her? Did he say anything incriminating? Was the ole tally-whacker out?"

"I'll give you the police report, counsel. I've got other things to think about."

...the victim observed the suspect acting in a menacing manner and fainted. When she woke up she observed the suspect next to her, behind the counter. The victim sought to get away while screaming. The suspect talked menacingly...

The girl's name was Connie Bret, from Whitehaven. Something about her story bothered Tuke. Women don't faint and then scream but the other way around. He gazed out his office window toward the river and thought about it. The line of cottonwoods reflected on the far bank, pale and insubstantial, and beyond them, the deep green of oaks hung like cumulus massed on the floodplain. In the evening the sun would descend, bloody, cyclopian, into the mid-American continent.

He rode the elevator down, crossed Main Street, and pushed through the door of Kress's. Two men in shirt sleeves had finished their coffee and they exited by the lingerie aisle. Tuke opened a menu, watching the girl in the green uniform nudge the stove with her pelvis, her hair netted, wearing flats mashed down in the back. Her calves needed shaving. She was not a natural blonde, this skinny girl from the wrong side of the tracks, but she was pretty.

"Connie?"

She turned and took in his jacket and silk tie, loose at the neck, the half spheres of gold in his shot cuffs — miniature golf balls with red dots. She smiled. "Do I know you?"

"Don't think so. I'm Tuke Harrington, I practice law across the square."

"You with the cops?"

"No, I'm just concerned about what happened to you the other day."

"How'd you know my name? The paper didn't carry it."

"Friends," he said.

"Well, I don't need no lawyer. And I ain't supposed to talk about it." She fished a pack of Luckies out of her uniform pocket. "The newspaper got it straight enough."

"I was just wondering exactly what he said to you, the menacing part."

She took a drag. "I got these patties to fry," and turned her back to him.

Tuke went straight to county records and from there back to his office, where he called Cooper Paine.

"Soliciting," he said, "a young sailor from Millington. He had ordered apple pie, not a slice of Miss Bret." After the pause, he added, "The lad reported it to Vice, they sent somebody over to Kress's, and she solicited him, too. You know about this, Coop?"

"A counter girl who hustles on the side can't get raped?" Cooper had a new-fangled speaker on his desk that allowed him to walk around while talking on the phone. He sounded like he was inside a barrel.

"I suppose she could. But takes something away from the charge, wouldn't you say? When Connie Brett testifies her whoring's bound to come up."

"We need to talk about this," Cooper said. "I don't want a trial. But we're not letting the perpetrator off."

"Even if he didn't perpetrate?"

"And he tried to get served at the counter. In the white section."

"Why can't you just charge him with disturbing the peace and let it go at that?"

"You want it all over town that a colored boy's sitting down where he shouldn't?"

Tuke and Cooper had played ball opposite each other in college, double-dated, shot quail over Rebel on the rare occasions when the house-bound dog could find a bird. Both men came from old Memphis families, belonged to the Episcopal persuasion, and Osiris of Cotton Carnival fame. "You can't charge a man with something he didn't do," Tuke said, and hung up.

He sat up late that night on his patio, drinking and listening to the revels over at the club, the women's gay voices carrying better than the men's. There were two kinds of southern women, those who sought to turn the transparent needs of southern men to their advantage, and those who didn't. His wife had been one of the latter. He had met her in a Nashville speakeasy while he was still in law school, Lois one of a line of rangy Upchurch women who had bolstered their middle Tennessee and southern Kentucky husbands for a century. Tuke had said to her when they met, "Stand up so I can see how tall you are," and she had.

In the months following her death, he had felt not just loneliness but also abandonment. He thought of her at the club on bridge day, seated in broken sunlight falling through the high windows of the card room. After her death, Tuke had looked into the room, knowing she wouldn't be there but doing it as if she would be. He then had to go and stand for a moment in the alcove where the water glasses and silverware were kept, tears in his eyes. A colored waiter had discreetly approached him. *Can I get you a little something, Mistah Harrington?*

That man had been Harmon Brown.

6

Dove shooting on the Buxton place over in Arkansas was anticipated by all those favored with an invitation. The day began with scrambled eggs and loving cups at the house, then the men were driven out into the fields on a flatbed truck, each with a folding stool, a shotgun, and a glass. Tuke loved hunting over soybeans and sunflowers. You could talk to your neighbors and breathe good air touched with the smell of autumn, and then the birds came and tested your skill, lost in blue sky and the rattle of gunfire.

Negroes with dogs retrieved and piled the shot birds in the shade and a pick-up moved slowly up and down the line, the tailgate mounted with big metal coolers. Tuke was flanked by Cooper Paine and St. Elmo Spence this time, a member of the University Club who had graduated from no university. St. Elmo said, "I hear you're representing that nigra," and Tuke gave the answer he had decided upon: "Word gets around, doesn't it?"

Cooper asked Tuke, "What did Harmon say?"

"He won't plead."

"Then you better get out of it."

"I already took him on."

"Un-take him."

"I can't do that."

"Since when," asked St. Elmo, "can't a lawyer un-take a nigra?"

A station wagon crept over the field, driven by another stalwart — UT, Hunt and Polo Club. He wore a cowboy hat and next to him, in an alpaca suit, sat Boss. The car stopped while a handy Negro set up another stool in their blind. Boss got out, leaning on a black umbrella. He had no shotgun.

"Ain't this a beautiful place?" he said to no one in particular, settling precariously on his stool. "That colored boy giving you trouble, Tuke?"

Tuke didn't answer. The estate owner was making his way here, too. He wore a new shooting jacket with suede patches and accompanying him was Buff Wallace, carrying the Fox he had turned on Tuke. Everyone stopped talking when a single dove appeared. They all hunched their shoulders and watched the bird beat downwind, tilting, already shot at ineffectually.

"Here comes another'n," said St. Elmo Spence. "Too high."

But Tuke waited until the bird was near past, then threw up his double, went to the second trigger, quartering away, and fired. Feathers marred the sky. The plummeting quarry was dead before it bounced.

A black man retrieved the dove from the stubble and added it to the growing pile. Boss gripped the stool with a tendon-riven hand, and said, "The thing that bothers me about this Kress's business is the timing. Not the boy's brazenness. Not that he just set himself down where he wasn't supposed to be. Our nigras don't do that. If I didn't know better I'd have said that's an outside nigra. No, it's the timing, with what all's going on up in Washington, the Supreme Court looking at a case where Communists said nigra schools aren't as good as white ones."

No one was expected to add anything. "The South," Boss continued, "will never stand for any tampering with the way we live. Separate is the way things are, will always be. We can't let the socialists and mixers in Washington think otherwise, or it would just encourage them. We can't have them snooping around down here, finding run-down nigra schools and so on, agitating. A agitated nigra then goes into a white establishment and tries to prove something."

"He wasn't trying to prove anything," said Tuke. "He just wanted a Dr. Pepper."

"You know, Tuke, I gave the nigra the vote in this town. When they couldn't vote in Miss'ippi, Arkansas, the rest of Tennessee, they could vote in Memphis. I've probably provided more payroll jobs for nigra choir members. I'm responsible for the killing of more catfish to feed nigra picnics. There's nothing I haven't done for Memphis nigras. Nobody can say I'm prejudiced, but we're not gonna have a bunch of them in the front of buses anymore or agitating with communist garbage men. So, what should we do with this boy?"

"Drop the charges," said Tuke.

"I don't know but there's an example to be made."

Tuke felt flushed. He was expected to go along, and for once he couldn't. "I thought we were here to bang dove," he said, "not take care of goddamn *bidness*," and he walked away, across the yawning field.

Dudley Fairchild piloted his ancient truck through Orange Mound. It was heavy with old refrigerators loaded by his temporary employee whose massive black arm was planted on the passenger window sill. Both men stared straight ahead — at the Abundant Life Temple, the Mount Ararat Baptist Church, Mount Pisgah, Robert's House of Beauty, Hull and Norfleet's Bar-B-Q, Beulah Electric and then at signs praising hair straightener, Prince Albert, Dr. Pepper.

Two patient women with outsized purses and head rags paused to let the hauler buck the intersection. Dudley plucked a half-pint of Four Roses from between his legs, pulled the cork, and drank. Honeysuckle grew thickly along dilapidated fences and the clapboard church's steeple tilted in the heat. The truck rolled past an abandoned sedan crouched in the gutter, without wheels, its seats having been hauled out onto the sidewalk.

Dudley's hired man sweated profusely. While he had loaded the refrigerators Dudley had read about the black man in Kress's and he still hadn't gotten over it, his Adam's apple going up and down in his parched throat. When black boys swarmed around the lumbering truck on their bikes, Dudley asked mirthlessly, "Know the definition of mass confusion?"

"Sho' don't, Mr. Dudley. Don't care to, nuther."

"Father's Day in Orange Mound."

Dudley laughed bitterly but the black man's face remained unaltered. They cruised past the corner grocery and slowed to a crawl while Dudley ran a bony white finger down the clipboard. He further studied the narrow shotgun houses until he found the one with the missing front porch. "I do believe," he said, "that this gentleman has an appliance of mine and has stopped making the requisite payments. I do believe that said appliance is holding up this gentleman's very walls."

One boy passed in front of them on a stripped Schwinn, pedaling furiously, grandly indifferent, his baseball cap reversed and his pants leg rolled to avoid the chain. Dudley swore quietly and persistently. The truck rolled straight across what might have been a lawn to a pair of beat-up metal chairs on a concrete slab.

Bantam roosters in the shed next door crowed, flanked by old tomato vines in tin cans that had grown pale and stalky. The sun was dropping, the sky a lethal white radiance despite summer's end. Both men's shirts stuck to their backs and both felt, as they stepped down from the truck, the concrete's heat through the soles of their shoes.

Dudley rapped on the back door of the house but nothing happened. He tried again, with the same result. "What you do is," he said, "is you go to a neighbor and inquire within of the whereabouts of the miscreant."

He crossed to the next house and pounded on more unpainted boards. A skinny old black woman in a colorless gown opened the door.

"I'm looking for Mister Brown," Dudley said.

"He gone."

"Well, I have something for him. I'm from the insurance agency and I have a check for a handsome dividend for Mr. Brown."

"Leave it," said the woman. "I might be seein' him."

"Can't do it, not allowed. You happen to see Mr. Brown, you tell him I'm waiting on him over at the house."

Walking back, the man said to Dudley, "You ain't from no insurance agency."

"What a perspicacious observation."

They walked right into the kitchen this time without knocking. It was dark and smelled of ashes. Light from inside the refrigerator flooded worn linoleum as the door swung open. Dudley took another draft from the half-pint and re-stowed it in his back pocket, gazing up almost in reverie at the photograph on the wall of a light-skinned Negro woman.

"Pretty little bitch," he said, lifting from the refrigerator a single covered pan and a Mason jar of pale green liquid. "How do you know you're repo-ing a refrigerator in Orange Mound? Because said refrigerator is full of pot liqour."

He removed the contents, pulled the plug and taped the wire to the back. "All right, let's move her." But he made no effort to assist the black man who grasped the appliance like a lover and walked it out from the wall. It was he who went to the truck to fetch the dolly, he who tipped the big appliance covered with rust spots so he could slip the blade underneath and then muscle it up to the loading ramp. It was he alone who wrapped it with a thick cloth belt, secured that to the wench mounted on the cab, and began to crank.

Slowly the refrigerator moved up toward the truck bed. The man deftly righted and spun it, strapped it to the railing, and turned to Dudley. But his boss was no longer watching. Instead, the smirk had dissolved while Dudley stared at his clipboard, his skinny white finger dug into a name he had recognized at last.

"I do believe," Dudley said at last, almost too softly to be heard, "that we have chanced upon the residence of the attempted raper written about in our august newspaper."

7

Harmon had never been close to a courthouse except the day his father took him there, on an errand down in the Delta. His father had been scared of something and this had frightened Harmon even though he didn't know what it was. That had been an office, not a big courtroom like this one, but Harmon remembered the tremor in his father's hand, too slight to be seen but not to be felt by a little boy holding onto the frayed cuff of a pale blue work shirt.

Now there were seats all around, like church pews, high desk on a platform and a fenced-off chair. A gray-haired man in a back robe came in, and everybody stood up. The judge was announced by another white man in a tight-fitting suit and tie, and then everybody sat down again. Harmon knew the man in the robe was Mr. Corrison Jones and that he had served the 30th district of the law for thirty years and was acquainted with the family of Tuke Harrington, his lawyer.

Mr. Harrington sat close to Harmon and he stood and told Judge Jones, "We move that this case be dismissed on grounds that the defendant was simply trying to help a young woman who fainted."

Harmon moved his feet nervously. They still had no laces and were a constant embarrassment, as was the ill-fitting prison issue. Everybody else in the room was well dressed except the men in the far back, who Mr. Harrington called courthouse regulars. Harmon was clean-shaven, at least, and kept his eyes on the judge, listening to the sound of traffic coming in through the open courtroom windows, under ceiling fans that barely stirred the air.

"Denied," said the judge.

"Then the defendant insists on having a jury of his peers."

"Are you out of your mind?"

Mr. Harrington said that he was not. In fact Harmon hadn't insisted on anything but he didn't say a word or look at the jury, made up of two middle-aged women dressed like secretaries and ten men, two in suits and the rest in short-sleeved shirts. The women jurors held fans printed with the words, *Bellview Baptist*, said to be the world's largest, and they declined to look at Harmon but the men looked at nothing else.

"Your honor," Mr. Harrington said, "there are no Negroes in the jury pool."

Harmon could have told him there wouldn't be. The judge took off his glasses, and said, "If your client wants his story heard it will be heard by good and conscientious Memphians. Now sit down."

At the table next to theirs sat Mr. Paine, the district attorney, who wanted to go to Congress up in Washington. He stood and told the jury what he was going to prove. The fact that he was trying this case himself meant it was important, Mr. Harrington had said. Mr. Paine wore an unwrinkled seersucker suit and his hair was carefully combed, a sign, Mr. Harrington had said, that he expected to be photographed for the newspaper. Harmon had served this white man scotch whiskey many times — Haig and Haig, he remembered — and he had nothing against Mr. Paine until he started talking.

"The defendant went around behind the counter and got right down there on the boards preparatory to forcing himself on the witness. Her screaming stopped him. The witness has by all accounts quite a good set of lungs," Mr. Cooper added, "something we can all be grateful for."

The paper fans speeded up and people smiled. Then Mr. Harrington's turn came. "Ladies and gentlemen," he said, friendly sounding, "there's been a mistake here, pure and simple. My client is a poor black man who badly needed a drink on a hot day. He went behind the counter not to assault anybody but to help a young woman who had fainted. She woke up and became hysterical."

The district attorney talked some more, and then the judge. Mr. Harrington and Mr. Paine talked one after the other.

The arresting officer, sprawled in the front row right behind Harmon, came forward chewing gum and wearing a starched blue shirt hung with a badge and a loop of braided leather for his whistle, bringing back the memory of Harmon's arrest and the fear and anger he had felt. Harmon tried to keep these things out of his face, as he had been told to do, and that was hard.

Mr. Paine led the police through the whole story, except that what Mr. Paine said wasn't what happened. Then Mr. Harrington, Mr. Paine, and the judge were all talking at the same time. Finally Mr. Harrington asked the police, "Did Harmon Brown resist arrest, Chick?"

That must have been his first name and it didn't fit what Harmon knew to be a violent man. Mr. Harrington's being familiar with Chick didn't please the police, who just said, "Yeah."

"How so?"

"He tried to run off."

"You say 'tried.' Why didn't he?"

"It's hard to run when you're settin' on the sidewalk with your hands cuffed behind your back."

Judge Jones ignored the laughter in the courtroom. Two of the women on the jury smiled.

"Wasn't that because you clubbed him in the shins?" Mr. Harrington asked. "And in the face after he was arrested?"

Mr. Paine reared up. "Objection! A law enforcement officer may use or threaten to use force that is reasonably necessary to accomplish the arrest of an individual suspected of a criminal act who resists or flees. That's the law."

"Repeatedly striking a suspect after you have him in custody is against the law," Mr. Harrington said, and Harmon couldn't help but nod.

"Objection!"

The judge said, "Granted. Your client is on trial here, Mr. Harrington, not the police."

"I know that, your honor. But I think they misunderstood what had happened. Did you feel threatened by the defendant?" Mr. Harrington asked Chick.

"You never know what they'll do in a situation."

"Answer the question, please. Did you feel threatened by a skinny old man in handcuffs, one who already had been whacked across the shins."

"Yes," Chick said, hating to have to claim he was afraid of Harmon. Then he stepped down. Everyone waited while the district attorney shifted papers around on his table. Something had happened but Harmon wasn't sure what. The windows were opened wider because the morgue was under the courtroom and somebody down there was using formaldehyde, the smell of it rising through the floor boards.

The women looked at Harmon now, but not one of the men. They were intent on the waitress who had charged Harmon, seated in the front row with her thin, bluish hands folded in her lap. She wore a bright yellow dress and looked pretty, Harmon thought, and she blushed as she approached the stand.

"Are you comfortable, Miss Bret?" the district attorney asked her. "Would you like a drink of water? Now Miss Bret please tell us what happened last Tuesday in Kress's."

"Well, I was washing dishes and I turned around and seen this nigra here, on the other side of the counter, lookin' at me. I fainted." She twisted her handkerchief.

"I deeply sympathize with you, Miss Bret. Why do you think you fainted?"

"I never had a nigra look at me like that. And then when I woke up he was on the floor right next to me."

"Did you feel menaced?"

"I'm telling you."

"How did the defendant do his menacing?"

"He was reaching for me."

Mr. Harrington objected again and the judge overruled that one, too.

"What did you do then?"

"I screamed."

Harmon lowered his eyes. His own wrists looked like broomsticks sticking out of old, striped cloth. Mr. Harrington set a battered black book of Tennessee statutes on the table in front of them, next to two glasses of water for slaking their thirst. But Mr. Harrington didn't say anything.

Mr. Cooper asked Connie Bret, "What do you think he would have done, if you hadn't screamed?"

"Objection," yelled Mr. Harrington. "Leading."

"Granted. Please rephrase the question."

"So the man's demeanor and actions, the things that made you faint in the first place, made you scream?"

"Yeah."

There was more arguing. Then the judge said, "I'm going to get myself a sandwich and a Coke. I want to finish this up after lunch."

Back in the lock-up, Harmon asked, "You going to ask her about me sitting in the white section?"

"We're not getting into your integrating unless we have to." The smell of frying cornmeal seeped under the door of the consultation room, and Mr. Harrington added, "You're looking puny, Harmon."

"I ain't eating that trash."

"You have to take care of yourself."

"I don't like that durned jury. Somebody in jail told me I can wave 'em off, if I want."

"You mean waive your right to a jury?"

"That's right."

"Well, a jury can be let go at any time. But the judge's free after that to do pretty much as he pleases."

"Seems like he's doing that anyway. What do you think, Mr. Harrington?"

"I'm not sure. We better get down there."

Mr. Harrington thanked Miss Bret for testifying. "You have told us that you felt menaced by my client. Did Harmon Brown say anything to you at any time that made you think he'd harm you?"

"It ain't what he said."

"Did he hit you, or even touch you?"

"Better not have."

"Your honor, according to the law..." and he picked up the black book full of bits of paper, "...section one oh seven eight eight says '*a battery is an essential element of the assault and battery with intent to commit rape under the statute and a conviction is not authorized unless the indictment charge, and the jury so find, that a battery attended the attempt.*' The witness has admitted that no such battery was even attempted."

"Well," said the judge, "the court will take all that into consideration. The fact that he scared the daylights out of the witness should also be taken into account, don't you think?"

He adjourned without finishing up, after all.

8

The next day the trial was put off until afternoon, and the courtroom full. Stories had appeared in both newspapers, and Tuke stood up immediately to take full advantage of the crowd. "Your honor," he began, "there's one thing that needs to be clarified before we continue. Why isn't the defendant being given nourishment?"

"What are you referring to?"

"The jailers of Shelby County, 30th judicial district, are not taking proper care of this prisoner. So the defendant wants to waive his right to jury trial, in part so he can get something decent to eat."

"Are you. I repeat. Are you out of your mind?"

"I am not."

"The jury's been sworn and put to work. We're almost done."

"My client also believes the jury is prejudiced against him not because of the charge but because of the color of his skin. He's willing to let you decide on the evidence."

"Is this your idea?" the judge asked Harmon.

"Yes, sir." It was the first time Harmon had spoken. One of the colored men in the back sang out, "Yeah, tha's right."

The judge dropped his gavel once, then asked Harmon, "Do you understand that I would be the sole judge of the facts if you do this?"

Harmon said that he did, and from the back of the room there came a chorus: "*Yeah, he gon' jedge it now.*" He knew word would go out in Orange Mound and along Beale Street of a black man rejecting the ways of whites and tying the law in knots. A black man who did not eat.

Jones told the panel, “You are hereby dismissed. Thank you for your time and attention. Do not think the court shares the opinions of the defendant in this matter. Please step down. This court is adjourned — again — when it needn’t have been.”

That night Tuke stopped by the club. Men he knew well sat around the heavy pine table with removable boards in front of each player, the felt strewn with bills, chips, cigarette packs, heavy glass ashtrays, cork rounds with the club’s initials to keep the drinks from sweating on polished wood. Dr. McNeely was saying, “I guess a pair of threes is worth ten dollars in this bereft ordeal.”

Someone called and the doctor turned over the third queen. “Read ‘em and weep,” he said.

“Doctor had the tre,” said Guston Kinswanger, tight as usual, “That’s what you get, playing poker with a man’ll stick a finger up your ass.”

They all laughed. Guston turned to Tuke. “How’d you get messed up in all this, Tukie? I’m not above helping a colored boy, lending a hand. I grew up with them. Little black boy, forget his name, best friend. But why this colored boy, Tukie?”

McNeely said, “Hush up, Gus.”

“I’m sorry. Got to get a drink here. Clarence! But what I don’t understand is, Tukie, the nigra got himself into the scrape, let him get himself out. That’s what a lot of people are saying.”

At home the phone was ringing. He walked into the study and answered it. “Hope I’m not bothering anything.” It was Boss.

“Not at all,” said Tuke.

“I’d be sorry that little lady’s other profession came to light. I don’t like to think of a prostitute serving a grilled cheese sandwich to a Memphian. I suppose you feel you have to do that.”

"I do."

Boss was silent. Tuke thanked him and hung up, the first time he had ever done so, and the phone began to ring again. A man whose voice he didn't recognize said, "Harmon Brown's gonna receive due reward for what he's wrought, one way or the other. And if he gets off, his ass is grass."

The next morning Tuke called Connie Bret to testify again. He asked her politely, "Miss Bret, have you ever been arrested?"

Cooper was on his feet. "Objection! What's that got to do with the charge?"

"What're you up to?" the judge asked Tuke.

"The complaining witness's account is all we have to go on. It's important that the court know something about her."

"It better be relevant."

"I think it is, your honor. Now Miss Bret, on April twelfth of this year, weren't you arrested?"

Connie Bret's handkerchief was already a hank of damp twisted cotton. She narrowed her eyes but didn't answer.

"Soliciting for prostitution, I believe it was. Two counts?"

"I was just being friendly."

"Didn't you plead guilty to the lesser charge of pandering? Didn't you pay a fine of twenty dollars, Miss Bret?"

This time she couldn't answer because Judge Jones gaveled loudly and announced, "Court is adjourned until tomorrow, goddamned *again*. And Mr. Harrington" — no more familiarity, Tuke noted — "and Mr. Paine I want to see you both in my chambers."

Harmon heard the deputies in the corridor just before lights out. They let themselves into his cell and as he was about to get off the bunk when the little one, Tiller, said, "Stay."

He carried a bucket with a lid and a tin funnel and the big deputy carried a spoon. He put a knee on Harmon's chest and held his wrists against the bunk frame.

"Open up now."

Tiller held Harmon's head and pried at his clenched teeth with the spoon. "He's too polite to eat when he's got company."

Harmon tasted steel as the spoon went in.

"Git the chute."

He felt the funnel's sharp edge against his tongue. The deputy removed the lid on the bucket and lifted it, Harmon thrashing and trying to bellow. He recalled another hand on his forehead, pushing him down into the cattle pond when he was small, and warm water pouring over his head. *Dearly beloved, forasmuch as our Saviour Christ saith, None can enter into the kingdom of God except he be regenerated and born again of Water and the Holy Ghost…*

Cold prison fare filled his mouth, but he refused to swallow it. There was a pause, then spoon and funnel rose on a torrent of pea soup. The men fell back, spattered. "Why, you done messed up this shirt."

They were about to go at him but were stopped by shouting up and down the corridor, the prisoners' complaints so loud they drew the deputies to the bars. Thrown magazines, cups, cigarette butts, shoes, rolls of toilet paper even loose change rained on the lock-up's otherwise scarred, scrubbed concrete.

9

Tuke rose early and dressed in anticipation of the finale. He crossed a downtown dry as cobwebs, eager for rain. Crabgrass festooned the cracks in the pavement, sickly yellow, and everywhere growing things encroached on the implements of civilization: untrimmed bushes swallowing wrought iron fences, creepers on telephone lines, weeds at bus stops, all stymied by the drought.

He went into the courthouse and found spectators gathering. But the wooden sign indicating when court was in session stood in the corner, like a truant. Tuke opened the heavy door to Jones's chamber. It was deserted.

"What's up?" he asked a passing bailiff.

"Jones called it off." The man kept walking.

In the clerk's office the secretary was bent over the mimeograph machine, working on the dockets. "What's going on with the Harmon Brown case?" Tuke asked her.

"Dismissed," she said, turning the crank, releasing the sharp chemical smell of the ink.

Tuke passed through the double doors at the end of the hall and went directly up the stairs. The black trusty sat on a stool, his hand thrust through the bars where he enticed music from the radio on the sill. Tuke said, "I want to see Harmon Brown."

"He gone."

"What?"

The trusty found the station he had been searching for and the room filled with guitar music. Tuke turned and went back down the stairs and into the sheriff's office. Deputy Tiller sat with the *Press-Scimitar* spread on the duty desk, open to the comic section. Didn't the man ever sleep?

"When was Harmon Brown released?"

Tiller considered the name as if he had never heard it. He checked the ledger with elaborate diligence, his lips moving as he read. "You just missed him."

"Where'd he go?"

"How the hell would I know?"

Outside on the steps Tuke watched cars pass, Adams Avenue traffic much as it always was, and people taking care of business. Stepping into the street, he was blinded by the sun over the civil courts building, and he thought, if only it would rain.

Harmon saw the cruiser too late, the slack-gutted driver and the one called Chick. They saw him, too. While they went screeching around the block he hustled south on Second. They caught up to him at the light but Harmon turned and crossed the street, his shoes beating on the cobbles, and entered the alley, smelling barbecue pork from the cellar tavern. Ribs laid over split hickory, meat dark with fire and paprika. He thought he smelled the funkiness of greens and fatback, too, then biscuits made with Martha White flour. How did that jingle go?

Baptize with butter, sop your
way to the Promised Land…

Cars moved faster on Union and the cruiser caught up with him again at Main, pulled past and into the intersection, turned left and eased to the curb. That's where they would try, before Harmon could reach Beale, but he wasn't getting into that car again.

He turned toward the river, crossed the railroad tracks and headed south, a boxcar between him and the cruiser. It picked up speed and bumped over the tracks, the police rocking in their seats. Chick saw Harmon, braked hard, put the car into reverse. So Harmon crossed Beale on the overpass instead, the cruiser below him now, and he followed the dirt path angling up the bluff toward warehouses and the back of the abandoned brewery.

He saw the cruiser bounce over the curb below and the police get out. Chick hailed him angrily, gesturing, but Harmon held his ground. The police talked together and then Chick started up the bluff after Harmon.

The river below looked drained, the sandbar on the far side skeletal in the morning sun, the waters confused. Atop the bluff two dogs screwed in the shade of a mimosa. Harmon's heart pounded as he waited for Chick to get close enough for Harmon to see that the pistol was still holstered. A black man running was a problem at any time, but Harmon wasn't running anymore.

He turned and walked on up the bluff, Chick's shouts bouncing off the old brewery's blind facade.

Tuke had Harmon's address and found the house without difficulty. He expected Harmon to be home but he wasn't. The empty little house was more desolate than he had expected, a skeletal smoker sitting out back, lid raised, the sort you saw in the yards of colored residences everywhere, filling whole neighborhoods with smells well beyond the ken of Morningside Park and Chickasaw Gardens.

He left the Cadillac in the weeds and approached the back door, aware of a curtain moving in the house next door. He knocked. There was no response, but the unlocked door swung inward and he followed it out of the ferocious sun. In the kitchen, his eyes adjusted to the shadows and he made out a pot on the table, an off-kilter calendar above the stove, and next to it a photograph of a young woman in a cheap frame, her smile hazed by years of stove smoke but affecting anyway. Pretty woman, Tuke thought, sitting down.

He was sweating, tired for no reason, and he loosened his tie and ran a hand over his sparse hair. He wished he had a clear alternative to lolling around a strange house. Orange Mound was a mystery to most people he knew, known as "over there" though it was one of the oldest neighborhoods in the city. It lacked services like regular garbage collection and, in many cases, plumbing. Untouched by the niceties that had made Memphis the cleanest city in America, or so people claimed. The judges must not have made it south of the Southern Railroad tracks.

Looking again at the photograph, it occurred to Tuke that Harmon once had an existence far from his duties at the Memphis Country Club. It must have gone back a long way. Manual labor as a kid, some kind of farming, most likely. Something in the black man's demeanor — patience, dignity, contrariness — suggested a connection to land far beyond the city, but how had Harmon's long journey led from there to the calamitous present. Had the woman in the photograph been part of it? Her liquid eyes, the set of her soft mouth, spoke of expectations Tuke couldn't fathom.

He tipped up the lid of the pot and saw it was full of dark, moldy mustard greens. What an ever-loving mess they had made of Harmon Brown's life.

He slept soundly that night but was awakened early by the almighty telephone. The same man said, "Brown's house has preceded him to the nether regions. Brown's next," and the line went dead.

Tuke dressed and went downstairs. Without a word to Carlin he got into his car and drove back to Orange Mound. The charred remains of the house confused him until he realized it was what remained of

Harmon's, now all rendered clapboard and shingles that stank. Only the cooker remained, triumphant in the weeds.

Not a soul came to look at the ashes, as if just seeing them could visit the same fate on neighbors. He drove to the sundry store on the corner and dropped a nickel in the pay phone under the roof's overhang. A Negro stared out the store window at him and then, like a big bass finning back into the shadow of a cut-bank, he disappeared.

Cooper Paine's secretary answered and switched him immediately to the D.A. Tuke told him, "Somebody torched Harmon Brown's house last night."

"Maybe it was an accident. Those old wood shacks..."

"'...'go up like tinder,'" said Tuke. "Not by themselves they don't. Looks like the fire department didn't even show up until it was too late."

Cooper didn't say anything.

"Why don't you call the police commissioner, Cooper?"

"I suspect he's already heard about it."

"Well, you ought to get somebody over here."

"You've got some nerve, Tuke, telling me what to do. I warned you about this. Maybe if you hadn't grandstanded in court..."

"Maybe if you hadn't pushed that bogus charge."

"Maybe if you had listened to reason."

"Maybe if you had stood up to those sorry-ass cops."

They were both shouting.

"Tuke, I never thought I'd see you doing damage to your town and to the people you know."

"I never thought I'd see Cooper Paine prosecuting a man for something he didn't do, just to get further up the flagpole."

"There always was something wrong with Tuke Harrington, wasn't there? Always a little too quick to laugh at things, to get in a scrape. Something makes you want to tear down the things others built up."

"Law and order aren't being preserved in Memphis, Coop."

"You can't leave this alone, can you? Well, it's going to finish you." Cooper hung up.

Tuke stood surveying the alien landscape and its latest wound. Night-riding was done to accomplish that which could not be accomplished in daylight: houses burned, people lynched. But Harmon's house had contained no telephone, so there was no listing in the phone book. His address had never appeared in a newspaper, so how had the arsonist found his house? It had to be someone with access to the jail's file, Chick or more likely the squat, gap-toothed deputy, Tiller.

He picked up the receiver again, fed it another coin, and dialed. Someone said, "Shelby County lockup."

"Tiller, please."

"He's gone home."

"He still live in Whitehaven?"

"He ain't never lived in Whitehaven. He lives in Raleigh. Who is this?"

Tuke rolled up Main Street, passed the cement works on Jackson Avenue and made his way north to the Wolf River bridge. He had found Tiller's address in the phone book and now the road snaked east from the blacktop through dwindling stands of oak and poplar and tangles of cut-over land too poor to plant.

The name was hand-lettered on a mailbox welded to a tire rim and the house squatting at the bottom of the lot. Windows shaded, low porch eaves strung with gourds. Tuke drove down, heralded by a chained dog of no discernible breed, standing in the dirt. When Tuke got out of the Cadillac the dog turned and ran into its tarpapered retreat, its muted howls comical.

He walked past a pick-up with a missing tailgate and stepped onto the porch. He knocked but no one answered. There was no neighbor to inquire of, no motion beyond the gourds swaying in the breeze. This was country life without its fundaments: no boat, tractor, crops, or decent hound.

Tuke walked around the house, thinking of what he might say if he encountered the deputy. The shed at the back contained a jumble of trenching tools, barbed wire, a fence stretcher. Tiller had some project in mind, a couple of beef cattle, most likely. Tuke called, "Anybody home?"

He entered, careful where he put his costly loafers. Jumper cables hung from a nail, and a double-bitted ax. He was looking for a gasoline can, rags, any evidence of arson. Tuke picked up a rake and probed the collection of pails in the far corner, aware of the futility, the presumption, of a lawyer poking around in another man's effects, whatever might be suspected.

He dropped the rake and was turning back to the door when he saw a figure to his left, in shadow, moving toward him. Instinctively Tuke brought his right hand across, leaning into the blow, and a body went down across the handle of the power mower.

He had tried for most of his life not to react so quickly; a big man can do damage. Now he recognized the voice — *"You son of a bitch!"* — and Tiller's ashen face. In his out-thrust hands was a large pistol, a .45 semi-automatic, government issue like those Tuke had seen in the Pacific. It would produce a finger-sized hole where the bullet went in and a bloody cavern where it emerged.

He watched Tiller cock it. Tuke's life was supposed to pass before his eyes but instead Tuke saw a version of Tiller's: married at seventeen, assigned to a foxhole in France or North Africa, then to the back roads of west Tennessee and finally to the county lock-up. Tuke stared at the little man's white knuckles and the gun's steely sheen, the bluing long since worn away. "You're not going to like prison," Tuke said softly.

"You done attacked me. On my own property."

"You won't get electrocuted, but you'll be in there with some boys you arrested. They'll get to you."

During the long pause Tuke wondered who would he call if he got into trouble. Not the district attorney, or Boss. He said, "I'm not armed. That's not going to look good, either. The jury'll be unhappy to learn you shot me while I was here on legal business."

"What bidness?"

"Somebody burned down Harmon Brown's house."

Tiller lowered the gun. He thought about it, then gave himself up to the joke. When he had stopped laughing he said, "So that's it. Well, I'll tell you something. I'm glad his house burned down. I wish't he'd been in it. But I ain't the one you're looking for. Now git before I blow you out the back side of Jesus."

10

The rain came from the west, darkening the streets of Orange Mound, singing in the leaves. For a time there was no run-off, just the steady suck of dry grass, and then water began to puddle and to run in the gutters. It piled up at the bottom of the block and scooted through the weeds, toward the railroad tracks.

Harmon watched from the shadow of his neighbor's shed as a car passed, the driver bent over the wheel, but he kept going. Harmon's house had stood on what was now a black, foul-smelling slick, the gaunt iron cooker presiding over the loss of chairs, flatware, old photographs in the split-spined album that for years had stood behind the flour can, photos of Harmon and 'Simmon outside Peewee's, and Claudet eating sugar ice at the corner of Second and Beale.

Harmon used to play his guitar for her in the mornings, out on the porch, while she made coffee. She liked it best when he sang, far from the clubs and anybody to judge him. Then she would pull a chair up close and put her feet up on the post, light a cigarette, and smoke with one hand while keeping a grip on Harmon's trousers with the other.

He wished more than anything that she had kept that grip. He could still feel her in his hands, in his mouth, even, those pretty nipples like blackberries. The smell of her lived in his head, more durable than all others. Memories were all he had now but he couldn't get away from them except by writing songs he had sung at night, too, in this house that was a house no more. The rage would come, he knew, but right now there was only pain.

Louella Mae emerged from her house next door and stood on the porch like a bunch of old chicken bones in a used flour sack. She stared at Harmon, seeing not a man but some evil saint in need of mojo-ing. Louella Mae would walk through the neighborhood with her old grocery cart and encounter things other people couldn't see. She would take a pod from a catawba tree and strip it like a string bean and give it to you for the purge. Once she fed some to the rooster that stretched him out stiff as a board.

After a while Louella Mae raised her hand. "Harmon?"

He crossed the yard. "How you, Louella?"

"Oh, Harmon, he burned it right up."

"Who done it, Louella Mae?"

"I felt all hot inside, just knowing somethin' would come along."

The rain had slackened. In all these years Harmon had never stood on Louella Mae's porch as he did now. Louella Mae thought mockingbirds were people. If you got bit by a copperhead, kill and hang it over a tree limb before sunset and if the thunder don't roll you're as good as dead.

"That sun went down white," she began, and he knew it would take a while. "I heared the car, that engine shet down. Heard the car door open, then the trunk. I thought maybe it was you. Then I seen him carryin' a big can. A bunch a' light jumped under my door, I seen these old feet" — she looked down at her lace-less tennis shoes — "shadows dancin'. Them tacked-up magazine pictures liked to jumped off my wall. My door handle got warm to the touch, him still standin' out there like he's cookin' chicken, his face all lit up."

She moaned at the memory, raking her face with long broken nails.

Harmon repeated, "Who, Luella Mae?"

"When I look agin, he gone. I can hear that fire. I cain't call no department 'cause I don' have no phone, Harmon. I'm thinkin' them men'll come along presently, running up the street in them hats like horse haids. I hears somebody shootin' but it ain' no gun, it's them boards poppin.'"

"Who?"

"Then I seen sparks. Light dancin', I smellin' smoke. Law', I hates the smell of smoke of a evenin.'"

"Louella Mae…"

"Don't you know, Harmon?"

"You never said."

"I thought you knowed. I thought ever'body knowed. It's the 'frigerator man."

"The 'frigerator man?"

"Yeah, you know, that skinny white man with the truck and all them old iceboxes. The one you owe money to, Harmon — Mistah Dudley."

There was a pause during which Tuke heard race music in the background. He held the receiver closer, and Harmon said, "Mr. Harrington, you still my lawyer?"

"Yes, of course."

"Well, I found out who done it."

"Burned down your house?"

"Yes, sir."

Tuke waited, not sure he wanted to hear this. The *Commercial Appeal* had published a more thorough account after the *Press-Scimitar* led the way. "How did you find out?"

"You want to hear it, you got to meet me. I ain't telling it over the telephone."

Tuke followed his directions, easing the Cadillac through a clutch of streets back of Beale: barrels full of bottles, sagging stoops with kids sitting on them like notes on tattered sheet music, windowsills draped with clothes. Up there, white eyes in dark half-faces gazed warily down at this stranger. "Where the hell?" he said aloud.

A skinny black man with salt-and-pepper stubble and an up-raised, cleaver-like hand came from behind. At first Tuke thought it was a panhandler, but then the man smiled and Tuke braked.

"Get in, Harmon."

He did, sitting bolt upright, staring straight ahead. Tuke asked, "What happened after you left the lock-up?"

Harmon waved away the question. "The refrigerator man done it," he said. "You know that raggedy-ass looking white man sitting in the back of the courtroom that last day? Well, his name's Dudley and he sells old appliances out of a warehouse just west of the Mound. Last name of Fairchild."

"I know that name." The Fairchilds were one of those old Mississippi families that fell from the stirrup cup taken astride a fine horse to peddling iceboxes.

"Well, Louella Mae seen him plain in the light of the fire he set."

The Fairchilds had drawn endless credit from Memphis cotton brokers and ended up losing everything but a dilapidated mansion in a no longer fashionable part of downtown. He hadn't heard the name in years. "Son of a bitch," was all he could say.

"You got that right. Hateful man. Sold me a refrigerator, then come and took it while I was in jail. Now he's burned down my house. Can you get the police on him?"

"Will your neighbor talk to them?"

"No, can't bring Louella Mae into this."

"I can't do anything without a witness. In the old days I could have called somebody." But no longer.

"Don't tell nobody about Louella Mae. Promise me that, Mr. Harrington. I don't know what that man might do to her if he knew she saw him."

Harmon's budding beard, unshorn hair and shirt with pointy old-fashioned collars, picked up in some church basement, gave him an ageless look. "I don't know what's going on in that head of yours," Tuke said, "but don't you try to take this any further, Harmon. You're not in any position. You've been through the system once and got clear, but that's not going to happen again. Keep out of sight and let me think about this. How can I get in touch with you?"

"Come round to 'Simmon's." He scribbled an address on a piece of paper in his pocket and handed it across.

"You must need some walking around money," and Tuke was reaching for his wallet when Harmon got out of the car and headed up the alley, a gaunt figure turning into the passageway next to a juke joint.

From directly above the car came the sound of music, loud but unidentifiable. At that moment an object struck the hood of the Cadillac with force. Tuke saw a lump of damp fur with disjointed legs and rheumy eyes: a dead cat, flung from a rooftop.

Harmon stood outside 'Simmon's house with his back against the doorframe, as he had been instructed to do, wearing an old felt snap brim Artice had given him. In the first hour after midnight a change came over the neighborhood, not just in the volume and variety of the music — the keening of singers unlimbering, the throb of the bass and drum spilling out of the clubs over on Beale, the heavy beat Harmon didn't care for.

Too much voice, too little soul, but that was the voice the audience wanted today. Those musicians had been boys when Harmon played in the same places and not a one of them had planted crowder peas, chopped cotton or hauled water from a rusty pump. On pavement all their lives, they drank too much and smoked too much stuff, jumped the bones of too many pretty young things in skimpy dresses and never learned that it began with sun-blasted row crops dwindling toward the horizon and a real fear that the distance might not be covered in a lifetime.

There were radios on the alley, too, tuned to some preacher reminding the world that everybody would fry in hell if they didn't shut the doors and turn off every station but the preacher's, cork the bottle, put their trousers back on and commence praying. There were Victrolas on which records spun and from which came sounds as different from one another as day and night, all of them fighting to be heard. And when the front door finally opened there was Persimmon Smoot's voice, not as strong as the others but rising and falling like a little bobber on a windy pond.

Harmon could hear 'Simmon clearly even though outside. The old house was alive with heedless laughter, 'Simmon on his cushion, that big belly contending with the guitar as the rightful occupier of the same space. People passed Harmon, paying him no mind, and went in. Every now and then Artice came to check on Harmon, stationed on the porch so he could warn her against the police. Everything's fine, he would nod, no cruiser in the alley. If it wasn't fine he was to rub his back against the door jamb, a signal for Artice to lock up and turn off the lights.

Artice's Saturday nights brought an unusual mix of people, some as worn out as Harmon and 'Simmon, others bright as new money. Artice got a little from them at the door and they paid a little more for a glass of whatever it was she was pouring. They paid considerably more if they wanted to "rest up" which involved the back room and an old mattress for couples with nowhere else to go. The young ones were in love and the older ones hiding from husbands and wives.

The prettiest black girls did not have to pay to get into the house but they did have to pay to get out. Harmon watched the one called Petunia through the window: slim, high-toned, teeth very white when she laughed. Skirt so tight that when she danced she had to take little steps unsuited to those long legs and spike heels. 'Simmon's music was not for dancing but people danced anyway, assuming a blind man wouldn't know, soon forgetting all about him and his blues guitar.

Watching Petunia, Harmon felt the past, faces coming up like fruit on a slot machine. Claudet was gone but he still thought of swapping Memphis for St. Louis, finding her, starting over again. How he would do that without money, in a strange city? It had been years. Were there country clubs in St. Louis that needed waiters? Might he figure out a way to get back on a stage, any stage?

He saw the cruiser too late, sitting right there in the alley, headlights out. Behind the windshield were the hated silhouettes and for a second Harmon thought he would choke. No time to run and nowhere to go if there had been. He rubbed his back furiously on the doorjamb, trying to get Artice's attention, watching her leaning down to 'Simmon with the port, oblivious of Harmon's signal.

The front door opened and a customer came out, saw the police, turned on a dime and went back inside. The police were out of their cruiser now, hauling on their belts, looking around. Harmon hoped they would turn into another doorway but they came on, kicking bottles out of their path. Harmon's back rose and fell more slowly against the jamb, then stopped altogether.

"Back itch, boy?" asked one police, but before Harmon could answer they were passing him by. They hadn't recognized him from the mugshot that had appeared in the *Press-Scimitar* because the hat was tight to his eyebrows.

The music inside died, and Artice opened the door, her eyes shrunk down to little points. The police walked right past her too, one of them hollering, "You all be quiet now, you hear?" They were ready for some entertainment beyond 'Simmon's guitar and high-pitched voice and it was a good thing Petunia had already gone to rest up with a young man in an iridescent green jacket. If they found her they would take her out to the cruiser, but Harmon wasn't waiting for that.

Before he reached the end of the alley he heard the cruiser doors slam. The car laid down rubber and when Harmon looked he saw receding taillights and a haze of blue smoke.

11

Harmon awoke at first light, the words of the song by Son House going round in his head: *I got a letter this mornin'...* He left the resting up room that still smelled of Petunia and made his way to the front of the house. Artice and 'Simmon lay together in an unconscious heap, around them paper plates piled with chicken bones, cigarette butts, half-filled amber glasses.

Hurry, hurry, how come the gal you love is dead?

He rummaged around in Artice's kitchen drawer until he found the pad and a pencil stub. He sharpened it with a butcher knife and sat down and began to write: *I had some trouble, Claudet. If I was to come up there I would need work and a place to stay for a while.* He folded the letter, unfolded it, and added words never spoken. *I'm sorry about all that happened. What came after was just about what you said it would be.*

He refolded the paper and put it in his shirt pocket. He took it out, re-read it, tore it in half, and in half again and dropped the pieces into the brimming garbage can.

Behind him, Artice said, "What you doin', Harmon?"

"Nothin'."

"You writin' to her, that's what you're doin'. Well, don't. Claudet's gone. Even if she ain't, it wouldn' be the same."

He turned away from this strong, railly woman half falling out of her dress. She went to the stove and turned on the gas. "Want coffee?"

"I don' mind."

"How come you never sang, Harmon? I want to know. If you had a sung you might have shet ole 'Simmon up now and then and gotten us onto the radio, into better places. How come you never did?"

He didn't answer.

"I know you got a voice. Claudet liked it, used to talk about it. How come, Harmon?"

"Didn't want to."

"That ain' no answer."

"It's the only one you gonna get, Artice."

"You must be the stubbornest man alive."

She made that blowing noise, shoveling grinds into the water. It would be river-boil coffee, dark as death, a big spoon standing in it to settle the grounds. Egg shells would be better but don't expect eggs at Artice's.

Wrapping a blanket around him, Harmon went out the front door and into the alley. Cats everywhere but not another person. He hadn't opened his mouth in public all those years because, in truth, he was afraid, so afflicted with stage fright that in the early performances he had looked at the ceiling to avoid the sea of bright eyes intent on his picking. This fear forced his mind and his hands onto the strings, and the anguished sounds that came from them were enough.

People loved the sight of music being made, balancing with 'Simmon's flailing, raunchy style. Harmon could play the guitar as well as any man alive but he couldn't bring up that voice. The very idea of it slicked his underarms. He had smoked Chesterfields through performances, a further guarantee that singing wouldn't be possible, breathing haze like some fiend, eyes up-cast, hands touching secrets he himself couldn't define. He still wrote bits of songs on scraps of paper, carrying them in his pocket, in a shoe until he lost them. Someday, he always told himself. Someday.

He walked past mounds of trash and out into Beale. The sun touched the top of the marquee on the Daisy Theater. The doors of the clubs were all chained, tottering on the curbs out front were dented cans laden with empty bottles. Far up the street, a severe figure in a black suit stood on the steps of First Baptist in a black hat much like Harmon's discard. It was a vision of an unforgiving minister who might well be looking around for the likes of Harmon.

The recording studio on Second Street, next door to the bail bondsman, had the same moth-eaten lettering on the window he remembered: *Big River Recording*. It was open on Sunday mornings and Harmon stashed his blanket in the alley next to it and concentrated on the photographs in the window. Chet Atkins and the Raymond Brothers but also Furry Lewis. White and black, they seemed touched by some inner light.

He pushed through the door and stood for a moment, waiting for the woman at the desk to notice him. She was talking quietly but intently on the telephone, one hand shading her eyes. The dark line in the part of her hair told Harmon she wasn't a natural blonde. The skewed halter top revealed a purple bra strap when she hung up, and only then did she see him. "Oh my," she said.

"I used to cut some acetates here, long time ago." He knew it sounded as crazy as he looked.

"You don't say."

"Learned to play at home," amazed to hear himself say it. "Outside Tupelo, when I was a little thing. Stood on a folding chair at Delvane Baptist, with a borrowed guitar. Heard my voice come back at me over a loud-speaker and I fainted."

The door at the back of the studio opened and a heavy-set man in a Hawaiian shirt came in. His shoes were made of little strips of woven leather, his pink face ridged with muscles that showed as he chewed gum. Harmon glimpsed a raised platform in the back and a bunch of kitchen chairs and bar stools up against one wall. The cloth over the speakers was torn. There was a clock, a bunch of colored lights, a microphone, and a sign that said *Can It*.

The woman angled her chin in Harmon's direction. "He said he used to record here."

"Not much," said Harmon. "Once or twice."

"Oh, yeah?" said the man. "I've heard that one before. Who'd you play with?"

"Persimmon Smoot and the Boys."

"Well, we don't record race music now. What'd you play?"

The woman said, "Guitar."

The man reached behind the partition and brought out an old Stella, scratched from all the handling. Winking at the woman, he came around the desk and offered it to Harmon. "You said you can play, so let's hear something."

Harmon took the guitar out of politeness, wishing he hadn't spoken. It felt warm in his hand, solid. Needed new strings but no matter. He hit a few, as natural as the wind, and before he knew it he was backing the absent 'Simmon with somebody else's melody, hearing the words only in his head:

I send for my baby and she don' come...
You made me love you,
now your man have gone...

Then came one of his own compositions, Harmon still mute, missing a lick, going back, squinting at the box. He let out one searing chord, vocally — more like it let itself out — and then another, looking up when done to see them both staring.

The woman said, "Missip'pi John."

"Jumpier," said the man.

"Hell, Robert Johnson."

The man asked Harmon, "Why don't you sing a little more?"

But Harmon set the guitar on the desk, nodded, and turned.

"What's your name?"

"Harmon Brown."

He opened the door, and the man called after him, "Don't go way mad, Harmon."

The statement thrilled him. Did this white man recognize a former blues player, or the Negro charged with attempted rape behind the counter in Kress's department store.

12

Tuke was surprised by his sudden popularity as an attorney, not for white Memphians but for black ones — a preacher, an undertaker, and a maid trying to get her son out of jail. He also sought new drinking friends, with less success, not at the Memphis Country Club but at the Tennessee Club after hours and when this proved too depressing he moved to the Peabody Hotel. After watching the ducks march from the fountain to the elevator every evening, to be whisked upstairs to their abode on the roof, he tired of that, too, and sought solace in the Rendezvous's dry-rubbed ribs that won out over Carlin's cooking many nights.

Otherwise he drank in his office, going over torts and murky deeds to near-worthless property and wondering all the time about Dudley Fairchild. His night riding was of no interest to anyone else, but Tuke's own research indicated that Harmon's house was but one of a string of burnings over the years that had not been investigated. He suspected a connection existed between the torchings and the refrigerator trade, but he couldn't find it.

The only logical thing to do, he reasoned illogically, knowing it, would be to have a drink and then take his suspicions to the source.

As if Tuke had thought it up, the Fairchild manse rose out of the grainy darkness of south Memphis as he turned into an overgrown driveway. He saw patches of wood showing through a slate-covered mansard roof, and plywood covering half the windows. He drove past the iron palisade fence, the lance points rusted, everything overgrown with honeysuckle. Scrap collectors and roving bands of teenagers had certainly taken a toll on the Fairchild's once glorious real estate.

In the headlights loomed ornate pedestals and a yard full of old, overturned furniture. Tuke got out, feeling the night air soft on his face. The week before he had almost gotten himself shot in Tiller's tool shed and vowed to refrain from such stupidity, yet here he was again in the middle of another Harmon Brown dilemma.

On the porch a swing dangling by a single chain, the raffia back staved in. At the bottom of the steps was the traditional hitching post for non-existent horses, the paint mostly gone, the iron darky's face eaten away by rust but the up-turned eyes still beseechingly bright.

A shadow crossed the light deep in the house and Tuke called out, "Anybody home?"

He switched off the headlights and walked toward the back of the house, past more hedges gone wild and a *No Trespass* sign. He called out the Fairchild name this time, but there was no response.

A big delivery truck stood in the driveway, and an ancient Oldsmobile with Mississippi plates. Light from the kitchen window fell across the back stoop and a collection of tin cans licked shiny. A clothesline stretched into the darkness and appended to it were half a dozen cat carcasses in antic attitudes. Tuke watched the crack in the kitchen door widen and heard the sound of a television set. Two black holes — the barrels of a side-by-side shotgun — brought him up short.

"Mr. Fairchild, I'm Tuke Harrington. I'd like to have a word if it's not too late."

The door closed, throttling the newscaster, and swung open to reveal a room devoid of furniture, cracked linoleum stacked with newspapers, and the television set resting on a crate. A gaunt Dudley Fairchild stepped aside and with a flourish waved Tuke in.

Propped against one wall were pillows, the slips still fringed with bits of old lace. The television viewer's position, Tuke noticed, was below window level and out of any line of any possible gunfire. A nauseating smell, ammoniac, filthy, assaulted him.

"To what do I owe this honor?" asked Dudley. "I assume you're one of the law-practicing Harringtons." His Adam's apple had performed a mesmerizing routine.

"That's right. I represent Mr. Harmon Brown."

"I know that, of course. As does most of Memphis, I might add." The accent was toffee-thick, the voice itself undeniably cultured. "The question, of course, is why?"

"Mr. Brown was wrongly charged and needed a lawyer." Tuke's blood had already risen; he must be careful, an old refrain.

Dudley revealed more bad teeth and made a low sound akin to laughter. The shotgun rested on the edge of the sink now, a fine old double, possibly a Purdy. Turned walnut stock wrapped with masking tape, elegantly engraved hammers browned with rust. This would have been inexcusable to Dudley's forebears, but inexcusable was the foot and a half of the gun's business end that had been removed with a hacksaw.

Dudley closed his eyes completely and wiped his hands on his trousers. His words came stickily. "I suppose we should retire to the drawing room." He was very drunk.

Tuke followed him down a hallway full of newspapers, his host rebounding from succeeding stacks. The passage ended in a large room dark as coal dust. Dudley slapped the old-fashioned button on the wall and light descended from a web-girded chandelier. The settee had no cushions — those must be in the kitchen — and faded drapes were full of holes apparently blasted with the Purdy. That explained the plywood over the windows.

"So," said Tuke's swaying host, "what brings you uptown this evening?"

"I know who burned down Mr. Brown's house." Tuke wanted to get it over with.

"Why in the world would I have to do with such a thing..." but Dudley was interrupted by a decisive sound from above. A large rat would explain the smell, but Dudley seemed oblivious of both.

"Because you did it," said Tuke, "and people know about it." Three, anyway. "I've come to say you have one chance to make this right, Mr. Fairchild," framing the argument as he went. "Pay for his house to be rebuilt and no charges will be filed."

But Dudley's eyes were shut. He rocked in silent mirth. "Why would I want advice from a rapist's lawyer? You've found yourself a fine client there, Mr. Harrington. But you people never did have any real standing in Memphis, did you? Wasn't your great-grandfather a barrel maker, Mr. Harrington? Wasn't your mother a low-church Georgian, and your late wife" — he made a chuckling sound — "from *Kentucky*?"

How the hell did this man know so much about Tuke's family? He must have done due diligence as soon as Tuke's name appeared in the newspaper, Dudley one of the madder Fairchilds whose only standing and pleasure was debunking social pretenders.

The mention of Lois had made Tuke mad, and Dudley stepped back, the smirk gone. "I must now ask you to leave, Mr... Ah, is it Harrington Junior? Of course my family never used that pathetic patronymic. But then we didn't have to."

Dudley headed unsteadily back to the kitchen. "I could tell the authorities that you forced your way into my home and threatened me," he said as he walked. "This would, of course, justify self-defense of even the most radical nature."

"I'll give you twenty-four hours to do something about this." And Tuke stepped past him, picking up the shotgun. "I'll leave this on the front porch so you won't hurt yourself," and he went back out into the night.

As he passed around the house he saw faded curtains jerking as Dudley followed his progress. Before Tuke got back into the car he flung the Purdy toward the porch, the gun turning lazily in the air and landing flat. Matching black barrels swept the night, two cones of fire and a deafening blast separating the head from the hitching post and sending it tumbling among the weeds like a spent cannonball.

13

Harmon got off the bus on Airways and stood under the awning of the abandoned hardware store, looking across the street at words burned by the sun and picked at by the weather until barely legible on the flaky old clapboards: *Bluff City Appliances*. The door to the loading ramp had been rolled up and a handful of refrigerators stood back in the shadows. There wasn't a soul in sight.

The blinds on the door of the corner office were drawn. Harmon pulled down the brim of his hat and crossed the street. He mounted the steps, knocked, and heard Dudley Fairchild holler, "Around the side!"

Harmon walked around to the loading ramp and into the office. Bundled newspapers mounted to the ceiling, and a desk was scattered with invoices, bottle caps and assorted trash. Behind it sat a shockingly skinny white man in a butt-sprung chair, his thinning hair messed and his hands in his lap. They were wrapped around a half-pint bottle, Harmon saw, not a pistol. If Dudley Fairchild had recognized Harmon in his droopy snap-brim and ten-day beard, he would be reaching into a desk drawer for some kind of weapon. Instead, he asked, "You in search of a good icebox, boy?"

Harmon shook his head. So he hadn't been recognized

"I just got a rebuilt freezer in, could give it to you at a considerable reduction. *Con-si-der-able*. Put all your ribs and chicken and fresh condiments in there. A whole catfish for that matter. Save you significant money in the long run." Dudley drank from the bottle. "Ten dollars down, and she's yours."

"I don't want it," said Harmon.

"Well then, what do you want? I don't have all day. Oh, I get it. You want a job."

"I might," said Harmon, thinking fast.

"Know how to rewire a motor?" asked Dudley. "Put gas in a cooler coil?"

"No."

"That's the problem, see? You want a job, but you don't have the skills. You don't want to put in the time to learn. Know how to push a broom though, I bet. Know how to keep your eye on the door? These boys around here'll rob me blind if they get the chance." Dudley looked him over speculatively. "The old ones are better than the young ones, though. This I have deduced. What's your name?"

"I go by my initials."

Dudley laughed at some old joke. "All right, Bominitious it is." He stood and led Harmon out to the warehouse. The refrigerators were all second-handers touched up with white paint. "I can't deliver these things myself. Got a bad heart. Couple of boys come in here and load for me. You're too slight for that kind of work, Bominitious. But there's plenty else you could do."

He grabbed a push broom and handed it to Harmon. "Start with this. Up one side and down t'other." He stopped talking, then started again, like a broken water pump. "You're not gonna get rich here, Bominitious, I hope you know that. I'll give you twenty-five cents an hour and nothing down on an icebox if you'll sign for it right now."

"Don't want no refrigerator," said Harmon

"Have it your way, your very own way, Bominitious."

"Could I stay in that storeroom?"

"The tool repository, you mean? Why the hell not, Bominitious? Yes or no?"

The storeroom door could be locked from the inside. In the middle of the first night he couldn't tell what made the noise, rats or human beings, but he wasn't about to lift the two-by-four snugged into metal brackets. He just rolled over and struck the door with the flat of his hand, sending a deep drumbeat out into the void. It stilled the intruders for a time and he was back asleep before racket resumed.

It was comfortable lying on the mattress spread with a blanket. His clothes stayed packed in the duffle bought at Army Surplus to serve as a pillow. The next night he ate Vienna sausage and beans from a can warmed in the Sterno's blue flame, using a spoon engraved by its rightful owner: *Boliver State Mental Hospital.*

Harmon washed under the tap out back in the mornings, after hurling the contents of the covered bucket onto the crushed stone under the railroad tracks. During slow periods, which was most of the time, he sat on the bed, his salvaged coat over his knees, his back against the duffle, and the bare bulb overhead giving the impression of heat, and smoked a hand-roll. Using a pencil from Dudley's desk he wrote on the backs of pages torn from old appliance catalogues lines and sometimes whole songs. He dropped them to the floor, picked them up later, re-read them and then usually tossed them out with the trash.

There were exceptions made for those lines that still touched him on the third reading and these went into what had once been a wallet and was now ragged bits of leather strung together with black thread. A life-long habit from all the times he had no money, which was practically speaking his entire life.

Sometimes the words surprised him. They weren't about women or hooch or the brightness of Beale in his time, but about the absence of light and the seeing this brings with it. He had learned in jail that you do not understand how things are until you are helpless. Only then does the world reveal itself and you realize that unappreciated things are what really matters, particularly the ones you can't get back. As songs his scribblings didn't amount to much, but he couldn't keep from making them. Each thought made him pause and look back at it after he had written it down, and sometimes to sing it aloud.

On the coldest night he would pull the duffle under the blanket with him, as a kind of backstop. Sometimes he held it, thinking about Claudet. But mostly the nights were getting warmer and shorter, daylight cutting through the high window with a new intensity, telling him that another spring in an endless line of them was here and he would have to get through this one, too.

"What exactly do you see as your role in this establishment, Bominitious?"

"Sweepin' up. Keepin' hootch-heads away. Carrying out dead rats."

"If I'm not mistaken," continued Dudley, in that way he spoke when the effects of the whiskey had peaked and he was about to fall off the other side. "I am your boss, your superior in every way, and still you will not do as I instruct you. How can this be, Bominitious?"

"I ain't getting inside no freezer."

It stood in the gloomy warehouse where it had been deposited by two black men hired by Dudley. They had quit the day before, but before going had come to Harmon to speak about his recent court appearance. Dudley was too drunk to notice that these younger men spoke to Harmon with a respect he wasn't used to.

Dudley went on, "I order you to get in this freezer someone has used as a swimming pool and pull out whatever it is blocking the drain. I order you to do this now or I will have to terminate your employment and apply your back wages to advertise for your replacement. And…"

"Go ahead," Harmon said. "And where you gonna find somebody else'll deal with all this?"

Dudley glared, his back against the wall. His trousers were dirty, his hair a mess, the man himself both hung-over and drunk again at 10 in the morning.

"Don't you get uppity with me."

"I'll git anything I want to git."

"That's the trouble with you people. Give an inch, you take a mile."

"You don't have a inch to give."

"Now you listen here. I'll fire you where you stand, Bominitious." But if Dudley did he would have nobody to look after the warehouse and Dudley himself, who had become Harmon's other job. Locking down the big garage door and turning off the lights at night was often followed by propping up Dudley with his feet on his desk and a pillow behind his head.

Disgusted, Harmon turned and walked to the back and stretched out on his mattress. He stared up at exposed rafters to which clung a wad of old wasp nests. Dudley stood just outside swaying and muttering. Finally he said, "Give me a hand, Bominitious. I think I can sell this freezer if I can get it unstuck. People forget how hot it gets, that food has to be kept and no better place than a nice secondhand freezer."

Harmon relented. Dudley's toolbox stood in the middle of the floor, next to a bucket of rags, and a broken mop handle held up the freezer lid. Dudley thrust a screwdriver into his belt and climbed onto the stool, gripping the edge of the freezer with bloodless, trembling hands. "Give me that stuff when I'm ready."

Throwing one leg over, he lowered himself, lost his balance and tumbled. "*Goddamn it!*"

Harmon peered into the freezer. Dudley lay lengthwise on the bottom, up on one elbow, gasping for breath. He pulled out the screwdriver and poked at the drain.

"Chewing gum. Can you beat that? A freezer's not some kind of bathtub."

"People will do most anything to get comfortable in summer."

"What they ought to do is fix up those places and stop using appliances for things they weren't intended for. Some of those houses they ought to just tear down and start all over again. Fetch that bucket."

Dudley had risen to his knees. Harmon said, "Or burn 'em down."

"Better yet. The bucket, I said."

"Maybe you ought to help 'em."

Dudley's mouth was showing more of his teeth than usual. "What're you talking about, Bominitious?"

"That you're pretty good at burning down folks' houses."

Dudley stared. He started to get up but Harmon said, "Un uh. You stay right where you are. Don't you know who I am, Dudley? Don't you know by now?"

Dudley tried again, but Harmon leaned over him. "I'm Harmon Brown, the man whose house you set fire to. In the middle of the night. Not something a man ought to forget. That's right, the one whose icebox you took, too."

Dudley whispered, "I'll have the police on you."

"No, you won't."

Dudley shrank back, trying to cram himself into the far corner of the freezer. Harmon leaned in further. "You ain't gonna do nothin' but what I tell you to do. And that's this. Admit to it, admit to it right here, right now."

Harmon took pleasure in Dudley's befuddlement, backed up as he was against the ring of dirt left by water in which colored children had frolicked. Harmon had thought an admission and an apology would be enough, but now he wasn't sure. For the first time in Harmon's life he glimpsed what he was capable of, but Dudley had gone all gray in the face, his eyes dreamy in the pale evening light coming in through high scumbled windows.

As Harmon watched those eyes rolled up, showing more red veins in the yellowish orbs, and his hands pressed against opposing walls of the freezer. Then they slid slowly down, leaving trails in the muck.

"Mr. Dudley..."

Harmon leaned in, his feet coming off the floor. He prodded Dudley with a finger, lost his balance, and tumbled in on top of him. He felt the softness of those parts where the vitals lay, and the hard edges of a man who rarely ate. Gasping, he pulled away. Dudley's eyes were motionless. Harmon felt first where Dudley's heart should have been, then Dudley's neck, the skin cool and underneath it utter stillness.

Harmon climbed out of the freezer and sat on the floor, his back propped against it, staring up at the windows. In so little time everything had changed and the long odds of his continuing life were longer still.

He got to his feet. Dudley looked like he had been dead forever, not just a few minutes. There was nothing to hear but traffic, the squabbling pigeons high up, and Harmon's own heavy breathing.

He took the rag out of the bucket and wiped the freezer clean, then the handle of the toolbox. The biggest problem was the broken mop handle holding up the lid. Harmon didn't like the idea of leaving a body exposed to rats and whatever else came along. Dead people don't shut themselves up in freezers, he told himself, but one could have nudged or kicked the stick away. Harmon elbowed it inside, and the lid fell with a sickening thud.

Moving quickly, he went to the back room, stuffed the duffle, and stepped out the back door. No one to see a vagrant climbing a trash-strewn embankment to railroad tracks leading far off to the east, coming together just short of eternity.

14

Carlin was waiting in the kitchen doorway when Tuke came home. That fact alone told him something unusual awaited. The shadow of the leafing elm closest to the house lay across her slightly averted face. He asked, "What is it, Carlin?"

"Somebody waitin'."

Tuke saw Harmon at the kitchen table. Ordinarily a black man — and Tuke was surprised Carlin had even recognized this wooly-headed itinerant out of the Old Testament — would have been told to come back another time or at best given a seat on the bench in the entranceway and told to wait. But Carlin had seated him at the table and poured him coffee.

Hands folded in his lap, a duffle at his feet, Harmon was watching him. Two things were certain: Harmon didn't have a red cent, and he hadn't touched the cup before him.

"Evening," Tuke said.

"Evenin', Mr. Harrington."

"Keep your seat, please."

Carlin said impatiently, "It's Harmon Brown."

"I know who it is."

"That trash pile at the bottom of the yard," Harmon began, as if they had been discussing it, "somebody ought to do something about that. Spring's the time to burn them cut branches, and to clean out the beds. Looks to me like nobody's worked them for the longest. The hedges are stalky. Excuse my sayin' so but there's a lot of pruning needs doing. The mulch pile behind the garage is all broken down. I used to do that stuff at the club, and the edge work. I looked after all the flowers by the parking lot."

It was the longest speech Tuke had ever heard him make. He glanced at Carlin, who was rapt before Harmon's indirect proposal. "Well," said Tuke, "I suppose the place is a mess. I lost my yard man."

"I owe you and this could be a way of working some of it off."

"Well," said Tuke, "if you want to take that up, Harmon, that's fine."

"Could I sleep out yonder over that garage? That's what I was wondering."

"You can stay above the garage, no problem. Carlin can give you some meals and we'll see how it goes."

"Ain't no sheets out there," said Carlin.

"I'll bet you could find some."

She went to the stove and began to noisily perform. Tuke stood. "We can work out what all that's worth later, Harmon, but not tonight if you don't mind."

"Thank you, Mr. Harrington."

And that was that.

In the beginning the work seemed inexhaustible, full of hard edges and things that weighed more than they should have: sodden leaves, piles of old rain-soaked branches, weeds that came up with mud balls attached to the roots. Harmon realized how long it had been since he had done any real labor. His hands chaffed and got that powdery look from exposure to the wind. His nails broke but he didn't care, liked it in fact. At quitting time his clothes were dirty and his joints ached but he felt like he had done something and cut into his obligation.

In the room above the garage he filled the old footed bathtub with hot water and sat for the longest, taking his time. Afterward, wrapped in the towel, he washed his clothes in the same water, clean rinsed and then draped them over a stout cord he stretched from the bedstead to the handle on the toilet door.

He ate whatever was on the covered plate Carlin handed him as he passed the big house. After supper he got into bed stark naked, turned off the light and stretched out in such a way that he could see any cars coming down the driveway. He went to sleep with a dim vision of his own shirt and trousers dancing in the heat rising from the register. After the first night he had no dreams, or none that he could remember.

It was no problem staying at the bottom of the yard, out of sight of the street. The trees were thick and there was enough work to keep him busy. All the while he watched passing vehicles and those that sometimes turned into the Harrington driveway — deliverymen, postman, a utility truck — and made sure they passed out again. Except for Carlin the big house was empty during the day, which seemed a shame with so much space where children might have played, had there been any.

Harmon moved on to clipping suckers off the little trees that were trying to flower, and trimming low-hanging boughs on the elms and dogwoods. He hauled the cuttings to a back corner of the yard and burned them with the aid of gasoline from the can in the garage. He went about other tasks associated with a colored man in such a neighborhood, and nobody paid him any mind as pale blue smoke wafted up against a bluer sky.

On Saturday, Mr. Harrington left money in an envelope, and Carlin handed Harmon some old clothes. "These're too big," she said, smiling broadly, "but they'll do. Here's some newspaper to stuff into the shoes."

Harmon cleaned up early and walked over to Southern Avenue and caught the bus uptown. He got off at the foot of Beale, where the action was already underway in front of Johnny's and the Green Castle.

Harmon went into Schwab's and bought two pairs of cotton work gloves, extra socks, a hat with a brim that would keep the rain off. The girl at the register put all this into a paper bag with handles, and out on the street Harmon tarried under a succession of dangling gold balls, studying the guitars in the windows.

Unable to resist, he stepped into the one he knew from another life, past racks of saxes and clarinets, toasters and silver plate punch bowels, radios, Victrolas, television sets with spikes attached, tuxedos with stars on the lapels, and snakeskin cowboy boots.

The white man behind the counter watched him through glasses with heavy black frames, smoking, his elbows resting on the counter, using a bottle cap as an ashtray.

Harmon said, "I want to look at them guitars."

The man got up and came around and without a word went to the front of the shop, set the footstool, and stepped up into the window case. "All righty," he said, "which one?"

"How much is the Gibson?"

"One hundred and fifty dollars."

Harmon shook his head. "Can I see them two little Martins?"

The man handed them down, one at a time. The first was prettier, but Harmon didn't like the action. The strings were too high for the fingerboard, meaning the whole piece was probably warped and expensive to fix. The second Martin was all beat up, with fingernail scratches and what looked like a cigarette burn, but the action was fine. He thumped the back, checking for body cracks, and the bridge, to see that it was glued down right.

"You'll never find another one like it," said the man.

Harmon had heard that line all his life and had seen more just like it than he cared to remember. He gripped the neck and raised his right hand, and saw that it was trembling. Nothing for it now but to play.

"Go on," said the man.

Harmon struck a solid E chord and listened to it ring.

"What you want for this old box?" he asked.

"Fifty-five."

"I'll give you forty." It was all the money he had, except for bus fare.

Harmon followed the man back to the counter and handed over the bills and wrote out his name on the form attached to the clipboard because that was required. So was an address, and after hesitating he added the address of the Harrington house, all the while gripping the neck of the Martin. Then he asked the man if he had any picks.

"This ain't a music shop."

"Oh, you got some, you're just a few years too young to know. Reach up under there," and he tapped the counter top, "and feel around."

The man just looked at him.

"I been here a long time and I know. Just reach up to the underside and run your hand along to where the two-by-four's nailed to the front, you'll find something."

Reluctantly the man reached. He would have a pistol under there, that was certain. But he reached a little further. "Higher," Harmon said, "and a little bit to the right."

Expressionless, the man withdrew his hand. In it was a paper cup, yellow with age. He upended it and half a dozen guitar picks fell out. "Well, I'll be damned," he said.

They were mostly steel and plastic, but Harmon put his finger on another and shoved it across. "That one's real turtle," he said, "worth more than the rest of 'em together."

The man examined the tortoiseshell and dropped it into his shirt pocket.

Harmon fitted old steel picks to his index and middle fingers and ran them across the strings. The guitar had a real good sound. "How much you want for these?" he asked, of the picks.

The man studied Harmon's name on his clipboard. He said, "You can just take 'em."

Tuke rolled out of the Caddy and for a moment breathed in early spring: wet earth, forsythia, that unidentifiable greenness. Blossoms just peering out at the extremities of the Japanese cherry looked like tiny snowflakes in a painting. Even as he looked their whiteness receded within the mass of dark branches. Had Lois still been alive, there would already be annuals in the ribbons of mulch Harmon had put down.

He didn't want to enter that big house. Carlin had probably already walked down to Southern Avenue and caught the bus. Then he heard it, music carrying in from somewhere, someone playing a stringed instrument. It was close, emanating from the cubicle above the garage where no light shown in the early evening, a thin keening of what at first he thought was a harmonica. Then he realized it was a human voice — Harmon's. Tuke stood in the pea gravel and listened, most of the words eluding him, but not the feeling: a yearning, beyond articulation, wild, disturbing, and quite beautiful. Chin lifting, arms dangling, Tuke's fleeting memories in half-tone, were too brief to fully grasp: a youthful Lois clinging to him in his father's house one illicit night, then Lois descending the stairs, much later, in a smartly-cut jacket and heels. What had he done with his life since then? Was there any other way things might have gone?

Tears filled Tuke's eyes. To his own amazement he began to sway in time with the strange music, a release he hadn't felt in years, an enthrallment in an alien lament from a black man in a dark room who didn't even know that Tuke was out there, listening.

15

Chick and his partner rolled east on Lamar Avenue. They had received the complaint the day before but had been too busy to look into it. They had more important things to do than check out run-down establishments supplying second-hand appliances to colored riffraff. The complaint had come from a car dealer up the street: warehouse door left open, people off the street going in and out.

"So what," he said again, "if a bunch of darkies take some sorry-ass appliances?"

"Oh, you better be careful," said his partner, settled back. "You're bein' *insensitive*. You're kindly *deficient in evaluation skills*, too."

Their laughter was bitter and it didn't help at all. They had to watch themselves these days because of the publicity surrounding the Harmon Brown case. It had affected the department and so was doubly bad for the two of them. "Nobody had the balls to fault us," said Chick, words familiar in the cruiser. "The captain had no problem with what we did when we did it. No sir. And now we have to listen to some fruitcake talk about *community relations*."

"No we don't."

They eased into the lot and for a time sat looking at the building and the ghostly words, *Bluff City*, over the half-open door of the loading ramp. Blinds were drawn in the office, and an old truck sat askew by the fence. "Let's go," said Chick at last.

They crossed the lot, adjusting their belts and their weapons, and mounted the stoop. Chick said, "Push that door on up," and his partner did, a heavy man who never passed Leonard's without taking on a load of pulled-pig and a double slaw. They entered a big room lit from above, empty except for a big, battered freezer sitting dead center of a concrete floor. A pigeon beat listlessly against the window pane above and there were deep shadows at the rear amidst a jumble of rope.

Chick led the way into the office: newspapers stacked against one wall, a desk scattered with foolscap and wrappers from candy bars and Mrs. Drake's store-bought sandwiches. The desk drawers were all closed. Chick jerked one open and revealed a half-dozen empty Four Roses bottles, pints and half-pints. He slammed it and opened another. Contracts, product guarantees, maintenance manuals, more bottles.

He slammed that drawer. "Nothing here."

They crossed the warehouse, passing on either side of the freezer. A toolbox stood open and empty. There was an overturned bucket and a mop gone stiff. Chick smelled something sweet and putrid.

"Rats," said his partner.

They found a mattress in the storeroom, and a moldy overcoat gone in the cuffs. A naked bulb at the end of a dust-clotted cord, a scrap of paper on the floor. Chick's partner picked it up and together they squinted at words written in pencil.

"Some kind of poetry." The paper fell from his hand.

Back out into the big room they inspected corners, reluctantly gravitating to the freezer. They stood staring at the ceiling, waiting for resolve. In times like this the future could be plainly read but they weren't inclined to read it. Let someone else do the reading, the miserable finding and the writing up. But sometimes this couldn't be put off and these made their lives much harder and their dreams bad ones.

Chick looked at his partner's large hand on the handle of the freezer, watched as he jerked it upwards and instantly engulfed them in a stench so powerful it set them back a step. Chick had seen some awful sights in his day but nothing to equal this blue-gray thing stretched out in the bottom of the freezer, fingers contorted in decomposition, clutching clothing darkly soiled, its translucent eyes locked onto Chick's.

Together the two men wheeled, foreheads colliding, raising hands as if to fend off the smell. The freezer lid dropped and the exhalation from that dank space of rotting flesh reached down to knot their innards. Chick could make it outside if he could just get past his partner, but the two of them collided a second time, clawed at each other, vomiting all over each other's shoes.

The call came to Tuke at the office. Cooper Paine, without the usual preliminaries, said, "I've got some bad news."

Boss was ill, the word going out to all who mattered, though Tuke no longer did. "Cops found the man you think torched Harmon Brown's house. In one of his own appliances."

"Dead?"

"More like compost, from what they tell me."

Tuke waited, possibilities racing through his mind, none of them good.

"How long's it been since you saw this Brown."

"Weeks ago," Tuke said.

There was a long pause. Why was Cooper Paine interested in the death of a nobody like Dudley Fairchild? "He had had a heart attack," Cooper went on. "Question is, how did he get inside a second-hand freezer? Tell me, Tuke, might Brown know something about this?"

"No. Why would a demoralized black man who had been beaten and barely escaped going to prison for something he didn't do shut up a white man up in a freezer?"

Tuke waited while Cooper decided whether or not to let this be.

"You hear anything," said Cooper, "you give me a call."

Harmon heard footsteps on the stairs and sat very still, gripping the neck of the Martin like a throttled chicken. He had heard no car. The knock that followed was respectful, persistent.

"Who's there?"

"You gon' open up, Harmon?"

He lay the guitar on the mattress and stepped to the door. Carlin stood in the dim little corridor at the head of the stairs, holding a plate covered with tinfoil. He said, "All right," as if she had enquired about his health, and she said, "I brought you some supper."

Harmon did some of his own cooking on the hotplate, much as he had at the warehouse. Not having a refrigerator was a problem, with the weather turning warm. "What is it?" he asked, trying to be sociable.

"Ain' no hot tamales," she said. "Ain't no 'Red Hot.'"

"You know that song?"

"Oh, yeah. I heard him sing it once, when I was little. My daddy played harmonica. You might have heard of him — Calvin Knox?"

Harmon remembered a big man in coveralls. Big smile, bigger voice. "Oh yeah," he said. "They called him Cruise."

"That's right!"

"He reminded me of John Lee Williamson," said Harmon, still standing in the doorway. "Not quite as good, if you don't mind my saying so, but then nobody was."

"Daddy got stabbed behind Peewee's. At noon on a sunny day."

"I'm real sorry."

"He got over it, though."

"That's more than you can say for John Lee, murdered on a back street in Detroit, I heard. I always wondered if somebody didn't mistake that shiny silver instrument in John Lee's pocket for a gun."

"Harmonica was dangerous business for some reason."

"So was guitaring," said Harmon. "Ole Robert Johnson sang *Hot*

Tamales, innocent-sounding as a child, and then died on his hands and knees, poisoned by somebody's jealous husband, barking like a goddamn dog."

"Anyway, this is just a pork chop and a piece of cornbread but I don't think you'll have no trouble gettin' it down."

"I thank you." He could see a trace in her of her father in her dark eyes. Spanish, Indian, something.

She asked, "Ain' you gon' let me in to set this down?"

He offered to take the plate but she walked right past him and placed it on the scarred enamel tabletop. Her white maid's uniform was gone and she wore instead a dark skirt and some kind of blouse with puffy sleeves. Not bad looking, as he had noticed before, but there was a lot of her.

"You gon' eat it?"

"Later. I'll bring the plate over in the morning."

"Where'd you get that?" She raised her chin at the Martin.

"Downtown."

"I heard you playin' it."

"Uh huh."

She walked over and sat at the foot of the bed and leaned over the guitar like it was dangerous. "Play me something, Harmon"

"I'm plumb wore out this afternoon."

"No you ain't. Come on, I heard you. Just a little something." She turned on him a broad face that felt like a headlight. "If you don't I might have to take that plate back to the kitchen."

Harmon sat carefully at the other end of the bed and picked up the guitar, wondering what to play. What did she expect? People were so easily disappointed and that would make him feel bad, so he played a few bars of nothing in particular and kept his mouth shut. He set the old instrument back on the bed.

She said, “That’s nice.”

“Glad you liked it.”

“How’d you learn?”

“Oh,” he said, “that’s a long story, Carlin.”

She settled her hips the way a woman will. “Well,” she said, “I got time. Tell it.”

16

One afternoon Tuke turned into his driveway and saw a a strange car parked in the turn-around. Gray and unwashed, without markings, it supported the backside of a young man in a jacket and tie, leisurely smoking. Tuke parked and got out of his Caddy, and the other fingered his cigarette into the gravel and came crunching forward, his manner deferential. The suit was wrinkled and the shoes scuffed. A policeman, Tuke assumed, probably Vice. "Can I help you?"

"I knocked," said the man with a thick delta accent. "Nobody's home."

Carlin was but she must have seen him and decided not to open up. There was no sign of Harmon.

"I'm looking for Harmon Brown," said the man.

"Well, I'm not him."

"I know that." He laughed, fishing another Camel out of his shirt pocket. He lit it with a wooden match, the yellow residue of tobacco visible on thumb and forefinger. Tuke asked, "Who are you?"

"Billy Chritchfield."

He didn't offer the stained hand but used it to beat his jacket pockets, then reached inside and fished out a card. He handed it to Tuke.

"What's the Society for the Preservation of Southern Folkways?" asked Tuke.

"Largest cultural reservoir in the Mid-South," said the young man. "Headquartered in Oxford. We mostly record people, some going way back, so their stories and work won't be lost. We do good work, Mister…"

"Harrington. I'm sure you do, but I'm not going to make a contribution today and neither is Harmon Brown."

"Oh, I'm not looking for contributions. I just want to talk to him. I finally found him in the pawn shop's logbook."

"What about?"

"Music."

"Sure you've got the right Brown?"

"No, but I hope so. If I could just talk to him for a minute."

Tuke hesitated. "Okay, come on."

He led him in through the kitchen, past the scowling Carlin propped against the sink, arms crossed. "Go get Harmon," Tuke said.

"He ain't here."

"Yes, he is. Get him, please."

Tuke left Billy Critchfield in the living room and came back into the kitchen to wait. Presently Carlin returned, followed by Harmon in his new coveralls. Tuke said, "There's a man here wants to talk to you, Harmon. I think it's all right. If it's not all right just walk out. He says he wants to talk about music."

"What about it?"

"Don't know. Says he records things."

Harmon followed him into the living room. Billy Critchfield was still on his feet, still smiling. "You the Harmon Brown that played with Persimmon Smoot?"

Harmon nodded.

"I knew it! I've been looking for you for a long time, Mr. Brown. You got no idea how happy this makes me."

Tuke left them and went upstairs, where he took off his suit and put on old golfing pants and a short-sleeved shirt with an alligator over his left pectoral. Harmon and Billy Critchfield were between him and the liquor cabinet, so he decided to wait a bit longer. When he looked out the window he saw the trunk of Critchfield's car standing open and the man muscling out a big tape recorder.

Tuke went back downstairs and through the living room and poured himself a drink. Harmon sat on the edge of the couch, closed as a stone, but Tuke went into the kitchen for ice and a look at the *Press-Scimitar.* Critchfield passed behind him with his machine.

The next time Tuke looked Harmon and Critchfield were both on the couch, staring at the revolving tape reels. Critchfield said something about a Memphis Minnie, and Harmon grunted in the affirmative. Then Critchfield asked, "Was it Persimmon Smoot or Robert Johnson wrote *Since My Baby Left Me*?"

"Wasn't neither one of 'em. I wrote it."

Tuke took his drink out onto the patio. The iron lawn furniture was still covered and he stripped one bare and sat facing the golf course. A foursome of husbands and wives was on the twelfth green but he couldn't tell who at this distance. He heard the back door slam and saw Harmon crossing to the garage, and then coming back carrying his guitar.

From deep within the house came the sharp lament of vibrating strings. Tuke put his hands behind his head and looked up into the trees, enjoying the music that followed, song after song, all without lyrics but pleasant in a way he had never considered.

He heard tires in the gravel and wished he hadn't. A car door slammed. Someone began talking to Carlin at the kitchen door, and Tuke got up and walked to the edge of the house. A large man in a gray suit was reasoning with the Harringtons' formidable maid. It was the worst possible guest at the worst possible time.

"Coop."

The district attorney swiveled. In little more than a month Tuke had seen one of his oldest friends age and in the process lose something Tuke had once thought forever Cooper's, the aura of absolute assurance.

But Cooper had decided not to run for Congress, a fact that couldn't be blamed entirely on Boss's death or the Harmon Brown case, though they were connected. Boss's political machine was already coming apart and taking people down with it.

"Sorry to bother you," Cooper said. "Something's come up."

"Oh?"

"Look, I'm sick to death of this thing and know you are, too."

Then Tuke noticed the uniformed driver in Cooper's black Lincoln, not a chauffeur, a cop. "You still talking about Dudley Fairchild dying?"

"Yes," said Cooper. "Buff Wallace called to say there's a fella working in your yard he thinks is Harmon Brown. Looks like he's disguised himself, Buff said."

"Jesus." Even a hint of misgiving could now be fatal. "He's sitting on my couch with a man from some cultural organization. They're talking about music."

Cooper ran a hand over his face, and for an instant Tuke almost pitied him. "You ask him about Fairchild, Tuke?"

"No. But why don't you ask him?"

As they passed through the kitchen Tuke avoided Carlin's eyes. The conversation in the living room had been replaced by more guitar-playing. Billy Critchfield sat on the edge of the sofa, one knee on the floor, a Camel in his mouth, staring at the turning spool of tape.

The French doors stood open, letting in the fresh air, the lawn and trees beyond it framed by fine woodwork. The rug had been folded back to allow the doors to open. Harmon's guitar stood against the coffee table, the wood burnished by the light of the sun, the scratches bright as lightning strikes. There was no sign of Harmon.

Cooper said, "He's fleeing an interview."

"He must have seen your car with a cop behind the wheel. Can you blame him?"

"If he's done nothing wrong he's got nothing to fear."

"Oh yeah? Do you really want to start this circus all over again, Coop? Harmon didn't kill Dudley Fairchild. And he'll talk to you, I'll see to that, just hold off until tomorrow."

"Ten o'clock," said Cooper, and he let the screen door slam behind him.

Tuke was sprinting across the lawn, newly mowed as a futile warning to the elements. Low-hanging tree branches raked his shoulders. He broke free at the edge of the golf course, close enough to the two couples to recognize them. They were within chipping distance of the green, but they were staring at a dark, running figure on the far side of the fairway. Harmon had spotted Tuke and turned toward Southern Avenue, and angling across open savannah. Tuke ran faster, shrubbery and weeds in the rough flailing at his pants legs. He imagined an open downfield devoid of a football field's white lines, could almost hear the cheering, nothing between him and glory but space and light.

Hips pivoting, knees pumping, elbows swinging, he called out, "Harmon! Wait!"

But Harmon didn't. The Dupreys and the Darlingtons on the thirteenth tee froze in the midst of club selection. In passing Tuke saw Trish Darlington's lips distended in disbelief and her husband gripping the handle of the ball-washer with both hands as if trying to save a crashing airliner.

Tuke was close enough to see the studs on Harmon's coveralls. He reached, but Harmon swiveled and mounted to the green. Tuke, heaving for breath, lunged and took down the knobby collection of arms and legs, rolling on the costly manicured turf.

"Git. Off'a. Me!"

Harmon stood, but Tuke had him by the pant leg. "Harmon..."

Tuke's constricting chest shut him down. He felt pain, not much, but maybe this was it. His innards felt fast in wet concrete and the first ease of running had turned into suffocation. "You can't… keep… running… Harmon."

He let go and rose to his hands and knees. The green felt lush beneath his fingertips. Then he felt a hand on his shoulder. "Better to stand up," said Harmon. "I seen this before. It ain't a heart attack, you're just out of shape."

Tuke heaved himself erect and leaned on Harmon. "We have to talk," he began, but Harmon said, "We got to get you home first."

Tuke asked Carlin, "Would you like to get some scissors?"

Billy Critchfield was gone and Tuke and Harmon sat drinking water at the kitchen table. Soon Harmon's shorn hair began to gather on his shoulders as Carlin snipped away. Then she went for Harmon's beard, first with the scissors and then with Tuke's razor, the extra blades nearby.

On impulse, Tuke asked if Harmon would like a drink, and he said, "I wouldn't mind, Mr. Harrington."

Tuke went to the liquor cabinet and brought the bourbon bottle back with him, noticing that the golf course had been cleared as if by a violent storm. Tuke would no doubt be hearing from the board of stewards of the Memphis Country Club, but there were more important matters at hand.

He poured Harmon the drink and then one for himself. What the hell, he thought, pouring a third for Carlin. He put it on the counter where she was making dinner without asking and the next time he looked it was half empty.

"All right, Harmon, do you know anything about Dudley Fairchild ending up dead in a freezer? That's what Cooper Paine was here about."

"Yes sir."

Tuke closed his eyes. Please no, he thought. But before he could speak Harmon was telling the story and, once started, he couldn't stop until finished. Then Harmon drank his bourbon straight off.

Tuke poured himself another drink but Harmon raised his hand against a second. Carlin set the table for all three of them, without being asked to do so, and when the grillade and grits were ready she helped them up and set three plates on the table. Nothing like this had ever happened before and they all knew it but there was so much that could have been said about it no one said a word.

"There's only one way to deal with Cooper Paine," Tuke said, after they were all done eating, "and that's head on. I'm going to get you out of this, Harmon, I promise. But you have to tell the story again — some of it — to him and you have to tell it my way, not yours."

"All right."

"We'll leave here at nine in the morning. Please find Harmon a clean shirt, Carlin, and make it fit somehow if it's one of mine. And now I'm going to bed."

He awoke to a dark and silent house. But there was a light on in the room above the garage and when he opened the window he heard not music but the sound of splashing water. This was followed by a whoop, and it wasn't Harmon doing the whooping, but a woman. It was Carlin.

Tuke knelt and propped his elbows on the window sill, hoping for the sound of the guitar, but the light went out and all he heard was the raucous tumult of a nascent spring.

17

The array of framed mementos on the wall of Cooper Paine's office — citations, degrees, awards, photos of Boss and congressmen from Memphis to Chattanooga — were bracketed by the Tennessee flag in one corner and the colors of Cotton Carnival in the other.

Cooper sat at his desk in shirt-sleeves and suspenders; he hadn't stood when they entered. Tuke took a chair and Harmon did, too. The district attorney looked him over as if for the first time, and indeed Harmon had been transformed: not just hair clipped and beard shaved off. Tuke said, "I've told Harmon about Dudley Fairchild's body being found."

"So what you got to say, boy?"

"I ain't a boy."

Tuke quickly added, "My client has nothing to say about who might have killed him, in the unlikelihood that anybody did. Only that he didn't."

"That's right," said Harmon.

Cooper shifted in a swivel chair built to withstand earthquakes. "I can damn well make him have something more to say."

"Actually, Coop, you can't. Not unless you charge him with something and start up the circus again. What you might do" — speculatively, as if the idea had just occurred to him — "what you could do is ask Harmon to tell you what he knows, since he worked for Dudley shortly before he died."

"He did what?"

"That's right. Tell him what you did for Mr. Fairchild, Harmon."

"Fairchild hired *you*?" Cooper asked.

"Yes sir, he did. He needed somebody to sweep up and keep them thieves out, some of 'em, anyway. And I needed a job. I already knew him because I bought a 'frigerator off him once. He had big fellas around to do the heavy work."

"Well, I want names."

"I never heard 'em," said Harmon. "They come and went as fast as Mr. Dudley's Four Roses bottles. I got fed up and left, too."

"I want a date."

"Well, can't give you one exactly. Some weeks, best I can say."

"You telling me you didn't know Dudley Fairchild was a suspect in the torching of your house?"

"I know it now," said Harmon carefully. "He probably burned down other houses in the Mound, Mister Paine, but I can't testify to that, either."

"A white man's dead," Cooper declared, "maybe a homicide. Property stolen, you working there before Mr. Harrington took you on again. You telling me you don't know anything more about this?"

"Only that it was a sorry situation, him drunk all the time and sicker than anybody knew. I don't think he reported half the robberies out of that place."

Tuke said, "Dudley had no liver left to speak of, and a bad heart, apparently. There were no witnesses, no useable prints, no weapon, nothing."

"Somebody put him in that freezer," said Cooper.

"Probably he was already in there, cleaning it. Wasn't there a stool next to it, and a mop or something?"

"What about motive, counselor?"

"Apparently half the population of Orange Mound had a motive to kill Dudley Fairchild. It's a wonder none ever did. Harmon was working for me, anyway." That was not exactly a lie.

Cooper picked up the sheaf of papers and scowled at it. He harrumphed in that way of his, meaning that the discussion was over and he not entirely happy with it. "If I have any further questions I'll be in touch, Mr. Brown. Don't leave town, and… oh, never mind." He dismissed them with a wave.

Outside, Harmon asked Tuke, "What happened to that gal said I tried to rape her?"

"Connie Brett? Kress's fired her but she got a job at Britling's cafeteria. That's what I heard."

"That cafeteria at mid-town?"

"That's the one. Why'd you ask?"

Harmon didn't answer the question but said instead, "Mr. Harrington, I appreciate all you've done for me. You didn't have to do none of it, and you did. I owe you and always will."

Before Tuke could say anything more Harmon was headed down Union Avenue.

The cafeteria's bright interior was easily viewed from the street: polished railings, food steaming in metal trays, tables neatly set and already dining ladies with hair looking bluish in the morning light. The waitresses did not include Connie Brett, but it was early.

Harmon lowered himself onto the stoop of an abandoned storefront to wait. After almost an hour he saw her step from the lurching, mostly empty bus, her uniform pressed and a handbag banging against her thigh. She was about to pass him when he stood and said, "Missy."

She seemed to swell up at sight of him, but he went on, "I'm sorry about what happened that day in Kress's. I'm sorry I made you faint and I'm sorry you got called out in front of everybody. I just wanted you to know that."

At the corner he looked back and saw her still standing there, watching him.

Tuke stood at the iron railing around the country club pool as the swallows dipped to luminous green water. The evening was warm, the men playing poker in the air conditioning of the locker room downstairs and the women playing bridge upstairs, in the light. Southern men are children, he thought, and the women like it that way. Though he had lost access to the easy fellowship of those men below, they wouldn't ostracize him since they all had foibles, too, and the ever-useful excuse that alcohol makes men do things they shouldn't, not the men themselves. This could be the source of forgiveness and sometimes even of redemption.

His last trumpeted escapade — apprehending Harmon Brown on the fourteenth green — had been so outrageous as to defy categorization, engendering a kind of grudging respect from even the most outraged. It was just too much trouble to keep up that level of indignation, day after day, when there was golf, cards, wing shooting and money-making to keep track of. All arguments and animosity eventually pale before the absolute power of ease.

He opened the gate and crossed the flagstones to a chair under the lifeguard stand. There he sat and crossed his legs, watched by the waiter, a tall young man in a red jacket. The pool had closed and the waiter clearly disapproved of a member in street shoes transgressing at this hour.

Tuke called to him, "Bring me a Jack Daniels on the rocks, please."

The waiter eventually emerged from the cabana with the drink on a tray, opened the gate and bore down on Tuke with unspoken disapproval. He set the glass on the little three-legged table and offered the receipt book with long, slim fingers.

Tuke signed and handed it back. The glass was already cold to the touch. He looked from its amber beauty up into the the dense canopy of overhead branches and a sprinkling of budding stars, sipped, and was struck by the bourbon's sweet, instant sway.

The cacophony of tree frogs replaced the recorded music from the outdoor speakers and for a time there was no other sound but the gurgling of the pool. The lights went out in the snack bar, then in the pool itself, swallowed by depthless shadow.

The waiter appeared again and stood over Tuke with outstretched hand. Tuke felt the urge to toss his glass into the pool, as he had done almost a year before. The allure of such unburdening was as powerful as ever. The dark eyes above him expanded to reveal more of their whites, and Tuke relented. "Thank you," he said, and watched the waiter walk away in his tight trousers.

Tuke left the confines of the pool and walked around to the putting green. Little white flags in the practice holes winked at him. His reflection in the card room window dissolved to reveal the bridge ladies playing, their clothes bright and their hair perfect in every way. It was an affable state of alertness that did not threaten their sociability, something that came harder to the men down in the locker room.

Then he saw, facing him, the lovely presence of Onie Gay Wallace, her bosom impressive as always, her exemplary Appalachian bone structure — the one thing mountain culture contributed to Tennessee womanhood — highlighting that stellar smile. It was unabashedly directed at Tuke, who had not seen her so close since that Sunday her husband shot Tuke, which felt like a lifetime ago. He smiled, too, and Onie Gay canted her head in that way that said so much and that he remembered so well.

He turned slightly on the iron bench, still in plain view. The bridge party was just breaking up. Would Onie Gay push open the door to the patio and come out to him? Not as audacious in its way as Tuke going to her in his bathrobe on a Sunday, but close. He suddenly wanted that more than he had once thought possible.

He kept his gaze on the shadowy landscape beyond the fairways where in a subtle altering of light and shadow he thought he saw a dark, fleeing figure. But the more he looked the less convinced he was. He heard the sound of Onie Gay's high heels on the patio behind him, and whispered to himself, "What a beautiful place this is."

18

Billy Critchfield carried a chair across the stage of the Daisy Theater in both hands, the cigarette bleeding smoke into his anxious eyes. He had rented the place for two hours and brought together musicians most people didn't know were still alive. Harmon had come to trust him when he learned how long Billy had worked to locate him, 'Simmon, and Ozell Stiles, the slide harmonica player. The young man had grit, and he had a mission.

"Try this one, Harmon," Billy said.

"Don' be obligin' Harmon, Mr. Critchfield," said 'Simmon, already settled into the soft chair and rolling those big, milky, unseeing eyes. "Harmon, prop up yo' hard ole ass and let's hit it."

How can a blind man know so much about what's going on around him? Harmon held his own guitar lightly as he and 'Simmon tuned up. They both wore jackets fresh off the rack, Harmon's too tight but 'Simmon's looking like a faded plaid tent with pockets. He whipped the red handkerchief out and wiped his already sweaty face. "Artice!"

"Right here, 'Simmon."

Artice in white net stockings was something to behold. She handed 'Simmon the port bottle. "Now," he announced, "I's ready."

Billy Critchfield was fiddling with his recording machine while the big bass player recruited from Club Handy down the street hit another string. He was too young for this bunch. Ozell, born in another century, wore a porkpie hat and a jacket missing many sequins. What was left reflected the overhead lights onto a velvet curtain hiding them all from the gathering audience.

Judging by the sounds coming from the other side, more than a few had wandered in off Beale to watch the sorry remains of Persimmon Smoot and the Boys. They were making history, that's what Billy Critchfield had told them. The moan of Ozell's slide harmonica coincided with Harmon's memories of the Daisy, but the stage felt smaller than he remembered, and the light man high above dribbled ancient dust down through the beams of light every time he shifted his feet on the scaffolding.

The bass hit another lick, and Harmon started to feel better. Billy asked them, "You gentlemen got everything you need? Mr. Smoot, could you play something? I need to check the sound."

Persimmon strummed.

"A little vocal, please."

Squeeze my lemon 'til the juice
runs down my laig…

Billy lit a Camel off the last one. "Now Mr. Smoot," he said, "you promised. Nothing dirty. This is a cultural moment. The recording should reflect not purity exactly but this moment's historicity. Please remember who will be listening to this in the days and years and decades ahead."

Billy turned and stuck his head through the curtain, and Ozell asked, "Wha's *histor-icity*?"

The bass player said, "Who'll be listenin' to us in the days and years and decades ahead?"

What Harmon wanted to know was who would be listening to them that night.

"Hootch-heads," said Ozelle. "It's free, ain't it?"

"We're getting' paid," 'Simmon reminded him, "free or not."

Billy turned. "They're coming in, all right. Why don't you all play something before the curtain goes up?"

'Simmon started with *Cross Road Blues* but it was raggedy-sounding. Harmon's hands were sweating and he played too fast. He took a deep breath and watched 'Simmon fret, moving his slide up and down the strings. Garden spider on a bucket of flies. 'Simmon's high-pitched lament faltered, like he had been performing all night instead of one short practice session. But the light man above them was tapping his foot.

Suddenly the curtains were open and out there was not a sea of faces exactly but more of them than Harmon had expected. Not all were colored, which was a surprise. White people were packed tightly in the middle and up front.

Billy Critchfield came out from the wings and announced, "Ladies and gentlemen, Persimmon Smoot and The Boys!"

People clapped, looking round like they weren't sure they were supposed to. Derelicts sat in the back, but there was one white man in a coat and tie and the man from Big River Recording, still in his Hawaiian shirt.

The tempo picked up. Then 'Simmon's voice broke again and they all came in to cover. Harmon saw black faces out there he knew but couldn't name. They became not a collection of the curious and down-and-outers but people in snappy clothes from the late 'thirties. Harmon looked for Claudet, knowing it was crazy, but who he found was Carlin, her soft, broad shoulders exposed, smiling and giving him a little wave.

'Simmon was starting to squeak already, looking around for more back-up, blinder than a bat. What manner of man was the Harmon Brown who lived in 'Simmon's head? Harmon had depended on him for so long, but now, it seemed, he was depending on Harmon.

"You okay 'Simmon?" he asked, when the song was done.

Sweat ran off 'Simmon like water. Harmon had been afraid of

this happening and had even considered standing with his back to the audience and corner-loading, an old trick to bounce the sound of a voice off the walls. But the Daisy stage no longer had corners, and maybe never had, and hiding his face tonight would have been shameful anyway. Billy Critchfield had helped him see that.

On impulse, Harmon reached up and took Billy's cigarette and put it between his own lips. Head-banging strong, but good. He exhaled, smoke momentarily shielding him from all those bright, staring eyes.

"Come on, Harmon," 'Simmon said. "It's time, son."

Harmon dropped the butt on scarred boards and ground it beneath his heel. The creases in his trousers were tight, the way he liked them, though the trousers had belonged to someone else. The strings felt good beneath his fingers, which were still quick. Steel and flesh, moving together.

Looking up into that domed ceiling.

Taking a deep breath.

Singing.